A Fool Among Fools

John Terracuso

For Ken Page, who taught me the prayer,
and Wendell Wyatt, who answered it.

Horace Vandergelder's never tired of saying most of the people in the world are fools, and in a way he's right, isn't he? Himself, Irene, Cornelius, myself! But there comes a moment in everybody's life when he must decide whether he'll live among human beings or not — a fool among fools or a fool alone.

As for me, I've decided to live among them.

— Dolly Levi
in Thornton Wilder's
The Matchmaker

PART ONE

1
As Seen On TV!

I realize now that I made two mistakes on my twenty-ninth birthday. The first was deciding to go in to work. I had planned to take a vacation day to do the things I never had the time for, like going to a museum or browsing my way through Macy's. I would have settled for the luxury of sleeping late. But when the day actually arrived – May 27, 1986 – I knew I couldn't afford the time off from work, so I dragged myself out of bed. I stuck to my decision to go in even after I looked outside and discovered that it was pouring rain.

I was a junior copywriter working on an awful piece of business – the Skin Therapy Moisturizing Gel account. All of the work we had just completed had been killed, and now we had to start over again and come up with a new commercial.

If I had to go to the office on my birthday, then I wanted a reward. So instead of ordering my usual bran muffin from the Lexington Avenue Gourmet, I asked Ida, my favorite of the three people who worked at the counter, for English Breakfast tea with milk and a chocolate croissant. She came back with the tea, and told me they had just sold the last croissant.

No croissants? Signs! Warnings! It was *raining* on my birthday! Where was I looking? I should have gone right back home. Instead, I settled for the bran muffin, and left the store trying to convince myself that it was all nothing more than bad timing, not some kind of omen.

I walked into the lobby of the Chrysler Building and waited for an elevator. Working in that beautiful old deco building was the only compensation I could come up with for staying in a job I hated. I couldn't figure out why I was still there. I was twenty-four when they hired me; five years later, my explanation was that I had grown up, but still didn't know what I wanted to be.

As its name implies, Malcolm & Partners Worldwide is a huge ad agency with offices in just about every major city. "We Think Global" went the company slogan, and grammar notwithstanding, they made millions and millions of dollars doing just that.

We had Sparks Cola at Malcolm. It was a huge account and we did big-time work for them. You know the commercials: healthy muscular types gulping down the stuff on a beach somewhere, looking bronzed and gorgeous but never gaining a pound from something that was basically carbonated high-fructose corn syrup with a few suspected cancer-causing secret ingredients tossed in for color.

We also had a lot of packaged goods clients. If you could buy it over the counter or take it off a shelf in a grocery store, we probably did the commercials that bullied you into trying it. Or, considering most of the projects I worked on, the commercials that not only made you hate the product without even buying it, but also made you want to murder the people on TV trying to sell it to you.

I had worked in the Production department at another, smaller agency before I came to Malcolm. It was not a pleasant experience, and I was fired before the end of my first year in one of those terrible Black Fridays that happen when an agency loses a major piece of business (in this case, we lost a big personal computer account back when home computers were still a novelty).

I managed to find another job at Malcolm as a secretary in the Creative department. I had wanted to be a copywriter anyway, and what better place to learn the business (or so I thought at the time) than in the center of it all.

Most of the people were fun to work for, and they didn't care what I wore or that my hair was longish or that shortly after I was hired I grew a beard. But I wasn't on the job too long before I realized that I truly hated being a secretary. I was good at it, though, and most of the people I worked for knew I wanted to be a writer and eventually gave me small assignments.

But there were some in the group who saw a secretary – especially a male secretary – and thought "imbecile," and nothing I did or said could change their minds. Richard Eisenstein, for example, not only thought I was an imbecile, but also thought I was his *personal* imbecile. He was a quietly menacing creative group head who seemed to delight in humiliating me by demanding that I get his morning coffee every day from the Lexington Avenue Gourmet, even after I explained to him as nicely as I could that it upset the other people in the group when I was away from my desk on a coffee run and their phones were left ringing off the hook. All the other people I worked for made do with the coffee in the break room, which Richard called "that horrible hot brown liquid." I couldn't understand why he didn't just buy his own coffee on his way into work. When I politely suggested it to him one morning when we were still on good terms, he said, "But that's why *you're* here."

After that conversation, Richard always insisted, and since he was fairly senior, I always went. That he thought I wasn't capable of doing much more than getting coffee and taking messages was obvious in the way he'd explain the simplest of chores to me.

"Now, Michael," he'd begin, which was an improvement, since for the first four months I'd worked there he kept calling me Robert, "I have to go to a meeting upstairs," he said, enunciating each word carefully. I wanted to point out that I *could* hear, and that English *was* my native tongue, but I knew it would only get me into trouble.

"I'm expecting an envelope of chromes from the photographer. You know, *slides?* It's going to have my name on it, and they're going to deliver it by messenger to the receptionist. When the envelope gets here, she'll call you. Make sure you get the envelope and leave it on my desk in my office."

"No, Richard," I told him, "I'm going to walk down Fifth Avenue wearing it on my head next Easter. What else would I do with an envelope that has your name on it?"

Richard told me I had an attitude problem, and got back at me by making me get him coffee every afternoon as well. I was saved when he left Malcolm to take a creative director spot at a smaller agency downtown, a challenge he described with the same relish and enthusiasm, I imagined, as Hitler had probably used to describe Poland.

I stayed at that terrible job for a year and a half. I kept trying to find another one the whole time, but no one would consider me for a spot as a junior writer at any of the other agencies I tried. They only wanted writers who were already recognized as such, not ambitious male secretaries with portfolios full of spec ads.

After a while I stopped searching, and focused instead

on moving up at Malcolm. I asked for more assignments, and sought advice from anyone who had the time to give it. I still wasn't convinced I wanted to work in advertising, having spent all this time watching from a ringside seat, but I didn't seem to have any other options.

I got a promotion of sorts when the agency landed the Muscovy Vodka account and formed a new creative group to handle the work. Leif Andersen was taken off Sparks Cola and appointed associate creative group head. Gwendolyn Hammond, one of the people in my group, went with him as senior art director.

Gwen suggested me for a position that she was calling creative group coordinator, but which was really more like secretary with wings. The bait was a small raise ($600 a year, if you can believe it) and some vague promises of writing assignments mixed in with a job description that Gwen seemed to be improvising.

Although I had an ethical problem with working on a liquor account, it was small potatoes compared to my more pressing practical problem: I was broke. The only chance I had of ever making real money if I stayed in advertising was as a copywriter – and here was someone offering to train me. At least it wasn't a cigarette account.

Gwen had a reputation around the agency for being difficult, although I had never really seen that side of her. She always seemed genuinely interested in my career, and often took the time to critique my spec ads. If she was fighting with people, she was doing it behind closed doors as far as I knew. I got along with her just fine. The most I ever had to do for her was to answer her phone and submit her expense reports. And she never made me get coffee.

I took the job, figuring a raise was a raise. Jack Russo, a senior writer from Sparks Cola, joined us, and two new art directors – Henry Barnett and Jenny Lynch – were hired to round out the group. We settled into our own corner of the sixtieth floor. I got a desk outside of Gwen's office and I waited for the writing assignments to come rolling in.

Just after my third anniversary at Malcolm, Leif was offered a better job in San Diego and left without a second thought. This created an opening for a new group head, which Gwen naturally wanted. That decision was left to the agency's creative director, Howard Nielson.

Now, Howard despised Gwen. True, he was always pleasant to her, but that's the way Howard operated. He was like some smiling Borgia, handing you a cup of poison and toasting your health. Howard liked to think he was too nice a guy to fire anyone. If he didn't like someone, he simply stopped giving him assignments, hoping he'd take the hint and find another job. When that didn't work, he'd have his assistant, Fran Rotunda, fire him.

When Gwen approached Howard about taking over Leif's job, Howard told her he didn't have any time to make a decision, as he was in the middle of an emergency campaign to keep the Sparks people from pulling the account and taking their lovely hundreds of millions of dollars to some other lucky agency. Muscovy Vodka was a trifle by comparison, so Howard told Gwen to run the show for the time being.

Gwen assured Howard that he could count on her, and then came after the lot of us with morale-boosting speeches and a glazed look in her eyes. That she had grown up in England listening to Churchill on the BBC while the other kids were out playing Red Light Green Light was evident in her "rally 'round me my soldiers" harangues. Deep down, I think she wanted to be the Margaret Thatcher of advertising, but as it turned out, with her hatchet-sharp features, long black hair (usually pulled into a tight French braid or a feeble Gibson girl) and untreated personality disorders, it was closer to the truth to call Gwen the Margaret *Hamilton* of advertising.

"We have to make this client believe they can't live without us. That's our *mission*," she implored, blowing cigarette smoke in my face. Gwen smoked an obscure Canadian brand of cigarettes that smelled remarkably like an electrical fire, and the sharp stench they generated clung to her like cheap cologne. She was not at the top of my list of people to spend lots of time with.

Muscovy Vodka was a new brand with a lot of money behind it. The client, stuffy Dover Spirits, had finally decided to change with the times and introduce some new lines to their venerable Scotches and whiskeys. They claimed to have unearthed the original formula for Czar Nicholas's favorite vodka and wanted us to treat this discovery like it was a secret recipe hidden for years in some file cabinet in the Kremlin. Others could claim to have once been the official purveyor to the Russian court, but Dover's brew was the private stock the Czar liked to swill when no one was looking. They demanded at least a nod to that heritage in advertising and packaging.

They approached the marketing people at Malcolm with the intention of launching the new brand as Standart, after the Romanovs' imperial yacht. The marketing people convinced them to go with a more contemporary look and campaign, telling them it wouldn't be easy to sell a vodka named after a boat, authentic formula or not, particularly a vodka made outside New Brunswick, New Jersey.

Someone came up with the name Muscovy, and the client bought it, and there we were, sitting on top of a $15 million account with an acting group head who really hadn't a clue what she was doing. Gwen was sure she could make it into a $20 million account, and get herself promoted in the bargain, by capturing more of Dover's business.

Dover had, in its vast inventory, an interesting little item called Old Atlanta Peach Schnapps, which seemed to be languishing on liquor store shelves. Gwen truly believed she could revive this neglected brand and leave her mark on the history of advertising at the same time. The night she made us all stay late and taste it, I thought she had lost her mind.

"This is vile, Gwen," said Jenny, our junior art director and the youngest in the group, as she choked down her first sip. Jenny already had a history with Gwen. From time to time, Dover ran price ads for Muscovy in local newspapers – benign little blurbs advising consumers that there was a reduced price for a limited time. The ads followed a format: price in the lower right-hand corner under a blowup of the label art, the Standart in silhouette (a subtle reminder of the brand's Russian heritage the client refused to part with, even after we changed the name to Muscovy). When I suggested it implied that the vodka in the bottle tasted like marine diesel fuel, Gwen asked me to kindly stop voicing that opinion.

The ad always ran in the same vertical format, and only the dates of the sale ever changed. One day, Gwen announced that someone at Dover had asked to see what we could do with a horizontal format, and asked Jenny to stay late one night and "have a go at redesigning it."

When Gwen came in the next morning, Jenny presented her with three new designs. Gwen didn't like them, and told her to keep working.

Jenny spent the rest of the day at the copy machine making ships smaller and blocks of type bigger, and kept rearranging the elements of the ad like puzzle pieces – only to have Gwen veto each subsequent version. She wanted perfect, she said, and these layouts were merely good. She kept Jenny there until midnight that night, until four the next, and then, on the third and most terrible night, they simply worked together around the clock. I came in and found Jenny still in yesterday's clothes, her face tearstreaked and her office littered with rejected ads and crumpled-up paper.

"Don't ask," she said, holding up a hand to stop me. "Don't even talk to me because if you do, I'm going to start to cry again."

"Can I get you breakfast or something?"

And Jenny started to cry. I went in and closed the door.

"Michael, it's been horrible. She keeps telling me she's so hard on me because she wants me to be a better art director. I'll be a *dead* art director if I don't get some sleep. It's a lousy little price ad! What does she want to do with it, hang it on a wall in the Museum of Modern Art? She said she won't let me go home until I get it perfect."

The client thanked us for "perfect" when Gwen finally presented it, the ink barely dry, and filed it away somewhere. Nothing was ever said about the horizontal format until a month later, when someone in the account group told us that Gwen had misunderstood: The client never really wanted to change formats. Gwen laughed it off, telling Jenny, "Oh well. It was a good design exercise for you. You can put it in your portfolio."

Jenny came in the next day with an Astroturf doormat she'd bought at Woolworth's, glued big white block letters on it that spelled out JENNY where it should have said WELCOME, and put it down in the hall just outside her office door.

So when Gwen invited us to stay late that night and have a drink in her office, I think we all suspected what she was up to. Usually, she drank alone in her office.

Her idea was to pitch the Old Atlanta Peach Schnapps business using a *Gone With the Wind* campaign. I took a sip, and had to agree with Jenny. It was terrible.

"I don't think it's going to work, Gwen," I said. "I can see why they don't advertise this hooch. The only way I can think of to connect it to *Gone With the Wind* would be to show General Sherman using it to set fire to Atlanta."

I should point out here that I spent my adolescence in front of a TV set watching old Warner Bros. films on *Million Dollar Movie*, and that I generally identified with whatever character Eve Arden was playing.

"You're not helping, Michael," Gwen said. "And you don't have to work on this assignment if you don't want to. I just thought you might like something else for your portfolio."

Henry Barnett, the more senior of our new art directors, attempted a second diplomatic swallow. "This really isn't very good, Gwen."

Henry was roughly my age. I don't know which bothered me more, the fact that Henry had already come this far in his career and I was just his secretary, or the fact that I was also Jenny's secretary and she was only twenty-two and fresh out of art school.

"I happen to think it's tasty," Gwen said, blowing cigarette smoke at us and refilling her glass. "Now, I thought of a great campaign line today at lunch." She produced a napkin on which she had scrawled with a felt-tip pen: OLD ATLANTA PEACH SCHNAPPS. IT'S THE RHETT STUFF. "Get it?" she chirped. "Rhett Butler? Georgia peaches? We call it 'The Rhett Stuff!'"

I gagged on my second swallow. "Yes," I sputtered. "It's the *Rhett Stuff* to use to unclog the pipes under your kitchen sink."

"Gwen, you can't be serious about pitching this junk with that awful line," Jack said, finally speaking up. Gwen turned on us.

"I'm quite serious! It's a dying brand because they don't advertise. If we do something great, they'll give us the account and we'll save it for them. Now, I want you people to do a campaign using that line, and I want it to look like something out of *Gone With the Wind*, and if you don't like the idea, I'll bloody well do it myself!"

That said, she dismissed us.

I wanted no part of this assignment, and begged off when Jenny asked if I would work on it with her. I'd help everyone get the presentation together, but I wouldn't touch Gwen's horrible slogan.

Back at my desk, I watched as the lines on my phone lit up – first Henry, then Jack, then Jenny, each probably canceling whatever plans they had for the evening. I called Irene.

"Hi, Lambie. What's up?"

"What are you doing now?" I asked.

"What am I doing? Me and seven other college girls are testing Neet. What else would I be doing in my office at 5:30?"

"I mean, can you get time off for good behavior and meet me for a drink?"

"Isn't tonight a gym night?"

"No. Actually, I disappeared at lunch and went. I was planning to work on the play tonight."

I was writing a play about life in an ad agency called *Dial Nine to Get Out*, but couldn't seem to get past the first act. I looked for any excuse to avoid working on it.

Irene was an editor at a big publisher across town. She put in long hours, mostly on a series of lusty historical novels by one Mara Everds, the titles of which I could never remember, whose hoop-skirted heroines always seemed to be fleeing someone – their gowns torn but their virtue intact. I used to beg her to get me dates with the men who posed for the cover art.

Irene was two years ahead of me at Georgetown, but somehow our paths never crossed until after I had graduated and returned to New York. After months of trying unsuccessfully to find work in film as a production assistant, I gave up and, out of desperation, took an entry-level job at a small book publisher where Irene was already working as an editorial assistant. We started talking in the hall shortly after I was hired, quickly established the college connection and branched out to having lunch together. We found we had a lot in common, especially a passion for old movies, and became friends.

Things began to get awkward when I realized that Irene wanted more than friendship from me, and didn't seem to sense that friendship was the best I had to offer her. I always thought I wore being gay like a red picture hat, but some people need to be told. Irene practically had to be clubbed.

"I can meet you at six," she said. "I shouldn't leave yet, but what the hell."

"Great! I've got a good story for you. Meet me in the Village?"

"Michael, I'm not going to Uncle Charlie's Boystown with you again."

"Uncle Charlie's *Downtown*, and that was your idea. Anyway, you said you had fun that night. All those guys wanted to know where you found those big Bakelite brace-lets. No one paid any attention to me."

"Well, let's go someplace tonight where if a man notices me it won't be because I'm wearing fabulous antique jewelry, okay?"

We settled for an outside table at the Riviera Café. Irene let me have the view, provided I alerted her if anyone cute, straight, and preferably tall with glasses walked by. I told her all about Gwen's idea for Old Atlanta Peach Schnapps.

"The Rhett Stuff," Irene said. "Is she kidding?"

"I wish! Thank God I don't have to work on it."

Our drinks arrived, Cape Codder for me, Screwdriver for Irene, both made at my insistence with Smirnoff, just to spite my friends at Dover.

"Well, this will put O'Hara on your chest!" she toasted, and sipped her drink.

"Oh, that's perfect. Let's get Gwen on the phone."

"Wait," Irene said. "I have a better one: As God is our witness, you'll never go thirsty again!"

"No," I said, laughing. "Don't wait for tomorrow, buy some today!"

Irene smiled. "Drink enough, you'll turn Scarlett!"

I let out a big laugh and almost knocked my drink over. The waiter shot us a dirty look.

I kept laughing the rest of the week. Every time I looked at the empty schnapps bottle in Gwen's office, I wanted to say, "Puts O'Hara on your chest!" But Henry, Jack and Jenny were not in the mood to laugh. They worked late every night for a week and a half, churning out comp ads using that dreadful line, each layout more terrible than the last.

The work was presented a week later. The client was very polite, thanked Gwen and probably filed it away in the same drawer with the redesigned Muscovy price ads.

We did get the account, but that was only because the CEO of Dover and the senior account manager at Malcolm were old golf buddies. The CEO said we could have the account only if we did a recipes campaign, showing how to cook with Old Atlanta Peach Schnapps as well as make mixed drinks with it. He made us promise not to make him reconsider "that godawful *Gone With the Wind* idea."

The recipe ads ran until Thanksgiving, when consumers discovered that turkeys made "plantation-style, basted with Old Atlanta Peach Schnapps and other authentic down-home Southern ingredients" tended to explode after about an hour in the oven. The ads were pulled and the product was withdrawn, which was a pity, considering what we had up our sleeves for Christmas.

2

Buy One, Get One Free

Jack found another job about two months after the Old Atlanta Peach debacle and resigned, leaving us without a writer. Gwen, hoping to be promoted into Leif's still-vacant job, told Howard there was no need to fill Jack's spot, since I wanted to write, and could take on whatever assignments Jack would have done. Not only was she saving the department an extra salary (a fact she planned to mention when making her case for a promotion) but she was also solving a problem for Personnel and showing Howard what a good manager she was.

Howard, who was still trying desperately to hang on to Sparks Cola, probably agreed just to get Gwen out of his office.

Gwen took me aside to tell me that Howard had approved her idea. This was the first I had heard of it. Now I was going to be the copywriter for the group, in addition to what I was already doing.

"Does this mean more money?"

"Not just yet. Howard wants to see how you work out."

"What about giving me Jack's office, then? We could

have the phones put in there, and my files..."

"We couldn't *possibly* give you an office, Michael."

"Why not? It's empty now, and it belongs to our group. It's hard to concentrate out at my desk. *You* try writing an ad with a million people buzzing past and someone always interrupting to ask you to order a stapler or take something down to the mail room."

"It just wouldn't be fair to the other secretaries."

"The *other* secretaries don't write copy. And I'm a coordinator, not a secretary. There's supposed to be a difference, remember? At least make them add 'copywriter' to my job title."

"I should think you'd be satisfied with an opportunity to write."

"I've been writing since I took this job. You and Howard are giving me something I already have."

We compromised. I could use Jack's office to write when I had an assignment, but had to perform the non-creative duties of my job at my desk in the hall.

But Gwen changed her mind after we tried it once, because no one answered the phones while I was away from my desk writing. We got into a huge argument over it, but she wouldn't give in. I did the mature thing: I called in sick the next day and went to a Bette Davis double feature at the Regency. Gwen retaliated by having Office Services move all the Dover files from the hallway into Jack's office while I was out, turning it into a workroom and storage area for props and artwork.

The writing assignments finally started coming in, and Gwen made my life miserable with each one – picking apart everything I wrote and making me do countless revisions for even the simplest ads.

Things finally came to a head the week I also had to run a casting session for an upcoming shoot. Gwen asked me to "get people who looked like the young Kennedys, and interview them on videotape." This way, she could inspect them at her convenience.

I called in all the young Kennedys I could find, plus a few favorite male models in the Ford Men book that I had always wanted to see in the flesh. The casting session went just fine: They found all the people they wanted for the shoot from the sixty models I auditioned. But at the end of the week, when I was finally getting to the ad I had had to put off writing, Gwen called me into her office first to coyly ask for it – then feigning shock when I told her that it wasn't done yet.

I told her I just couldn't do everything – especially not for what I was making. Jack made twice my salary just for writing, and now I was doing his job plus whatever Gwen decided she didn't have time for.

Gwen told me I had no choice: She was the boss and that was the end of the discussion. She waited until I was back at my desk, and then called me to add that the files were getting a bit sloppy, and would I please straighten them up when I had a chance, and would I please also remember to take care of her plants the following week while she was at the shoot. I think that was when I started watering them with Muscovy.

Things got worse as the year wore on. My then-boyfriend, Tim, and I broke up – largely because he couldn't stand to see how upset working for Gwen was making me. We had more arguments over whether or not I should quit than I care to remember. Then, shortly after we broke up and he had moved to California, I got promoted again. I had just turned twenty-eight.

Howard had reorganized the Creative department and accounts were being shuffled. The Dover Spirits group was being absorbed into a larger group on the sixty-first floor under a recently hired creative group director, Ellen McCarthy.

Gwen barely looked at me when she told me I had been made a junior copywriter. "We're all moving upstairs to work for Ellen, and since there isn't a vacant secretary's desk, I told Howard that we may as well promote you." Gwen certainly knew how to toss off a compliment.

I slipped into the writer's office and prop closet and called Irene.

"What's up, Lambie?"

"Irene, I just got promoted!"

"That's fantastic! What are they calling you now?"

"'Sweetheart.' No, really, I'm a junior copywriter."

"Congratulations. Does this mean you write junior copy?"

"No, it means they only had to give me a seven-hundred-dollar raise."

"So what does that bring you up to now? A whopping eighteen thousand a year?"

"Seventeen-seven. Can you stand it?"

"J.H. Christ! They couldn't throw in a lousy three hundred more and give you some dignity?"

"Look, I'm getting an office with a door, and that's dignity enough for now. I'll beg for a raise in six months."

As far as Gwen was concerned, it was a promotion in name only. She still came to me with a million clerical things she needed taken care of, until I pointed out to her in less than polite terms that she now had a new secretary to torture. She accused me of being insubordinate. I told her that if she had something for me to write, I'd be happy to help her out, but I wouldn't do any of this administrative stuff anymore, and that was that. She stormed out of my office leaving her signature cloud of smoke and ash behind, didn't speak to me for a week, and refused to give me any assignments. I came in every day and worked on my play.

But a week later, the problem was solved. Howard told Ellen to find a group head for Muscovy, and she gave the job to Ralph Graham, someone she had worked with at Ted Bates years ago. Ralph was in, Gwen was out. All she had been doing was keeping the seat warm for two years. Ralph's first official act was to kick her off the account, with Howard's blessing.

Needless to say, Gwen was devastated. Here she had been doing the job all this time, thinking that sooner or later she would be promoted by default, and instead they gave it to Ralph, whom Gwen had the nerve to call a hack, a word coined with her in mind.

In spite of the fact that she had mismanaged the account from the start, they promised to make her a group supervisor on the first new piece of business they got. This after she made noises about lawsuits and Malcolm's being unsupportive of women.

It had nothing to do with the fact that Gwen was a woman. It had everything to do with the fact that she was an incompetent manager. Every Muscovy ad we produced under her supervision had gone way over budget. She would make the photographer overshoot every setup, rearranging the models into every conceivable combination – "Now you hold the Bloody Marys and you hold the pitcher and you pretend to be surprised; now *you* hold the Bloody Marys and *you* hold the pitcher and *you* pretend to be surprised" – all to make sure her ass was covered when we got back to the agency and tried to pick the final shot.

Yet no matter how many slides she scrutinized with her 8X Loupe, she could never find one that she liked best. She was notorious for picking three or four slides and creating a master "Best Of" transparency. She'd combine the girls from one slide with the guys on another and the background of the third and through the unconvincing miracle of retouching, another mediocre Muscovy ad was born. We did five terrible print ads while Gwen ran the account, all under the horrible campaign line "Good Times

Start with Muscovy." In every one of them, a group of friends was shown doing some cornball thing like the-guys-shovel-the-snow-while-the-girls-build-a-snowman-and-someone-brings-them-Muscovy-cocktails-using-icicles-as-swizzle-sticks – all carefully (and unconvincingly) choreographed to create what Gwen liked to call "that magic moment" so you'd stare enviously at the page and think to yourself: Aren't they just the cutest bunch of cut-ups *and* they all drink Muscovy! It was one of the worst campaigns to come out of Malcolm & Partners, and just why the client liked it was a mystery to the rest of us.

My personal favorite, and truly the runt of the litter, was the fall ad: a Halloween scenario in which everyone wore funny costumes. The two husbands in the shot were laughing like idiots over their Muscovy cocktails because they had both turned up in identical clown outfits. Brilliant stuff. As in every "Good Times" ad, someone had his mouth open and head thrown back, the very model of mirth, although if you stared at them too long, they started to look more like they were in pain.

And what happened when we got back from the shoot and had reviewed more than a hundred slides? Gwen couldn't find one person in the agency who understood the scenario. The shot she had picked – two men dressed like clowns flanked by their wives, dressed as Marie Antoinette and a cowgirl, with confetti and black and orange balloons everywhere – provoked the same response: What are those two clowns laughing at?

Gwen's solution? Call the retoucher! They decided that the idea would come across better if they stripped in an arm from another shot, so the clown who was laughing the hardest could be *pointing* at the other clown, who was merely chuckling while holding his Muscovy on the rocks. I thought it made the ad read, "Look at what that clown's *drinking*," but Gwen told me to shut up.

She badgered the retoucher and made him do the work over and over. Five thousand dollars later, she had her clown with a pointing arm. The client signed off on it. The ad ran. And then the letters started pouring in: they had given the clown a second left arm, and if you lowered it, his hand would reach his knees. And Gwen wondered why they gave the account to Ralph?

I worked on Muscovy for only a few months after that. Gwen was right about one thing: Ralph *was* a hack. I knew I was in for trouble when we had our first briefing in his office. It was an altar to organized sports. He had every kind of bat, stick, club, puck and hat from every professional team within a fifty-mile radius. All he needed was bunk beds and model airplanes hanging from the ceiling to complete the picture.

You can imagine Ralph's reaction to me. Obviously I wasn't the sort of writer Ralph had in mind for his team.

He sat with his feet on his desk and his chair tilted back against the wall, tossing a baseball from hand to hand as he outlined what he wanted to do with the account. He was attractive, if you like thugs. He was also incredibly arrogant. How he got promoted was another of Malcolm's mysteries. Being Ellen's friend certainly helped. His big claim to fame was a series of commercials he'd done some years ago for a national real-estate chain, using Arthur Godfrey as a spokesman. Hardly award-winning stuff.

We started off on fairly good terms, but as time went by, he became less and less receptive to my ideas, and more and more critical of my writing. He used to read what I'd written, crumple up the sheet of paper and toss it across the room to see if he could bounce it off the wall and into the wastebasket, like he was some hotshot on the Knicks, and then tell me to go back to my office and try again. Worse, it had come back to me that he referred to me as "that little faggot I'm stuck with."

Finally, he just stopped talking to me directly if he could avoid it. He generally gave assignments to Henry or Jenny, and told them to fill me in.

I knew I had to get out of Malcolm, but to find another spot as a copywriter, I had to have a TV commercial. It was that simple. And my chances of doing a commercial while still on Muscovy were pretty slim, especially since you couldn't advertise liquor on TV back then. I went to Ellen and asked to be taken off the account, saying I had been on Muscovy since it came to the agency, and I was getting tapped out. I asked if she needed a writer on one of the accounts where I'd get a crack at TV and radio. She said she was glad that I came to her, and that she liked to see her people hungry. I resisted the temptation to ask if "starving" wasn't a more appropriate way to describe what her people were. I didn't say a word about what was happening with Ralph, which I thought was professional of me. Malcolm being the gossip mill it was, she probably knew anyway.

"I have two accounts I could put you on," Ellen said. "I need a writer on Whatta Wheat crackers. It's Forster Foods. We're making Gwen Hammond group supervisor on that. You'd be reporting to her."

"Umm-hmm," I said, trying to swallow my terror at having to work with Gwen again. "What's the other one?"

"Lakeland Labs Skin Therapy Moisturizing Gel. It's a pool-out of the existing campaign, but someone's gotta do it. You know Jo Fuller?"

"I know who she is, but we've never actually met."

"Well, go talk to her and tell her I thought you'd be good on this."

Jo was born in Sandusky, Ohio – how long ago she wouldn't say, but I suspected she was somewhere around my mother's age. Her first name was really Josephine, but she never liked it, and insisted that everyone call her Jo. She came to New York City after graduating with a B.A. in

English from Vassar sometime in the 1940s. She started working as a copywriter when most of the women her age were still secretaries, and in the years since had worked on just about every major cosmetic account in New York. Her campaigns were legendary. She was creative director of the Paris office when Malcolm called her back home to pitch the Lakeland business. They promised her a vice presidency and her own group to handle the work, but a year later, neither had been delivered. Jo won the account, but every attempt to frame the products as something cosmetic was rejected. And worse, Jo had to answer to Ellen, who had no cosmetic experience at all and was at least ten years her junior.

Undaunted, Jo came to work every day in classic Chanel suits she'd picked up in Paris, always with a colorful Hermès scarf knotted around her neck. She still wore her hair in the efficient Margaret Sullavan bob she'd had all her life, except on days she just couldn't be bothered and hid it under a silk turban. "I'm in an Adrian mood," she'd announce, striking a pose in my office doorway.

Jo and I hit it off from the start. She was delighted to finally have a writer in the group, since no one wanted to work on the Skin Therapy account and she had been doing all of the writing herself.

Lakeland Labs, our client, had been forced to move the account after they were bought out by a French conglomerate in one of those awful "merger and acquisition" deals, which caused a conflict of some kind at their original ad agency. It was a corporate decision, not a creative one. They had been very happy, and were less than thrilled to suddenly be doing business with a giant like Malcolm.

As much as Ralph disliked me, I think he still resented my leaving his group for Jo's, and suspected me of maligning him somehow to Ellen. At first he refused to let me go. A flurry of memos went back and forth between Jo and

Ralph and between each of them and Ellen before it was all resolved. Ralph finally relented, provided I wrote one last ad for Muscovy – a Valentine's Day Sale price ad. Ellen was exasperated, and told me to write the ad so he'd get off her back, and then I'd be free.

I stuck a piece of paper in my typewriter and wrote:

VALENTINE'S DAY SALE!

> *Roses are red,*
> *Muscovy's clear.*
> *Why not give both*
> *To your sweetheart this year?*

I drew a big red heart around the copy, and left it on Ralph's desk with a note that said: How 'bout them BoSox! Ralph never responded. But they *ran* the ad.

3

At Fine Stores Everywhere

Jo managed to get Henry Barnett assigned as art director on the Lakeland Labs Skin Therapy Moisturizing Gel account, and the three of us had spent the winter and early spring trying to persuade the client that it was time to retire their current campaign, which had already been running several years. They wouldn't listen. Jo met with Ellen, who recommended that we do some new work for them in an attempt to get them to move on, although she warned it would be for nothing, since, as she so delicately put it, "They think what they have is hot shit."

What they had was a campaign created by someone at their former agency, probably as a joke, and Lakeland laid it at our door like some rotting carcass, insisting we revive it. The basic structure of their commercials wasn't the problem: they usually found a bland actress who looked like that young mom living just down the street from you, or your kid's favorite grade-school teacher; she had dry hands, she used the product, and then she didn't. It was the demo that was causing all the trouble. The product was designed to moisturize skin that was so dry, it actually flaked off – a dire, life-threatening condition they called *handruff*. Every one of their commercials was designed like a donut, with a hole in the middle for the same tired demo: The spokeswoman would rub one hand over the back of the other, and we'd cut to electron microscope photography of dead skin flakes falling through the air and bouncing off a tabletop in slow motion. Handruff! Then we'd see her rub the stuff onto her hands and we'd cut to the same microscopic view and – problem solved – no more flakes!

It was one of the worst campaigns on television and now we had it, and anyone who worked on it at our agency referred to it as "handjob."

"Look at her," Jo sneered, as we screened the original commercial for the fifth time. "I just want to hit her. Who picked out that blouse she's wearing, anyway?"

The woman in question was speaking to the camera with deep sincerity. "Dry skin, *really dry skin*. You know, so dry it actually flakes off. It's called 'handruff!'"

With that, there was a cut to a close-up of her wringing her hands, and we cut to the horrible demo.

"Ugh! It gets worse each time I see it," Jo said, laughing.

"It looks like a snowstorm on Mars," I said.

The client believed the spot was brilliant because it was memorable. We told them it was memorable because it was disgusting, adding that a bus accident was memorable too, but people didn't want to see one over and over again on television.

And when it became obvious that they loved the idea and that nothing else we could come up with was acceptable, Jo just sighed and said to us, "This is it, kiddies. I've tried and tried but they won't budge. Go give me another one where her skin flakes off in slow motion."

Henry and I tried to do something humorous, figuring that if we were stuck with this premise, the least we could do was to go for a laugh on our way to the jugular. We wrote a spot called "How Dry Was My Skin" to be shot in black and white like a scene out of *Mildred Pierce*. We had a Joan Crawford type walking around a tremendous beach house all upset because her man has left *and* she has handruff. Her friend, a ringer for my buddy Eve Arden, tells her about Skin Therapy Moisturizing Gel. Joan uses it and gets relief – no more flakes! "And maybe *he'll* come back," she says, looking off hopefully into the sunset. "Even if he doesn't," Eve offers, "you'll still have softer hands!"

The client thought I was crazy when we showed it to them, and told us to come back when we had a spot with a spokeswoman in it. The fact that they already had one didn't matter. They wanted another.

And that's what brought me in to the office on my birthday. With a deadline looming, Henry and I still had nothing to present. We really needed the time to work if we were going to have something to show to the client.

Irene says part of my problem is that I'm always taking inventory: Where was I at this time last year? Have I done all the things I set out to do this year? That sort of thing. I know I was doing that in the lobby of the Chrysler Building waiting for an elevator. Twenty-nine and where was I? Still single, still sharing an apartment I could barely afford, still paying off a college loan for a liberal arts education that was basically worthless in the New York job market. Most of my problems stemmed from being perpetually broke, I rationalized, and that would change when I got a better job. I was convinced that if I could hold out at Malcolm for just a little while longer, I could do one or two really good TV commercials, which would be my ticket out. It was all just a matter of time.

"Please, God," I muttered, "don't let this be another year of bran muffins when I really want chocolate croissants."

The doors opened and I stepped into the art deco elevator cab along with Sandy, the receptionist on the executive floor. The ornate doors slid shut, revealing the outline of a huge penis hastily carved into the wood paneling.

"Oh, for God's sake!" I said.

"What's the matter?" Sandy asked.

"Look at that," I said, pointing to the crude phallus scratched on the door.

"I seen bigger," she said, casually.

"No, I mean, who does a thing like that? This is a landmark building! This isn't just wood paneling, it's *art*. I can't believe someone could be so destructive!"

The doors opened on the sixty-first floor. She shrugged as I got off and said, "It's New York," as if that explained everything. Actually, it probably did. I'm sure she thought I was a little crazy, to be going on and on about a couple of scratches in some old two-tone wood zigzags in an elevator cab. But then, I was getting off on one of the two floors occupied by Creative. As far as the rest of the agency was concerned, we were all crazy there.

"Have a nice day," she offered, as the doors slid shut.

I walked through reception and turned down the hall toward my office. I was late. Well, I'm always late. Rose, my mother, says I haven't been early for anything since I was born.

"Hi, Karen," I said, breezing past my secretary.

"Happy Birthday, Michael," she said.

"How did you know?"

"I remembered from last year. And besides, your brother just called to wish you a happy birthday, and so did Irene Lucca. Your brother said to call him back."

Marco had a meeting every morning at ten and I'd miss him if I waited much longer. I touch-toned his number, then uncovered the tea and threw the teabag away, while his phone rang and rang.

My older brother was the yardstick against which everything I had ever done or accomplished was measured. He was named Marco after Rose's father. I got the bland American name; he got the sexy Italian one. I got looks they call boyishly bookish and Marco got stud. He was a star swimmer in high school and was bright enough to get into SUNY Cortland. He majored in business administration, minored in screwing and was the NCAA champion in the 200-yard butterfly in his junior year.

He picked up his phone and barked, "Gregoretti!" then softened his tone when he realized it was me on the line. "Oh. Hi, Michael," he said. "Happy birthday. I meant to send you a card, but it's been really busy."

"Don't worry about it."

"Are you celebrating today?"

"And how. Lunch with Irene. Dinner with Tim. And Friday night, Anthony, Frank and his lover Billy are taking me out."

"Tim? I thought he was in California."

"He's in for the week."

"Oh," he said, not doing much to hide the disapproval in his voice. "You're still coming home on Sunday, though, right?"

"Um-hmm," I said, sipping my tea.

"Well, I have to run. I'll see you then."

Rose was a working mother long before it was the norm. When we were still little, she used to put Marco and me into the tub after dinner to soak, then run around the house doing all the chores she'd been unable to do during the day.

From time to time, she'd check in on us to make sure Marco wasn't holding my head under water. Later, when she had finished what she had to do, she'd come back and wash us and get us into bed.

Marco always sat in the front of the tub. Since he was four years older, he decided that this entitled him to "work the controls." If the bathwater got cold, he would run the hot tap and warm it up again.

One night, he decided to tell me a secret. This was a major event in my life: Marco was telling me a secret! Most of the time he wouldn't even talk to me, saving secrets for his friends only. Now he had one for me! It must mean that he was my friend too.

I didn't realize that the secret was just his way of making sure I'd always sit in the back of the tub. I never did find out why this was so important to him, but I guess the thought of my someday getting to work the controls bothered him.

"See these ladies?" he asked me. He was pointing to the frosted figures etched on the sliding glass shower doors. Each panel showed the same underwater fantasy: a tiny castle with two angel fish and a lovely mermaid swimming near it, little air bubbles rising from their mouths. Marco touched the mermaid on the door near the front of the tub first.

"This lady is the good mermaid. She's very pretty and wears her hair in a ponytail."

Even then, Marco was an expert on the female sex. He considered all ponytails to be signs of great beauty and refused to even talk to the girls with pixie cuts.

"But this one," he warned, as he pointed to the identical mermaid on the other sliding door, the one in the back of the tub, closest to me, "this one is a *bad* mermaid. She's very ugly."

I was already confused. The bad mermaid looked just

like the good one as far as I could see. She even had a ponytail.

"This mermaid is so bad, she would kill you if she could get down off this door. But she can't. *Unless you do one thing.*"

He took a dramatic pause here. I was growing terrified at the thought that there was something I could do, at age three, that could get me killed in my own bathtub.

Leaning toward me, Marco took a deep breath and continued in sinister whispers. "If you ever take a bath without me, and you sit in the front of the tub, that mermaid is going to jump off the door and drown you. Then she's going to chop you up into little pieces and feed you to the angel fish. Only they're not angel fish. The ones on *that* door are devil fish."

Of course, I believed him. I can still see Rose leaning in on her elbows at the foot of the tub with a bottle of Prell in one hand, trying to coax me to move forward so she could wash my hair. I was having my first solo bath after learning of the dangerous mermaid, and refused to leave the back of the tub.

"Move up, Mikey," Rose pleaded. "I can't reach you back there."

I was too afraid to tell her *why* I couldn't move forward, and kept casting worried glances at the bad mermaid to see if she was about to spring from the door and drown me, hoping Rose would somehow catch on to the danger lurking to my immediate left.

I outgrew my fear of the bad mermaid, but my brother would have another chance to pronounce my fate years later. Marco graduated college with vague career goals. He moved back in with Joe and Rose, and decided to spend the summer working out and going to the beach until something inspired him.

A few weeks later, he had lunch with a college friend

who was working at *Wide World of Sports* at ABC. They were staffing up for the Olympics, and he offered to get Marco an interview – his first and only interview since graduation.

Needless to say, Marco got a job at ABC Sports as a desk assistant. It was a combination of right college degree, right athletic background, right time, right place. And Marco's smoldering good looks and the fact that his shoulders were practically bursting out of his jacket certainly didn't hurt his chances either.

Rose was delighted. Her firstborn was working at ABC Sports! Was it near the news division? she wondered. Maybe one day he would get to meet Rose Ann Scamardella!

Marco spent the rest of the summer commuting on the Long Island Rail Road. He left each morning with a frown on his face and came home with his tie loosened and his expression unchanged. The trains were hot, his boss was an idiot, and he hated wearing suits in the middle of August.

He plodded along, and as time went by, they gave him more responsibility. Soon he began to believe that his "I'm going to be the next Jim McKay" fantasy might just come true. At least they were paying him enough so that he could rent a small studio apartment on the Upper West Side and finally move out of my parents' house.

By the time he was twenty-seven, Marco had been made an associate producer. He complained that it hadn't happened fast enough: He should have been a full producer by then, he claimed, blaming all the time he had wasted as a desk assistant. The fact that he never would have started at the network any other way was never acknowledged.

I went through college assuming that Marco would help me get a job at ABC. But when I graduated from Georgetown and asked him to help me get an interview, he said, "There's nothing I can do," as assuredly and finally as when he told me I'd drown at the hands of a bad mermaid.

I tried to get into one of the other two networks on my own. I was not successful. I decided that if I couldn't get into TV, then film production was the next logical step. There were so many things being shot in the city, I thought finding work as a production assistant would be easy. It wasn't. I drifted into publishing next – more out of economic necessity than a love for books, but the whole time I was there, all I could focus on was that I wasn't working in film.

Finally, figuring it was as close as I would ever get to film production, I moved into advertising. I knew that if I couldn't get a spot in the Production department at some agency, I could certainly get something in Creative. I was an English major, after all, and had grown up watching some of the greatest commercials the industry would ever produce. How hard could writing commercials be? They were like thirty-second movies, but with much more product placement. It seemed like a surefire career path either way when I started. But now, at twenty-nine, I wasn't so sure. I was nowhere near to matching Marco's success, and I didn't think I ever would be.

4

Use Only As Directed

And now we come to my second birthday mistake and the bigger of the two: saying hello to Gwen Hammond. Up until that moment, I had avoided any social contact with her. In the same elevator, I would study the woodwork. Passing her in the hallway, I would pretend to be focused on something else or read whatever piece of paper I happened to have in my hand if I was lucky enough to have a prop. I was just so grateful to be away from her.

Everyone else from our original group felt the same way. Jenny said she would never forgive Gwen for the way she tortured her on Muscovy and refused to even look at her. I should have followed her example. The whole time I worked for Gwen, I would have gladly pushed the woman into traffic without a moment's hesitation. But time passed and memories faded, I guess. I had even started defending her, saying things like, "Well, she *was* the one who gave me my first job as a writer, and as miserable as I was, at least I got promoted." And, since it was my birthday and I was feeling benign if not absolutely happy, I started the whole avalanche sliding with a simple "Hello" as I passed her in the reception area.

Fatal, *fatal* mistake. I should have stayed mad. Gwen misinterpreted the greeting I casually threw her way to mean she was forgiven. I had no idea that at that very moment she was desperately searching for another copywriter to work on a presentation, and went straight to Ellen with my "Hello" still ringing in her ears to have me reassigned to her group. Knowing our history, she still wanted me. In moments of delusion, I like to think that she saw past our difficulties and appreciated my talents, but the truth was probably something more clinical: Gwen loved a victim.

So when I turned from my typewriter to see who had knocked at the door, I nearly fell out of the chair – there was Gwen, with a folder in her hand and that glazed smile on her face.

"Gee, hi!" she chirped. "Got a minute?"

"Um, yeah," I said, trying to think of an excuse to keep her from coming into my office.

"Henry told me that the two of you are working together on Skin Therapy Moisturizing Gel. How's that going?"

"It's not. The client hated all the new work we did, so we have to give them another spokeswoman spot. They practically wrote it. All we'll do is change a couple of words in the spot they have already and find a new actress to say it. I don't know why they're even bothering." Sensing I was setting myself up, I quickly added, "But then again, they may come around and do one of the other spots we pitched."

Too late.

"Well, I have an assignment for you and Henry that I think could be a lot of fun. You could really do something *terribly* creative on it."

"I'm not sure I have the time to take on anything new right now," I lied. "I have some other things working, and when they do approve the Skin Therapy spot, we'll be going into production right away."

"Okay. Maybe I can talk to Ellen about getting you off some of the other things so you can work on this. It really would be fun, and with your sense of humor, I think you'd be perfect."

"I'll talk to Ellen myself, okay?"

"Let me tell you about this assignment," she said, lighting one of her foul Canadian cigarettes.

"Well, Gwen," I hesitated, "I have a meeting to go to in a couple of minutes."

"Oh, this won't take long. The product is a really good one. It's new. It's a butter."

"A butter?" I asked.

"Yes. But it's a *low-fat* butter. In a *can.* Come to my office, and I'll show you what we've got so far."

"Well, Gwen, I really – "

We were interrupted by Karen, who came in with my mail, asking, "What's burning in here?" There was an awkward moment when she realized it was Gwen's cigarette. "Here's your mail, Michael," she said, trying not to laugh as she left.

"I'll have to talk to Ellen about it, Gwen. I mean, I appreciate your thinking of me."

"Well, you really should catch her today. She's going to be in meetings all day tomorrow."

"Okay, Gwen. I'll get to her right away."

"*Grácias!*" she said, and left.

I tried to rationalize away my guilt for lying to her. I was busy, but I wasn't swamped. It was just self-preservation. TV or not, I didn't want to work with her on this or any other project. Before I could sort things out, I was interrupted by a phone call from Gwen.

"Michael, Ellen's in her office, and I told her you needed to have a chat. Why don't you go on in there now?"

"Oh, great. Thanks, Gwen."

What was I going to say to Ellen? She hadn't been at Malcolm long enough to know my history with Gwen. As I walked down the hall to Ellen's office, I tried to think of a way out, but I forgot all my lines the moment she looked up from her relatively new Apple Macintosh. Only select, very senior people in the agency had them. The rest of us were still clacking away on battered IBM Selectrics from the 1960s while these titans of industry compared notes on their computers with each other like they were talking about dick size. The sight of Ellen perched there and glaring at me could only have been more intimidating if she had remembered to wear her crown that day. But no matter – if you hadn't already figured out that she was advertising royalty, the four Clio awards displayed behind her on a strategically placed shelf (built to hold several more awards she was anticipating winning) made sure you got the point.

Though in her mid-fifties, she could still pass for much younger, thanks to lots of cosmetic surgery and never having any time or desire to eat meals. Her hair was an unnatural shade of red and she wore it in a shoulder-length pageboy that reminded me of a 1940s Hollywood screen siren by way of Boston's South End. She had been married and divorced years ago and had a daughter who was a freshman at Mount Holyoke. She didn't talk a lot about her life, but did mention once that she had been a washout as a wife because her career was more important to her, and that ultimately, she was happy with the way things had worked out.

"Gwen tells me you're too busy to take this assignment," she stated, matter-of-factly. Her words froze me in the doorway. She motioned me in, and I sat down on her couch. I decided to be just as matter-of-fact.

"Ellen, I know you're really busy now, and the last thing I want to do is turn down work. I only said that to

Gwen because I didn't want to hurt her feelings. But the truth is, I just can't work with her."

"You have to."

"But you weren't here when I worked with her before. She made my life miserable."

"Michael, Gwen was under a lot of pressure then, and she was very disappointed that Howard didn't give her the Muscovy business after all the time she put in. But all that craziness is behind her now. I wouldn't have promoted her otherwise. She isn't the same."

She smells the same, I thought.

"Besides, this is a really good assignment. Half the agency is working on it, and the team that comes up with the winning campaign gets the account. It's a new product, and Forster Foods has a lot of money to throw at us. It's a chance to do something truly breakthrough. And it's television, Michael. Even if they don't use your commercial for the campaign, they've agreed to produce three spots for test. You may get a finished spot for your portfolio."

She knew exactly which buttons to push. I had heard about her performances at client meetings, and there I was in a house seat for a matinee. I almost believed her. If this pitch had been a commercial, she would have just scored a fifth Clio.

"And anyway," she continued, "putting you on this wasn't entirely Gwen's idea. Fran Rotunda suggested it."

True to her last name, Fran was quite round. She was also a force to be reckoned with, ever since Howard had turned over the duty of doling out assignments to her. Fran had her list of favorites. The basic rule of thumb was that if you were tall, male, blond, straight, and didn't wear underwear, Fran gave you the best assignments – like big-budget Sparks Cola shoots in Barbados in February – so I was surprised she even thought of giving me this crack at TV.

"And," Ellen continued, "Gwen's job is to make sure the work gets done on schedule, and that's all. She's a supervisor only. She doesn't make any creative evaluations. I do that. You'll hardly even see her."

I wasn't convinced, but I was trapped. I needed television and Ellen knew it.

"Well, Ellen, if that's the way it's going to be, I guess it's okay."

"I promise you, it'll be fine. And the minute you feel you have a problem with Gwen, I want to hear about it. I think you have a lot of potential, Michael. Now go tell Gwen you're on the account."

Why hadn't I taken the day off? More to the point, why hadn't I been able to stay mad at that witch? By now I was sure this was going to be a disaster. There was nothing I could do but find a seat and wait till the decks started sloping and the life belts were handed out. Some birthday! As I turned the corner, Gwen stepped out of her office and into the hall.

"Hi," I said. "I spoke to Ellen – "

"I *knew* we could convince you to clear your schedule. This is going to be fun, you'll see!" I imagined a giant ring on a string coming out of her back. She sounded like some demented Madison Avenue Chatty Cathy doll.

"Now let me tell you all about Project Fofolofabu! It's a code name."

It seemed like every time we got something new at the agency, they had to give it a code name. My favorite was when they got the Duncan Hines line of boxed cake mixes, and the code name for Moist & Easy was "Dolores."

"Project what?" I asked, stalling.

"Project Fofolofabu. Project Forster Foods Low Fat Butter. It's a code name we'll use around the agency. It's top secret."

"If it's such a top secret, why are we talking about it in

the hall?" Some secret! Hadn't Ellen just told me that half
the agency was working on it? "Why don't you just call it
'The Gadget'? It would be a whole lot easier to pronounce
than Project Folafluffaloo."

"Project *Fofolofabu*," she corrected, steering me into
her office. "We'll call it that so no one will know what
we're talking about."

"I sure don't," I said, trying to figure out how I could
get away before she started writhing on the floor. She was
already babbling in tongues.

"Gwen, can we do this later? I think you should brief
Henry at the same time so you don't have to repeat
yourself."

"Oh, Henry knows most of it already. I told him I'd fill
you in."

"But later, okay? I have a lunch appointment and a
meeting after with Jo Fuller," I lied.

"Okay, fine," she said, drifting out the door. "*Grácias!*"

I looked at my watch and realized how late it was getting. Irene was probably on her way already, so there was
no chance of making our lunch date later. I had to talk to
Henry about what had just happened with Gwen, and that
definitely couldn't wait. But there was no reason Irene had
to wait in my empty office if she got there before Henry
and I had finished. At least something good might come out
of this situation if I timed it right.

I told Karen that Irene was on her way and to just send
her over to meet me in Henry's office when she got here,
then ran down the hall. The more I thought about what had
just happened with Gwen, the more worked up I got. I
steamed into Henry's office, closed the door halfway, then
planted myself in his guest chair, saying, "What is this
butter we're on now, and why does Gwen want us?"

"Well, come on in and sit down, Michael," Henry
drawled, adding, "I think it was Ellen's idea. Gwen is just

supervising it."

"Do you believe that for one second? You know her as well as I do."

"Well, I was a little surprised when she asked if you were available," Henry said, chuckling.

"What is this stuff, anyway?"

"Someone in R&D at Forster Foods found a way to make low-fat butter out of yogurt, egg whites, corn oil and some milk by-products."

"That's the most repulsive thing I've ever heard."

"Me, too. But wait, there's more. It's in a *spray* can."

"Gwen said that before, but I was hoping it was just her dementia talking."

"She speaks the truth. They whoosh it all up with some percentage of real butter and they end up with a butter substitute that's low-fat and low-cholesterol but tastes like the real thing."

"Except it shoots out of a can like Silly String."

"Well, more like Reddi-wip, but yes. They want commercials so they can test-market it next year."

Henry told me everything he knew about the project, which wasn't much more than Gwen had already told me. He agreed to attend Gwen's briefing with me, so at least I was relieved that I wouldn't have to face her alone. While we were talking, there was a knock on the door. It was Irene. She asked if she was interrupting and offered to wait in my office if she was. She was holding a shopping bag with lots of tissue paper poking over the top. Irene had an eye for vintage clothing, and today she was wearing a rust-colored tweed jacket that was very 1950s Christian Dior. She looked particularly fetching, and I introduced her to Henry.

Henry was one of the few art directors at Malcolm who still came to work in a suit every day. His one conces-sion to the lax dress code on our floor was his selection of ties – all loud, all vintage and all truly fabulous. Without them, you might mistake him on the street for a cute, lanky account executive with wire-rim glasses. The ties and the rolled-up sleeves made him look right at home behind his drafting table. He had a great sense of color, and I was glad Irene had worn that jacket. He stood up and shook her hand.

"Oh, Henry! It's so nice to meet you. Michael tells me so much about this place, I feel like I work here. I loved that *Mildred Pierce* commercial you two did. Michael showed me the storyboards."

"Thanks. Too bad the client killed it."

"Are you sure I'm not interrupting?"

"No, you two go. Michael and I were just finishing up."

At lunch, Irene did what she always did. She listened to me rant, calmed me down, and gave me clear, rational, step-by-step ways to deal with the situation: If A, then B, just like the good Jesuits taught us. Knowing my history with Gwen, Irene agreed that it wasn't going to be much fun, but she reminded me that this time Gwen had to answer to someone. There was no Ellen to play "good cop" the last time we worked together.

"So when she starts acting like Medea, just go in there and tell Ellen that you can't work with this dame anymore and get yourself on to a different account. But don't go in and whine."

"I don't whine. When do I whine?"

"When *don't* you? Let's move on to another topic," she said, producing a largish package from the shopping bag, now stowed under the table. "Happy birthday."

I took the gift from her. Irene did such a beautiful job wrapping presents that you almost didn't want to unwrap them. Almost.

"What could be inside this *fabulous* package?" I

wondered aloud, pausing briefly to appreciate the ribbons and paper before tearing into it. The gift was a framed color lobby card of Gregory Peck in *The Man in the Gray Flannel Suit* that Irene had found at Ron's Now and Then on Fourteenth Street.

"Oh, perfect! *This* is going on the wall in my office today," I said, and gave her a peck on the cheek. "Even if you and I are the only two people in the world who get it. I love it, I really do."

"I'm glad. Now tell me more about Henry. First, please tell me he's on my team."

"Yes, Irene, he's straight."

"And you've been hiding him from me?"

"I wasn't hiding him. There was a serious girlfriend for about a year. But I noticed a few weeks ago that the framed picture of her had disappeared from his office. And then he told me one night when we were working late that it was over."

"And you thought the two of us might hit it off?"

"Why do you think I made sure I would be in his office when you got there today and told Karen to send you over?"

I went back to the office after lunch feeling like a condemned man. Even though I was working on other assignments, I couldn't stop thinking about this butter thing.

Henry and I went down to Gwen's office late that afternoon. She was on the phone, smoking what must have been her ten thousandth cigarette of the day. She made an elaborate pantomime of waving us in. We sat at her conference table and waited for her to finish the call.

"Right. Riight. *Riiiight.* Yes! Riiight..."

Was she having phone sex?

"Well, listen, I have people in my office. I'll ring you back shortly. *Ciao!*"

"Well, hi guys!" she bubbled, hanging up the phone. "I suppose you're here to learn about the butter."

No, we came for the free beauty tips.

She handed us sheets of paper on which she had written the headline: INTRODUCING THE HEALTHY WAY TO ENJOY BUTTER.

"Sounds like something Marlon Brando might have said," I muttered.

"Sorry?" she asked, not catching it.

"Nothing."

"Well, anyway. This is what I think should be the strategy statement. This is a new product. If the timing goes as scheduled, it'll be the first low-fat butter on the market."

Henry looked at the statement again, and then looked up at Gwen.

"What exactly is the name of this product, and is there any in the agency for us to taste?"

"Oh, we have lots of names. I made up some of them myself. We're assigning three names to each of the teams working on the product. You two can start with Homestead Acres Dairy Spray."

"Dairy *Spray?*" I blurted.

"Well, it's butter that you spray."

"Gwen, Homestead Acres Dairy *Spray* sounds like something new from Glade that farmers use to freshen the air in the barn." I could have gone on, but Henry gave me a shut-up kick under the table.

"Okay, call it Dairy *Spread* then. I guess that's closer. It's got an applicator nozzle and you can make a sort of pat of butter with it. Or more like a ribbon."

She would, over the next few months, keep changing her mind about what to call the yellow-gray blob that the can dispensed. "The Ribbon" and "The Pat" were her favorites, but every so often she would call it "The Dollop," "The Dab" or "The Smudge." For consistency's sake, Henry and I always called it "The Stain."

"You can either make up two more names, or I can give you two more from my list," Gwen continued. "If you do come up with a name, it should be something that says 'light' or 'first' or 'healthy.' But for now, you shouldn't call it a low-fat butter."

"Why not?" I asked.

"It's a legal thing. You can call it a spread, and you can call it dairy. You can also call it a blend, but it isn't technically a butter as far as the FDA or the FTC is concerned because it doesn't have enough milk fat in it. They're working on getting around that, since it's really made from butter. You can say some weasely thing like 'It gets its goodness from butter' or 'It does everything butter does.' Only for goodness' sake, don't say it fries like butter."

"We can't show people frying with it?" Henry asked.

"Oh, God, no, because it doesn't fry. You can melt it but if you try to fry with it, it just sizzles, and then the water and the oils separate and splatter like mad. It's one of those bugaboos their research people couldn't quite iron out. They're still trying, though."

We went on like this until past five. She smoked and lectured, and read the entire marketing strategy memo aloud, making sure we understood every nuance. The only option was to let her drone on until she finished what she had to say. Asking questions was inviting trouble and I had already caused enough today.

Then she handed us a schedule that outlined when she wanted to start seeing ideas, when these ideas would be presented to Ellen, when spots would be shown to the account group, and so on, right up to a tentative air date for finished commercials.

"Now have fun with it, guys!"

As soon as we got back to Henry's office, we both started laughing. Henry slumped over his drafting table. "Lord, why me?" he moaned. "It took her almost two hours to tell us this crap. Two hours to say, 'The product is a new, low-fat butter, and you have to give it a name and come up with an introductory campaign.' I've got so much other stuff to do today, and I'm stuck sitting in Ding Dong School with Miss Frances instead."

"Do you believe this 'healthy way to enjoy butter' thing? It sounds like a safe-sex guideline." I went into my breathy Gwen voice. "Try massaging it into his nipples. Write dirty words on her tummy with it, then lick it off!"

"Sounds kinky," Gwen said from the doorway.

How long had she been standing there? I felt my face go red.

"I forgot to give you these," she said, handing each of us a folder of information from the client. "It may prove useful. Well, I'm off! Have a good night."

I looked at Henry, but waited until I was sure Gwen was out of earshot to speak. "Do you think she heard me? I mean, I *know* she heard what I said, but do you think she knew I was doing her?"

"Nahhh," he said with a laugh. "The look on your face..."

"It happens every time. You'd think I'd know better. Oh, screw her. If she doesn't know by now how much I hate her, she's certifiable."

5

For A Limited Time Only

While Tim and I were together, we used to eat at least one night a week at Charlie's. It was an actors' hangout in the West Forties – the kind of place where you could get a burger or a bowl of chili, then run across the street for an 8:00 curtain. Tim discovered it just after moving to New York, and dined out for a year on his story about the time the man scribbling away at the next table turned out to be Jerry Herman, working on the score of *La Cage aux Folles*.

It was one of my favorite places, but after we broke up, I avoided it because I didn't want to run into Tim. And after he moved, it just brought back too many memories, so I stopped going in altogether. Tim wanted to buy me dinner for my birthday, and wouldn't even consider eating anywhere else.

The place had more or less emptied out, and would stay that way until the after-theater rush. Tim sat at the bar with a beer, talking to the bartender and one of the waiters, both of whom were actors and old friends of his. They turned when I walked into the room and smiled. The bartender and the waiter waved. Either they knew something I didn't, or the three of them were about to break into a chorus of "Hello, Dolly."

Tim looked great. He hopped off the chair and hugged me. He had been working out, I noticed.

"Happy Birthday, MG!" He held me away from him at arm's length, giving me the once-over. "I see you've still got that beard," he said, as if he'd just noticed. "And you need a haircut."

"Tim, whatever happened to 'Michael, it's good to see you?'"

"I'm sorry. I don't like you in a beard. It's just not the man I fell in love with."

I was starting to feel a little conspicuous. "Why don't we sit down?" Tim took his beer and our waiter took us to a table. I asked him for a glass of white wine. Tim was staring at me again.

"MG, are you all right?" he asked. "You really do look awful."

"Did you fly all this way just to insult me? You could have saved the airfare and called."

"I'm sorry. I didn't mean it that way. You just look so tired."

"I've been working too hard, that's all. I'm fine. I'm depressed, but I'm fine. You look wonderful."

"My new agent. He made me lose a little weight and join a gym. I feel great."

I wanted to ask why he listened to the agent in California, but had told me to stop nagging him when I gave him the same advice in New York.

"You should move to California," he continued, "you'd love it."

"'Hate California. It's cold and it's damp.'"

"How can you hate someplace you've never even seen?" he asked defensively, missing the joke.

"I live in New York. You're *supposed* to hate California. They put it in your lease."

"Well, you should give it a try. I love it." And it showed. The waiter came back with my wine, took our order, and left.

"So what's going on? What are you doing back here, anyway?"

"Try not to sound so happy to see me, Michael."

"You know what I mean. You were so mysterious on the phone. 'I don't want to talk about it, but I'll be in New York the week of your birthday.' Are you delivering stolen microfilm, or what?"

"I'm up for a part. I didn't want to jinx it."

"Here? You got a part in a play here?"

"I'm auditioning."

"Tell me."

"Okay. Remember when I auditioned for the tour of *Torch Song*? They liked me and kept me in mind and called to ask me to read for a part in Harvey's new play, and that's all I'm saying."

"That's great. You should be flattered."

"I don't want to talk about it anymore until after the audition," he said, absently running a hand through his sandy blond hair. He was just so gorgeous. Why didn't we last?

"When is it?"

"Friday morning. So how's your family?"

"Fine. I'm going out there Sunday. Joe is baking an apple cake, and Rose will probably prepare the usual feast."

"And how's your brother?" he asked, practically spitting the words out. Tim and Marco took to each other instantly. Marco thought Tim was arrogant and Tim said Marco was a homophobe. I got them in the same room exactly once.

"Marco's fine. He's dating some woman from the Research department at NBC News."

"Are they serious?"

"Who knows? Rose says that Marco had better get married soon, or the mother of the groom is going down the aisle on a walker."

Tim laughed. "I love your mother, I really do."

"She liked you." I didn't tell him that she liked him only until he broke up with me. Then she got very protective and started saying he was a jerk for letting me go. I usually let her go on for five or ten minutes. It was nice having one person in my life who held me totally blameless for the split.

"And how are you? Really?"

"Same as the last time I spoke to you, Tim. I'm broke. I hate being single. They're making my life miserable at Malcolm. I hate my job, and I can't find a new one."

"You've got to get out of New York, Michael."

"Listen to him. You used to love it here."

"Well, I found a better place. I only came back for the audition, and I wouldn't have done that, except my agent thinks it would be a good move for me. I don't know why you stay here."

"I don't either. It's home, I guess."

"What have you got to lose? Try something else."

"I can't leave now. I just got my first crack at a TV commercial. Today." (I didn't dare tell him who with.) "I have to stick it out a little longer, Tim. No one's going to hire me in California, New York or anywhere else without a couple of commercials in my portfolio."

"If you stay in advertising."

"I've invested all this time in it – I'm going to quit now? And do what?"

"What about the play?"

"I'm working on it."

"You've been working on it since before we met."

"I finished the first act."

"When are you going to finish the whole thing?"

"What am I, on trial here? We're supposed to be having a nice dinner. I don't have to come here for abuse. I can stay at the office for that."

He reached across the table and took my hand. "Michael, I will never love anyone as much as I loved you. As much as I still love you. But maybe now you'll understand why I left. You don't want a lover, you want a father. You want someone to solve all your problems for you. The only one who can help you is you. You're the most brilliant man I've ever met."

"Tim —"

"You *are*. I don't think you realize how much you've got going for you. Why do you settle for this stupid life? You hate that agency. You could temp and make more money, and then you could write."

"I don't want to temp. I don't ever want to be a secretary again."

"They have other things for temps to do besides secretarial assignments. I made a bundle word processing."

"And what about health insurance? I have a great plan at work, and I don't think this is a good time to give it up."

"You're not going to get it, Michael. Stop finding excuses."

The waiter came back with our food. I wished Tim would let go of my hand. The waiter sized up the situation and winked at me. If it had been an RKO movie, he'd have said, "Chin up, sister." He put our plates down on the table and left.

"You should be writing, Michael."

"I don't have anything to say."

"I think you have a lot to say. You just don't know where to start."

I didn't have an answer for him. "Eat your food before it gets cold."

"Yes, dear," he said, like a henpecked husband.

"Tim, please don't do this to me."

"What?"

"What! You're here five minutes and you're all over my back because I didn't pick up the Pulitzer Prize for drama this year and I look like hell."

"I'd love to be all over your back," he said in that sexy voice he usually used on soap opera auditions.

"Stop it."

"He's blushing. I'm glad I can still make you blush. I wonder what else I can still make you do?" he said, smiling his little schoolboy grin. The thing I hated most about Tim was the fact that he knew he could charm me every time, just by smiling at me.

"So how about letting me come over tonight and watch you shave."

"I'm keeping the beard, Tim."

"I'll shave you. First we'll shave the beard, then we'll shave the chest, then..."

"Eat your burger."

"I'd rather..."

"Don't even finish the sentence."

He didn't have to. I knew what he was thinking by the way he was grinning. We finished the meal on better terms, and then the waiters brought out two slices of cheesecake with candles and harmonized a "Happy Birthday" to further mortify me.

Tim asked me if he could spend the night, and I said no all the way down to the Village. We finally agreed on a nightcap in Christopher's, though I told him I had had enough to drink.

"Not yet," he said. They say no one is seduced who doesn't want to be.

We sat at the bar, and the bartender asked us what we wanted. I asked for a Perrier, but Tim said, "Two glasses of champagne," adding, "on me."

The bartender set down the flutes in front of us. Tim picked up his and said, "I hope we stay friends for the rest of our lives."

"You're really pushing it, Laughton," I said, lifting my glass to him in a toast.

I looked across the room and saw Anthony, my roommate, at the other end of the bar. He had been waiting to catch my eye, and now waved at himself with an imaginary fan and batted his eyes.

"Tim. Anthony's here."

"Where?"

I pointed and Anthony waved. Compact, cute, street-smart – a tough guy with affectations, Anthony DeLorenzo was a sweet kid who grew up in a bad Brooklyn neighborhood where everyone called him "Antney" and tortured him because he was gay. But Antney was scrappy. What he couldn't defeat with his fists he could destroy with caustic sarcasm, and local terrorists soon moved on to more passive targets. He went through life doing and acting as he pleased, with no apologies to anyone. He was, in short, a good old-fashioned Brooklyn queen, and I knew the moment I met him that I had made a friend for life. When he finally ended a disastrous four-year romance with an antiques dealer and part-time sadist named Vic, Anthony kept the rambling two-bedroom apartment they had shared on Hudson Street. "Part of my divorce settlement," he explained, grinning like Paulette Goddard. A month later he asked me to move in.

Tim got off the barstool, walked over to Anthony and gave him a big hug. He put his arm around Anthony's shoulder and took him down to our end of the bar.

"Where are you staying?" Anthony asked, playing the innocent.

"Uptown. With my old roommate."

"How *is* Barry?" Anthony asked. (He once confessed to

having a major crush on Barry. "He's my type," Anthony
had said. "Yes," I deadpanned. "He has a penis.")

We got caught up for a few minutes, and then Tim
excused himself and headed for the bathroom. Anthony
waited until Tim was far enough away not to hear.

"Are we having a houseguest?" he asked, coyly twirling
the lemon wedge in his drink with his index finger. "I
would have dusted behind the armoire."

"I don't know, Anthony. He certainly wants to."

"So why don't you?"

"I have to work tomorrow, for one."

"Not good enough."

"No clean sheets on the bed?"

"Tim's idea of heaven."

"I'd be lying if I said I didn't want him to."

"So give yourself a birthday present. Have a good time
tonight."

"Tonight's not the problem. The problem is after he
leaves."

Tim spent the night. And the next night, too. It was
getting too comfortable too quickly. He had his audition on
Friday, and he joined Anthony and Billy Altman and Frank
Donovan, a couple I'd met through Irene, in taking me out
for another birthday dinner that night. And we slept
together again.

Tim called his agent on Saturday and found out that he
didn't get the part. He said he didn't care, and was glad he
was going back to California the next day. The weather had
turned cool, and we stayed in Saturday night. Sunday
morning I left for Long Island and Tim flew home. It had
been perfect, I suppose, because there was a limit to our
time together. It was just sleeping with an old boyfriend.

But I never felt as alone in bed as I did that Sunday
night.

6

Look For Our Ad In Sunday's Paper

I was sitting in my office the next day with my feet on the desk and a yellow legal pad in my lap, jotting down some thoughts about the butter. Henry and I were planning on tossing some ideas back and forth, but so far, I hadn't had many. I looked down at my pathetic stabs at headlines, each one worse than the one above it. I was disgusted with the whole thing already and we hadn't even started. I added one more headline to the list: PROUDLY SERVED ABOARD THE ANDREA DORIA.

I heard Fran Rotunda in the hallway asking Karen if I was in my office. A visit from Fran! Usually she summoned you to her office. I quickly put my feet on the floor where they belonged and tried to look like I cared about what I was doing.

"Hi, Michael," Fran said, poking her head in the door. She was eating an apple. "Ellen told me you've decided to work on the butter after all, and I just wanted to thank you for helping us out."

"No, Fran. Thank *you* for thinking of me for it." Okay, Michael, I told myself, don't spread it on too thick. "I mean, it's TV. Why turn it down?"

"Exactly. Anyway, I'll let you get back to work."

She crunched her way down the hall and I went back to my legal pad. Ten minutes later, Gwen was at the door.

"Knock, knock!" she said, as she breezed into my office. My eyes went involuntarily to the cigarette in her hand. She must have caught me, because she took a step back and stuck her arm out the door. I had thrown away the ashtray long ago, hoping that once she realized I didn't want people smoking around me, she'd stop. But she didn't. She would just let the ashes fall onto the carpet, sometimes grinding them in for good measure, other times letting them sit there like long-dead caterpillars. Today she must have thought she was being fair by keeping the burning part in the hallway where she could poison Karen, and only exhaling in my office.

"Michael, I had an idea I thought you and Henry might want to play with. Since you're doing a spot for the name Homestead Acres, I thought it might be quite clever if you did some talking cows."

"Talking cows?"

"Right. Can't you just picture it?" She started talking in this Margaret Dumont dowager voice that was supposed to be a cow, chatting with one of her friends. "Frankly, I'm udderly *mooo-stified!* Imagine! A butter made from yogurt!"

I don't remember the rest of it. I suggested showing Elsie Borden getting into a snit, but she took me seriously, and said she didn't think Borden would let us use their character since Forster was the competition.

"No, this has to be an original cow. Maybe we could call her Flossie Forster?"

"It's brilliant, Gwen," I lied, "but I don't think I could improve on what you've already done with it. You should tell Ellen about it yourself, so she'll know it was your idea."

"But I'm *giving* it to you. With your imagination, it would be super!"

Super. She was the only person I knew who still described things as "super" or worse, "groovy."

"You don't think it's a good idea, do you," she said, wounded.

"It's fine, Gwen. I just don't think I could do it justice. You should write it."

"But I'm telling you to write it," she said icily, taking another step into my office and bringing her cigarette in with her for good measure.

"I'll mention it to Henry and we'll see."

"Yes, we will, won't we? I don't care what else you and Henry come up with, but I want to see talking cows!"

She turned on her heel and went striding away, leaving ashes and clouds of blue smoke in her wake.

"Well, *I* want to see a blur fly past my window and find out it was you jumping out of the tower like Kim Novak," I said under my breath. I got up and went down to Henry's office to tell him what Gwen had said.

"Let her talk, Michael. We'll tell her we tried, and we just couldn't do anything with it. What is she going to do to us?"

But later that day, Ellen stopped me in the hall. "Gwen tells me that you and Henry are doing a talking cow for Homestead Acres Dairy Spread."

"Actually, it was Gwen's idea."

"Well, I think it's great. It's breakthrough." ("Breakthrough" was Ellen's favorite buzzword. A commercial was breakthrough if it grabbed attention by being interruptive or different and broke through all the other clutter on TV. Sort of like the sirens you'd expect to hear when the U.S.S.R. finally pushed the button that sent its nukes our way.) "You stick with Gwen, Michael. She'll teach you a lot. She's got good instincts."

And a big mouth, I wanted to add.

In addition to giving us the terrible talking cow assignment, Gwen asked us to write commercials around two other names for the product she dreamed up: Premiere and First Light. She told us to write a commercial for each where the name could be switched with any later choice, and one commercial for each name that could not be switched. Five commercials based on her thoughts and ideas didn't leave us much room to do anything on our own.

"What are we going to do about the talking cows?" Henry asked one night – the first of many in which we found ourselves still in the office after nine, surrounded by empty takeout cartons from the Chinese place around the corner.

"I would like to grind up the talking cows for hamburger. I would like to send the talking cows away on an all-expense-paid vacation in exotic Hawaii, with luggage by American Tourister, and hotel accommodations provided by the posh Ala Moo-ana Hilton…"

Henry interrupted. "Hey, why don't we show cows all around the world?"

"What do you mean? Like French cows: *Ooh-la-la! Zees new Om-staid-A-cra ees très, très magnifique?* Forget it."

"Well, no. Suppose they were glamorous cows? They were fat cows but they started eating Homestead Acres Dairy Spread instead of butter and they got slim and gorgeous, and now they're like international cows."

"That's so twisted, I'm afraid of it. If Gwen hears that one, she'll make me write the dialogue. I'm not writing lines for international cows."

"*Gwen* is an international cow," Henry said.

"Okay, let's come back to the cows later. What are we going to do for First Light? I think this one might be easier to sell. We could take the name literally – first light of day – mornings, breakfast?"

"Sure," Henry said, catching on. "Breakfasts all across the country – soft guitar music – sunrise over the farm, cut to the farmhouse. Happy Farmer and Happy Farmer Family eating home-baked, oven-fresh bread stained with First Light. Dissolve to a city. Sunlight peeks through the steel canyons as corporate types in starched striped shirts and suspenders sit down to power breakfasts. And what are they spreading on their bagels?"

"FIRST LIGHT!" we shouted at each other.

"Except it can't be a bagel. The client will say bagels are 'too New York,' which is code for 'no Jews.'"

"English muffin, then," Henry said, scribbling little drawings on a newsprint pad as he spoke. "Anti-Semite *bastids!* Okay, I think we have one here. Hey, can I ask you something? Is your friend Irene seeing anyone?"

"Why? You want her number?"

"Well, if you wouldn't mind and you think she might be interested."

"No, I think she'd be glad to hear from you. Only I don't want details. Don't put me in the middle of it, okay? She's my best friend. And don't break her heart."

"Michael, come on. You know me. She seems nice and I'd like to take her to dinner."

"Okay. She loves sushi, by the way."

By the end of the week, Henry and I had covered every inane idea Gwen had. We hated the work, but hoped that if she saw what she'd asked for, she'd look kindly on any original work Henry and I had done.

For the name Premiere, we had come up with two truly terrible ideas we knew she'd love. One was to show people getting invitations to some posh premiere, and then when they arrive in their evening clothes, lo and behold! They get to taste a new butter. It was pretty hokey, but our

second idea was even worse. This involved the same premise, but this time, the premiere was a red-carpet event,
where glamorous people in beautiful clothes have to stop
on their way into the theater and say some witty thing to an
emcee at a bank of microphones. So we made up all these
terrible characters with names like Laura Lean, Larry
Lowfat, and Lina Lowcal. It was a scream. I had the emcee
ask Lina Lowcal, "Who designed your dress?" and she told
him "Oleo!" We hated the name Premiere for a butter, but
at least we finished the week with everything Gwen wanted
to see, and just enough time left to work on something the
two of us could live with.

When we got together on Friday morning, we
reviewed all the ideas we had come up with and used or
abandoned, then started talking about new ones.

"You know, maybe it's just me, but I always feel a little guilty when I use butter," I said.

"Guilty? Why guilty?"

"Cholesterol. It's like getting a tan now, or eating a
cheeseburger. You know you shouldn't do it."

"So what are you saying? We have guilt-free butter
here?"

"In a way. I mean, when I use butter, I practically
shave the stick to make the thinnest slice possible. I even
keep it in the freezer. It's harder to use that way."

"You're kidding!"

"Isn't that the sickest thing? It drives my roommate
nuts. Compulsive mind at work. But you can take smaller
slices when it's frozen."

"Sounds like a World War II housewife trick —
rationed butter lasts longer if you freeze it."

"I guess it is like rationing. But then, I'm using so little
when I do have some butter, I won't have to worry about
calling Roto-Rooter in thirty years to come over and unclog
my arteries. Now if you told me that you had taken out the

fat, but it still tasted the same and did everything butter does except kill you, I'd slather it on everything."

"You know, that's what we should do. Show people doing weird things, like spreading paper-thin slices of butter on toast..."

"I don't think that's so weird!" I said like Peter Lorre.

"You know what I mean. People go through elaborate tricks to use less butter because it makes them feel guilty when they use too much. Then, along comes new whatever-we-name-it, the low-fat butter in a can, and great googly moogly! Ribbons, dollops and stains all over the place!"

And by the end of the day, we had the one spot we both loved. "Eating Less" was funny, on strategy, and best of all, our own idea. We had done what Gwen wanted, and cranked out talking cows and rising suns and jet-setters attending low-fat premieres – ideas I wouldn't touch if they were taped to Dennis Quaid's abs – but at least we had one spot she couldn't say was hers. We were working on the last few details when Gwen poked her head into Henry's office.

"Hi, guys. Ellen expects to see work first thing Wednesday, which means I should see it sometime Monday. That gives you a day and a half to fix them, in case I have any little nitpicks. Is that comfortable for you?"

"Sure. We're just about done." Henry said. "We've got six spots."

"*Six!* Didn't I tell you? Ellen only wants to see *two* from each team."

"So we'll show her all six and she can pick the two she likes. I'm sure she'll kill something anyway," Henry said.

"She wants you to present your *best* two. That's what our little meeting on Monday is all about. I know what Ellen wants, and we'll see what each team has that comes the closest and just weed out the rest. However did you come up with so many commercials?"

"Gwen, you practically dictated the copy for five of them! They're what you told us to do!"

"I don't like your tone of voice, Michael."

"That's too bad. We've been here late every night this week busting our asses on this assignment, and then you tell us it's been for nothing? We either present six spots to Ellen or I'll rip them all up right now, and you can go in empty-handed."

"Michael, calm down," Henry said. "Look, Gwen, we have some stuff that's pretty good, and some stuff we wouldn't mind seeing die. Maybe we can weed out two spots before we see Ellen. Then she'd only have to look at four. I can't believe she would want to eliminate work without even seeing it first."

"She's very busy, you know. She has a lot of client meetings to go to and..."

"For Chrissake, Gwen!" I shouted. "They're thirty-second commercials, not full-length screenplays! They'll take all of ten minutes to present. Give us a break!"

"I think we should all take the weekend to chill out. It's been a bad week for everyone, and we're all a little tense. Now I'll see you both in my office on Monday morning."

She turned and walked out.

"Michael, why did you do that?"

"Because I hate her, that's why. It frightens me. You know how she treated me when we worked on Muscovy. I swore I'd never work with her again. So look what happened."

"Okay. Calm down."

"You wait and see. She'll make our lives a perfect hell until this project is over, and the work will be terrible. I keep hoping it's a nightmare and I'll wake up screaming. She's a manipulative, condescending, no-talent fraud, and everyone but Ellen is on to her. I'd like to know who she's sleeping with. Or which client she's related to."

"Michael, come on."

"I'm sorry. I just see it starting all over again. And by the time this project is over, one of us will have tried to murder her."

"I think I can predict who that will be," Henry said, throwing an Artgum eraser and hitting my shoulder.

I screamed in mock pain, clutching my shoulder, and fell theatrically to the carpet. "My typing arm! I'm done for! I'll never finish my play!"

"I'm glad to see you haven't lost your sense of humor," he said, shaking his head.

"I haven't lost my sense of humor," I said, sitting up. "Just my mind."

7
Relieves Itching

The next night, Anthony decided that what I needed was to get out of the apartment. He dragged me to a double bill of *The Awful Truth* and *You Can't Take It with You* at Theatre 80 St. Mark's.

Moving in with Anthony had turned out to be one of the few things I'd done right. We would go to the bars together every so often, but we never took it seriously. Sooner or later he'd say something like, "Woof, woof. All the beauties must be on the Island this weekend. It's *faccia brutta* everywhere you look," and we'd leave, laughing but empty-handed.

He was convinced we'd be roommates into old age and had it all planned out. The two of us would end up in some retirement village in Florida, "the oldest queens in Fort Lauderdale," he would say, "sitting in the sun, watching shirtless boys jog by and bickering over who starred in which old movie."

"Yes, Anthony. I can just see us now. Big Edie and Little Edie with palm trees."

Anthony's mother once asked him why he couldn't bring home a nice boy like me — or better still, why he couldn't bring *me* home. Anthony replied, "Michael? Michael is my *sister!*" He enjoyed his pose as world-weary queen giving advice to the new kid on the beat. He was overprotective and, sensing how upset I was getting over the impending Homestead Acres disaster, he sprang into action, making me go to that double feature with him instead of letting me sit in the apartment as I had planned.

"Are you still depressed?" he asked. We had decided to walk back to the West Side.

"Depressed is the wrong word. It's just the office, that's all. I thought it was going to be fun once I started writing, but it isn't."

"Michael, let up on yourself. Remember two things: You're young and you've got your health. Oh, I sound like someone's old grandmother. But you know what I mean. It'll all work out." Realizing that the movies hadn't helped as much as he'd hoped, Anthony suggested his other standby: men.

"Come on. I'll take you to the Spike."

"Anthony, I have lived in New York all this time without ever going into the Spike. I think I'll keep it that way."

"What have you got to do that's more interesting? Go home and wash a shirt, maybe?"

"Something tells me I'll stick out at the Spike."

"Why?"

"I'm not wearing any leather, for one thing. Don't they have a dress code there?"

"You don't have to be in leather."

"Maybe another night. Let me work out for another five years first."

"Michael, come on! It'll be fun."

"I can't go to the Spike, Anthony."

"Why not?"

"Guys in full leather seem so...menacing."

"Menacing! Oh, honey, *please*. They all stand around

there looking so butch, but it's a big act. Take any one of those queens home, and she'll show you how to reupholster your sofa. Now stop arguing with me. You'll love it. I'll get you inside, you'll get one whiff, and I bet I'll never get you out again."

So we went to the Spike. As we walked in, Anthony leaned close and muttered, "Just don't ask for Perrier with a twist. Let your hair down and have a beer."

"I'd much prefer a strawberry daiquiri or a mai tai," I minced.

"Michael! Can you butch it up just a little?"

"That's homophobic and self-loathing. I embrace my nelly side. However, now that I look around, I think we should have stopped off at the apartment first so I could stuff a sock in my underwear."

Anthony got us a couple of beers, and we found space on a wall to lean against.

"God, I haven't been here for so long. I practically lived here in the '70s."

I felt so self-conscious. Well, more self-conscious than usual. I couldn't have looked more out of place in this bar if I had been wearing a lavender ball gown.

"That guy likes you, I think."

"Which one?" I knew which one – the guy in the black leather jeans, open black leather jacket, black tank top, black hair and black beard, with a pair of eyes that could have given Elizabeth Taylor a run for her money. Breathtakingly beautiful, built like a swimmer on steroids, and what the hell did he want with me?

"Him! Al Parker's little brother. He keeps looking over here."

"There's a clock on this wall, Anthony. Maybe he's just trying to see what time it is."

"He isn't looking at the clock and he isn't cruising me, honey."

"Which one are we talking about? The dark one in leather, or the dark one in leather?"

"Oh, you're never gonna let me forget that I took you here, I can see it!"

Our new friend crossed to the bar and got a beer, then turned and leaned and stared and smiled a smile that spoke volumes, mostly unprintable.

"He's hot," Anthony said.

"He looks like a gay ax murderer. Body by Nautilus, hair by Kenneth."

"What's wrong with him? That he likes you, maybe?"

"He has a tattoo on his chest, for starters. See it poking up over the tank top? It's a dragon, I think."

"So? What's wrong with that?"

"Anthony, when I was growing up, only two kinds of people had tattoos, convicts and sailors – and my mother said to stay away from both."

"Well your mother's not here and that guy is. Tell him to zip up the leather jacket while he does you and you won't see the tattoo, because he wants you."

"He's just trying to figure out who let these two girls in here."

"Michael, if you don't want him, then step aside. He's just my type." Then, in a fluttery falsetto that sounded like it came from the love child of Billie Burke and Topo Gigio, he trilled softly, "Oh, mystery man of my dre-ee-eeams…"

And Bruno just kept staring at us. I studied the floor. Thank God I still had the beard! I didn't have the body or the wardrobe, but at least I had the facial hair. And what if I did go home with him? Just what was I so frightened of?

"Go talk to him, Michael."

"I'll ask him what he's majoring in."

"Oh, I give up. I can see this was a mistake. Finish your beer and let's go."

"This isn't my kind of place, Anthony. I'm sorry."

"You hate it, don't you?"

"I don't *hate* it. But I feel like I went through a wrong door somewhere. The steward is going to come along any minute now and sneer at me and tell me this isn't my deck chair. I do better at Bloomingdale's."

We left the Spike and walked toward Eighth Avenue.

"Where do you want to go now, Michael? How about Ty's?"

"Home, I think. I'm just not up for this, Anthony. I feel bad enough about things as it is. I don't need to add rejection to the list."

"Rejection? You had the hottest number in the bar looking you up and down like you were ice cream in August and you're complaining about rejection?"

"Anthony, I wasn't interested in him. That's what always happens. The ones I like won't even look at me, and the ones I don't want won't leave me alone."

"What are we gonna do with you?"

We walked in silence for a while. It was a beautiful clear night. We turned onto Eighth Avenue and Anthony tried again.

"Just stay out another hour. We can go anywhere you like. Then you can go home."

"Caffe Sha Sha? I can get a chamomile tea there."

"How exciting! I meant somewhere where you can get *men*."

"You *said* anywhere I like."

"Fine. Maybe we can sit near the window at least and see who's headed toward Christopher Street."

We walked on a bit. Anthony lit a cigarette. "You should have given that guy a chance. He would have been fun."

"Anthony, please. He wasn't my type."

"Who *is* your type?"

"You know what I mean. I'll bet that guy never saw

The Awful Truth. He was hot, but not husband material."

"*Husband!* Michael, sometimes you just need to go home with someone and roll around a little, then say goodbye the next morning."

"I can't do that, Anthony. I never could. Someone hanging out at the Spike is not going to settle down with someone like me."

"You never know, Michael. You never know."

"I *do* know. I want the whole thing. Geraniums on the kitchen windowsill."

"You gotta have money to have a kitchen with a window in Manhattan."

"Who says we're living in Manhattan? Maybe we'll move to Connecticut."

"You gotta have money to have *anything* in Connecticut."

"Oh, really? Have you ever been to Bridgeport?"

"Well, you wouldn't last ten minutes outside of New York."

"I would so. I could leave the city in a second. I miss having a backyard and a garden. I want to live someplace where the leaves change color and don't just turn brown and die and drop off the trees."

I realized he wasn't listening. He was staring at something up the street. I turned in time to see a tall, absolutely gorgeous man in a yellow sweater and tight jeans ambling toward us. I mean beautiful – like Don Murray in *Bus Stop*. As he passed us, Anthony swiveled his head to the point of breaking his neck in order to keep staring at him. Dreamboat said something but I didn't hear it.

"Why didn't you say hello back?" Anthony hissed, lightly punching my arm.

"He said hello?"

"Yes. To *you*. Maybe if you weren't so busy studying your feet you would have heard. He's been staring at you for half a block."

I turned around to look back. He was doing the same, and stopped and gave me a big grin. I turned back to Anthony.

"He *did* mean me. Now what?"

"How many more chances do you think you're getting tonight? Go talk to him. He's waiting."

"On the street, Anthony? Just like that?"

"Oh, how long have you been gay? He knows we're standing here talking about him, so don't be stupid. You go talk to him, and I'll go to Sha Sha and get a table. See if he wants to come. Or go someplace with him for a drink and I'll see you later. Or tomorrow."

He walked away trilling, "Oh, mystery man of my dre-ee-eeams."

Don Murray was still waiting, so I walked the half-block to talk to him.

"I was hoping you'd stop," he said. The voice matched the face. Like FM radio down South. He shook my hand.

"I'm Craig Connolly." He had beautiful blue-gray eyes and a tiny diamond stud in one ear.

"I'm Michael Gregoretti. Nice to meet you."

"Do they call you Mike?"

"No. Mikes are taller. Everyone calls me Michael. Or MG. That was my nickname in college, MG. My mother calls me Mikey, but she's the only one. Anyone else calls me that, I feel like the kid who liked Life cereal." I made a mental note to shut up, already. He was grinning at me.

"You're an adorable kid."

"I'm no kid, Craig. It's the streetlights. I'm older than I look."

"What are you? Twenty-five?"

"I just turned twenty-nine."

"Have you always been so handsome?" he asked.

"Oh, you should have seen me before they removed

the hump," I said, patting the back of my neck. I was blushing, something I've unfortunately raised to an art form.

"I was heading over to Chelsea Transfer. Can I buy you a drink?"

"Umm, well, sure. A Perrier."

We started walking up Eighth Avenue.

"I don't do this, usually," I said.

"This?"

"Stop and talk to strangers on the street, then go have drinks. It's not something I make a habit of doing."

"I'm glad you did. I saw you and your friend – what's his name?"

"Anthony. He's my roommate."

"Anthony. I saw you and Anthony walking toward me, and you were talking away. I tried to think of something to do to get your attention."

"Anthony kindly took care of that."

"We'll just have to thank Anthony. Someday."

He held the door for me. It was crowded inside, but not packed to the walls. Craig squeezed into a space at the bar to order. The bartender brought the drinks, Craig paid and we drifted off toward the wall. He smiled at me, lifted his beer and said, "Cheers." Then he asked, "What do you do, Michael?"

"I'm a copywriter at Malcolm & Partners Worldwide advertising. I'm on the Skin Therapy Moisturizing Gel account."

"Did you do that commercial where the skin flakes off her hand in slow motion?"

"No, another agency did that before we got the account, but we're going to do another one just like it."

"God, that's a dumb commercial."

"I wish the client could hear you. We keep telling them that but they don't believe us."

I was having trouble concentrating. I was dazzled by

this man. "Where are you from? I mean, your accent…"

"I was born in Louisville, Kentucky. I grew up in Dallas and then Phoenix. I just moved here about four months ago from Santa Fe."

"What do you do?" I asked.

"I work at GMHC. In Financial Management."

"Really? That's great! I mean, I imagine it isn't easy, but it's good that you're involved."

"I like it. It doesn't pay a whole hell of a lot, but I feel good about what I do."

"Beats writing skin care commercials. How's that for social consciousness?"

After about half an hour, we hit an awkward spot where we'd both run out of things to say. I told him I needed to leave, since I had to be up early the next morning to catch a train to Long Island to visit my grandmother in the nursing home and have dinner with my parents. He gave me his card and said he'd like to have dinner sometime. I told him that would be nice. I didn't have one of my cards with me but told him I was in the book. If I wasn't the only Gregoretti in Manhattan, I was definitely the only one on Hudson Street.

He took my hand to shake it, but just held it instead. Then he bent down and kissed my neck. He flashed a sly grin and said, "Sorry. I've been wanting to do that all night."

"It's okay, really," I said, my voice fluttering like Judy Holliday's.

"He even blushes. I love it!"

"Well, good night, Craig."

"Good night, cutie."

I floated down Eighth Avenue smiling. It felt like the most magical, romantic night of my life. The only thing missing was Frank Faylen and Ward Bond on the corner singing "I Love You Truly." By the time I got to Caffe Sha

Sha, Anthony had finished one cappuccino and was smoking a cigarette and waiting for his second.

"What's wrong? What happened?"

"Nothing's wrong."

"Then what are you doing here?"

"I'm going to have a cup of chamomile tea, if that's okay with you."

"You know what I mean. What happened with Mr. Hunky?"

"He *is*, Anthony. He's so sweet. He's Southern. He has the greatest voice. Like warm honey."

"What's his name?"

"Craig Connolly. God, he was gorgeous."

"I noticed."

"He's got beautiful eyes and when he smiles he gets little crinkles around them. And that salt-and-pepper hair. He wears a little too much cologne, though."

"You can fix that after you hook him."

"We went to Chelsea Transfer and talked for a while, and then he kissed me. Oh, God, I sound like The Crystals!"

"He kissed you?"

"On my neck. I thought I was going to swoon."

"You let a man, a *stranger*, kiss you in a bar? You wouldn't talk to that stud in leather at the Spike, but you'll stop on Eighth Avenue for the Old South and go have a drink with him and let him kiss your neck. All my illusions are shattered! My sister has a sex life after all."

When we got home around one, the little light on the answering machine was blinking, so I played back the message, expecting it to be Irene.

"Michael? This is Craig. I just wanted to tell you again how glad I am that we met tonight. It's about half past midnight now, and I'm at home. I'll be up for a little while, I think. Call me if you get in soon." I played the message back for Anthony. He picked up the phone and handed it to me, ordering, "Call him now!"

"It's after one in the morning."

"He's waiting for you. If you don't, he'll think you were lying about getting back here so you can get up early tomorrow. Call! Then come tell me everything," he added as he headed to the kitchen.

The phone rang once and he picked it up. I asked if he had been sleeping. Craig told me that he was just lying there, "thinking about this cute Italian boy I met on Eighth Avenue." There was a pause and then he asked me if I would have dinner with him on Wednesday night. I told him I'd like that. He suggested meeting at his apartment, and gave me the address. It was right near the Chelsea Gym.

"Well, good night, Michael," he said. "I'm really looking forward to seeing you again."

"Me too," I said good night, hung up the phone, and dutifully rushed to the kitchen, where Anthony was having his last cigarette of the evening.

"Well?"

"We're having dinner on Wednesday. We're meeting at his apartment first, and then we're going to dinner. I can't believe I have a date with someone who looks like that. He sounds so sweet on the phone."

"He certainly looks like a good time."

8

The Medicine More Mothers Trust

Rose was waiting with the car when I got off the train on Sunday morning, and was already sitting in the passenger seat so I could drive. I got in and kissed her cheek.

"Hi, Rose."

"Oh, Mikey, that beard. I hate it. I wish you'd shave it off."

I started the car. The ride to the nursing home took about forty minutes, and if we didn't get off the topic of my beard, we'd end up riding out in silence.

My mother was a Depression child. She woke up the day after she graduated high school to find that my grandmother had enrolled her in secretarial school. My mother had wanted to become a nurse, but Grandma Renata would have none of it. No daughter of hers was going to empty bedpans.

Rose went to school, though not happily. And while she learned to type, my grandmother made arrangements to get her a job in the offices at the factory where my grandfather worked – no easy feat in 1938, but my grandmother had ways. Rose had been working ever since.

Born on the morning of the Feast of the Assumption in

1920, she was christened Assunta Rosa Milana. Assunta for the day, Rosa after my grandfather's sister. As a child, she insisted that everyone call her Rose.

She married my father when she was thirty. They had met at a high school dance and had dated on and off, but they never really got serious, as they say, until after my father came back from the Pacific at the end of World War II. My mother was working at Fabiani, a famous and very exclusive photography studio on Fifty-second Street in Manhattan. She was the office manager and wore tailored suits and hats to work, and patterned herself, I think, on Rosalind Russell.

Joseph Gregoretti was the youngest of five brothers. When he married Rose at thirty-four, he and two of his buddies from the 11th Bombardment Group had just opened an auto body and engine repair shop in Queens.

My parents were married on New Year's Eve at the Hotel Ambassador. They took an apartment in Brooklyn Heights and saved for a down payment on a house on Long Island. Joe drove to work every day in a red Studebaker, and drove home to Brooklyn every night picturing their life to come in the country.

The novelty of house hunting wore off quickly. Finding nothing they could agree on, they bought a vacant lot and found a builder who sold them on a basic brick-and-fieldstone Cape Cod. Contracts were drawn, loans were arranged, and my parents took possession some months later, with enough furniture for one room, and a thirty-year mortgage. The house cost them a then-staggering $19,000 to build.

"I bought Grandma Renata another opera tape, I said, breaking the silence. "*La Bohème*. I also got her a Carlo Buti."

"Oh, that'll make her happy. She hasn't really been herself lately."

The nursing home was clean and bright, but it wasn't home as far as Grandma Renata was concerned. She left Florida after my grandfather died and had come to live with us.

She seemed happy at first. But five years and two small strokes later her health had deteriorated: She progressed quickly from walker to wheelchair, and even with the help of a visiting nurse, Rose couldn't take care of her. Grandma Renata just couldn't navigate the chair, or gave up trying to, and getting her into the bathroom or the tub was a nightmare in our tiny 1950s house.

The solution was to put her in a home. Rose felt terribly guilty about this, but she wasn't in the best of health herself, and the strain of taking care of her mother for five years was beginning to show.

The nursing home was out in Suffolk County and Rose tried to get there as often as possible, but even after all those years on Long Island, Rose had never adjusted to driving on the Expressway, and her visits depended more and more on my coming home weekends.

My grandmother was never the stereotypical black-dress-gray-hair-in-a-bun-gold-tooth-Italian-lady I saw Esther Minciotti and Argentina Brunetti play in all those old movies. Before she got sick, my grandmother was a big, robust woman who looked like Ingrid Bergman and wore her gold around her neck and wrist. She was particularly proud of the gold watch on a chain her mother had given her the day she sailed to America on the Giuseppe Verdi, and always wore it pinned to her dresses.

When we were kids, Marco was fascinated by it. He would sit in Grandma's lap, lovingly inspecting it, and make Grandma tell him its history. Then Grandma would unpin it and dangle it just out of Marco's reach and say, "You like-a Teek-a-Tock, Marco?"

"Yeah, Grandma. I like Teek-a-Tock."

"Then when I die, I geeve you Teek-a-Tock," came the response. It was always the same. Christmas, Easter, Mother's Day. Every holiday Grandma spent with us, the ritual was repeated. Instead of asking why this night was different from all other nights, Grandma Renata would sit her husband's namesake on her lap and ask if he liked Teek-a-Tock, until the Thanksgiving when Marco, dressed like a little angel from heaven, looked up at Grandma with those dreamy brown eyes and sweetly asked, "Grandma, when are you gonna die?"

She screamed "WHAT?" so loudly, they probably heard her back in Senigallia. Marco tried again.

"When are you gonna die and give me Teek-a-Tock?"

Grandma put my brother down and said something menacing to my mother in Italian. My mother shot back in English, "Well, what do you expect, Ma? You keep shaking that thing in front of him and telling him you'll give it to him when you die. He's only a little kid."

Don't you know that a month later at Christmas, Marco was given a little Teek-a-Tock of his own. "Timex," my grandmother said solemnly, as she helped Marco slide the watch onto his little wrist.

Although Marco wore the watch until he outgrew it, he confided in me that Christmas, "I still like Grandma's Teek-a-Tock better."

My glamorous grandmother disappeared slowly over the years, replaced by this little woman who rarely combed her hair anymore and spent her days dozing in a wheelchair. We had bought her a tape player and had shown her how to use it, and I supplied her with any opera or Italian music cassette I could find. Her sight had begun to fail, and she could no longer read books. The music seemed to be the only thing she enjoyed.

"Hallo, Assunta," she said to my mother as we walked into her room. "And Michael! You come to see Grandma, too. Oh, boy!"

I leaned down and she gave my cheek three big chirping kisses. I gave her the tapes.

"What is thees?"

"Tapes," my mother said. "Italian tapes he gets down on Mulberry Street."

"Oh, but thees is too dear," she said, taking my hand. "You shouldn't spend you money on Grandma!"

"They're not expensive," I said. "And you enjoy them, so never mind what they cost."

We were interrupted by a tiny old woman who wandered into the room saying, "Where? Where?" She looked terrified.

"Oh, that one!" my grandmother said, with an annoyed expression on her face. "Go back to you room, you!" Grandma looked at my mother and added, "She's crazy, thees one. All the time, she's lost. Michael, you take her to the nurse, down the end there."

"Are you lost?" I asked the woman.

"Yes. Yes, I am!"

I took her arm gently and led her to the nurses' station at the end of the hall. As we walked, she complained about the turkey she had had for lunch. I noticed her handbag flapping back and forth between her hip and her elbow. Why would she possibly need a handbag in a nursing home?

I hated the thought of my grandmother spending the rest of her days here. I started thinking ahead. What if I had to put Rose in a place like this? And what would happen when I was this old? Who would come and visit me — Marco's grandchildren?

"Beatrice," one of the nurses scolded lightly as she came down the hall with the medication cart. "Have you been walking around again?"

"I wanted to go to the store, but this young man is taking me to Maryland instead."

"You can't go to Maryland today, honey! It's a holiday in Maryland. You'd better go back to your room. She lives in that corner room," the nurse told me, pointing down the hall.

When I got Beatrice back into her room, she gave me a dime. I tried to refuse, but she insisted, so rather than hurt her feelings, I took it.

As I walked back to Grandma Renata's room. I could hear an old woman screaming, "Mama! Mama!" I just hated this place.

Grandma was alone when I got there, listening to one of the tapes I had given her. Rose had gone back to the car to get a sweater she had brought for my grandmother but had forgotten in the back seat. The nurse I had just spoken to in the hall came in with a small paper cup full of pills and some apple juice to wash them down with. Grandma Renata took the pills and downed the juice. When the nurse left, she reached for a tissue from her night table and spat two pills into it.

"Throw away," she said, balling up the tissue and handing it to me. "Don't say nothing to you mother."

"Grandma, you shouldn't do that."

"They geeve too many pills in thees place."

"But this is your medicine. One of these might be your blood pressure pill."

"Is all junk," she said, pushing my hand away. "I never take what they geeve me. Throw away."

I dropped the tissue in the wastebasket. I'd mention it to Rose later. Grandma laughed to herself. "'La Commedia è finita,'" she said, sighing.

"No, it's not," I said, taking her hand and sitting down again.

"That's what you theenk. You like thees girl you brother keeps company with?"

"Carla? She's very nice."

"You theenk they gonna get married?"

"Maybe."

"She can cook, thees girl?"

"She's sweet but she doesn't look like she can."

"Oh, well. There's always Progresso soup. And what about you, Michael? You keep company with anybody?"

"No, Grandma, not right now."

"Somebody better hurry up and make me great-grandma!" she said, folding her hands as if in prayer and shaking them at the ceiling.

Rose was fairly quiet as we drove home. I had tuned the radio to WNEW, the Big Band station, and when they played Artie Shaw's "Begin the Beguine," I looked and saw that she was smiling.

"I love this version," I said.

"I was a teenager when it came out. I remember I wanted to buy the record, but we didn't have a record player. I wanted your grandfather to get one, but money was so tight. One day, I went out and bought it anyway. I don't know how long I had to save for it. I wanted to have 'Begin the Beguine,' and I knew I'd have a record player someday. I never thought I'd end up like this, though."

Her voice trailed off as she looked out the window. Rose seemed to be looking backward lately more than ahead, and a bitterness was creeping into her voice that had never been there before.

"All the things I wanted to do. I worked my whole life. What have I got to show for it? You want my advice? Enjoy yourself a little more, Mikey."

"I'm trying. I just wish I could find another job."

"You will. Sooner or later, someone will give you a chance. And your life isn't as terrible as you think. When I first started out, I worked three jobs to support myself. I used to eat lunch in Chock full o'Nuts every day. Same lunch – cream cheese on date-nut bread and a cup of coffee, because that was all I could afford. If I had a little extra money and I really wanted to splurge, I had a donut, too. They had these delicious whole-wheat donuts. I should be your age now. You think your brother has a big job? They wouldn't see my smoke. When I first went out on my own, I tried to get a secretarial job at Bonwit's. I had it too, until the guy in Personnel looked over the application and asked me what kind of name Milana was. I told him Italian, and he turned me down, just like that. It wasn't like it is now. So as I was leaving, I guess he felt bad, and he walked me to the door and said, 'You know, there are lots of jobs for Italian girls in the garment district.'"

"He said that to you?"

"Sure. You had an Italian name in those days, it was bad news. Bonwit's was all WASPs, I guess. So I said, 'Well, this is one Italian girl who chooses not to work in the garment district.' He wished me good luck, and I told him, 'I'll have it,' and a week later I got my break and started working at Fabiani on Fifty-second Street, where all the rich WASPs came to have their wedding pictures taken. By an *Italian*."

"I can't believe they got away with something like that."

"Are you kidding? There was a time when the *phone company* wouldn't even hire Italian girls. Now I look at AT&T and I think to myself, 'Good for you! You wouldn't hire Rosie Milana, you deserve what happened to you.' I just wish I knew why everyone had it in for the Italians. The only reason I voted for Mondale was because of Geraldine Ferraro, poor thing. There's another Italian girl who never should have married."

9

Just Heat And Serve

We assembled in Gwen's office the following morning. She had seen one team before us, and would see the others after.

"Well, did we have a nice weekend?" she asked.

"Yes."

Silence followed.

"So. Let's see what you've got."

Henry began presenting an overview of the spots we had done at Gwen's request: the talking cows on Homestead Acres, the First Light rising suns, and the two ideas for Premiere.

"And then there's the extra one we did. It's an introductory spot, adaptable to any of the names they finally select for the product. And it's campaignable," he said, trying not to oversell it.

We started with "First Light." Henry described it for Gwen before we showed her the rough storyboards he had drawn.

"This spot takes the name 'First Light' literally. We see lots of rising suns – sunrise over the city, sunrise over the farmlands, the Pacific coast. And after each sunrise, we see people living in that region of the country sitting down to breakfast with First Light."

"Hmmmm," she interrupted. I didn't give her a chance to jump in.

"It's introductory," I said. "We see this beautiful sunrise, hear this very tentative chord that leads into a beautiful guitar piece – the 'First Light Theme,' which would be used in all future spots..."

"And," Henry added, "we'd recommend that they design a sunrise logo of some sort on the packaging that would tie into the visuals in the commercial. You could do a great effect where the filmed sunrise turns into the logo, then we pull away from the logo on the box..."

"Well, that's been done a trillion times before," she said, lighting a cigarette.

"There are ways to make it look fresh, Gwen," Henry answered. "What hasn't been done a trillion times before, anyway?"

"What's the copy like?" she asked, exhaling smoke at me and barely managing to disguise her boredom.

I resisted the temptation to start coughing like Garbo. "It's very straightforward – introducing-announcing-presenting. We want to let the visuals drive this, and I don't want to stack the deck with too much copy."

She nodded and narrowed her eyes in concentration. I started reading. "Across America, people are discovering new First Light..."

"You know what I think?" she interrupted. "I think there's too much going on in this commercial. I mean, sunrise-sunrise-sunrise and people eating...there's no *intrigue*."

"Sure there is!" I could hear my voice getting that defensive edge. "What are all those people eating?"

"But you want it to be *compelling*, Michael. Why show all those sunrises? Show just one. One, huge, beautiful rising sun, with the theme from *2001* under it." And just in case there was anyone on the planet who didn't know the theme, she started singing it. "Bah, bah, bah-h-h-h, BAH-BUM! Now, people would watch *that*."

"No, they wouldn't," I said, "they'd be too busy throwing up." Henry gave me a shut-up kick under the conference table, but I wouldn't stop. "Talk about done a trillion times! People were sick of that music by 1969."

"But you're taking too long to get to the product. There's no intrigue in your copy."

"I say the product name in the first sentence. We show people eating it from the beginning. Mrs. Consumer sees them eating something and looking happy, I think she'll hang around a few seconds to find out what it is. Let me finish reading."

"But you haven't grabbed my attention. That's my point. By the time you get around to telling Mrs. Consumer what this product is, she's already in the kitchen using Parkay!"

This was the infuriating part of working with Gwen. She scrutinized every comma and period but never saw anything as a whole. I'd been through it so many times with her, you would think I would just let her talk instead of getting angry. Ellen had final say, after all, not Gwen. I was just afraid she'd ruin the work before Ellen got a chance to see it. Or worse, that Ellen would think what she was seeing was a commercial Henry and I created, rather than our damaged commercial as filtered through Gwen. I kept thinking of Ellen's guarantee that Gwen would only be supervising the work, not changing it. I wondered if Ellen could possibly be that naive, or if she just said that to shut me up, and had actually given Gwen a degree of creative control.

"You know what you should do, Michael?"

"No, Gwen. Tell me. What should I do?" I asked,

moving my legs out of the way so Henry could only kick the air.

"You should write a Hal Riney commercial."

"What?"

"Hal Riney. He did those wonderful commercials for Perrier. They were quite marvelous, really. You should sit down and watch them. Get into his head. Then write a Hal Riney spot."

"Gwen, I don't like Hal Riney. Hal Riney got Reagan re-elected with his damn 'Morning in America' commercial. They should have called it '*Mourning* in America' because Reagan is *killing* this country! So if you want a Hal Riney spot, Gwen, I suggest you go out and hire Hal Riney. I can only write Michael Gregoretti spots. And if you don't like the way I write, then why did you ask for me on this assignment?"

"Michael, I never said I didn't like your writing. I'm merely suggesting another tone for this commercial. Something more important."

"But that isn't what we're trying to do. This is a low-fat butter for people who want to watch their cholesterol. It's a great idea, but it isn't the cure for cancer, and I'm not going to position it like it is by writing something deep-dish and pretentious. We have five more spots to show you and we're still haggling over the first line in this one. Would you kindly let us get on with this?"

Henry was glaring at me. He usually approached Gwen in an entirely different way. He let her talk and talk and said yes, and then went off and did what he wanted to do. He knew Gwen just liked to give advertising lessons.

I don't know why it was such an issue with me. I couldn't figure out what was making me angrier – Gwen's nitpicking, or just the idea of having to work with her again. I could feel a headache starting.

Somehow, we finished the presentation. Gwen hacked

her way through everything we had done. She thought the cows were great, but debated with us for half an hour about whether to use claymation or animation to bring them to life. Henry wanted claymation, but Gwen kept insisting we'd have more control over animation. Henry finally made the point that the concept had to be approved first, then they could decide how to execute it. For now, whether we used claymation, animation, or taught real cows to speak English was a little beside the point.

She agreed with us that the two Premiere spots were awful, and not really worth showing Ellen.

"Well, let's have a go at the last one, then, shall we?" She was smiling her phony smile, and speaking in that cheery voice she used on account people that sounded like she was going to start singing "Getting to Know You" at any moment. By this point, I was so tired of arguing with her, I let Henry present it.

"Michael said using butter makes him feel guilty, and that's where the idea for this spot comes from. It's called 'Eating Less.' We thought we could show people in really wacky situations trying to cut down on the butter they use, like making wafer-thin slices with a scalpel, or using so little butter on toast that they have to use a magnifying glass to find it. We thought we would film it so the whole thing runs slightly fast..."

"You mean fast motion?"

"Just slightly exaggerated," Henry said.

"I'm not sure about that. This is a very conservative client. You've seen the other things we've done for them. It's always a housewife in the kitchen."

"But that's what *everybody* in this category does, Gwen," I said, quietly. "Everyone thinks if they want to sell to housewives they have to *show* housewives. What's wrong with doing something slightly offbeat that would stand out?"

"It's a very cute idea, Michael. I just don't know if it's

appropriate for this particular client. But why don't you finish up this board and the other two and we'll take all three into Ellen on Wednesday? I think you have a couple of winners here. Ellen will love the cows!"

Henry and I thanked her and went back to his office. I could tell Henry was annoyed at me even before he told me.

"Michael, do you have to make it so obvious that you hate her? It makes you look bad, and it makes me look bad too."

"I'm sorry. I just – I don't know what it is about her. I go in there with gold and I come out with lead. I don't understand how she got where she is. Her work was always so terrible. Why do they let her judge other people's ideas? I'm not saying there isn't room for improvement in anything we did. But improve it; don't make it worse because you don't understand it."

"She thinks it's her job. She thinks she's creative director, not creative supervisor."

"But she's so absolutely irrational about it. I remember one of the first assignments she ever gave me. Muscovy was doing this little insert in a Christmas Gift Guide in *Esquire*. A picture of the bottle, two lines of copy and a toll-free number to call so you could send some as a gift anywhere in the country. *Two lines of copy*. And it took two days to write because every time I went in to her with something, she would read it over and over again, and start editing. She made me rewrite it so many times, I thought I would lose my mind. Do you know what she made me do in the end?"

"I'm afraid," Henry said.

"I took the very first thing I did back in to her like it was something I had just written. She had heard variations on it so many times at that point, she thought it was new. I had written: 'This Christmas, remember your special friends with a gift of Muscovy Vodka. Once the vodka of the Czar, now it's everyone's favorite.' And Gwen decided she still had to fix it. She made me stick another 'special' in. So now it reads: 'Remember your *special* friends with a *special* gift of Muscovy Vodka.' She just couldn't leave well enough alone. She's starting it all over again."

"Some of her suggestions weren't bad."

"That's the problem. I hate her so much, I can't see past my own rage. If she walked in here right now with a glass of poison and said, 'Michael, don't drink this, it will kill you,' I'd snatch it out of her hand and gulp it down, just because she said not to."

"Michael, you have to learn when it's important to fight for this stuff and when it isn't. I know you want Ellen to like what we've done, and you think Gwen is ruining it, but she hasn't. We can get around a lot of the changes she asked for. What's the point of fighting with her now when Ellen could kill the work on Wednesday?"

"I don't know."

"Look, go to lunch. Take a walk somewhere. It's just not that important. Ellen will understand the stuff Gwen didn't, and then we'll be back on track. And if she hates it, we'll start over again."

"I'm sorry about being so nasty in the meeting."

"Actually, it was pretty funny. You're so insulting and it goes right over her head."

"She hears me. She just thinks I hate everyone, so she doesn't take personal offense."

After dinner that night, I started going through my notes for Act Two of *Dial Nine to Get Out*. I hadn't worked on it for almost a month, and I still hadn't decided how I was going to end it. I lost track of the time until the phone rang. It was Craig.

"I just wanted to say hi and see how your day went."

"About the only good thing I can say is that it's over. We're having trouble getting a commercial past the creative supervisor. She keeps changing things we don't want to change. How was your day?"

"Fair to middlin'. I'm working on a financial report now that's taking forever. But I keep thinking about this certain young man I'm having dinner with Wednesday, and it gets me through. I really can't wait to see you again. I guess that's why I called."

"I'm glad you did."

We stayed on the phone for about forty-five minutes, not talking about anything important. I think we were both testing the waters. I guess I passed, because he asked me if I wanted to get into a cab and come over and sleep with him. If it were earlier I might have, but by now it was almost midnight.

"Well, Butch, I guess I'd better let you get to sleep," he said. "Good night."

"Thanks for calling, Craig. I'm looking forward to dinner."

I hung up, gathered all of the papers back into the folder, and got into bed. I started thinking about Craig. I still couldn't believe that we had met, much less that we were going to have dinner together. He was gorgeous and sweet and flirty and I was getting that fluttery schoolgirl-with-a-crush feeling in my gut anticipating the next time I would see him.

"Love finds Andy Hardy," I said out loud, as I snapped off the light.

10
Easy-To-Follow Recipe

Henry and I spent the next day and a half refining the commercials Gwen had approved. We tried to incorporate all of her changes in a way we could live with and still keep our jobs, but there were a couple of changes we just couldn't make. Henry said we should bring all of the original storyboards with us in case Ellen didn't like the new versions, but what would probably happen was that Ellen would make changes in the boards and undo most of the damage Gwen had done. If we guided Ellen in the right direction, he reasoned, she would think she was making the spots better, when, in effect, she was only saving them from Gwen. And Gwen wouldn't be so stupid as to open her mouth and tell Ellen that she was correcting her own mistakes and not ours. I hoped he was right.

Gwen made a point of checking in with us from time to time to make sure we'd be ready for the presentation. She stopped by with bulletins from the client or further instructions she claimed were from Ellen, but probably sprang from her own head.

On Wednesday morning, as we waited outside Ellen's door to be summoned in, I did a quick review of what we

had, and what we were going to say about each spot. The
talking cows were embarrassing, but it was Gwen's idea,
and Ellen knew that. "First Light" could be interesting
unless Ellen liked Gwen's version better than ours. The
only one we really cared about was "Eating Less," and
Gwen already had her hooks in that too.

Ellen's door swung open more or less on time. She
had spent roughly half an hour with the first team, Steve
and Michelle, and they looked fairly pleased as they walked
out of her office. Gwen got up from the conference table
and motioned us in.

"Hi, guys!" She chirped. She excused herself for a
moment to borrow a cigarette from Nora, the secretary she
and Ellen shared. Ellen was on the phone. Henry and I sat
there like two idiots, watching the rain pound on the windows. At least the weather reports had promised it would
be over by noon. I was nervous enough about my date with
Craig. The last thing I wanted was to show up at his door
soaking wet and looking like some drowned cat.

Gwen streamed back in and closed the door just as
Ellen was finishing her call.

"No. No. *No* original music," she barked into the
phone. "You tell those assholes *stock* music, and tell them *I*
said it, okay?" She slammed down the receiver without
waiting for an answer, then looked up at us and asked,
"What have you two got?" out of one side of her mouth, as
if we had come in to sell her toxic Florida swampland.

We started with "First Light." In subsequent arguments with Gwen, we had compromised on two sunrises:
one on the East Coast, one on the farm. I tried to make the
copy a little more dramatic, but something was wrong with
it, and I could tell from the way he was presenting that
Henry wasn't too sure of it either.

Henry took Ellen through the visuals and I read the
copy. Ellen reacted by frowning. "What's that tag line

again?" she asked.

"'Finally. Butter comes to light,'" I repeated, trying to sound like I cared.

"I understand what you're trying to do. I'm just not sure this is big enough. The client expects something really strong to launch this brand. This spot needs something more." Ellen took the board and started rereading the copy. "The idea is good. I think it needs some romancing."

"Like a Hal Riney spot?" Gwen asked, as if it just occurred to her.

"Yeah. Do it like Hal Riney."

"I don't know if I'm comfortable with that," I said. "I mean, what's the point of mimicking what's already out there?"

"You don't have to mimic him. Just write something that *sounds* like him," Ellen said.

Gwen smiled victoriously from behind a cloud of smoke. Ellen asked what was next.

"Next we have the famous talking cows," I said.

"This ought to be interesting," Ellen said, as if she were anticipating yet another eye lift, only without anesthesia this time.

"Okay," Henry said, setting things up, "the scene is somewhere near the barn on Homestead Acres. We'd be using either claymation or animation – I lean toward clay-mation, but Gwen prefers animation. Anyway, we have these cows, and they're all excited, because they just heard that someone has invented a low-fat yogurt butter spray."

"You're joking," Ellen deadpanned.

"I told you about this spot, Ellen, remember?" Gwen asked hopefully.

"Did you? Did I like it?"

"You loved it," Gwen reminded her.

"Well, I hate it now."

"Do you want to hear the copy?" I offered.

"Not really. Forster will never buy talking cows, Michael. I'm sorry. Stick it in your portfolio."

My portfolio was the last place I'd stick this loser spot. Gwen looked crushed.

"Okay, what else have you got?" Ellen asked.

Henry picked up the "Eating Less" board and began explaining it to her. "We show a series of people in slightly exaggerated situations, all trying to use less butter, or no butter at all. We see one woman in her kitchen looking at a slice of toast with a magnifying glass trying to find the pat of butter on it. We see another woman making thin slices of butter with a scalpel. We see a couple arguing in a super-market. He picks up the butter and drops it in the cart. She keeps taking it out and putting it back on the shelf. Then we tell all of them about this new low-fat yogurt butter in a can that hasn't got a name yet, and wow! Everyone's using it and they're all happy! It's all shot in just slightly faster motion so you know we're exaggerating."

"I'm not so sure about the fast-motion part," Ellen said, "but so far, it's good. What's the copy like?"

Gwen lit another cigarette and looked bored.

"First of all, we want to use an older announcer with a little bit of character in his voice," I said.

"Mason Adams, Burgess Meredith, got it. *Read*."

"'Butter lovers,'" I began, trying to sound a little like Burgess Meredith but it was probably closer to Truman Capote with a head cold, "'have you been eating less of the butter you love lately? That's a good way to cut down on fat and calories, but you still miss that great butter taste, don't you? Well, butter lovers, here's something new. Introducing Homestead Acres Dairy Spread. The revolu-tionary low-fat butter in a spray can made from real butter and yogurt. It has fewer calories and less fat, but still has that great butter taste you crave. So now, you can eat all you want. New Homestead Acres Dairy Spread. It's butter

— made better.'"

Ellen was smiling. "That's pretty good. I hope you can say that 'butter made better' line. They'll tell us. I think the copy needs a little work. And take out some of these situations. You have too many little vignettes here before you get to the product. Stick to three at most. Do the lady making a tiny butter slice with a scalpel and a couple of the others. Pick the best ones. You can always save the ones you cut for future pool-outs if this campaign wins. Just simplify it. Also, I wouldn't do it in fast motion. Do it at normal speed."

"We were thinking about music, too," I added.

"Music would help, but don't be surprised if they say no."

Between the presentation and knowing I had dinner with Craig later, I was a basket case all day. I relaxed a little when it finally stopped raining.

The night before, Anthony knocked on my door and asked me what I was going to wear.

"Well, we're not meeting until after seven, so I have time for the gym first, provided I leave work at a normal hour. I'm bringing another shirt. I was thinking about this red polo shirt," I said, holding it up.

"Darling, you should wear black. Black is sexy."

"On you, black is sexy. On me, it looks like I'm coordinating my outfit to match the circles under my eyes. I'll stick to red."

"Red is too warm a color for this."

"Who are you tonight, Natalie Kalmus?"

"Fine. Wear the red. Are you wearing 501s?"

"Don't I wear them every day? Do I ever wear anything else? Do I *have* anything else? It's this or my gray suit. I'm wearing 501s and a button-down shirt and a tie to work, and after the gym, I'm changing to this *red* shirt."

"Okay, calm down. I'm just trying to help."

"I'm sorry. I think I'm getting a little carried away. Let's start over."

"What are you wearing, Michael?"

"I'm wearing a red polo shirt and 501s."

"Perfect."

"I'm glad you approve."

"Are you gonna sleep with him?"

"Anthony," I whined.

"Well are you? Be prepared, I always say."

"I don't know. I want to, but I don't really know him that well."

"Oh, honey, do us both a favor. You *need* to get laid."

"If I do it too soon, I never enjoy it. I'm too awkward the first time."

"You worry too much. Just let it happen. And take a rubber."

"What am I going to do, pull it out of my gym bag like a toothbrush? Then he'll know I was planning all along to stay over. He works for GMHC, Anthony, I'm sure he'll have one handy. Or we'll stop off and buy some."

"How romantic. Just try to have a good time, okay, pal?"

"I will."

I managed to get out of work by five that day and headed downtown to the Chelsea Gym. I had a decent workout, showered, and left for Craig's apartment. He buzzed me in and I started climbing the five flights of stairs. He heard me rounding the last flight and opened the door.

"Hi, there! I should have warned you about the stairs."

"Second workout tonight," I said, catching my breath.

"Well, come on in!"

He looked wonderful. He was wearing a white shirt, a red-and-blue striped tie, khaki pants, and tortoise-shell glasses. My first thought was that I shouldn't have worn the red polo shirt. I should have kept the shirt and tie on that I wore to work.

He let me into the apartment, closed the door, and slid his arms around me. "Hi," he said again, and gave me a long kiss. "I hope you don't mind," he said, his hands sliding down my back, "I wanted to do that since I met you."

"I don't mind at all," I said, resisting the temptation to add "Help y'self" in a Mae West voice.

"I have to change. Are you starving? Can you wait a minute? I just got in."

"Okay." Actually, I wanted him to leave on what he was wearing. He looked great. And the *glasses*! Wait until I told Irene.

"I want to put my contacts in, too."

Oh, well. He kept walking from the bathroom, past the living room where I sat waiting, into the bedroom and back again as he changed.

"How was your day?" he asked, whipping off the tie.

"Okay. We presented the low-fat butter stuff today. I'll bet the client kills it all. How was yours?"

He came back to the bathroom, now without his glasses or his shirt.

"Same old shit. Red tape and lots of meetings. I accomplished nothing. I didn't even have lunch today." He stopped talking and tilted his head back to put in one contact lens, then the other, then headed back down the hallway.

"I like your apartment," I said.

"It's not mine," he called from the bedroom. "It's a sublet. I got it through work." He came back into the living room, wearing a blue button-down shirt and a pair of faded jeans. "I told them they had to find me an apartment or I wouldn't take the job, and someone knew someone who knew the two guys who live here. They're filmmakers.

They're in Europe for six months, and I have to find a place of my own when they get back. This is all their furniture. My stuff's in storage, except I didn't bring a bed. I took the place sight unseen. They just said it's eight hundred dollars a month and I said okay."

"For this? It's huge."

"They pay even less. They've been here a long time. It's rent-controlled and they're making a profit on me."

"Still, it's a bargain in this neighborhood."

"I had an entire house in New Mexico for less. With a garage and a washer and dryer. But I wanted to live in the big city, so..."

"How do you like it so far?"

"I don't want to stay here more than a year or two. I hate the noise and the filth, and living behind so many locks. And the fact that I can't afford anything. I had a nicer life back home, but this job was too good to pass up. I do like the fact that there's so much happening here all the time. And the men are pretty," he said, running his hand through my hair. "So are you ready to eat, hot stuff?"

We walked down Eighth Avenue to Mary Ann's, a neighborhood restaurant he liked that I had never been to. I was worried that we'd run out of things to talk about, but we didn't. I loved listening to his voice. Eventually the conversation came around to the health crisis and our respective pasts.

"I'm thirty-seven years old," he said. "I spent a lot of time playing around and had a lot of fun. I haven't taken the test but I'm sure I'll turn out positive. I just don't want to know. So I live my life as if I could come down with it. I try to take care of myself." He shrugged and smiled. "I sure don't want to get sick, but there isn't too much I can do now to undo all the time I spent on my knees."

"I took the test," I told him. "I'm negative."

"You took it?"

"Anonymously. I don't know why I was being so paranoid, but my doctor said to take it under another name so I
used 'Judith Traherne.' I mean, I took so long to come out.
I knew I was gay when I was in college but I only slept with
one man. Just the one time. It wasn't that great, and I
decided to hold out for Love, but I guess Love didn't know
that. I graduated in 1979 and moved back home. It was a
while before I could afford to move into the city, and it's a
little hard to sleep around when you have to worry about
missing the last train for Long Island. And then around
1981 or '82, I started hearing about this GRID thing. I had
some older gay friends by then who sort of took me aside
and told me to be careful. God, two of them are dead now.
Then I met Tim, and we were together just about a year."

"Why did you and Tim break up?"

"Oh, lots of reasons. I think part of it was because he
hated New York. He's an actor, from Indiana. And his
career was going nowhere here so he moved to California.
His career's going nowhere there now, but he seems
happier. And I was really miserable at my job. It's bad now,
but for different reasons. It used to make him depressed,
too. He wanted me to quit. And I got frustrated with him
because I thought he wasn't working hard enough at acting.
He was making so much money temping, I guess he wasn't
hungry enough. Anyway, it was bound to happen. Sometimes I think we were just two very needy boys who found
each other and then couldn't let go."

"I was with Robert for five years," Craig said. "I came
home one day and caught him with someone in our bed.
Some friend of his who came over to do his laundry and
wound up doing Robert too. Turned out, he had been
cheating on me all along, and I never knew it. That's part of
why I decided to move here."

The check came and he paid it. We left the restaurant
and started walking up Eighth Avenue. "So," Craig said, "do

you think you might want to come back to my apartment for a nightcap or something?"

"I think for, 'or something.'"

"Oh, really?" he said, wrapping his arm around my shoulder.

Hours later, lying in bed with Craig, I remember wondering if this was the start or the end. I had tuned his clock radio to WNEW and "Moonlight Serenade" came on.

"I don't believe it," I said, sleepily. "That makes it perfect."

"What does?"

"This song. Glenn Miller. It's my favorite. If I were stranded on some island somewhere with only one piece of music with me, I'd want it to be this."

Craig kissed me again. I started thinking about how wonderful it was to be there – lying in bed on a balmy New York night with this handsome stranger and Glenn Miller underscoring the scene.

The song ended, and Craig whispered in my ear, "It needs a tambourine."

I should have realized then that it would never work, and politely rolled out of bed, got dressed and gone home. Instead we had sex again.

The alarm woke us at six the next morning. The idea was, I would go back to my apartment to shower and get to work on time. Instead, I stayed in bed with Craig and talked for an hour. When we finally got up, he offered to make me a cup of tea and breakfast – I had a choice of Pop Tarts or Frosted Flakes, so I politely settled for the tea, deciding I'd wait until after the wedding to change his diet.

"Now, I hope I *have* tea," he said, searching through the kitchen cabinets. "I think they left a box here somewhere. Aha! You sly dog, you, tea!" It turned out to be some awful peppermint rosehips ginseng concoction the filmmakers left behind, but I didn't care. I was in very big like with this man, and would drink any kind of tea he offered if it meant spending another ten minutes with him. When I finished the tea, I washed the cup, saying, "As much as I hate to go, Craig, I have to."

"I'm glad you spent the night."

"So am I."

"Can I see you again? Maybe tomorrow?"

"I'd like that."

He walked me to the door, and kissed me. "I'll call you later."

Anthony was awake when I got in, which was surprising. He managed Shades of Meaning, an antique lighting store on Christopher Street, and normally got up around ten and opened the store at noon. He was sitting at the table with a mug of coffee, smoking a cigarette.

"Well, well. It's about time you came home. Did you lift your skirts, Myrtle?"

"Oh, honey, right over my head! It was wonderful."

"Tell me."

I went into the kitchen and started heating a cup of milk for oatmeal. Then I started measuring out the oats, wheat germ, oat bran and apple pectin powder I always added.

"You're gonna make me watch you cook that mess you call breakfast, aren't you," Anthony said. "You should wear a cloak and pointed hat when you make that. You look like an alchemist."

"Just because your idea of breakfast is a cigarette," I said, spilling the oats into the hot milk and sprinkling in some cinnamon.

"A cigarette and black coffee."

"You want some too?" I teased.

"Are you crazy? Something healthy like that would kill me."

I made a cup of *real* tea. When the oatmeal was done, I scooped it out into a bowl and sat down at the table. I probably wouldn't get to work before ten at the rate I was going, but I didn't care.

"I'm so content right now," I told him. "Not delirious, just happy. I want this man in my life, Anthony."

"Well, it sounds like you're off to a good start. Just don't ever let him see you make breakfast until you've got a ring on your finger. You'll scare him away."

11
Serving Suggestion

The following Monday, Gwen sent a chart, a timetable and a confusing seven-page memo to everyone working on what was now called Project Forster, since no one working in the agency could either remember or spell "Fofolofabu." Her memo and the attachments were supposed to tell us about next steps, tentative meetings and requirements from each team, but they were worthless, since they were projected months ahead and would probably change in a week when we presented work to the account group. She shouldn't have wasted her time, but then, that's what Gwen did best.

Cocaine was in plentiful supply around the agency in those days and sometimes I wondered if Gwen used it. The rumor was that someone in Creative was the main provider to the rest of the floor. No one knew who it was — well, no one who wasn't a customer knew, and anyone who *was* a customer wisely feigned ignorance. This ghostly dealer was referred to as Casper. Whenever someone acted erratically, someone else might say, "Oh, I think she just had a meeting with Casper" or "He and Casper must have had lunch today" as a sort of sly code. Or, if the comment could be overheard, you would just slide an index finger alongside your nose and roll your eyes and everyone knew you were blaming whatever strange behavior we had just witnessed on cocaine. The one thing I did notice was that every so often, a box of powdered donuts appeared in the break room, yet no one ever knew who had brought them. This was believed to be either a signal from Casper that he or she had merchandise to sell that day or that, in addition to having merchandise, Casper was also providing a convenient cover story in case anyone got caught with traces of white powder on a lapel or a cocaine halo around a nostril. If Gwen and Casper *were* friends, it would explain a lot, but it wouldn't change anything. Cocaine or not, I still had to work with her and navigate her mood swings.

Henry and I had several meetings with her during the rest of that week to further refine (or more precisely, to further damage) the two spots. She liked "First Light" best, and decided to channel all of her energies into making that one perfect. I didn't mind, because she left "Eating Less" alone and that was the one I was hoping they'd produce.

Gwen phrased demands like suggestions. First, the farmer family and their country sunrise were cut. Next, she started calling in reels of rising suns from stock film houses, most of which looked like outtakes from *King Solomon's Mines*. She assured us it was "just for presentation purposes, because account people have no imagination."

I did write a pseudo-Hal Riney spot, or rather a parody of one. It must have been too subtle, though, because Gwen read it through once and said it was right on target, and sounded exactly like what Hal would do. She then took out her stubby pencil to make one or two refinements on Hal.

Gwen wanted to present to the account group right after the July 4th holiday, and informed us that she and Ellen were going to personally show all the work. She explained that there were too many people working on this assignment for all of us to be in the same room at once, and it was simpler for the two of them to sit down with the account people alone.

"Yeah, simple," Henry said as soon as she had left. "She'll *simply* present the ones she likes and sandbag all the others."

"Looks like we'll be doing the sunrise," I said.

"Do you care anymore?"

"Not really. This isn't going to be the commercial that gets me out of this dump, that's for sure."

"Let's just do it and get it over with and wait for a better assignment," he said.

"Oh, God. 'Waiting, waiting, waiting. I'll never get out of here. I'll *die* in Casablanca!'"

Gwen called us into her office the day after the presentation to the account group to hear the results. Five commercials had been picked to show to the client. Miraculously, "Eating Less" had survived. Unfortunately, so had "First Light."

The account group had asked for minor changes in the copy. Instead of calling it a low-fat butter, they asked us to call it a low-fat butter *product*, just to be safe.

I met Irene for lunch that day, although neither of us really had the time. We decided it was worth getting away from our offices for an hour just to breathe. She wanted an update on how things were going with Craig.

"It's hard to say. We've had exactly three dates now. We've spent more time talking on the phone, I think, than we have in the same room together. His schedule is awful, and mine isn't much better lately. He's been working nights and weekends. But he said last night that he thinks we have potential, and he wants to give it a chance. I guess I can't ask for more than that."

"It sounds like he's interested."

"I guess so. I want this to work, but sometimes I think I'm trying too hard to make something happen before it's ready. You know, like when you're baking a cake, and you're tempted to open the oven door and look inside, but you know that if you do, the cake will fall."

"Mr. Metaphor, that's you."

"You know what I mean. I don't want to ruin it."

"Michael, just stop trying so hard to make him like you. Obviously he's interested or he wouldn't have asked for another date. Give him time to get to know you."

But about a week or so later, Craig stopped calling. On the fourth straight day of not hearing from him, I called him late one afternoon from the office.

"Hi there," he said. "I'm sorry. I meant to call you. I was just thinking about it, as a matter of fact. I've been having such a bad week here, I guess the time got away from me." I could tell that he was typing on his computer keyboard as he spoke, and he sounded distracted. I wanted to ask him if he would like company for dinner or if he wanted to see me over the weekend, but I was afraid it would make him feel more pressured.

"I'll call you tomorrow, and we can talk about the weekend."

"Tomorrow *is* the weekend," I said.

"Tomorrow's Friday? Jesus! I'll call you tomorrow morning, okay? I just can't talk now."

"Okay. I hope things get better."

"I hope they don't get worse."

I wished that he had asked me over. I wasn't having such a hot day myself. Instead, I got a package of cookies from the newsstand in the lobby and put them in a big brown envelope with a note:

Sorry you had such a bad day.
Wish I could be there to make it up to
you, but cookies are the next best thing.
Love,
MG

I debated over and over whether or not I should leave the cookies – it just smacked of sixth grade. What the hell, I reasoned, I'd like it if someone did that for me. I got off the subway at Twenty-third Street and, on the way to the Chelsea Gym, taped the envelope to his mailbox. Then I waited for a phone call on Friday to say that he (a) got them or (b) got them and realized what a find I was and wanted to marry me.

Naturally, when he didn't call, I panicked. I thought I had done a dopey thing and had scared him away. At the end of the day, Anthony called for an update.

"No, I haven't heard from him yet, and I probably never will again."

"Will you calm down? He's probably having another bad day. He said he would call."

"He said he would call in the *morning*."

"So you call him, then."

"I'm tired of always being the one who calls. He has to call me this time. I left him cookies!"

"Maybe he never got them."

"Oh, God, Anthony. I hate this. If this one goes sour, I swear, I'm never going to look at another man again. I have enough bad stuff going on in my life without adding boy-friend trouble to the list."

"Maybe you should just stop making lists. *You* make yourself unhappy, Michael. He never said anything about ending it. He said he's busy, that's all."

"But it's Friday night. Am I supposed to assume we're

getting together? What happens if he doesn't call? Do I sit home alone because I didn't make other plans?"

"Look, I have nothing to do tonight. If Craig doesn't call, we'll get Frank and Billy and the four of us can go see *Ruthless People*, all right? Jesus! I wish I were there so I could throw a Xanax down your throat!"

Karen knocked on my door and poked her head in. "Craig Connolly just called you. I told him you were on the phone, so he said to call back." She backed out and closed the door.

"Anthony, he's been trying to call all the time we've been on the phone."

"You see?"

"You're trying to sabotage my love life by tying up the line so he can't get through," I said, laughing.

"You're crazy, you know that? You are one twisted bitch. Two seconds ago you were getting ready to cut yourself open like Madama Butterfly because he didn't call."

"All right, let me go. I'll call you back after I talk to him."

Craig was very apologetic about not calling, and thanked me for the cookies. He said, "I would rather have had you," which made me feel happy, then angry, because all he had to do was ask and I would have come over. He told me he didn't feel up to doing anything that night. I said that was fine since I was going to the movies, and hoping that was true, made plans to see him on Saturday.

The presentation to Forster Foods took place the following week in the executive conference room on the sixty-fifth floor. I hadn't met anyone from Forster, but I'd heard they were a fairly humorless bunch. We were making this presentation to Maxine Somebody, a middle-to-upper-level someone, who had brought two bland assistants with her. Gwen was running the meeting, and had decided to call in one team at a time. We were to answer all questions put to us and then leave. Maxine would take all the work back with her to Forster's offices on the West Side.

At least we were getting a chance to present our own work this time. I was still amazed that the account group had liked "Eating Less" enough to let us show it. Gwen hated the spot, and made no secret of the fact. She would have done anything she could to kill it. In fact, she probably already had.

Michelle and Steve were already inside presenting their spot. Henry and I were next, and as we sat there waiting for our turn to go in and do our soft-shoe for the client, I felt just like Eleanor Parker, about to appear before the parole board.

Waiting with us were two other teams: Barbara and Carolyn, both new to the agency, and strangers to me until we got this assignment; and Peter and Lisa, who had been at the agency longer than I had.

Peter was staring off into space, tapping his foot absently. Lisa sat with a pile of scripts in her lap, not looking particularly happy. Peter let out a long sigh and raked a hand through his hair. I said to Lisa, "What's the matter? You two look like you just had your last meal and it wasn't what you ordered."

"I keep hoping the client will throw up when I read these scripts," Lisa said. "Then I'll be done with this assignment, and no hard feelings. Of everything we did, I can't believe *this* is what we're presenting."

Peter and Lisa had put all of us to shame, showing up at Gwen's door with nine commercials, only to have them all killed before Ellen ever saw them. And what were they presenting today? A dairy farmer's wife sitting on a porch in a rocker, talking about how you turn yogurt into low-fat butter. In a can.

"Too bad Marjorie Main is dead," I kidded. "She'd be perfect for this." They didn't smile. "Tell me something. Was this your idea or Gwen's?"

Peter looked at me and frowned. "Michael, it stinks. Of course it was Gwen's idea. She said, 'Why don't you do a talking head, guys!' so we asked, 'Like who?' and she said, 'Oh, why not have a dairy farmer's wife talking about yogurt and how it becomes a low-fat butter.'"

Lisa picked up the story. "At first, we thought it could be a good spot. We tried making her funny but Gwen killed that idea."

"I know. 'This client doesn't appreciate humor.'"

"Exactly," Lisa said. "Anything I did that was any good got cut out three revisions ago. It's Gwen's commercial, and it's all we have left. I'm praying the client hates it. The farmer's wife actually says, 'Look for it in the dairy case!' at the end of the spot. I mean, where else are you going to find butter, in the detergent aisle?"

"She did the same goddamn thing to us," Barbara said.

Until then, I had never really sat down to compare notes with the other teams – we were all so busy. Barbara and Carolyn were also going in with a spot they hated, called "Better Mornings," in which actual pats embossed with the word "butter" kept magically turning into The Ribbon, embossed with the word "better." They had the awful tag line: Better mornings start with Forster. And where did the idea come from?

"Gwen," Carolyn said. "She killed all of our stuff and told us we were off strategy. She handed us 'Better Mornings' and she gave us that damn tag line."

"I wonder if she did it to Steve and Michelle too," I said.

"What have they got, anyway?" Henry asked.

"Their product name is Right. They have a jingle that

goes to the tune of 'Straighten Up and Fly Right' called 'Lighten Up and Try Right,' if you can believe it," Lisa told us. "Who'd buy a butter called Right? I wouldn't, and if I did, I certainly wouldn't sing a song about it."

"So we got the names First Light and Homestead Acres, you two got Better Mornings, and you two got what?" Henry asked Barbara and Carolyn.

"Ours is the generic. We're using Homestead Acres, but they can call it Drano if they want to and the spot still works. Gwen told me to be ready to reread the spot with whatever name Maxine pulls out of the air to prove the point."

"How about calling it New Poison?" Peter offered.

"Raw Sewage!" said Lisa.

"Try new Low-Fat Cow Manure Spread!" Henry said.

"Shh!" I hissed. "They'll hear us in there." When everyone had stopped giggling I asked, "How about new Low-Fat Creamy Oil Slick?"

The conference room door swung open and Michelle and Steve walked out, followed by a cloud of blue smoke. As she closed the door again, Gwen called after them, "Thanks a lot, guys!" Michelle looked at me and crossed her eyes. Steve was shaking his head like he'd just heard bad news. They joined us in the reception area.

"What's Maxine like?" I asked.

"Please," said Michelle, sitting down. "She never changed the expression on her face. She just nodded a lot. I think she hated the spot. Maybe it was my singing."

"No, I think she just hated the spot," Steve said. "She had never heard the song 'Straighten Up and Fly Right' to begin with."

"Linda Ronstadt just did it," I offered, trying to be helpful.

"I have a feeling she never heard of Linda Ronstadt, either," Steve said. "Wait till you see her."

"Well, good luck, folks," Michelle added, standing up.

The door opened again. Gwen called to us, "Michael? Henry? Why don't you come on in and meet Maxine?" I remember thinking that "Meet Maxine" would make a great title for TV's first lesbian sitcom.

Gwen ushered us into the dark and absurdly cold conference room. Maxine stood up to shake our hands. The woman was just dumpy. There was no other way to describe her. There she was in her little blue suit, her hair twisted up on her little head. One look at her and you knew this job was her whole life. She existed only between the moment she arrived for work and the moment, twelve hours later, when she left for her apartment. Like Brigadoon, she disappeared into the mist every night only to reappear with the morning coffee in another plain suit.

She had brought two younger, paler versions of herself, assistants named Fran and Ann or Sue and Lu. I don't remember their names except that they rhymed, and I never saw them again after that first meeting. It was possible they disappeared into the mist one night after work too, and never returned.

Gwen got things rolling. "Henry and Michael have two spots to show you today, Maxine. One is for First Light, and the other is for Homestead Acres. Guys?"

It was just another performance of the same tired scene as far as I was concerned. We had said the same things at so many other meetings, we almost didn't have to think about it anymore. We started with the First Light spot. Henry set it up, and I read the script from the enlarged color storyboards. When it was over, we looked at Maxine for comments.

She had scrunched up her mouth into a tight, concerned little pucker. "I don't understand this one. It isn't really an idea, it's more of an execution. You spend too much time on this sunrise. If there's something here, I don't see it."

"It's breakthrough!" Gwen said defensively, as if her child were being mauled. We all must have had the same blank look on our faces as we turned toward her. "It's visually compelling," Gwen offered as clarification. "People are going to see this beautiful sunrise and hear this voice of authority talking about 'something so revolutionary,' and they're going to be glued to their seats, asking 'What is it?' And then, *we tell them!*"

"I think," Maxine began, choosing her words carefully, "what you've done here is over our consumers' heads. Now, if I don't understand it, how is the lady out in Iowa going to get it? Maybe you need to universalize it. In the second half of the commercial, there's a family sitting down to eat their breakfast and they're using low-fat First Light. Why not show several families?"

"I understand," said Gwen. "But then you lose the punch."

"Forster Foods doesn't *punch*. We *invite!* We are friends of the families of America. We come to the side door with home-baked cakes, and we're always welcome."

This woman is a pod, I thought to myself.

"What I'd like to see is nice American families interacting with the product," she continued. "Lots of appetite appeal. Everyone fit and trim and happy, and a simple sell. Here's a new product that's low-fat, low-calorie, delicious like butter, and it's called First Light. Simple, direct..."

"Clichéd!" said Gwen. "We can do that if you want, Maxine. How about this? We write the spot that way, but you agree to take a second look at this one too and see which you like better."

"That's fair."

Why was she doing this? What was so important? The woman was sitting there telling us what she wanted, and Gwen kept trying to talk her out of it. It was Forster's money, for God's sake. I was thrilled because I knew I could just dust off my original idea for this commercial and she'd love it. I just needed to make it a touch homier.

Gwen made her point. Maxine seemed happy. We moved on to "Eating Less." Once again, Henry set up the spot and detailed all the visuals shot by shot. Then I explained that we wanted slightly comic music under and an older announcer with a little character in his voice.

I eased into the newly revised copy. "'A lot of butter lovers are eating less butter these days, as a way of cutting out fat in their diets. And it's not making them happy. Well, now there's new Homestead Acres Dairy Spray...'"

I really believed that our wacky visuals needed simple copy for counterpoint – you can enjoy this new product because it tastes like the butter you love, but with less fat and fewer calories.

Maxine sat and listened and nodded. Then she puckered again and cleared her throat.

"Of course," Gwen said almost apologetically, "none of these is a final commercial. We still need input to refine them."

"Yes, I know," said Maxine. "I have to say that generally, humor makes me nervous. I do like this commercial, but right now, I think it might be too whimsical somehow. There isn't enough sell. It's there, but it needs to be turned up a little. This is a great third commercial, but as an introductory, I don't think it's going to build enough brand awareness. Do you understand what I mean?"

"I thought it wasn't quite there," Gwen said, "but it was a good idea and I wanted the guys to show it to you."

"Well, here's what I think," Maxine said, pausing for dramatic effect. Gwen held her cigarette aloft and gazed at Maxine as if she was about to hear Moses read from the first edition of the tablets.

"You need to give this commercial a little harder edge.

That phrase you had in there toward the end – something about making people happy?"

"'Now that should make all of the butter lovers who couldn't give up butter – and a lot of the ones who did – very happy,'" I read back.

"Yes. That has to be rewritten. Also, both spots need much more appetite appeal. I want to see the product melting onto hot muffins and steamy vegetables and toast. But no bagels." I looked at Henry, who looked away from me and tried not to smile. "Bagels are too...*New York*. I *do* like these spots. I don't think they're quite right at this point, but if you'll work on them, I'd like to recommend both of them for production. Do you think you could make some of the changes I've asked for and tighten them up by the end of the week?"

"That's no problem," Henry said.

"Excellent."

"Well, thanks, guys," Gwen chirped.

We shook Maxine's hand, and then shook hands with Nora and Laura or whatever their names were and left.

Gwen made a point of stopping by our offices later in the day to tell us how impressed she was with the way we handled ourselves. She asked us if we thought we could tighten up the spots in two days, so we'd have time to run it all past Ellen (and Howard, who had suddenly decided to get into the act), and still make our next meeting with the client. It didn't seem like we had much choice, but I thought we could get the work done in plenty of time, especially if Gwen would leave us alone, and accept the changes we made when she saw the revisions. Knowing Gwen as I did, I don't know why I was optimistic at all.

Henry and I worked late the next two nights, rewriting, redrawing and rethinking our two commercials. We tried to tighten them up and address all of Maxine's concerns. For "Eating Less," we came up with a housewife bringing baked potatoes with birthday candles in them to the table on a tray, along with a can of Homestead Acres. As she walked in carrying the tray, the family would cheer. I took out the line Maxine had objected to and replaced it with, "Now, butter lovers, that's something to celebrate!" I liked the idea of these people being so happy about the product that they'd treat it like a special dessert. We also made sure both spots had plenty of appetite appeal but no bagels.

Henry started redrawing the boards, and I went back to my office to type up the new scripts. When we had finished, we took the work back to Gwen.

Gwen looked over the boards, took a long drag on her cigarette, and then blew smoke at the work in a dramatic, drawn-out sigh. "I don't know about this 'something to celebrate' line. I don't think 'celebrate' is the right word. And the wife coming out with candles in the potatoes is all wrong."

"Well, Maxine didn't like the line we had there about making all the butter lovers happy again, and we said we'd find a different way to say that. I really like it. I think it works."

"Steve and Michelle did one spot that didn't work out at all for the product name Lighten Up. I was really sorry to lose that name because it's so American. I hear people saying 'lighten up' all the time, and it's sort of a pun, since this is also a light butter. Anyway, Michelle wrote a line that said, 'So, America, lighten up with new Homestead Acres Dairy Spread.' I think that would work really well in your commercial."

"I'm not comfortable with using Michelle's line in my spot," I said. "I feel like I'm cannibalizing. And I also hate the expression 'lighten up.' I think it's hostile."

"You're not cannibalizing, Michael. It was a good idea that didn't work somewhere else, so we're using it here. It says something about the product. This candles-in-the-baked-potato business has to go."

"But it ties everything together. In the first half of the commercial, before they started using this stuff, she used to run around the table and give everyone just a thin wafer of butter scraped off the stick with a scalpel. But now they can all be pigs again with Homestead Acres, and they're celebrating, so she puts candles in the potatoes like it's a birthday cake."

"It's too complicated," she snapped. "There's too much going on in this spot."

Henry spoke up. "Gwen, we took out so much stuff that you and Ellen and Maxine hated. I really think this is a good idea, and that Ellen is going to love it."

"I think Ellen is going to tell you it's confusing, and to take out the baked potatoes with the candles. But if you feel so strongly about it, present the work the way it is. We'll see what Ellen thinks."

12

Imitation Flavoring

I was getting ready to leave the office on Friday when the phone rang. It was Craig.

"I know this is short notice, and I know I haven't called you in a while even though I said I would, but I was wondering if I could buy you dinner tomorrow night."

Craig's phone calls had become rare events, and when I called him, he was always too busy to talk and unable to commit to making a date. I had reached the point of giving up on him.

I tried telling myself not to give in, to be busy – but the truth was, I wanted to see him again. I found myself thinking about him at odd times during the day, wondering what he was doing. I missed him, and that was all there was to it. So I agreed to have dinner.

We met at Fedora in the Village. Over dinner, he told me about his week, I told him about the recent skirmishes with Gwen.

We went back to his apartment and wound up in bed, where he told me how much he enjoyed spending time with me. He talked about "us," and finally hit me with the fact that he wanted to keep seeing me, but wasn't sure if he could find the time. He had already told me that he couldn't spend Sunday with me because he was going to the office to get through some paperwork.

"Craig, look. I like you a lot. I'd like to get to know you better. I'm not asking you to move in with me. You don't have to see me every night of the week. I'm pretty busy myself. But how long does it take to pick up a phone just to say 'hi'?"

"I know," he said. "I'm sorry."

We had breakfast the next morning at the coffee shop on his corner. Then he left for the office, and I bought the Sunday *Times* and headed home.

We met with Ellen the next morning. She liked what we had done with "First Light," and said that she still thought it was the stronger of the two commercials. I told her I still liked "Eating Less" better. I didn't add that I thought "First Light" was pretentious, and that until you figured out what we were selling, you probably would have thought it was a commercial for some big bank or life insurance company.

Ellen agreed with Gwen on the simpler version of "Eating Less," and decided to do more damage to the spot by simplifying it further.

"Why can't you just cut back at the end to the grumpy husband from the first half?" she asked. "We saw his wife hand him a piece of toast with the tiny smear of butter and he looks at it with a magnifying glass, right? Now, he's standing there about to take a bite of this dry toast, and the wife's hand comes into the shot and takes that first slice away, hands him another slice on a dish and then she sprays a big glob of new Whatever-It's-Called on it, and he takes a bite and then he's happy as shit. The End."

"But that doesn't work with my line about celebrating. I thought that was a nice idea. I *liked* the happy family."

"It takes too long to set up, Michael. You use up a lot of time saying all this stuff about the product, and you want people to hear it. You can't rush that part. And if they have to sit there and look at the screen and try to figure out what she's doing with potatoes and magnifying glasses and scalpels, they're not going to hear one word of your copy. People are morons. I know you want to do something really funny here, but this isn't a Wendy's commercial. This client is too conservative, and it's a brand-new product. It's okay to make people smile, but save the laughs. Cute, but not funny. I'll put you on something else when this is over and you can do something funny, I promise."

I couldn't think of any other product on her client list where I could do anything funny. She wouldn't let me near any of the jewels in her tiara – like Buick or GE. I could just see myself sitting down, trying to come up with big laughs on Whatta Wheat crackers, only to have Gwen do the Mexican Hat Dance all over my copy. It was hopeless.

"I had an idea about changing that celebrate line," Gwen said in her annoying mother's-little-helper voice. "I thought we could say, 'So, America, lighten up – with new Homestead Acres Dairy Spread.'"

"'Lighten up.' I like that!" Ellen said, nodding emphatically. She would. "That's better, actually. The voiceover goes 'Lighten up' and the man gets the other piece of toast and he smiles and we cut to the product shot."

So much for guiding Ellen away from Gwen's ideas. They were on the same frequency. I sat there listening to my commercials being rewritten, and couldn't see past my own anger.

Maybe they *were* better. Ellen had those Clios, after all, and had been in the business as long as Speedy Alka-Seltzer. The most important thing was producing a good commercial, and so what if everyone had to add a word or a visual? But I just didn't feel like they were improving it. I felt as though they were changing it because they thought it was their job to change it, not because it needed to be changed. Malcolm was a giant idea factory where no one had any real creative freedom. You came into the office, gave birth to an idea, and sent it down the assembly line, and by the time it had been passed back to you, ten people had changed your cat into a dog. An ugly dog at that.

"I need scripts and boards on my desk by the end of the day," Ellen continued. "Howard wants to review the work tonight, and Gwen and I are going over to Forster Foods tomorrow to present to Maxine and Larry."

"Who's Larry?" I asked.

"Maxine's boss. He's the brand manager. Gwen worked with him last year, so that's good for us. But we can't troop over there with everyone who worked on this. They don't like it when we gang up on them. Just get me copies of the scripts and staple copies of the new boards to them. Then give me mounted color blowups. You only have to replace two frames on 'Eating Less.' The other one is fine the way it is. That's the one they're gonna buy."

"First Light," it turned out, was already dead. Gwen arrived at Forster without Ellen (who had canceled at the last minute because of yet another crisis on Buick) to find that the name hadn't cleared the Legal department's search. Someone else was already using it for a disposable cigarette lighter.

Changing the product name to something else wouldn't be a problem for any of the other spots, but in this particular commercial, it wouldn't make any sense to see all these sunrises and hear the announcer call it "Premiere." I was not sorry to see it go.

Our other commercial, "Eating Less," had survived Larry's scrutiny and the Legal department's name search for another Homestead Acres Dairy Spread. It was such a bad name, who else would want it? Gwen came back with the warning that if the client ultimately approved the spot, we couldn't go too far in casting. Henry had made the people in the boards look as offbeat as he could while still getting them past Gwen and Ellen. He compensated for being restricted in his characters by going a little overboard with the setting, adding silly touches like vintage appliances, souvenir potholders and odd cookie jars on the counters in the background wherever he could. Gwen and Ellen didn't seem to notice, and the client never said a word about the sets – just the actors. In no way could we cast people who looked like the ones Henry had drawn.

"But, Gwen. They're not supposed to be everyday people. They're *supposed* to be a little off," Henry said.

"I tried to explain that to Larry," Gwen offered, and we knew she was lying, "but you heard Maxine yourselves. Humor makes her nervous." I was rubbing my eyes at this point. I had another headache and I felt about a hundred years old. I kept telling myself it wouldn't be so awful. New York was crawling with actors. I was sure we could compromise and find people the client could live with who still had that slightly manic edge we wanted.

"The client also said we couldn't alter the speed of the action," she added, giving the words more weight than necessary. "They were adamant on that point. No faster than normal. And they're not sure they want music under it – at least not what you had in mind."

"Is it still about butter?" I asked sarcastically. The headache was getting worse. I didn't want to hear any more. I wanted to go home. I wanted someone to be there when I got in to make me a scrambled egg sandwich and give me a backrub. I tried to focus on Gwen again.

"It's not a total loss, guys. Ellen wants me to work with you to tighten up the spot. She thinks the client will agree to test it if we make just a few more adjustments. Just a kiss, here and there, and I think it's going to score like gangbusters."

"What's the deal timewise?" Henry asked.

"We've got a week, and then we go back with revisions. All we need to do is change the boards a little and tighten up the copy and cowabunga! But let's not worry about it tonight. You've both worked very hard, so go home now. We can start fresh tomorrow."

Henry and I started on what we hoped would be the final revisions for the "Eating Less" boards. We decided to compromise on the way the characters looked – but not to the degree the client wanted. Our thought was that if they hated the casting reels when it came time to do the spot, we could always say, "But you approved the boards and these actors are what we drew."

Gwen fought us on just about every one of the characters. Plump people got thinner. Old people got younger. One woman Henry had deliberately drawn with a 1940s Andrews Sisters hairstyle got a complete makeover and wound up looking more like the despised Nancy Reagan.

When Ellen saw the finished work, she said, "It's lost a lot of the charm, hasn't it?" As if her fingerprints weren't all over the revolver. I just looked at her and said nothing.

Henry was still somewhat hopeful. "I think we can save it with propping, casting, and the right director. I've been looking at a couple of reels, and I found someone I think really has a flair for this kind of thing."

"Didn't Gwen tell you? Forster always uses Ed Harmon Productions down in Chelsea. They do all their test stuff there. He's okay. He has a pretty elaborate setup."

"We thought we'd at least get to pick a director," Henry said. "I've been screening reels for two weeks."

I think Ellen could tell by our faces how disappointed we were, and how little enthusiasm we had left for this project. I also think she knew we felt she had let us down by having Gwen present the work instead of doing it herself. Ellen was known as a fighter and a brilliant sales-woman when it came to getting more creative ideas through.

And there was no denying Ellen's success. Clients, especially male clients, loved her gorgeous, tough-talking broad act, which unfortunately had taken a back seat to Gwen's wishy-washy Greer Garson style of selling. Perhaps she thought Gwen needed the experience of dealing with tough clients. I only wish Ellen had sent Gwen off with someone else's commercials in her briefcase, if that was the idea.

Or maybe Ellen just didn't care about this account anymore. She was focused on hanging on to Buick, and I knew we'd be seeing less of her in the future and more of Gwen.

13

Packaged By Weight, Not Volume

Two days later, Fran Rotunda called me.

"Michael, what else are you and Henry working on right now besides the butter?"

"The only other thing we have in the works is the Lakeland Labs Skin Therapy Moisturizing Gel spot, but that's been dragging on for months."

"Well, I want you and Henry to go talk to Jo. We just got another assignment from Lakeland. A new product. Jo will tell you about it. It won't get in the way of what you're doing for Forster. Can you do that for me?"

"Sure, Fran."

"Thanks. By the way, did Howard call you yet?"

"Howard? No."

"He looked over the Forster spots, and he wanted to know who did 'Eating Less.' He loved it. Don't be surprised if he stops by."

"Really, Fran? Thanks."

"I thought you'd be happy. Listen, I gotta go. I've got someone waiting out front for an interview."

I called Jo. "Hello, sweetie pie," she said. "I was going to call you. Have you spoken to Fran?"

"Just now."

"Great. I hope you and Henry can work on this with me, because I'd love to have both of you. Come over and see me."

Henry was free, so we walked down the hall to Jo's office for the briefing.

"Hey, kiddies! Come on in," she said when I knocked on her door. She sat down at her corner conference table and handed each of us a folder. "Lakeland has given us another modern miracle to crow about. It's actually a hand care kit. A tube and a little nail polish-style bottle, together in one package. They're still designing the packaging, but think Clinique – very sleek and modern. Now, as I understand it, you brush the solution on your nails first and before it dries, you squeeze out some of the lotion from the tube and massage it into your nails and onto your hands. The lotion makes the nail bed moist or something so your nails become less brittle. Then after you massage the second lotion into your nails, the first solution hardens, like a glaze. Apparently, it's got vitamin E and some miraculous protein in it. The second lotion does wonderful things for your hands and cuticles, they tell me, but I was so confused by then, I didn't *dare* ask."

"Sounds like a lot of trouble," I said.

"It is. Our job is to convince the women of America that it isn't. As a matter of fact, the less we say about how you use it, the better. They just want us to talk benefits."

"Why two tubes?" Henry asked. "It would make more sense to put it all in one, wouldn't it?"

"It would, except the stuff would harden in one tube like asphalt and you'd never be able to squeeze it out."

"Have they named it?" I asked, hoping to avoid what had just happened on the butter.

"Oh, have they ever! How does 'Lakeland Labs Total Hand Treatment System' strike you?"

"Ouch. That's terrible," Henry said. "'Lakeland Labs' has to be in the name?"

"It's like that on all their other products."

"It's just so horsey," I said.

"Well, don't get hung up on it now. We may be able to tell them it's too long to say in the commercials, and see if they'll settle for something else."

"What kind of timing do we have on this, Jo?"

"They just briefed us yesterday. The product is in the last stages of development. They still don't know what color it's going to be, and they haven't picked a package or designed a logo, but that isn't stopping them from thinking they're ready to do a commercial. They swear it will all be done by the time we shoot. And by the way, the Skin Therapy commercial you two did may not be as dead as we think."

"They want to produce it?" Henry asked.

"They're still talking about it as if they might. But what I need from the two of you for now is ideas for this new nail thing. And you know they're going to want a demo no matter what we write. You can just count on those fools. So start thinking of some way to show stronger nails and softer hands. That's going to be the worst part of it, so work on that."

My friend Frank called me on Friday afternoon just to see if I'd heard from Craig, and when I told him I hadn't, he asked me what I planned to do that night. I told him I was going to go home.

"No, you're not," he said. "Billy's out of town for the weekend on business and I don't feel like cooking. Come out to dinner with me."

Over omelets, Frank let me drone on about work, and mostly about Craig.

"Michael, any relationship that's causing you this much pain at the start isn't worth it," he counseled. "The beginning is supposed to be the fun part – when you can't get enough of each other. Maybe you should just cut your losses now and get out before you really get hurt."

Frank had brought work home from the office, and had to get up early the next day. I was exhausted, and had no problem with calling it a night after dinner. I got home just as Anthony was getting ready to go out. He tried to convince me to join him.

"Forget Craig. We'll find you somebody else," he offered.

"I don't want somebody else. I just don't think he's going to call me again. I'd like to know what I did wrong."

"I don't think you did anything wrong, Michael. I think he likes you and it's got him scared. They're all the same. They only want the sluts like me who show 'em a good time and disappear," he said. When I didn't laugh, Anthony cleared his throat and said, "That was your cue."

"Sorry. I'm a little out of it tonight, I think."

"Things will get better, pal, I promise."

After Anthony left, I sat in the kitchen for a while, just thinking. Frank's advice was good, but too late. I was hurt already, and wanted to cry. Then I decided it wasn't worth it, and refused to give into it. I got up, changed into a pair of shorts, put the 1960s Girl Groups tape Irene had given me two Christmases ago on the stereo, and cleaned the kitchen.

On Saturday afternoon, Anthony complimented me on how sparklingly clean the kitchen was, and asked me if I planned to do the bathroom that night. As a matter of fact, I told him, I was.

"Oh no, you're not. You put on something tight and we're going out."

We went to dinner and saw *Heartburn*, then stopped

off at Ty's for a beer on our way home. We got in around
midnight. Anthony headed toward the bathroom and I went
to check the answering machine. It was blinking to signal
one missed call.

"We have a message," I said so Anthony could hear.

"I'm not interested unless it's Harrison Ford."

"With or without the whip?"

I pressed the play button to see who had called. It was
Craig.

"Hi, Michael. I just wanted to see what you were
doing tonight. I was hoping to catch you before you went
out. Maybe we can get together during the week. 'Bye."

"Good for you!" I shouted at the machine. "I hope you
miss me and suspected I was up to no good with every man
in the West Village."

"Who are you talking to?" Anthony shouted from the
bathroom.

"Craig."

Anthony pulled the door open. He had smeared a blue
masque over half of his face.

"That was him on the machine."

"What did he say?"

"He wanted to see if I was available tonight. I'm glad I
wasn't. The last thing I want him to think is that I've got
nothing better to do with my nights than sit by the phone,
slowly counting to five hundred and praying for him to
call."

"Atta boy," Anthony said, turning back to the mirror
and doing the other side of his face. "If I were you, I'd let
him get my machine a few more times."

"He's got two weeks, Anthony, that's all I'm giving
him. If he doesn't get his act together in two weeks, I'm
not seeing him again. If he decides to pursue this, fine. But
if he doesn't, I'm not going to pieces over it. So much for
picking up men on the street. Next time I'll choose a more

likely place – an Audrey Hepburn retrospective at Film Forum, or an antique shop, or the Mrs. Fields counter at Bloomingdale's."

I returned Craig's call the next day and got his machine. I told him I was sorry I'd missed the call, didn't tell him where I had been the night before, and asked him to call me back. When he didn't, I decided to take Frank's advice and cross him off my dance card. But I didn't feel happy about it. "It's his loss," I kept telling myself.

Henry and I were sitting in his office tossing around ideas for Total Hand Treatment. We had been working on the assignment on and off since Jo's briefing, and had a few things to show her already.

"Knock, knock!" said Gwen, appearing at Henry's door. "Oh, you're both here. I've got good news, guys. The client approved your spot. You'll be getting a memo in the mail from Production with a schedule and shoot dates and all that, but I wanted to be the one who told you."

"We're producing it?" Henry asked.

"Just on tape. But even a test commercial is better than a storyboard for your portfolio."

"When are we going to shoot it?" I asked.

"The second week in September. They really want to get these things into test as soon as possible."

"What else got approved?"

"Besides your spot, they liked the dairy farmer's wife – Peter and Lisa's spot – and a new one that Ellen and I did."

"You and Ellen?"

"Well, they killed everything else we had, and we needed a third spot to test. So we stayed late one night and wrote a new commercial. I'll show you the boards. It's all food shots and voiceover." She had little else to say, but that didn't stop her from taking a half-hour to say it before leaving. Henry and I looked at each other. He dropped his jaw in mock surprise.

"When did Gwen and Ellen have the time to do a third board?"

"Much less run it past the account group and Howard, and then Maxine and Larry. Now watch. Theirs is the one that wins. Like Ellen really needs this."

"I don't care," Henry said. "At least we get to produce ours."

14
Nothing To Add!

Two days later, we sat down with Patty Copland, one of the agency producers, Peter and Lisa, Roger Howell from Casting, and Al Parson, the management rep on Forster, for the first of several preproduction meetings with our director, Ed Harmon. We met in the small conference room on the sixty-first floor.

Gwen had prepared a booklet for the meeting: scripts, boards and schedules, all neatly bound and indexed. And what should have been an hour meeting at most – a discussion of what we needed from Ed and what the client expected us to produce – turned into a three-hour marathon, thanks to Gwen.

After several minor skirmishes, Gwen managed to engage me in a full-fledged battle over casting. And it was brutal.

When Henry told Roger and Ed that we wanted somewhat offbeat people in the spots, Gwen reminded us that she had been told by the client to find everyday people. I tried to plead the case for casting offbeat types if the commercial was going to make any sense, since these people would be running around doing rather odd things, such as scraping sticks of butter with scalpels, but Gwen wasn't having it.

"You're giving Ed the wrong direction!" she said, slamming her hand down on the conference table for emphasis. "If we go back to Maxine with a tape full of loonies, she'll…"

"Damn it, Gwen! Will you please listen to me?" I didn't mean to shout at her, and I really shouldn't have. I had made up my mind that the spot was beyond repair already, and that I didn't care anymore. I guess in the end, it just wasn't true. I did care. I still thought I could save it.

"Michael, you watch your tone of voice around me."

"These are my characters," I said, evenly. "I know what they're supposed to look and sound like. If you'd just let me work it out with Roger and Ed, I think we can find some actors who won't make the client nervous."

Always the diplomat, Al tried to smooth over what had happened by saying that he thought we could compromise on real-looking people, instead of the usual model types.

"No. I want to see *character* actors," I said.

"That's exactly what the client doesn't want," Gwen said through clenched teeth.

"No, Gwen, that's what *you* don't want. I told you in the beginning that this was an offbeat spot. If you didn't believe in it, it should never have been presented. As it happens, it was presented and the client bought it. Now, I said we'd find the right people for this, and I promise you we will."

"I'm sorry, people," Gwen said, addressing the group. "I need to borrow Michael for a moment. Michael? I'd like to speak to you outside."

I got up, gathered my things, and walked out of the conference room. Gwen followed me and pulled the conference room door shut, then grabbed my elbow in the hallway and spun me around so I was facing her.

"How *dare* you speak to me like that?"

I pulled my arm back and started moving down the hall toward my office. Gwen followed, hissing, "You stop right there!"

She caught up to me as I reached my office, grabbed my arm again and ushered me inside.

"I have never seen such unprofessional behavior, Michael! And in front of Ed and Al! I'll go to Fran Rotunda! I don't have to take this from you!"

"Listen, Gwen, I'm sorry if I got upset, but you're ruining my first commercial. I can't stand what you're doing anymore."

"What *I'm* doing? You're in there behaving like an infant in front of all those people." She started imitating me in a mincing, baby-talk voice. "'I said we'd find the proper actors for this commercial and we will, and you better keep your goddamn hands off it.'"

"That's not what I said, Gwen."

"You listen to me, Michael. You forget who gave you your first chance to write around here. No one liked you, and if it weren't for me, you'd still be sitting at that little desk in the hall. I was the only one who gave you assignments. And this is how you pay me back? By humiliating me?"

"That's not true. Other people gave me assignments, too. Secretaries got evaluated every six months. Personnel had to tell me what was said when I had my review. Everyone but Richard 'Go Get My Coffee' Eisenstein said I should be promoted. Just because you gave me a break doesn't give you special rights to abuse me, Gwen."

"Oh, really? And who am I abusing? I have certain obligations to the client –"

"You have obligations to the work first. You don't have to give them everything they want. You could at least do me the courtesy of letting me audition the kind of actors I want in the hope that the client will agree with me for once. At least let me try. If I have to fill this thing with bland actors, it's going to fall flat on its face. It won't be funny."

"The client doesn't want funny."

"But it *is* funny, can't you see that? In spite of all the changes, it's still funny. Why can't you leave it alone?"

"I'm very unhappy about this, Michael. And when I see Ellen, I'm going to tell her how unprofessionally you've behaved."

"Go ahead, Gwen. But I have to tell you, back when you were trying to get me on this project and I kept telling you I was too busy, I went to Ellen myself. I told her that I thought you were impossible to work with. I told her that you made my life a living hell when we were both on Muscovy, and that I didn't want to take on this assignment if it meant working with you again. And Ellen promised me that I could come to her anytime I thought you were out of line, and she'd take me off. I didn't go to her, and there were plenty of times I could have. I felt this commercial was worth fighting for, and that it would work out in the end. So you go to Ellen, and have your little chat. But believe me, I've got a list of complaints about you as long as my arm. And even if I do have an attitude, no one ever said I was impossible to work with, or that I was crazy. If I were you, with your history in this place, I wouldn't want one more name added to the long list of people who said that about me — on or off the record."

"Fine!" she snapped. "If that's how you feel, the next time I have a plum assignment for a copywriter you'll be the *last* one I'll ask!"

"Don't even bother, Gwen. I'd cut my dick off in Macy's window before I'd ever work with you again."

She turned and stormed out. And, judging by the

deadly silence that followed, I knew that up and down the hall, no one had missed a word. I sat down at my desk. I had finally told her off, but for what? It would fall in on me sooner or later.

"Did you two have a nice heart-to-heart?" Karen asked, breezing in with my phone messages and mail.

"God, Karen, did the whole agency hear us?"

"Michael, everyone hates that witch. They were practically applauding. Lisa came out of that meeting to go to the copy machine, and when she heard Gwen yelling at you, she said, 'I hope he stabs her.' If it were anyone else, I might be worried. But Gwen? She's nuts and everybody knows it."

Henry told me later that Gwen returned to the meeting looking none the worse for wear. She finished what she had to say about casting "Eating Less," then moved on to the next spot. Meanwhile, I went to see Ellen.

"What's going on?" she asked. "I heard you just had a big shouting match with Gwen."

"Boy, there are no secrets at Malcolm & Partners," I said.

"What happened?" she asked, not laughing.

"Look, Ellen, I told you when we first started this project that I can't work with her. I don't respect her creative judgment. I think she's ruining this commercial. She's like a freight train. You can't stop her. If you try, she mows you down."

"I don't like my people screaming at each other in meetings, Michael. This business is hard enough without us clawing at each other's throats."

"That's my point, Ellen. I'm trying to do good work here, and I'm constantly being sabotaged by Gwen. I don't think she's making the commercial better just because she thinks she's doing what she thinks the client wants. She's ruining the idea and she doesn't even realize it."

"What do you want from me, Michael?"

"I need to finish this commercial without fighting with her anymore. You told me that her job was just to make sure the commercials got done on schedule, not make creative calls, but that's what she's been doing from the start. She prefaced every change she asked for with 'the client said' or 'Ellen wants,' and who knows if that was the case? This spot could still be saved with the right actors in it. Gwen won't even let me try. I'm sure we can find people who would make the client happy and would still work."

"Michael, I think Gwen has a better idea of what you're up against."

"But she just treats me like I don't have any idea what I'm talking about. It's my spot."

"When do you shoot this? In a couple of weeks? Just get through it and I promise I won't put you on anything else with her."

"I'm sorry, Ellen. I promised you this wouldn't happen and it did."

"Just don't pick any more fights with Gwen. Her personal life's a mess and I think it spills over into work. I'll take care of it. Just give me a winner, okay?"

"Okay, Ellen. Thanks."

I went back to my office. I had barely sat down when Jenny flew in and shut my door.

"I can't believe you told her off and I missed it!"

"What did they do? Put it in this week's *Malcolm Memo?*"

"Lisa told me," she explained.

"I don't know. Ellen didn't seem to be too upset with me, but I think I made a fool of myself. This is going to come back to haunt me, I know it."

"I just think it's great that somebody finally said no to that hag."

Henry knocked on the door and came in. "Want to hear about the rest of the meeting?" he asked.

Jenny excused herself and Henry sat down.

"Michael, I'm not saying you're wrong, but you can't lose it like that in front of everyone."

"If you liked *that* performance, you should have seen the one we played in here."

"I heard it was pretty awful."

"It was. But I gave as good as I got."

"Michael, you're going to screw yourself. This stuff isn't that important. Everyone knows she's an idiot."

"She's an idiot with power. That's what makes her dangerous. I can't stand what she's doing anymore."

"Michael, you won't win. You know her history. Nothing ever happens to her. I don't know who she's related to or who she's been blowing all these years, but she isn't going anywhere. Now she's got Ellen's ear. You make her angry, and she'll get back at you through Ellen."

"I already told Ellen what happened."

"I don't trust Ellen, and you shouldn't either. And I think you'd better go apologize to Gwen."

"Oh, puh-leaze! I just got through telling her I'd rather maim myself than work with her again, and now you want me to go in there and say, 'I'm sorry'? She'll think I just had a nooner with Casper. She's supposed to be the crazy one, not me."

"Michael, even if you don't mean it, things are only going to get worse if you don't apologize. We have to work with her for another month at least."

"I know, I know. Let me think about it."

I thought about it. I brooded. And then I called Irene, who had already heard all about it from Henry and agreed with him. So as I was leaving for the day, I poked my head into her office. "Gwen, I'm sorry about the fireworks back there."

"That's okay," she said, as if I had merely used the wrong fork at her dinner party instead of argued with her in a meeting. "We're all a little tense."

"It's just very important to me. This is my first chance at TV. I want it to be good."

"It's going to be fine, Michael. You just need to learn to take criticism better."

"Okay. I'm sorry. Let's just finish it and forget about the rest."

"That's fine with me," she said. "I'm sure you'll behave from now on."

"I'll see you tomorrow, Gwen. Have a good night."

"*Ciao!*" she called after me.

"'Oh, pernicious woman!'" I muttered to myself as I headed to the elevators.

Roger from Casting called the next day, and asked if I could come down to his office to talk about "Eating Less."

Henry was in the middle of some other client-induced crisis and told me to handle it alone. I took the internal staircase down two floors to Production rather than wait for an elevator and ran into Patty, our producer, who was on her way up.

"I was just coming to see you," she said.

"I'm going to Roger's office. What's up?"

"Ed Harmon wants to know if he can meet with you and Henry again to talk about your spot. He wants to bounce a couple of ideas off you."

"Does Gwen know?"

"She was down here when he called."

"What did she say?"

"She said she was too busy to meet with Ed, and that you and Henry could do it without her."

"She said that?"

"Yeah. I thought it was a little strange, since she always likes to be in on everything. She said at this point she felt we were all in agreement about what was left to be done, and just to keep her posted."

"Well," I said, trying to process this happy turn of events, "check with Henry first, because he's a little crazed today and I don't know when he'll have time. I can do it just about any day this week."

"Okay, Michael. I'll set something up."

Patty continued up the stairs. I headed down another flight wondering why Gwen had suddenly backed off. Had Ellen told her to cool it, or was she legitimately busy on some other project? Maybe she was just on a stronger tranquilizer today.

Roger was on the phone when I arrived at his office, but he waved me in and pointed to the chair. He had the latest Ford Men book on his desk, so I picked it up and started leafing through it to see this year's crop of male models. After about five pages of perfect beefcake in various stages of undress, I decided I had better stop before I got really depressed. Roger finished his call and smiled as I put the book back on his desk.

"Makes a great coffee table book, doesn't it?"

"Gorgeous. But can these demi-gods make a really good cheese omelet? Can they critique Hitchcock's use of the camera in *Notorious*? Can they balance a checkbook? Or fix a leaky faucet?"

"Do we care?"

"No. It's a self-defense mechanism. When I'm confronted with that level of perfection, I have to imagine flaws. So what's on your mind?"

"I wanted to talk to you about your casting. Now, what kind of people did we decide we want in this spot?" he asked, smirking. "You and Gwen seemed to be having a difference of opinion over that."

"Gwen and I could have gone four rounds at the Garden over that."

"I heard you went a round or two in your office."

"Yeah. She's like Rasputin, though. No matter what you do, she won't die. Poison cakes. Bullets..."

"She *looks* like Rasputin. They go to the same beauty shop, I think. So what am I doing here, Chief?"

"We want people who are slightly different, but in subtle ways, or we'll never get them past this client. You know Sedelmaier, the guy who did the 'Where's the Beef' ads? I would love to use the kind of people he uses, but you saw how Gwen reacted."

"Yeah. Like one of those people Sedelmaier uses. What the hell is her problem, anyway?" he said.

"I don't know. If you want to know the truth, I think she should be in an institution."

"Well, if it's any consolation, I don't think you're alone in that boat. Patty's worked with her twice before, and she's ready to pull out her hair over having to work with her again."

"See? I think everyone in the joint hates her, including the lady who vacuums the hall at night. I swear she's either some client's daughter or she's got some really serious dirt on Howard."

"So, okay," Roger said, getting us back on track, "you want not-too-goofy people in this spot, but not-too-pretty either. You want character actors."

"Yes. Like from 1930s RKO movies. When are the auditions? Patty didn't tell me."

"Voiceovers here, Thursday morning. Actors at Harmon Productions, Friday afternoon, Monday morning and Tuesday morning."

"Roger, just find me people we can all live with who won't spoil my commercial."

"I'll try, Chief. And by the way, it *is* a really good

commercial."

I liked Roger. He wasn't someone I knew well, and I had never worked with him on anything before. It seemed to me that there weren't as many gay men at Malcolm as when I started, and most of the ones who were still there were so deep in the closet, they may as well have been straight.

Now, everyone knew Howard was gay. Howard knew everyone knew he was gay. Yet he wasn't really out. I don't mean I expected him to come to work in a caftan and an Eva Gabor wig and call everyone "Honey," but he was about as senior at Malcolm — or any other agency, for that matter — as he'd ever get. The next logical step would be to open his own shop. He had money. He had a reputation for producing fairly good work. What was he afraid of?

And if Howard insisted on pretending he was straight, what kind of message was he sending to the rest of the boys at Malcolm? And how did Howard react to someone like me, whose office was practically a shrine to Matt Norklun, the Perry Ellis model? I had every ad in the campaign tacked up on my wall. I was grateful for Roger. At least someone else was out at Malcolm. It made me feel a little less like a pioneer.

We auditioned twenty-five voiceover announcers, made our selections, and then took the tape to Gwen. She listened to our first choice and said, "Hey! I think you've got him." When she heard our second choice, she said, "Go with the first one. I don't need to hear the rest of them."

Who was this woman? I saw no evidence of a recent lobotomy. We were in and out of her office in fifteen minutes. No arguments, no advertising lessons, no stress. And I got the actor I wanted!

Patty and I had to wait half an hour outside Ellen's

office until she could see us. Nora, her secretary, was standing guard, and asked us what we wanted before she'd let us knock on Ellen's closed door. When we told her we wanted to play the audition tape for Ellen, she told us she was in there briefing the Buick teams. She called Ellen and told her we were waiting, and Ellen told her to tell us not to go away. So we sat on the floor outside Ellen's door until the meeting broke up.

When we went in, Ellen was sitting at her conference table with her head in her hands. She had dark circles under her expensive eyes, and she looked like she hadn't slept or eaten for days. It was pretty shocking. She lifted her head and said, "Whatever you want, the answer is no, unless you're here to take me on vacation, then the answer is yes."

"We just want you to hear our choices for voiceover for 'Eating Less.'"

"Michael, if you found someone you like, I'm sure he's fine. I just can't do this now."

"Okay," I said.

"I'm not trying to brush you off or anything. This Buick thing's gonna kill me. It's hideous. And the last thing I want to do now is to listen to tapes. Whoever you've got, I approve, as long as he'll work for scale," she said, making a cross in the air like a bored bishop offering a blessing.

"Thanks, Ellen."

"When are you casting the actors?"

"Tomorrow, Monday and Tuesday," Patty said.

"Those auditions I have to see. But just your selects, okay?"

"Sure."

"Now go away so I can have my breakdown."

"'Wouldn't you really rather have a Buick?'" I offered.

"Get outta here, Gregoretti."

15
Accept No Substitutes

Ed Harmon Productions occupied a former warehouse building on one of Chelsea's less charming industrial streets. It was almost indistinguishable from its neighbors, with only a small brass nameplate next to the door to identify it. The building had been gutted by fire and was practically in ruins when Ed bought it. He transformed it into a state-of-the-art facility. There were two sound stages, one with a huge kitchen set, several production offices, and about thirty full-time employees.

Ed Harmon was somewhere in his fifties. He had started in the business as some sort of apprentice underling, gradually became a cameraman, and then started directing.

I showed up on the first day of casting and was greeted at the door by the studio manager, a vaguely familiar-looking woman named Leigh. She took me on a tour of all six floors.

Leigh supervised the catering, made sure equipment was ordered and in place, and also played official hostess and public relations lady. I decided after watching her in action for fifteen minutes that whatever they were paying her, it wasn't enough.

Patty was talking to two of the production assistants. I
went over to see if I could help.

"Hi, there," Patty said.

"Hi. How's everything going?"

"So far? Fine. Henry's downstairs on the set. He wants
you to take a look. We should be ready to start soon."

"C'mon, Honey," Leigh said. "I'll take you."

She walked me to the end of the hall and pressed the
button for the elevator.

"So, how long have you been at Malcolm?" she asked.

"Five years."

"Like it?"

"It beats mining coal."

"I guess it does at that."

The elevator doors opened and we got in. "How long
have you been working for Ed?" I asked.

"How long have I been working for him, or how long
has he been paying me?"

"Sorry?"

"I'm Ed's wife."

"Aha! The power behind the throne."

Leigh laughed. I studied her for a moment, and then
realized why she looked so familiar. "You know who you
look like, Leigh? Rita Hayworth! Do people tell you that?"

"Yeah. All my life. Except my hair's this color
naturally. They dyed hers."

We got off the elevator and walked down a less
opulent hall toward the doors that led to the soundstage.

"Sad the way she is now," Leigh said. "At least she has a
good kid to take care of her." She pushed open the door and
held it for me. "You're in the viewing lounge today, which
is just behind the kitchen set. Let me know if you need
anything."

"Thanks, Leigh."

Henry and Ed were talking on the set, and I didn't

want to interrupt, so I went to the viewing lounge, expecting it to be some cramped little cubicle. Instead, I found a Ross Hunter living room, lavishly decorated with expensive furniture and plush carpeting. It had also been discreetly soundproofed, so noise inside wouldn't leak out onto the set while cameras turned – the perfect place to squirrel away obnoxious clients and crazed agency types.

There was a conference table at one end facing a huge TV monitor built into the wall. At the moment, the monitor was showing a silent test pattern. On the table was a spread of fresh fruit, bagels, muffins, rolls, cheeses, jams, butter and cream cheese, all set up on platters. On a sideboard were pots of coffee and hot water for tea. There was a water cooler next to that, and a refrigerator filled with juices and soda.

Over the next three days, we sat in that room watching the Big Parade of Actors. We decided to recommend three actors for each part – first, second and third choices based on the auditions Henry and I liked, and not necessarily according to what Gwen told us to look for. Their auditions would all be edited onto one presentation tape. But as a safety, we made up a second tape of actors, this time two for each role, so that if the client or Gwen objected to our choices, we'd have someone else to show them right away (but *only* if they objected).

At the end of each session, Ed would join us to go over the day's tape and give us his opinions of the people we had chosen. I thought he seemed fairly sympathetic to our problem – finding people who wouldn't frighten the geniuses at Forster. He agreed with most of our choices. He assured me that he could get the performance we wanted out of just about any of the actors on either tape, and told me not to worry.

After the last session, Ed sent the two edited videocassettes to Patty. Late that afternoon, we sat in the conference room near my office, ready to do battle over casting with Gwen, who was late.

She finally breezed in about fifteen minutes later, cigarette in hand, sporting one of her lopsided Gibson girls that made her look like a thousand owls were nesting in her hair. "Gee, hi! Terribly sorry I'm not on time. Conferences with Ellen and all that. She wants to see your choices as soon as we finish here, and then we have to show the reel to the account guys."

"Tonight?" Patty asked.

"Ellen tonight, definitely. She'll be out at Buick for the rest of the week. The account guys can wait until tomorrow, I suppose. They'd like to take the reel over to Maxine at the end of the week."

"I looked into availabilities," Patty said, "and so far, all of the actors we like can work on the scheduled shoot date. I can start putting them on hold as soon as we get approvals. I'd like to be able to start booking them on Monday. Do you think we can have final approval by then?"

"It depends on what you've got. Let's see the reel."

I let Patty run the meeting. It was her show, anyway, since she was producing the spot, and the less I had to say, the less antagonism I'd arouse in Gwen. At this point, I needed whatever objectivity I could squeeze out of her.

While the audition tape played, I kept glancing at her for signs of disapproval. She just sat there smoking. Every so often, she'd nod or scrawl something on a pad. Patty stopped the tape after the three choices for the first part had played, but Gwen said she wanted to watch the whole tape before commenting. When it was over and we turned on the lights again, Gwen asked, "Who else have you got?"

I closed my eyes and prayed Henry would say something. He did.

"What do you mean, Gwen?"

"I mean none of those actors is acceptable, and I want

to see who else auditioned. How many times do I have to tell you people that the client does not want humor? They want housewives and their husbands, not Barnum's freaks. I thought you could handle this without direct supervision, but I see now I was mistaken. I assume you saw more people than you put on this tape. You were there for three days. Now who else do you have?"

"There are others, Gwen," he said, "but these are the ones..."

"Who are un-ac-cept-able," she said evenly, looking at me as if I had done this deliberately to taunt her.

We ran the second reel for her, the one with our compromise actors, and she hated them all. She demanded that Patty call Ed for the master reels containing all of the auditions – the ones she'd just seen plus the people who hadn't made either cut.

Patty moved her reading glasses up on top of her head and left to make the call. Gwen lit another cigarette and glared at us.

"If the two of you want to ruin your careers with this willful stubbornness, go do it on some other account. I won't let you drag me down, too."

"All we're trying to do, Gwen," I said, "is finish this damn commercial. We hoped you'd like these actors."

"Well, I don't. And I can assure you that Ellen won't and the account group won't, and the client certainly won't. I don't know what you told Roger you wanted, but these actors are wrong, wrong, *wrong*. This is what happens when junior people get a chance at TV."

"Gwen, when I was your secretary, I remember you telling me that you had to fight for everything you ever wanted to do here. You told me that no one ever listened to you and you hated to compromise more than anything else. So why are you doing this to me now?"

"I'm not doing anything to anybody. I'm doing my job,

Michael. Maxine wants three commercials and she doesn't want to laugh," she said, stabbing out the cigarette. She fished around in her blazer pocket for the pack, extracted another and lit it. "If you think I'm attacking your work, then let's show these tapes to Ellen and the account people. Do you really think Ellen's going to let me take a cab across town with this tape full of idiots to show Maxine?"

Patty walked back into the conference room, preventing me from saying, I wish Ellen would let you take a cab back to England. The master tapes would be there by messenger within the hour.

We decided to meet again in Ellen's office when they arrived. Patty went to wait in her office. Gwen went to do God knows what in hers, and Henry and I went back to his office.

"I just can't believe this," I said to Henry, slumping down in a chair. "Why does everything have to be so fucking difficult around here?"

"Look, we figured this was going to happen, Michael. See what Ellen says. And the account guys. And then we'll show it to Maxine. You can't do anything about it now."

I walked to the window and looked at the late afternoon sunlight reflecting off the buildings and the traffic sixty-one floors below.

"This is all such a waste of time," I said.

"You're just figuring that out?"

"I wake up in the morning, and I haul my ass out of bed and drag myself to a job I hate. What is so wonderful about advertising that I let myself get seduced into this? That I get to wear jeans to work and make noise in the hall? That it's creative? There's about as much creativity in this place as in the Army."

"It's a business, Michael. We're only as creative as they let us be, which isn't very much."

"All I keep thinking about is how much I hate this life.

I'm almost thirty and I feel like a hundred. I should be skipping down Lexington Avenue singing show tunes because I'm healthy and not hooked up to an I.V. in Saint Vincents. Instead, I'm sitting up here wishing I were dead. I don't know. Maybe I'm the crazy one and Gwen and the rest of them are sane."

"Michael, everything gets to you because you let it get to you. Why do you care?"

"I just want to get out of here, and I can't do it without one good, produced commercial. If I had any guts, I'd march into Fran Rotunda's office first thing tomorrow morning and quit and go finish my play."

I looked out the window again. I didn't think I'd ever finish it, and I was tired of thinking about it.

"Michael, you need to find something else to do. This place is too big a part of your life. Finish your play. Go work with AIDS patients. Go do anything that means something to you, because you're going to make yourself sick if you don't."

It could have been worse, I thought. I had been lucky getting Henry as a partner. I could have been working with a bully like Ralph again.

"Thanks. I really appreciate the fact that you've put up with me all this time."

"I'm not putting up with you, Michael. I like you. I like working with you. And if it makes any difference to you, I think you're very talented. I think of you as a friend. And you introduced me to Irene. And if nothing else, we both got some good stuff for our portfolios out of this. The finished commercial may stink, but at least the storyboards were good."

Patty called from Ellen's office to tell us that she had the cassettes and that Gwen wanted us to meet her there. Gwen was smoking away and frowning when we arrived. Patty sat in a chair with the cassettes in her lap. Ellen was scribbling on a legal pad at her desk. She looked up at us. "What's the story with this casting?"

"We're divided on the kind of people we should cast in my spot," I said. "I found some people I love and some people I can live with, but Gwen thinks I've gone too far."

"What do you think?" she asked Henry.

"I agree with Michael. We sat down with Patty and Ed Harmon and we all agreed on these actors."

"And as I just told Ellen," Gwen interrupted, "these people are not what the client expects."

"Why do we keep having this same argument? The client didn't write the spot, Gwen, I did. And these are the people I had in mind."

"Enough!" shouted Ellen, with more drama than was necessary. "I'm tired of this. Just let me see the fucking tapes."

When we had finished watching all of the auditions, the only thing we all agreed on was that the rejects weren't worth presenting to the client.

Ellen thought for a moment, and then said, "I love the people on your first-choice tape, Michael, but not for this client. If you show them this, they'll shit."

"I don't understand why no one supports us around here. You keep saying you want breakthrough stuff, and then when you get it, you all run the other way."

"How about letting me finish?"

"Sorry, Ellen."

"What I think you should do is show them the second tape. If you never saw the people on the first tape, you'd take the alternates, right? Well, let's pretend these were the best you saw, and send this tape to Maxine."

"I still think they're too offbeat, Ellen," Gwen said through a cloud of smoke. "Maxine specifically and emphatically said 'ordinary.' Michael is giving her freaks."

"I think 'freaks' is a little strong, Gwen. Show them

this tape, see what they think. If they hate it, then we'll do another casting session."

Gwen came to my office the day after her meeting at Forster, glowing with the news that Maxine hated the casting tape. The account people had tried to persuade Maxine to be open, but she wouldn't budge. Gwen seemed to be enjoying telling me all this, but stopped just short of adding "Nyah-nyah, I told you so." As soon as she left, I called Al, the management rep, since he had been at the meeting when Gwen presented the tapes.

"Michael, I'm not going to say she sabotaged the whole thing, but you could tell from her presentation that she thought the actors were wrong, and Maxine picked up on it. Maybe if you and Henry had presented..."

"Did she do it on the other two spots or just mine?"

"Maxine didn't like anyone on any of the tapes. We have to recast all three spots. Luckily, Maxine asked for it, so Forster's paying. But Gwen sort of presented yours like it was a problem we were having at the agency, finding the right people, and we needed her input. I think she wants to come to the session."

"When is someone going to say no to these people?"

"That has to be Ellen's call, and she wasn't there. Gwen sure as hell wasn't going to say it. If Maxine told her to jump in the East River, Gwen would be wet before she finished the sentence."

As soon as I hung up, Karen shouted from her desk, "Michael, call Roger back. He just called you."

I got Roger's assistant, who put me on hold. Then Roger picked up and barked, "What the fuck's going on?"

"Maxine hated everyone and now we have to cast again."

"This is unreal. I just got a call from Peter and Lisa, and they're telling me the same thing. I don't understand this. For a couple of lousy test commercials? What is this,

The Search for Scarlett?"

"Roger, I know. I loved the people you got for us. We had no trouble picking three good actors for every part. Unfortunately, no one agrees with us here or at the client, so we have to do it all again. In one day."

"How come no one ever says no to these clowns?"

"I asked the same thing myself."

Gwen had another meeting with Maxine, and then came back and issued a two-page edict on red-bordered interoffice memo paper regarding specifics for casting. The only good thing about the memo was that Maxine, who had been copied, felt that it addressed her concerns, and that if we followed it, she wouldn't have to attend the session. But Gwen had no intention of missing it this time.

16
Easy To Swallow

On Saturday afternoon, the two-week deadline I had set for Craig had just about passed when he called me. I was convinced I'd never hear from him again. He told me he was starting to look at apartments, since his sublet would be up soon, and was going out to Brooklyn to see one later. He asked me to meet him for dinner and I decided it was worth one more chance. I didn't have plans and I had to admit I wanted to see him. As soon as we said goodbye, I called Anthony at Shades of Meaning to tell him what had happened.

"I'm not gonna argue with you," he told me. "But you'd better have it out with him this time."

At six that evening, I walked up to Chelsea. He buzzed me in, and I started the long climb to his apartment. I still wasn't sure. I thought I was being so adult, writing him off and suffering nobly like Norma Shearer. Yet all he had to do was call, and I had forgotten everything and ran. If only I had met someone else in the interim.

He opened the door wearing just a pair of faded jeans. No fair showing skin, I thought to myself.

"I'm not ready," he said.

"That's okay."

He closed the door and looked at me and said, "God, it's good to see you. I really missed you." He wrapped his arms around me and kissed me for what felt like forever. He was so tall, I had to stand on tiptoe. "Maybe I can persuade you to stay overnight?"

"Maybe. But you're going to have to work awfully hard for it."

"I know you're mad at me..."

"A little," I said. "I thought you weren't going to call me anymore. If I don't make the call, I don't hear from you for weeks."

"I'm sorry. Things have been terrible at work, and I had to look at three apartments this week."

"Craig, I know you're busy, but you can't do this to me. I'm too insecure. I kept thinking about our last date and wondering what I did wrong."

He hugged me again. "You didn't do anything wrong. I really like you. I think we have a lot of potential, and I'd like to try harder. Let me buy you dinner."

I did. We went back to Mary Ann's and stopped for a bottle of wine on the way back to his apartment. When we got upstairs, I took the bottle into the kitchen and said, "Where's your corkscrew?"

"The young man wants my corkscrew," he said, laughing to himself. He dug around in a drawer until he found one. Then he put it down next to the bottle on the counter, and kissed me again. As much as I enjoyed being in his arms, my calves were starting to cramp.

"Wait a minute," I said, pulling back. There was a Manhattan Yellow Pages on a shelf with some cookbooks. I took it down and put it on the floor. "I saw Barbara Stanwyck do this in a movie," I said, stepping on top of it and gaining enough in height to kiss his cheek without pain.

"You are amazing," he chuckled.

"You're just easily entertained," I said. "Now where were we?"

We never opened the wine. In fact, we never made it out of the kitchen. He told me later he'd always wanted to do it on the kitchen floor. It was actually kind of fun, except for the toast crumbs.

After breakfast the next morning, he apologized for not being able to spend the rest of the day with me. He had to go look at another apartment, this time up near Columbia University. I walked him to the subway. He kissed me goodbye and said, "I'll call you during the week, I promise."

Please let him mean it, I thought.

On Monday, we went back to Ed Harmon Productions for the casting session. Whatever glimmer of hope I had that we could save the commercial was snuffed out when I saw the actors milling about in the waiting room. They looked like they were here to audition for a Sears commercial.

I went downstairs to the viewing lounge, and was buttering a bagel when Leigh breezed in. "Hello, cutie! I didn't expect to see you back so soon!"

"Hi, Leigh. No one liked the people we picked first time out."

"So I heard. Ed feels pretty bad."

"It isn't Ed's fault. We picked the actors. It's Gwen's fault."

"Is she the one with the dark hair and the blazer over her shoulders and the cigarettes?"

I rolled my eyes and groaned, "Yes."

"Jeez! Does she own a bathtub? She smells like a wet ashtray."

"On a good day. They wrote that song about her: Gwen, Your Magic Smell is Everywhere."

"Boy, I wouldn't want to be *your* enemy," she said, laughing.

"I don't have any, really. Just Gwen. I get out a lot of aggression on her."

"Well, don't let her get to you. Gives you wrinkles."

At the end of the day, Gwen reviewed the casting tape with us and made her selections quite clear. Henry and I didn't like any of the actors she picked, but knew we had no choice in the matter. They all looked so ordinary. Ed took us aside and told us not to worry, saying that everyone was stiff on auditions, but that he could pull laughs from stones if he had to. Gwen told us she was satisfied and that Maxine would be happy with these actors, but I just couldn't leave it alone.

"Maxine's a fool, then."

"That happens to be your opinion, Michael. But she's the client. She knows her consumers."

"Oh, come on, Gwen. Maxine doesn't live in the real world. Look at the way she dresses."

"You know, Michael, you have a terrible attitude."

"I can't imagine why."

"Well, you had better do something about it. It's going to be your downfall. You have all of the ego and very little of the talent that goes along with it, if you want to know the truth."

"I'm glad you think I'm not talented, Gwen. It must mean that I actually am." I grabbed my things and walked out of the lounge.

"**O**h, my dear, you *must* be joking!" Jo said over coffee Thursday morning. Timing was getting tight on the Total Hand Treatment campaign, and Jo had asked if Henry and I would meet her for a breakfast work session to show her what we had done so far. But she had asked what was happening with Homestead Acres, and Henry and I spent part of the morning filling her in. That's when I told her that Gwen said I had no talent.

"I can't believe that...*hack* had the nerve to say that to you. Or to anybody, for that matter. You should speak to Ellen."

"I've *been* to Ellen," I said. "I just have to get through the next two weeks, and then we're done, and I'll never, ever work with her again."

"Well, there's one good thing about Gwen," Jo said. "Every agency needs a villain. There has to be one person everyone can rally around hating. And Malcolm's got Gwen. She brings out the worst in everyone. About ten years ago there was a woman working here as a copywriter. Sweetest thing, they tell me. Gwen got her so riled up one day she threw a stapler at her. Broke a window. That story made it all the way to me in the Paris office. See? Even people in *France* despise Gwen and they've never met her!"

"I just wish she'd go find someone else to torture," I said.

"Well this assignment's not going to be much fun, either, but it can't be worse than what you're doing now. So let's see what you've got."

We had come up with two ideas. The first was about flowers – how petals are soft and the stems are sturdy, and how the secret to both is natural protein. It was a bit of a stretch, but we drew a parallel to the proteins and vitamins in new Total Hand Treatment that keep hands soft and nails strong. Still, Jo was enthusiastic about it.

"We could have some beautiful photography. Have you ever seen Irving Penn's flower book?" she asked. "I'll bring it in. Just fabulous. I'd love to see you use a tulip, though. Roses have been done to death, and anyway, Lancôme uses a rose on their packaging. I just hope they don't hate this because it's cosmetic. You know, at

Lakeland they keep saying 'We're therapy.' I'd like to slap them to sleep."

"We could make it a real therapeutic sell, copywise," Henry said, "and just make it gorgeous visually."

"'Talk tough, look pretty,'" Jo said. "It works for Ellen. Okay, so number one is a flower-and-protein story." Jo had begun to list our ideas on a pad. "What else?"

"I had an idea that I don't think Michael is too crazy about," Henry said.

"I *like* the idea, Henry. I'm just afraid the client is going to think it's too way-out."

"Let me hear it and I'll tell you what I think."

"Okay," Henry said. "What if we open with an overhead shot of a woman's beautiful hand with terrific nails. Camera starts moving down closer to the hand." Henry demonstrated this using his left hand as the hand in the shot and the sugar dispenser in his right hand for the camera. "Okay, so we move in faster, faster. Extreme close-up of the skin fills the screen, and now we see something on the hand. It's our spokesman in a suit, walking across the hand toward the fingers. So now we see this little guy on a giant hand, and he talks about the product."

Jo chuckled. "Oh, that's just *divine*! I think you should work on it. Except I think the hand can't be beautiful when you first see it. As the camera moves in, the spokesman says something like, 'Look at this dried-up, ugly old hand' — these aren't the right words, obviously — 'and those nails!' So then at some point we see the woman massaging this stuff into her hands and painting the potion on her nails and we dissolve back to the little man and now he's showing us how beautiful her hands are. See? Now you've made it problem-solution. It's still way out but you haven't lost any of the fun. Now it's just in a familiar format their little Lakeland brains can grasp. Definitely work that one up. Number two," Jo said, writing, "'Big Hand, Little Man.'

Oh, that's going to be such fun! Now, is that all?"

"For now. We've just been so tied up with all this casting and recasting."

"That's fine. You've got two good things here, and that's a start."

We ran down our respective schedules and worked out a time-table to get the work done and present it to Ellen as quickly as possible.

It was getting late, so Jo signaled for the check. When it arrived, she waved away our offers to split it. "I'll charge it to the company," she said. "For what they pay the two of you? They should give you a free breakfast every day."

By late Thursday afternoon we had finished both spots. I was getting my things together, happy to be getting out on time for a change, and looking forward to hitting the gym. I stopped and took Craig's card out of my wallet. I hadn't spoken to him since Monday when he called to tell me the apartment he had looked at was a dump, and that he'd call toward the end of the week.

I sat down and called him. He was glad to hear from me – at least he seemed to be. But he said he was going to have to work late on Friday, and probably on Saturday and Sunday as well. He didn't know when he would have time for sleep, much less company. I was disappointed, but said it was okay, and told him to give me a call if he changed his mind.

We met in Jo's office first thing Friday morning to show her the new boards. For the flower commercial, we had done pretty much what we had discussed. Jo made a few suggestions about the copy – things that could be said differently as a way of saving some time, and a faster way of explaining the fact that it was a two-bottle kit. She also suggested some visual changes. We had a shot of a woman's hand placing the twelfth tulip in a vase at the end of the commercial. Jo suggested that instead, we see the woman's hand take one tulip from the dozen at the opening of the commercial, then move through all the close-ups of the stem, the petals, the woman's hand and nails, and the product as a series of dissolves, and then end up with the hand laying the single tulip down in front of the product, with the tag line: "For hands that are naturally soft, and nails that are naturally strong." I loved it.

For the giant hand commercial, we opened with the tiny man strolling past a knuckle and asking, "What's worse than rough, dry, flaky hands?" He would step out onto the nail and answer, "Brittle nails!" And the nail would snap under him, sending him sailing off into limbo. We would dissolve to shots of a woman using the two-piece kit while the voiceover described how it works on both nails and hands, and then, when we returned to the giant hand, the man would be back on her finger. First he would pat the skin, saying, "Not only is it softer here..." and he would step out onto the nail and start bouncing up and down on the tip, as if on a springboard, and say "...but it's also stronger here. And that works for me!" Then we dissolved to the product shot and out.

"Oh, that's just *heaven!*" Jo said, clasping her hands together and falling back into her big leather chair. "They'll just *adore* it in the Corn Belt!"

17

Now, For Men

The next night, Anthony and I went out around six for pizza. It was absurdly hot for September, but, knowing that we'd soon be facing weeks of rain and frigid winds and wet leaves sticking to everything, I was grateful for a little more summer, even if it was the last. We passed Ty's on our way home and decided to stop in, and were rewarded with two empty stools at the bar. It was still early for a Saturday night. We had a round and watched the place begin to fill up. Anthony ran color commentary on each new arrival, since I was sitting with my back to the door. His comments ranged from, "Turn around and gaze at heaven," to "Oh, *that* one. He goes to my gym. I have never met a more negative person. It's like he's a 90-year-old trapped in the body of a 30-year-old. They call him 'Ancient Evenings.'"

At one point, Anthony kept looking away while I was telling one of my more involved stories, and when I shrugged off the object of his distraction as being "not so hot," he said, "It's a good thing we don't have the same taste in men. I could just see us getting into a bitch fight in the living room over some man one of us brought home."

We each ordered another drink. I was already getting

that giddy floating feeling you get in an elevator that starts moving too fast, and knew that I'd better not finish this one. Anthony had his back to the bar again. He was looking toward the front door, and squeezed my thigh and muttered, "Turn around."

I turned in time to see Craig move from the door to an empty space near the window. He was wearing a loud red Hawaiian shirt over a gray tank top, and the smallest pair of shorts I had ever seen. They were practically Speedos, and definitely something ordered from the International Male catalog. And he was not alone. With him was a shorter man in a white tank top and tight jeans who definitely knew his way around a gym.

"Oh, I don't believe it," I said, turning back toward the bar but keeping an eye on Craig's reflection in the mirror. I downed what was left of my drink in one swallow. "He's supposed to be working."

"Well, he's working *something*, honey. What the hell is that outfit he's wearing, anyway? He looks like Betty Hutton at a luau."

"Do you think he saw us?"

"He's acting like he didn't," Anthony said. "Who's the little muscle puppy with him, packin' a cucumber?"

"I have no idea."

In the mirror, we watched Craig start maneuvering through the crowd toward the bar.

"He's coming over here," I said. Anthony reached over and opened two more buttons on my shirt, and before I could object, told me to shut up. Craig sort of squinted in our direction, but still didn't seem to see us.

"He's not wearing his contacts," I offered.

"He's not wearing his underwear, either. Catch his eye in the mirror, Michael. Make him sweat."

"I'd like to make him *bleed*."

We sat there for a while trading caustic remarks and

wondering when Craig was going to decide that he had seen me and come over. He passed us and went into the bathroom.

"He knows you're sitting here. He won't look at you."

"He's probably afraid I'll give him the evil eye or something." I shifted around to face the room, turning my back to the bar. There was no way he could come back and not see me. "Let's get this over with."

Craig came out of the bathroom and did a Keystone Kop double-take. "Look who's here!" he said, grinning.

"Imagine. Working hard, Craig?"

"Actually, yes. We just came from the office."

"*We* did?"

"I'm here with Eric, my assistant. I told you about him, didn't I?"

"You mentioned that he slept with his real estate broker to get an apartment."

"Oh. There's no air conditioning in the office on weekends," he said, I suppose to explain the outfit. "It's as hot as a firecracker up there."

"Craig, this is my roommate, Anthony DeLorenzo." Anthony held out his hand grandly and said, "How do you do?" like the First Lady of the American Theater. Craig shook it sheepishly, and then glanced above us at the mirror.

"Well, it looks like someone's getting ready to molest Eric. I'd better go rescue him."

"You do that little thing," Anthony drawled.

"Stop by on your way out."

"Sure," I said.

Craig went back to his corner, and I turned around toward the bar again. "He went to the *office* dressed like that?"

"Where's his office," Anthony asked, "behind the Port Authority Bus Terminal?"

I kept checking the mirror, hoping Craig and Eric would leave. When it became obvious that they weren't going for a while, I asked Anthony if we could find another bar.

He finished his drink and we started moving toward the door against the tide of men. I turned to Anthony and said, "We have to say good night."

"No, we don't."

"*Yes. We do.*"

We worked our way over to them. Craig introduced us to Eric, who, while easy on the eyes, turned out to be someone who definitely moved his lips while reading, if he read at all. It was so awkward. I had caught Craig in a lie and he knew it, and here we were commenting on the heat wave and how crowded the bar had become. Being so polite was wearing me out, and I finally said we needed to leave.

"Heading home?"

"No, this was just the first stop," I said.

"Well," he said with a laugh, reaching inside my open shirt for a quick grab at a nipple, "maybe you'd better button up. Heading out onto Christopher Street like that!"

I resisted saying, "Look who's talking," and instead said, "Well, you know what they say – it pays to advertise. Good night, guys."

We went through the door and headed across the street to Christopher's. "Cripes! Remind me never to play the *femme fatale* again, Anthony. I should stick to Thelma Ritter parts."

"You did all right, kiddo. I think he got the message." We got club sodas and moved away from the bar to talk. "You should get an Academy Award for that performance," he said, trying to cheer me up, adding, "I would have broken a chair over his head." When I didn't say anything, he asked, "You still love him, don't you?"

"I'm trying awfully hard to convince myself that I don't, but..." I shrugged.

"You need to find someone who'll appreciate you, Michael. Not someone like that who kicks you around."

"I don't want anyone. This is it for me, Anthony. No more men. I draw the curtain!"

"I'll remind you the next time he calls."

We had an 8:00 call at Ed Harmon Productions on Monday morning to shoot "Eating Less." By some miracle, I managed to get there at 7:30. Ed had scheduled all the food and product shots first to get them out of the way. We were required to show at least three different shots of Homestead Acres spread on food, shot in close-up. Henry and I privately referred to this as the Appetite Appeal Clause.

They were still fussing with the lights and the camera and no one needed anything from me. I headed toward the viewing room and ran into Leigh, who was going in the same direction with a platter of bagels and rolls.

"Hiya, cutie!" she called. "Are you hungry?"

"Always. How are you, Leigh?"

"Crazed, as usual."

"Can I give you a hand?"

"Just hold the door for an old lady, will ya? Thanks, hon."

She had already loaded the table with fruit and cheese and pastry. There was barely room for the bagels and rolls.

"Leigh, my God! How many people are you feeding here?"

"Well, I like variety, don't you? And whatever's left over we donate to the church on the next block. Keep that under your hat, though. I'd hate for a client to find out they're feeding the homeless when they think they're only catering a shoot."

Leigh started taking plates of cream cheese and butter from the refrigerator. She also took out several jams and jellies.

Gwen poked her head in to ask, "How's it going, guys?"

"Just fine," Leigh said, offering her something to eat. Gwen walked up to the table, frowned, said she'd be right back and left.

"I guess she wasn't hungry," Leigh said, shrugging it off.

"No, I think she'd rather root around in the garbage cans out back."

"You really can't stand her, can you?"

Leigh started arranging silverware and napkins on the table. I turned to make a cup of tea. Then Gwen sailed back into the room, singing, "Here we are!" and placed a can of Homestead Acres on the table. "What would Maxine say if she came in here and saw us eating butter instead of our product?"

Henry and Patty walked in, and Gwen addressed all of us.

"We need to see ribbons of Homestead Acres on whatever we eat today. Maxine will be here shortly and I think it would make her very happy if she saw us enjoying Homestead Acres on our muffins."

"Gwen," I said, "how is she going to know what it is we're enjoying on our muffins? Is she going to come around to each of us and ask for a taste?"

"She'll know," Gwen explained with a demented grin, "because I asked her to supply a few extra cans just for us. I told her we could barely keep it in stock when we had it at the agency."

"You told her *that*?" Henry said, laughing.

I remembered everyone asking to try it once, but only because they had to, in order to have something to say about it in commercials. But I never noticed crowds clamoring for seconds. In fact, I didn't remember anyone finishing their firsts.

"So make sure you eat some in front of her," Gwen said, as she discharged enough Homestead Acres onto a muffin to cover all of Texas. She took a bite and said, "Mmmmm. It really is rather tasty!" and turned out of the room, looking as if she had just had a vision.

"Is she on medication?" Leigh asked.

"Now maybe you understand why I can't stand her," I said. "They don't *make* medication big enough for what she has." I picked up a paper plate and started making a small mound of Homestead Acres on it.

"MMM-MMM-MMMMM!" I enthused, in my best Gwen-doing-a-housewife-in-a-bad-commercial voice, "even paper tastes better with the buttery-rich goodness of new Forster Foods Homestead Acres Dairy Spread! Made from yogurt plus the milk of virgin cows, which is a miracle in and of itself, new Homestead Acres is the nutrition sensation of the century: fake butter! Talk about your skim milk masquerading as cream, this is positively the *transvestite* of butter! Why, it looks, tastes, spreads and melts just like butter. BUT FOR CHRISSAKE, DON'T TRY TO FRY WITH IT, OKAY? Just enjoy the buttery-rich goodness on your whole-grain breads and delicious fiber-rich veggies. It's butter living through chemistry!"

I got a healthy round of applause and took a bow. Then I pitched the plate into the trash.

"I don't know about the rest of you," I said, moving toward the food, "but I for one am going to have cream cheese and jelly on a bagel, and I'm going to sit next to Aunt Maxie while I eat it."

"Yes," Henry added, "and she'll say, 'Funny, you don't look Jewish.'" He looked at Leigh, explaining, "Our client says that bagels are 'too New York,' which really means bagels are too Jewish."

"I know. We work with them all the time and they're a bunch of Nazis, if you want to know the truth. Old man Forster was a real anti-Semitic pig. But they throw us a lot of business and they pay their bills on time, and that's show biz!"

We all got something to eat and filed out past the kitchen set. Henry made one last adjustment to the grouping of Homestead Acres cans for the tabletop shot. There was an empty spot in front of them where, just before we rolled, a plate with a slice of toast and a smudge of Homestead Acres would be placed in the frame. For the time being, they were using a fake plastic stand-in for the smudge so they could compose the shot and adjust the lights without worrying about melting the product.

As soon as they had taken this first shot, they would move on to a shot of one of the actress's hands spraying a little blob of Homestead Acres on a slice of toast. This shot was a little more complicated, because the camera had to move in slightly at the same time the can discharged the product. After that came a shot of a dollop being discharged on a steamy hot muffin, followed by shots of all the foods you could use this stuff on – broccoli, corn on the cob, a baked potato. The trick was going to be getting the right amount of product out of the can in each shot, then capturing it on tape before it melted. Gwen had very specific ideas about just what The Dollop should look like.

As if on cue, Maxine trudged onto the set, wearing yet another dumpy suit with a sailor blouse. Her hair was tied back today with a big black velvet bow. She looked like a middle-aged Gigi. "Good morning, all," she said, primly.

Gwen grabbed her Homestead-Acres-covered muffin and shot to Maxine's side. "Gee, hi! You timed it perfectly." She took Maxine's arm and started leading her toward the viewing lounge. "We've got all kinds of goodies. And plenty of Homestead Acres, too!"

"Oh, I never eat it," Maxine said, as they rounded the corner of the kitchen set. "It gave me a rash."

We tried not to laugh. Henry turned toward the video monitor and began studying the package shot. He didn't like the shadow on the side of one of the cans, and asked Ed if something could be done to warm up the shot.

Maxine came back from the viewing lounge with a cup of coffee and a corn muffin. Gwen was busy introducing her to the crew. I sat in a chair eating my bagel, knowing they were headed in my direction.

"And you remember Michael Gregoretti, our copywriter?"

I wanted to correct her and say, *junior* copywriter, but didn't. It killed me that they referred to me as "the copywriter" when the client was around but made sure they said "*junior* copywriter" in every other situation, especially any conversation about salary. I wondered how this woman would react if she knew the agency had dumped her business in the lap of someone they considered a trainee.

I shook her hand and said something vaguely pleasant. Then Gwen noticed my jelly-smeared bagel and said, "You're eating *another* bagel, Michael!" I didn't know what she was talking about. She turned to Maxine and said, "I swear, when we put out the Homestead Acres this morning, Michael was the first one to have some on his bagel. He just loves it, don't you, Michael?"

"I do. That's the truth, Maxine. I've even taken some home and used it as a personal lubricant during sex."

I watched as clouds of horror and disbelief passed over Gwen's face like warring storm fronts. Satisfied, I broke the silence and touched Maxine's arm. "I'm sorry. That was a very bad joke. I just can't resist a good straight line. I don't use it as a personal lubricant."

"Good," said Maxine with a grin. "How do you think I

got that rash?" She broke into a laugh – a cross between a cackle and a giggle, actually. I was amazed. The woman had actually made a joke! Maybe I had Maxine all wrong. I laughed too, but Gwen just forced her lips into a tortured smile without making a sound. She still had that animal-in-a-trap look around the eyes, though, and she steered Maxine away from me and over to the monitor where Henry stood. He had finished positioning the cans and was satisfied with the lighting. As soon as she was sure that Maxine wouldn't see, Gwen shot me a look of death.

Ed began rolling tape not too long after that. We started with what would actually be the last shot of the commercial: a slice of toast with a tasteful dollop of Homestead Acres on it sitting in front of some Homestead Acres cans. The trick here was the butter had to look like it was *just* starting to melt but not vanish completely into the bread, which happened faster than you'd think it would, thanks to the heat from the studio lights. The toast was actually cold. Eileen, the food stylist, would put the blob of Homestead Acres on it first, then plop the toast onto a heated dish just before we placed it in front of the camera. That way, the butter would glisten and look delicious long enough to get what we needed on tape, before vanishing into an unappetizing wet spot. When we edited, we would add the super "It's butter made better" at the bottom of the frame – the tag line which, fortunately, had survived the Legal department at Forster.

"Cut!" Ed yelled, a few seconds into the shot. "Stop tape. The butter is starting to melt."

"Everyone keeps calling it butter," Maxine said to Gwen in a worried tone. "Tell them it's a low-fat butter *product*."

"Sorry. The low-fat butter product is melting," Ed said, not without sarcasm. Eileen picked it up replaced it with another dish and fresh toast slice, and Ed called "Roll tape!" again.

He kept it rolling until the second dollop began to glisten.

"It's starting to sweat again, but I think we have enough, folks. Stop tape." We turned to the monitor for the playback. There we were, fifteen adults scrutinizing an image of a slice of toast with a blob of fake butter on it in front of a couple of cans of Homestead Acres, as if it was the long-lost footage from *The Magnificent Ambersons*.

"I think we need to raise the camera just a hit, Ed," said Gwen.

"Really, Gwen? I think it's fine," Henry said.

"We don't settle for 'fine,' Henry. By raising the camera just a *kiss* more, the butter product becomes more centered. It won't take that long to fix."

It took forty-five minutes to set it up to Gwen's satisfaction and another half-hour to shoot. I couldn't tell the difference between the new footage and what we had shot earlier, but Gwen was satisfied and we moved on.

Getting the next shot should have been easy, since it was just a slow move-in on the cans using the setup we already had. But Gwen made Ed do the shot at least twenty times. She asked for a faster move, a slower move, one starting out fast and moving in slower, one starting slow then moving in fast, and every other conceivable combination. After an hour of this, I had had enough.

"Let's do one where we start on a street in Mexico, cross the border, come to New York, come through the stage door and circle the package," I offered. "All in one take. We can call it 'Smudge of Evil.'" Gwen glared at me. "Well, how many of these do we need? Henry and I were satisfied three thousand takes ago."

"Can we take a break, guys? I'd like to speak to Michael off the set."

"Here we go again, boys and girls," I muttered.

Gwen and I went to the viewing lounge. She slammed the door and turned on me. "Michael, if you insist on humiliating me in front of Ed and Maxine, I'm going to have to order you off the set," she shrieked.

"Listen, von Stroheim, this is not your production. You are wasting valuable time by demanding things that aren't necessary. If you ask me, it's Henry who's being humiliated."

"Henry doesn't seem to know what he wants."

"I think he's doing just fine."

"Well, as group supervisor, if I'm not happy with what I see on the screen, it's my job to step in. And we can all carry on without any more of your bitchy comments. You're not as clever as you think you are, Michael."

"I'd like to remind you that this is my commercial, and Henry's. Not yours. We're going to shoot it our way, and if you don't like it, piss up a rope, lady."

"I won't allow you to speak to me that way! I'll go to Fran!"

"Do that. I'll deny ever having had this conversation with you and everyone will think you're delusional. Next time, get a witness. Now, if you'll excuse me."

The look on her face, and I caught only a glimpse of it as I left the room, will stay with me forever. I never saw such pure hatred anywhere before, and I hope never to see it again.

When we broke for lunch, Gwen didn't come with us. She said she had things to attend to at the agency, but would be back in time for the afternoon session. I was sure she was going to call Ellen in Michigan.

As soon as we came back from lunch, we started getting ready for the next shot: A woman's hand holding a can of Homestead Acres would drift into the frame and apply "The Dollop" to the waiting slice of toast. This shot would come just before the one we had already shot, where the toast is seen in front of the cans of Homestead Acres. While that sounds simple enough, it wasn't simple at all, partly because The Dollop had to more or less match the little square of it we used in the first shot we made, partly because we had to set up the whole thing again after each take — new naked cold slice of toast on a warm plate — and mostly because Gwen came back to the set.

We had just finished adjusting the lighting when she breezed in. The hand model was making practice blobs of Homestead Acres on a big rectangle of foam board and seemed to have perfected getting the applicator to discharge just enough product in a square shape.

"How was lunch?" Gwen asked the group. "Did you go someplace fun?" She was trying too hard to be Miss Congeniality. I knew she had spoken to Ellen. The question was: Who was in trouble, Gwen or me? She moved to the monitor to examine the setup. Maxine was already there. I could see that Gwen was pointing out things to Maxine, but she was talking in such a low voice, I wasn't sure if she was being critical or finally liked what she saw.

Ed started taping. Gwen and Maxine were still huddled in deep conference in front of the monitor, analyzing each take. I wished we were shooting with sound so that Ed could shush them.

After about a half-hour, Gwen asked for playback, and we all gathered around the monitor to watch five different slices of toast get buttered. Finally Gwen said, "You see?" and stood up triumphantly. "Ed, what's happening here is that the hand model — what's her name again?"

"Sarah," said the hand model.

"Thank you. What's happening is that Sarah's application of the product doesn't seem to be fluid," Gwen said.

"Fluid?"

"Yes. She brings the can into frame in a very deliberate manner, but when she makes The Dollop on the toast, it seems tentative. It takes much too long. Isn't that so, Maxine?"

"Yes."

I couldn't believe this was happening.

"It should be like a waltz. One-two-three-and-one-two-three-and-down-kiss-leave. Sarah just isn't doing it gracefully enough."

Ed looked at Henry. Henry shrugged his shoulders, as if to tell Ed that he should handle it. He thought for a minute, and then asked someone to get him another piece of foam board.

"Sarah, here's what we're going to do. I want you to just keep making squares of product on this board for practice. Make twenty blobs. Make thirty. In waltztime. I'll shoot it. Gwen, you watch the monitor, and tell me when she's got it."

My respect for Ed kept growing. He rolled tape and Sarah started making smudges of Homestead Acres. Gwen assumed the role of director, shouting encouragements at Sarah with each swipe. "No. Nope. Too fast. Better. Smoother! Yes. YES! That one was perfect! COWABUNGA! DO IT JUST LIKE THAT! Except she has to be careful to make sure The Dollop she's applying here matches the one on the toast in the next shot. Continuity, you know."

Henry jumped in and insisted that a dollop was a dollop, and that as long as they were roughly the same size and shape in each shot, no one was going to run up to the TV screen with a ruler yelling, "Liars!"

When we got to the food shots, it was more of the same. There wasn't enough steam coming from the vegetables. Then the vegetables looked too hot. Then The Dollop kept sliding off the vegetables as it melted. In anyone else's universe, all of this could have been fixed in the editing room.

At 10:00 that night, when we started taping the seg-
ment where the product was applied to a hot muffin, Gwen
said she didn't like the way it was melting. The muffins, she
warned, were too hot, and the product looked like it was
separating, not melting. Finally, it was Ed's turn to yell at
her.

"Gwen, this is a two-second shot of some fake butter
melting into a goddamn muffin, not the Odessa Steps
sequence. Would you please let me make the fucking shot
so we can all go home?"

We wrapped forty-five minutes later. We had been
taping for thirteen hours, and had completed six different
shots — roughly fourteen seconds of the commercial. I
didn't even want to think about what we would have to pay
the crew in overtime.

18
No Unpleasant Odor

We had an 8:30 call the next morning, and I was late. I was exhausted and didn't want to go, knowing it would only be a replay of the day before. If ever there had been a day that I wished I could have connected with Casper to score a powdered pick-me-up, this was it. I found Henry and Patty in the viewing lounge having something to eat. "I hope that's Breakstone's you're putting on your bagels, not Homestead Acres," I said.

"Hi, Michael."

"I'm not ready for this," I said, making a cup of tea and looking over the food on the table. I was lusting after the apple turnovers. "Another banner day in the world of advertising, and you are there!"

"Al called Ellen in Michigan last night," Patty said. "He told her that Gwen was completely out of control yesterday, and that it's her fault we went into overtime."

"What did Ellen say?"

"Supposedly she called Gwen and told her to back off."

"God, I hope so," I said, finally settling for half a bran muffin.

We were going to tape the actors on the kitchen set

that day. Ed's crew had added a table and chairs in one corner, and Carl, the prop man, and his assistants were busy dressing the set. They had cluttered it up with a variety of interesting objects: an old-fashioned toaster and vintage blender on one end of the counter, a big clown cookie jar on the other, and some not-too-healthy-looking plants on the windowsill. They had put up some tacky polka-dot curtains and were adding a few last-minute touches when I walked in. Carl had found this really awful calendar and was looking for a prominent spot to hang it. It was the first encouraging thing I'd seen. We didn't even have the actors on the set yet, and the kitchen looked like something out of a *New Yorker* cartoon. I sensed Henry's subtle hand, and asked, "Has Gwen seen any of this?"

"Not yet," sang Carl, anticipating the same battle I did.

I went back to the viewing room to tell Henry that I thought the set looked great.

"I called Ed after the last pre-production meeting, and told him to do everything he could think of to keep this spot looking the way we wanted it to look," Henry explained. "Gwen never asked to see any of the props. She was too busy fighting with you on casting, so I approved everything when I came here for the pre-light. Wait until you see the wardrobe."

"Are we going to get away with this?"

"I have standby normal-looking stuff if we don't, but I won't tell Gwen unless she backs me to the wall."

The actors we had chosen were relatively ordinary people. At first I thought they'd look wrong in the dopey set. But when I saw them in their costumes, I wasn't worried. The hairdresser and makeup woman worked in a little exaggeration at Henry's prodding. They overteased the housewife's hair and gave it that dated look we wanted. They put a funny pair of glasses on the husband. Now if they could act, we had it made.

Gwen and Maxine finished whatever they were doing in the production offices and came down to the set. As they turned the corner, the prop people were hanging a cuckoo clock in the kitchen. Ed and his crew were positioning the camera, while a second crew started focusing the lights.

"Are these the same actors we saw on the audition tape?" Maxine asked, looking perplexed.

"Yes, ma'am," Henry said.

"But they look so...*different*." Then she noticed the kitchen. Carl was covering the table now with a gaudy tablecloth that said 'Visit Florida' and featured a big map of the Sunshine State with illustrated points of interest. While a lot of this stuff would never read on camera, it went a long way to help establish the offbeat mood.

Gwen said, "Henry, can I borrow you a minute, please?" And off they went to the viewing room. I knew it was Henry's turn for a lecture from Mother Superior. I stood next to Maxine with my muffin and tea. "What do you think so far?" I asked.

"This is for the scene where the wife takes the tiny slice of real butter and then drops it on her husband's toast with tweezers, right?"

"That's right. Then we shoot the 'after' scene where she switches the toast with the butter for the toast dripping with Homestead Acres and he smiles and eats it."

"You don't think it's a little too exaggerated?"

"Well, they are doing silly things. You kind of expect silly people to have a silly house. It's just like the storyboards."

"I'm not sure about this. I have to see what it looks like on the monitor."

I asked Ed how long until we'd have a picture, and he said it would only be a few minutes. Maxine had disappeared while I was talking to Ed, so I went over to Patty and asked her if she thought we'd get away with it.

"I don't know, Michael. Maxine looks awfully nervous. And Gwen is probably furious. I'd like to hear what she's saying to Henry right now."

"Well, they approved the actors, so what are they going to do? Change their minds ten minutes before the shoot?"

"They could ask us to tone them down a bit. The actors don't look exactly like they did on the audition tape."

"True, but the thing is, Maxine doesn't seem too concerned. Gwen is probably beating Henry up in there, but Maxine hasn't said a whole lot. She didn't say all that much yesterday, either. Henry and I never got to go to any of the meetings with them at Forster. Now I'm beginning to wonder just how many of the changes we made were actually Maxine's, and how many were Gwen's ideas that she passed off as Maxine's."

Gwen came back onto the set, red-faced and smoking a cigarette. Ed shot her a look, but stopped short of asking her to put it out. Henry came back from the viewing lounge with a cup of coffee and a healthy chunk of crumb cake. He smiled at us, so I assumed we were in the clear. I wanted to drag him off somewhere for the scoop, but with Gwen puffing away not ten feet from us, I couldn't say a word. He just mouthed, "It's cool," and passed me. I would have to wait until Gwen moved off the set to pump him for information.

It wasn't a long wait. Carl unpacked the final touch, a goofy ceramic teapot shaped like a camel, and set it on the countertop. "Isn't this great?" he asked me.

"Oh, where did you find *that*?"

Gwen stamped out her cigarette and stormed off the set without a word. Patty and I cornered Henry.

"You should have told me you were going to do this," I said. "If you had, I wouldn't have been fighting her so hard."

"Yes, but then Gwen could accuse you of being in on it, too. If I hang for this, I swing alone."

"What did she say to you in there?" Patty asked.

"She did her how-dare-you-undermine-my-authority-in-front-of-the-client rap. I told her I wasn't undermining anything. Maxine had approved the storyboards. No one had ever told me to tone down the sets when they saw the boards. I acted very surprised. Then she launched into her after-all-I've-done-for-you routine, and threatened to go to Fran."

We were interrupted by Al, the account executive. "Someone want to tell me what's going on? Gwen claims both she and Ellen told you you couldn't exaggerate the set like this."

"If you look at the storyboards, Al, I drew all these kooky gadgets and old appliances in the background," Henry said. "As a matter of fact, what we've done here is tame compared to the boards. If they wanted me to make changes, they never told me."

"Maxine is a little nervous about this."

"All she said to me was that she wanted to see it on a monitor first," I said.

"Hey, folks, we're ready to rock and roll over here," Ed called. "Let's get the actors on the set."

We were doing the medium shot first – the wife putting the plate of toast on the table in front of her grumpy husband. Next we'd move in for the two close-ups: his reaction shot and the opening of the commercial (the business with the wife and the tweezers). Although Maxine had returned to the set, Gwen was still missing. We gathered around the monitor for our first look.

"What do you think?" Al asked Maxine. The two actors had taken their positions. She looked at the image, turned toward the set, then looked back at the monitor.

"I was very concerned that you'd gone too far. I like

the way it looks on the monitor, though, I have to admit. But to be honest, I'm not sure."

"Is it too much clutter on the set, or is it the actors?" Henry asked.

"It's not any one thing. The actors and the set work, and I understand what you've done. I like what I see here, but I'm a little thrown by it. It's just not Forster Foods."

What was the problem? Was she looking for a reason to change it or a reason to shoot it? I gambled. "Look, Maxine. Your big concern with this commercial when we first presented it to you was that it had too much whimsy and too little sell. We beefed up the copy. We added gorgeous appetite stuff – you saw what we shot yesterday. You have to admit that the food stuff looks delicious. But your consumers are going to remember this product because they're going to remember the people in the commercial."

"You don't think we're going too far?"

"I think people are going to laugh *with* them, not at them. They're lovable and kooky, but not scary."

Ed came to my rescue. "I tell you what. Let's shoot it this way. But I'll also give you a couple of takes where we tone it way down so you'll have protection footage available when you edit."

"Let's try it this way first," she said.

I wanted to call *Adweek* and tell them to send down reporters and a photographer to cover this pivotal moment in advertising history: CLIENT BUYS CREATIVITY! Sticks Neck Out for Good Idea.

Ed had had a short conference with the actors, and was now ready to begin. We did about ten takes of the actress setting down the dish with the toast on it in front of her husband. She played it sweet at first, and then got a little broader. Ed was encouraging. He'd say "nice" and "good" after each take, even if it wasn't true.

Satisfied that we had enough "safe" footage, Ed started nudging the actors in the other direction. "Now let's try it another way. Come in and drop the plate in front of him. Sort of annoyed this time. I mean, don't break the dish — you're not angry. Everybody ready? Roll tape please. And... action!"

The actress sauntered into frame and dropped the plate in front of the actor with a little Alice Kramden flourish. It was a good thing we were shooting this sequence without sound because Maxine let out one big "Ha!"

We went on trying different moves, and finally agreed that we had plenty of good takes — some broad, some subtle, but enough of each to please both camps. Ed asked Maxine if she wanted to make any changes before we moved the camera for the close-ups. She asked to see the playback, and we gathered once again around the monitor. She watched what we had taped and said, "Let's move on," and then turned to find something in her briefcase.

I looked at Henry. He made a quick pantomime of shouting "Hooray!" and waved his hands over his head. I decided to take advantage of the break and call the agency for messages. I ran into Leigh on the first floor.

"Hey, what happened to Gwen?" she asked.

"We sort of mutinied."

"Well, she ran out of here muttering about an hour ago."

"Oh, cripes. We're going to be in big trouble when they get wind of this back at Malcolm. This may be my first and last commercial."

"Honey, is your client smiling?"

"Yes."

"Then I wouldn't worry."

Without Gwen there to interfere, we got everything we hoped for. In a way, the fact that the actors weren't what we were looking for probably worked in our favor. If we had hired the types we first said we wanted, the spot might have ended up too broad.

I finally cornered Henry and asked, "Okay, what did you say to Gwen this morning?"

Henry had tried reasoning with Gwen at first. Gwen told him she would call Ellen and tell her we had disobeyed her instructions and stop the shoot. "On what grounds?" Henry finally challenged. "We used the actors you wanted. The set looks like the storyboards. Maxine certainly isn't objecting. Go talk to Ellen if you want to, but you can't stop the shoot. You're stuck."

The next morning I went to the recording studio and had the announcer lay down a voice-over track. Then it was back to Harmon Productions to assemble a rough cut in the small editing suite on the top floor of the building.

Gwen had left town to supervise the "Dairy Farmer's Wife" shoot in Connecticut, and after that, would be tied up shooting and editing her own commercial, "Good Foods." She couldn't possibly show up while we were editing ours.

It took only a day and a half to pull it all together. Once we had selected the best takes, it was just a matter of putting them all down on a master in sequence. All the optical effects – dissolves and fades – were added as we went.

Karen saw me coming down the hall when I got back from the editing session, and waved me over to her desk. "Ellen called you about an hour ago," she said in a concerned whisper. "She's back from Buick, and said she wanted to see you the minute you got in. She said to make sure you went to her office."

"How did she sound?"

"Like she always sounds. Pissed off."

I went down to Patty's office and asked her for the rough cut, thinking that if I was going in to see Ellen, I should have the commercial with me. Then I called Ellen and told her I was back.

"Come down here. Now."

I walked to her office, trying to think of every possible thing she could accuse me of. Undermining Gwen? Gross behavior in front of the client? Fran was sitting in Ellen's office. Ellen looked up at me from her desk.

"Come in and close that door." She indicated the sofa near the monitor, and said, "Take a seat." I knew better than to make small talk. The last thing I wanted to know at this point was how the weather in Michigan was.

"Gwen went to Fran about your behavior on the set. She also called me out at Buick, which I really didn't appreciate. I left this assignment in her hands so I could go put out fires. What the hell did you and Henry do to me?"

"I couldn't help it. I told you she brings out the worst in me."

"But she said you completely ignored her instructions – that you and Henry went ahead and did the commercial the way you wanted and not the way you were told to do it, or the way the client wanted it."

"Maxine was there. We got her approval on everything before we shot it."

"You handled it all wrong, though. You and Henry," Fran said.

"Ask Patty or Al or Ed Harmon. The first day was a nightmare. Gwen had to get her hooks into everything and all she did was get in the way and push us into triple overtime. She wouldn't let Henry art-direct his own spot. If she hadn't stormed off, we'd still be there shooting."

Ellen pointed a manicured finger at me. "You were supposed to shoot this commercial in a style we all agreed on previously, correct? Instead you went ahead and did just what you wanted."

"Within the limits that were set by you and Gwen and the client. But we didn't really change anything. It still looks like it did on the boards. Actually, it's tame by comparison. The announcer copy is the same. Maxine and Gwen had the final say on the actors and we used the ones they picked. I just did my best to make the finished spot look and sound the way it did in my head. And I think you should at least look at the rough cut before you nail me to a cross."

"I'm not nailing you to a cross, Michael. I don't know what to do with you yet, because I still don't know what happened."

Fran chimed in. "Gwen said that you were abusive and that Henry ordered her off the set."

"Leaving the set was Gwen's idea. And I wasn't abusive. I can't help it if I hate her and don't care if it shows. I'm not going to get an ulcer standing by and smiling while she ruins my work."

"Enough, Michael," Ellen said. "Is that the rough? Let me see it."

I put the cassette in the big Sony U-matic VCR and played it for her. She watched it without saying a word. Then she lit a cigarette and told me to run it a second time. When it stopped, she said, "Did Maxine see this yet?"

"Not this cut, but she saw everything we taped on the set and watched all the playbacks."

"What do you think of this?" she asked.

"It isn't what I wanted to do originally. But considering all the limitations placed on it, I'm happy with it."

"I think it's fine," Ellen said flatly. "I think it's really good, actually."

"You do?"

"There are things I would change — I think you may have to find some alternate takes. The food looks great.

The people are funny enough without making me nervous and if Maxine is smiling, so am I. *But.*" She stopped to take another drag on her cigarette, making the moment as theatrical as possible. "I don't think it's going to be worth all the trouble in the end. You have to get this through two levels at the client. And they'll never buy it."

"Maxine approved what we did on the set."

"Maxine is nobody. She's only the first hoop we jump through. Her boss, Larry, is a real fuck. They'll probably never air this. Not the way it is now, anyway."

"That's their loss, then. It's a good spot, you said so yourself. And isn't that the point? Aren't we supposed to make good commercials here? Work we're proud of?"

"Not at the expense of losing clients. They don't care what we want to do. They sign the checks and they want what they're paying for."

I was wrong no matter what I said. If I did what the client wanted, I would have hated the result. By fighting with Gwen, I had alienated her mentor, Ellen.

"So what happens now?" I asked, expecting to be fired.

"What else are you working on?" Fran asked.

"Skin Therapy Moisturizing Gel and Total Hand Treatment System," I told her.

"Michael," Ellen said, "you're too young to get a reputation for being difficult. Let's just say you had your first whack at production, and it went to your head a little, okay? Your intentions were good. You wanted to keep certain ideals alive. But this isn't *The Fountainhead* here. They don't call this a whore's business for nothing. I wasn't at the shoot, and I'll never know what really happened. Let's just get these things approved and shipped for test and forget it."

I knew she was angry. And I'd probably never get a good assignment from Fran again. I only hoped that after they talked to Henry and Al and anyone else who was there, they'd have to admit that someone had to say no to Gwen. Maybe what Ellen was mad about was that I had been the one to say it. I was, after all, this little junior making his first commercial and a *test* commercial at that. What I didn't know was that Gwen, at that very moment, was bringing the dairy farmer's wife to tears in Connecticut.

The weather had remained ridiculously hot for September, but since the commercials were scheduled to air all winter, Mrs. Dairyfarmer had to be seen wearing some kind of coat. It wasn't a problem until they had to keep reshooting the same lines over and over again: "Imagine! Making a low-fat butter from yogurt! I said to my husband, 'Well, what will they think of next!'"

According to Lisa and Peter, Gwen kept badgering Ed for retakes. She made the actress emphasize "imagine." Then she asked for emphasis on "yogurt." Then she wanted her to punch both words. Then just "low-fat." So for an hour and a half, this poor forty-eight-year-old character actress, who normally played kindly schoolteachers pushing vitamins for kids and plump benevolent aunts making slice-and-bake cookies for Christmas, sat sweating on a porch in a heavy shearling coat in eighty-degree weather, pretending it was winter while trying to match the inflection of the voices Gwen heard in her head. And finally, after take ninety or ninety-one – Peter and Lisa couldn't remember which – she just snapped and shrieked at Gwen, "What the fuck do you want from me, you crazy bitch?" and stormed off the porch. She started walking – back to Manhattan, I suppose – muttering to herself as she trudged down the country road. Ed and Maxine had to chase after her, calm her down, and promise her that Gwen wouldn't open her mouth again.

By the end of the week, we had shown the rough "Eating Less" to everyone at the agency who was supposed to approve it – from the head of Production to the people in Account Services. The comments varied, but overall, everyone liked it. They all agreed that it needed music, and we had found two stock pieces that worked. I would have preferred an original piece, but it wasn't in the budget and stock was better than no music at all.

Gwen still wasn't happy with the dairy farmer's wife's performance, and wanted her to come back and rerecord some of her lines. The actress demanded triple scale for her time – over a thousand dollars – for what would be no more than an hour's work. Her agent claimed that the agency had abused her, and she wouldn't come back unless we paid her the rate she wanted. It was blackmail, although I thought she should have asked for more. Gwen solved the problem by hiring another actress to come in and dub the whole commercial for scale.

Henry and I met with Ellen and Peter and Lisa the night before the three commercials went over to Forster Foods. Ellen screened the spots so that each team could see what the others had done.

Ours was first. "Good Foods," the commercial she and Gwen had done, followed. It was gorgeous – heavy on the appetite appeal, with lots of delicious things to eat and steamy melty buttery shots. "Dairy Farmer's Wife," Peter and Lisa's spot, was pretty boring. Gwen's bad idea translated into a bad commercial, and the dubbing was obvious and didn't help.

"I want to congratulate all of you on some very nice work," Ellen said. "I hope they're going to like this stuff over at Forster. And 'Eating Less' is the spot the agency is going to recommend for full production."

I was shocked. I had thought all along that they would recommend "Good Foods." Of the three, it was the least problematic, and the one that addressed the product most directly – this is a low-fat butter and here's what you use it on. But Howard, who had the final say, liked ours best. This too was surprising, because he normally appeared to have no sense of humor. Maybe he just hated the other two more and we won by default. Whatever the reason, I wasn't going to complain.

Gwen sat in the corner blowing smoke into the air. She smiled and congratulated us with that sickly-sweet grin on her face, and I felt like I was being cursed.

I walked out of the meeting feeling better about the way things had gone. Henry clapped me on the shoulder and said, "Part one is over, at least."

"Now for our friends at Forster," I said.

As predicted, Larry at Forster didn't like the rough cut. He phoned Ellen to say that we had gone too far. Ellen made a case for testing our cut, but he wouldn't budge. We wound up going back and cutting in the less comic takes, and gave them a vastly toned-down version for test. *Without* music. By the time we finished the commercial at the end of September, Henry and I felt like a couple of whipped dogs. Gwen made us give the client everything they wanted, and kept twisting the knife by telling us we should have listened to her in the first place.

Henry managed to get our original version finished, scored and mixed at the same time as we finished the client's, and Forster obliviously picked up the bill. No matter what happened with the test version, at least I had my cut. Finally, I had a TV commercial in my portfolio.

19
Quick And Easy!

Jo had run the work for Total Hand Treatment past Ellen, and she had asked for some minor changes. The account group, however, was not enthusiastic about the work.

Beth Boyle, the senior management rep, kept insisting that they'd never go for either of these spots, especially not the "Big Hand" commercial. Worse, she told us that lately they'd been making threats about pulling the account and taking it to Ogilvy & Mather.

"You need to come up with something else. You know how they are over there. This is the worst client I've ever worked with! Fat Tom Dolgen will never understand this," Beth whined, waving her copy of the storyboards for emphasis, adding, "I'm *serious*," as if there were ever a moment when she wasn't. Presenting work to her was like talking to the George Washington face on Mount Rushmore. She made Maxine and Larry look like Harpo and Chico.

Jo tried to make a case for presenting the two spots, but Beth wasn't buying.

"Frankly, Jo, the tulip thing isn't very good and the guy walking around on the hand is too bizarre. Show it to them if you want to," she said, "but they won't buy it. Neither of these spots focuses on nail strength."

"You don't think that little man jumping up and down on a nail says strength?" Jo asked, tossing her glasses down on the legal pad in front of her for emphasis.

"Look, if you want to know the truth," Beth said, "you're going out there with nothing. They'll kill the tulip because it's cosmetic, and cosmetic makes Tom nervous. And they'll kill the little man because it's too weird."

Jo wore Beth down eventually, and she agreed to take the two spots we had on the condition that we do two more.

Henry, Jo, and I spent the next three days and nights huddled around her conference table, trying to come up with more commercials.

"What about Cinderella?" I asked.

"A cartoon?" Jo asked.

"No, live action. We update it. She's in a modern kitchen and she talks to the camera. She says, 'Do you love it? Here I work my fingers to the bone for these three,' and then she points to a picture on the wall of the stepmother and the two stepsisters."

"Okay, then what happens?"

"She says, 'And now they won't even take me to the Prince's Ball!' and she shows us the invitation. It's stuck to the refrigerator with a magnet."

"Okay," said Jo, politely. I don't think she was convinced, but she was willing to hear me out.

"So she goes on. 'They told me: With *those* hands? You'd be lucky if they let you in the kitchen!' So then the Fairy Godmother appears – a real 1940s glamourpuss. And Cindy says, 'Oh, Fairy Godmother, will you help me get to the ball?' and the Fairy Godmother says, 'Well, I'm not here to read the gas meter, honey!' And she waves her magic wand and the Total Hand Treatment kit appears and she tells her to use it to make her hands lovelier – all the legal stuff, blah, blah, blah, fine Arabian protein, and then we cut to the ball and the Prince, who's adorable, is kissing Cindy's hand and he says, 'Where have you been all my life?' and Cindy says, 'Oh...around.' And the stepsisters and their mother are looking on jealously and one of them says, 'How'd she get those beautiful hands?' and the Fairy Godmother appears behind them. Then the stepmom says, 'Must have been magic!' and the Fairy Godmother shakes her head 'no' and waves her wand. Then we cut to a tabletop in limbo, all swathed in pink satin, and the magic wand passes over it and we hear harps, and the product appears and we say 'New Lakeland Labs Total Hand Treatment System' and out."

"That's probably four hours long," Jo said. "I'm willing to present it if you can make it happen in thirty seconds, but you know they'll just *despise* it."

We sat silently for a minute or two, each trying to come up with another concept.

"What are things you do with your nails that would imply strength?" Henry said.

"We could show two women sitting on a banquette having lunch at the Colony in big hats," I said, "and one of them says, 'Oh, there she is now, that bitch! I'll scratch her eyes out!' and she turns to the camera and says, 'And I can, too, because I've got ten great nails...'" I got a laugh, but it didn't solve the problem. "Okay," I said, returning to Earth. "How about gardening? That's rough on your hands."

"It's been done," Jo said. "Besides, women sitting at home seeing a woman complaining about what gardening does to her hands are going to yell, 'So wear gloves, you dope!' at their TV. *I* would."

We thought a little longer. Then Jo said, "I always break my nails opening my luggage. Whenever I go to Europe, I end up having to have a manicure the first day there."

"What about soda pop-tops?" I offered.

"You know what might be great?" Jo said. "We get some piece of music under this, and show all the ways you break a nail. The copy is something like – it's no good having soft hands if your nails are always broken and split and your cuticles are a disaster, or something like that. We keep showing women breaking their nails. Then we see the product and how you use it, and then you see a woman with absolutely marvelous hands and she does something *fabulous* with her fingernail to show how strong it is."

"Like what," I asked, "pick a lock?"

"Don't laugh. That could be it. Some wonderful something that says really strong nails. Women would just die for that. But we do it with lots of style – really chic women, fabulous clothes."

By the end of the third day of this, we had thought up and thrown out numerous ideas for commercials. We settled on two to take to Lakeland for presentation.

In one, we decided to show a slow-motion, extreme close-up shot of a nail actually breaking when it's pressed down onto a marble table top. Then we'd move on to beauty application shots – gorgeous hands applying lotion and brushing on the solution. Then we'd show another nail moving into frame in slow motion, only this time, it would gently flex when it hits the marble instead of breaking.

In the second spot, I gave Lakeland their old standby: a spokeswoman. It wasn't bad, actually. When Jo suggested it and I made a face, she said, "All right, pretend you could have any actress in the whole world to do it. Any living actress. Who would you pick?"

"Kathleen Turner," I said.

"Oh, yes," Jo said. "Wouldn't she be *ideal!* So, go back to your office and pretend you're writing for Kathleen Turner."

I did, and it would have been the best thing she'd done since *Body Heat*, as far as I was concerned.

Jo called us in to her office the following Monday.

"Is this good news or bad news?" Henry asked.

"Well, it's news. It's not that bad. It seems your favorite client and mine…"

"Lake-land Laaaa-aaabs," Henry and I sang, off-key, in a parody of their signature theme.

"None other. They've decided to go ahead with all that work you did way back on Skin Therapy Moisturizing Gel."

"With changes," I said.

"With changes," she confirmed. "Unfortunately, the way it looks now, they want us to film it about a week after we do the nail kit commercial."

"When are we supposed to find the time to do all this?" I asked.

"It won't be that bad, Michael. The Skin Therapy spot is practically written. It'll just be a matter of finding a production company and an actress, really. I just wanted you to know it was coming. In the meantime, Howard has asked Ellen to show him the nail commercials."

"*Now* he wants to see the work? It's going to Lakeland on Thursday. Since when is he so interested in this account?"

"I guess there's nothing to do on Sparks Cola. Maybe Gabrielle called him and said she was taking '*air beez-neez to Oh-goul-vee*' for the thousandth time since we got the account. Anyway, Howard wants to see the work tomorrow. Can we be ready by then?"

"It's no problem unless he starts asking for changes," Henry said.

"I don't think he will at this late date. He just wants to see what we're going to present. I think someone upstairs must have said something to him about neglecting other accounts, because all of a sudden he seems real interested in what everyone else is doing. Something's up."

20
Why Pay More?

We sat waiting in the reception area outside Howard's office the following afternoon. Howard was impossible to see, and was seldom on time for appointments, but at least he was the first one to admit this, and had had a reception area set up outside his office for his staff to wait in – nervously – until he was ready to grant them an audience.

The area consisted of five overstuffed gray club chairs on casters arranged around a round coffee table. Someone in Creative had dubbed it "Newark" shortly after it was set up, because waiting there to see Howard was like being stuck in a holding pattern over Newark Airport. Until he called you in, you waited.

Ellen told Jo to call her when Howard was ready. We had been sitting there for quite a while when Howard finally rounded the corner, head down, tie loosened, muttering to himself.

"Hi, people," he said, passing by and stopping at his secretary's desk for messages. "I'll be right with you, I just need a second." He went into his office and started scribbling something on a sheet of paper, and singing in a low voice. Obviously, he was writing another jingle.

Howard had built his career on jingles, and firmly believed: if you can't say it, sing it (although I personally felt that he'd gone too far with his "Can't Help Lovin' That Van of Mine" for Chevy). Voltaire's observation, "What is too stupid to be spoken is sung" was obviously lost on Howard.

The latest Sparks Cola jingle was his. So were those memorable jingles for the frozen cream pie, the nondairy whipped topping that was probably made out of the same chemicals as the plastic container it came in, the toaster oven pancakes, the instant mashed potatoes, and that orange liquid toilet bowl cleaner.

Jo called Ellen to tell her that Howard was back from his meeting and more or less ready. Ellen dropped whatever it was she had been doing in her office and came over, knowing that the window of opportunity might not open again.

Howard called, "Come on in, people," from his office, and we joined him at his huge mahogany conference table. Ellen and Jo brought him up to date on the history of the account and what we had to show him, then turned the meeting over to Henry and me.

After we acted out a commercial for him, he'd nod noncommittally and say, "Aha, uh-huh, what else?" and we'd continue, not really knowing if we were laying an egg or if he liked what he saw. After the last spot, he said, "This is good work." He rubbed his chin and asked, "What was that, five spots?" We nodded. "That's too many. Give 'em four. Kill Cinderella."

"'Cinderella' is my favorite," Ellen said.

"It's too silly. You don't need to go over there with five spots."

He wrote down the titles of the four remaining spots on his legal pad. "Personally," he said, not looking up, "I love this Big Hand thing. It's breakthrough!"

That word again!

We drove down to Lakeland's headquarters in Raritan, New Jersey, in two cars for the presentation – the account group in one, Henry driving Jo and me in another. We arrived early as planned, and after signing in and getting the tacky visitor badges they insisted we wear, went to the employee cafeteria for coffee and a quick review of the presentation.

"Now, I want to caution you again that all this may very well be an exercise," Beth said guardedly, once we had settled around a corner table.

I got tired of listening to Beth drone and started staring at Donald Miller, her assistant on the account. He was sporting his usual power look today: striped shirt, suspenders, European-cut suit and slicked-back hair. I still couldn't make up my mind about him. He was definitely gay, but was always so careful around all the incriminating pronouns and cultural references (although I thought he was overdoing it the time I brought up the subject of Judy Garland and he pretended to have to pause and think for a moment who she was before responding).

I ran into him once on a Saturday afternoon in the Village. He was wearing a denim jacket, jeans and boots. He hadn't shaved and his hair was blowing in the wind. I was beside myself – he was just adorable when he wasn't buttoned-up. But the whole time we were talking, I had the feeling he was hoping no one else from the office would see us.

In the brief time we spoke, mostly about work and the situation on the account, I realized how much he really hated the place. He confessed his secret desire: to become a chef, pierce his ear and open a French restaurant. I said to him, "You should," and he looked at me and said, "Yeah, someday," and shrugged, and we both knew he never would.

That conversation was never acknowledged. I had said we should have lunch someday, but he never called. We went back to our usual routine, talking Lakeland business in the elevators, and confining phone conversations to scheduling meetings and coordinating transportation to and from Raritan. Sad, because I found him so appealing that day in the Village.

My thoughts about Donald were interrupted when Gabrielle's secretary came to escort us from the cafeteria to the conference room. Visitors to Lakeland's offices were treated like spies from Chesebrough-Pond's, and were never permitted to stroll Lakeland's hallways alone.

We presented all four commercials, and as predicted, sold nothing. Gabrielle couldn't bear to see a nail break, so she killed both the slow-motion spot and "Big Hand." We tried arguing that the "hand" was really a giant model, and that the nail that broke wouldn't be real, but she refused to budge.

Tom added his opinion. "That flower thing is definitely out. I don't want cosmetic, and flowers are cosmetic."

Jo took off her glasses. "But don't you agree, Tom, that women buy products they think will make them feel more feminine and attractive? You have something here for a woman's *hands* – something she can use to make them more pretty. If that isn't cosmetic, I don't know what is."

"But I keep telling you people that Lakeland Labs does not manufacture cosmetics. We are therapy. Skin *Therapy* Moisturizing Gel. Hair *Therapy* Moisturizing Shampoo. The word 'therapy' is in the name of practically every product we sell."

I tuned him out here and started wondering what Donald looked like naked, until I realized that the meeting was taking an ugly turn. Gabrielle had interrupted to say she was inclined to agree with Jo.

"Gaby, maybe in Paris, France, the women want glamour, but when you're here a little longer, I think you'll realize that Americans worship technology," said Tom. "We put a man on the moon with technology and we can cure dry skin and give you stronger nails with technology. Our products are the result of technology. So don't give me any more of this faggy flower shit!"

Was it my imagination, or did he look right at me when he said that? Jo said later he didn't, but I was sure he did.

"I want therapy!" he shouted. I was inclined to agree that he needed some. "Sell 'em progress, not beauty. Therapy! Therapy! THERAPY!" I was waiting for him to spit on the table like Sydney Greenstreet in *The Hucksters*.

Ellen wanted a recap of our meeting at Lakeland and asked us to meet with her the next morning in the conference room. Donald and Beth were sitting with her drinking coffee when we arrived. Ellen wanted to review what we presented and see what we could do with it.

"Unfortunately," Jo said, "they told us they wanted a spokeswoman but not the one we presented, and they're not interested in anything else. Tom wants us to come back next week with something that stresses therapy and technology."

"Tom Dolgen is a stupid, fat asshole," Ellen said. "I'm sick of the whole bunch of them. I wish they *would* give the account to Ogilvy. Now here's what I think we should do. Let's take the spokeswoman and make her the voice of technology for Tom." She picked up a copy of the script and gave it a fast scan. "You know, I'd rewrite this, Michael. See this line here where she taps her nail on the table and says, 'If I did that before I started using Total Hand

Treatment, this nail would be a memory now'? Keep that and rewrite the commercial around it. But this description of her you have in here as Kathleen Turner is all wrong. They couldn't afford Kathleen Turner and she'd never do it anyway."

"I *know* she'd never *do* it, Ellen," I said. "But I had to give them a name so they could picture the type of actress we wanted when I read the copy."

"Okay, so rewrite this spot, keep that line, but warm it up a bit. Think of someone else. And I'd like to go back there with one more spot if we can. Any other thoughts?"

"Does anyone know Leroy Anderson's 'The Typewriter?'" I asked. Only Jo knew it, so I had to whistle the melody for the others, pantomiming the part where the typewriter joins in. They got the idea. "What if we show an orchestra playing 'The Typewriter' and the soloist is this beautiful woman in a black velvet gown, and she's typing away on some old Royal manual, but she never breaks a nail because she uses the product."

"How do we know she uses it?" Ellen challenged.

"Maybe we open as the orchestra is tuning up," Jo said. "All the musicians are doing scales and she's rubbing this stuff into her hands. Then the conductor goes tap-tap-tap with his baton, and they start playing and she starts typing."

"And if she puts the kit down right next to the typewriter just before they start playing," Henry added, "we could have lots of shots where you see the product in the foreground while she types on the keys."

"I think we could also get away with very little copy," I said. "You know, 'For stronger nails and more beautiful hands, try new Lakeland Labs Total Hand Treatment.'"

"You could do it like some program on PBS," Ellen said. "While they're tuning up, you see a title that says, 'The Typewriter, presented by Lakeland Labs.' This could be a lot of fun, and it says nail strength. It doesn't say much about beautiful hands, though."

"I'll tell you what," Jo said, smiling. "They finish the piece, and you hear the audience applauding and you cut to a two-shot of the conductor and the soloist. He takes her hand and kisses it. Very continental. *There's* your beauty."

"Well," Ellen said, "if we can make it all happen in thirty seconds, and we can get the rights to the music, it would be great. Work on these two, and make sure you leave yourself enough time for turn-around if Howard has changes after I see it."

I met with Jo at the end of the day to talk to her about the new spots. Henry was tied up on something else, so we decided to concentrate on the spokeswoman spot. We finished it at eight that night, but neither of us liked it very much. I finished "Typewriter" the next day with Henry, and we met with Ellen and Howard the following day to go over the work. Donald was down at Lakeland Labs, so Beth came solo. We presented "Spokeswoman" first, and Howard and Ellen unenthusiastically approved it. Ellen felt compelled to act like she cared about the spot, purely for Howard's benefit, and asked me if I'd "held a watch to it." I assured her that I had, and she said, "Well, it sounds a little long to me. Trim a second and a half from it to play it safe."

Henry had done some rough sketches, which he had enlarged and mounted to make presenting "Typewriter" less complicated. We had borrowed Ellen's boom box, and when I played the Leroy Anderson recording, Howard's face lit up.

"Fantastic!" he said. "I can just see her sitting down at that typewriter. Not only is it fun, but it's like a thirty-second demo. If they don't buy this, they're assholes."

"They *are* assholes," Ellen said through one side of her mouth. "They'll hate this. It doesn't pool out and you can't make a fifteen-second spot out of it, and there's no copy.

It's a cute spot, but I think we all know what's going to happen here."

"You're right," Jo said. "I just think it's important to keep going back there with good work." She had said the same thing to me in her office two nights before, except she didn't repeat it to Ellen quite the way she told it to me – that it was important to keep going back there with good work because when the time came that Lakeland pulled the business (and Jo was certain they would), no one could honestly point a finger at us and say it was Creative's fault. Not that anyone was honest, however.

And so, on the second Thursday in October, we went back down to Lakeland's sprawling, ugly home office.

They hated "Typewriter." Tom said he didn't like it because there was no copy, and couldn't understand why she was typing away at an old-fashioned manual typewriter. Jo suggested switching to an electric typewriter (rolling her eyes at me surreptitiously first) and adding a crawl at the bottom of the screen in a typewriter font that would make the viewer think that the woman was writing about the product. Tom said no.

Next we tried offering to add more announcer copy. He still hated it. In a last-ditch effort, we suggested cutting away to beauty application shots, then cutting back to the symphony hall. Tom said, "The whole thing is contrived. And who ever heard of a typewriter in an orchestra?"

"It's a classic piece," I said. "I've seen the Boston Pops do it on public television."

"Our consumers aren't all secretaries," Tom snarled. "It's unrealistic. They don't sit around typing all day."

"They don't brush dead skin flakes off their hands in slow motion, either," Jo said, taking a slap at Tom's definition of reality via the campaign he had helped create.

But Tom wanted a spokeswoman, and that's what we sold. A safe, boring, talking head in a peach blouse. Then he suggested finding one actress to do this commercial *and* the new "handruff" spot, so that we could shoot both in one day.

And then he pulled the last rabbit out of his hat full of stock tricks, and asked, "Where's the demo?"

He firmly believed that the swirling skin specks footage had sold millions of bottles of their Moisturizing Gel, and wanted something equally brilliant for this product. We had decided to keep the demo simple, and told Tom that the spokeswoman would simply tap-tap-tap on a tabletop with her index fingernail in a close-up when she said, "while it strengthens your nails."

We had done this for a variety of reasons, mainly because the product didn't work. It didn't actually make nails stronger; it made them less brittle, and therefore more flexible and less likely to break. A weasel if ever I heard one.

Tom felt that we could get away with saying nails were stronger if we showed something that implied flexibility, and asked us to also shoot one of our earlier demos as an alternate. Instead of tapping the fingernail, she would press down on the tip and make it bow slightly. He'd decide which one would ultimately air after he saw the footage.

He also asked me to rework the copy.

"You can't say 'bigger' in the opening. Women are going to think we're just introducing a larger-size Skin Therapy Gel, and not watch the commercial. Why would you say 'bigger than that,' anyway?"

"It doesn't refer to the size of the product," I said. "When she says 'it's bigger than that,' she means it's big as in 'big news.'"

"Well, take it out. And here," he said, flipping to the third page of the storyboard, "where she's rubbing it into her hands and says, 'What this does is soften your hands and give you stronger nails.' That should be softens your *rough*, *red, dry* hands."

"You left out 'raw, cracked and bleeding,'" Jo said, taking off her glasses in her signature gesture of disgust.

"Well, you know what I mean," Tom said. "And why do you say 'what *this* does' instead of 'what *it* does?' Don't you think it should be 'what *it* does,' Gabrielle?"

Gabrielle! He was asking *Gabrielle!*

"*Oui*," she told him.

The ride back to Manhattan was post-funereal, at best. We knew we were doomed to shoot not one, but two terrible commercials. I tried not to think about it. I went in expecting the worst, and had not been disappointed.

Jo said to me, "Sweetie pie, it's not so bad. Get that look off your face."

"What look off my face?"

"Like Jackie Coogan in *The Kid*."

"This happens every time. When I got into this business, I thought it would be fun. I grew up watching those great commercials like 'I can't believe I ate the whole thing' and Jimmy Durante singing 'Inka-Dinka-Doo' in a Volkswagen. I thought I could write things like that. Instead I'm torturing America by showing close-ups of nails that don't break and dancing dead skin flakes. Cripes! Why don't we just recycle the old Bic pen spots? 'We've strapped this woman's hands to this man's ice skates to prove how strong her nails have become since she started using new Lakeland Labs Total Hand Treatment.' Then we show some dame getting dragged around the rink face down, with close-ups of her nails cutting ten little grooves into the ice."

"The trouble with that," Jo said, "is that they'd buy it, and then we'd have to do a pool-out and shoot a woman out of a cannon into a block of wood, nails first."

"The third one where they stick her hands in fire might be fun," Henry offered from behind the wheel.

21

Your Money Back If Not Completely Satisfied

The next day's *Malcolm Memo*, our weekly red-bordered update of who was moving what mountains on Lexington Avenue, carried two bombshells. First, Forster Foods had decided to withdraw Homestead Acres. Although test groups responded favorably to the commercials the agency had produced (Ellen had even told Henry that our commercial had scored the highest and would probably be the one that launched the product), those same people were not responding favorably to the product itself. I thought it might have had something to do with the fact that you couldn't fry with it, but Henry said more likely, it had to do with the rash it gave Maxine.

I had barely grasped the significance of this first blow when I came to the second bit of news – an announcement about Gwen Hammond. She was being promoted, it said, to associate creative director, and taking over the Forster Foods account.

Jenny must have been reading her memo next door at the same time, because I heard her let out a shriek. I ran into her office, clutching my copy.

"Did you see this?" she said. "They *promoted* that bitch!"

"Did you read all of it? They're killing Homestead Acres. Cripes! All that work down the toilet."

"God, I'm sorry, Michael. But I'd still like to know what Gwen did to get promoted." She mimed a little shiver of disgust. "You know what this means? If Gwen is what they promote around here, we'll be juniors forever."

"You know what else it means? Now I'll have to dance with her at the Christmas party!" I balled up my copy of the *Memo* and threw it through the doorway and into the hall, adding, "'That's all of Tara *you'll* ever get!'"

I was still brooding about all of this as I walked home from the Chelsea Gym that night. I had decided to take the scenic route – Seventh, then down Christopher Street to Hudson – but it wasn't improving my mood.

I thought about stopping at Ty's for a beer, but just kept walking instead. It was chilly, colder than I thought it would be when I left for work that morning. But it was a beautiful clear night. The moon hung low and huge over Hoboken, and the breeze blowing toward me smelled like coffee. They were roasting beans over at the Maxwell House plant across the Hudson. I used to love watching their gigantic animated sign with its three neon blinking good-to-the-last-drops falling out of a neon coffee cup in succession and, presumably, into the river.

As I turned onto Hudson Street, I told myself I was being silly, and that I should go back to Ty's and stop off for a half-hour anyway. There was always the chance that I'd meet somebody.

But then, I still wasn't quite convinced that I wanted to meet somebody. Anthony, Frank and Billy had been trying to drag me out for weeks, but I just hadn't been in the mood. The weekends came and I felt exhausted. I was happy to stay home and unwind and try to write. The truth was, I missed Craig, and I wished I had either stayed home the night I had met him instead of going out with Anthony or had gone home with that guy in the Spike. I had been doing very nicely, thank you, before we met. I wondered, as I put the key in the door, which would take longer to get over – my disappointment in Craig or the disastrous end to all that work on Homestead Acres.

Anthony was somewhere in the apartment. The stereo was on and Margaret Whiting was singing "All the Things You Are." I picked up the pile of mail from the little deco table in the foyer that Anthony had rescued from a Dumpster and lovingly restored. Right on top of all the bills and junk mail was a card from Craig. The return address sticker had a little cartoon bear on it and an address in the West Forties. I opened the envelope. It was one of those gay fantasy hunk cards. On the cover was an airbrushed drawing of this impossibly handsome guy with blue eyes and dark hair, shirt unbuttoned almost to his waist, heroic bulge in his jeans. The type who always looks right past me in a bar.

"What does Craig *Cannoli* want from you?" Anthony demanded, as he came out of his room.

"Here," I said, handing him the card. "Read it for yourself."

"'*Dearest* Michael?'"

"It gets better."

Anthony read the card out loud, seizing the opportunity to add commentary. "'I think of you often and would like to see you again.' Why? So he can treat you like shit? 'Dinner or a drink,' hmmm? Is that all? 'I hope you'll call.' Nertz!" He handed the card back to me.

I stared at it for a moment. "I was just thinking about him on the way home, I swear! I was wondering what ever happened to the two of us, and here's a card." I put the mail back on the table and took off my jacket.

"Are you gonna call him?"

"I don't know, Anthony. I'd be lying if I said I didn't want to. I mean, there hasn't exactly been a line of men around the corner waiting to take me out lately."

"Well, maybe if you didn't lock yourself up in this apartment like Miss Havisham every Saturday night, there might be. You're not exactly Lon Chaney, you know," he said. "So what are you gonna do?"

I called. Craig told me he had hoped that I would. He kept it as light as possible for as long as he could, then told me that he missed me and wanted to know if he could buy me dinner. We settled on a night the following week. Then he repeated how glad he was that I called, and we hung up.

Anthony was waiting for me at the kitchen table.

"Well?" he challenged.

"He's buying me dinner after work next Thursday. Some place on Fifty-seventh Street."

"Personally, I don't think it's a good idea."

"Maybe after all this time he's grown to appreciate me. Or is that too adolescent?"

"I think you're gonna get hurt again."

"I won't get hurt because this is just going to be dinner."

"You'll sleep with him."

"Maybe. So what?"

"I don't think I like Craig."

"It's a *date*, Anthony. One night."

"Just don't lose your head."

I was about fifteen minutes late for dinner. I looked in the restaurant windows to see Craig standing at the bar having a drink and looking devastating in his red tie. He smiled when he saw me come through the door, and put his drink down. I walked up to him, not expecting the public hug and kiss he gave me. I apologized for being late, and by the time our table was ready, we had gotten most of the small talk out of the way.

"I'm so glad you agreed to this," he told me over the top of his menu. "I really missed you."

"Tell me about your new apartment," I said.

"It's one room with a separate kitchen and bathroom. They're calling it a one-bedroom but it's really a studio. I got it through Andrew, someone I met at GMHC. He knew I was looking for a place, and when he got too sick to take care of himself, he asked me if I wanted to sublet it while he went home for a few months. He got my name on the lease somehow, and about a month later, he died. I got a call from his mom, and she said to keep whatever Andrew had left in the apartment. I already had dishes and my own furniture, so I donated most of his things to Goodwill. I kept his bed, even though it's shot. I can't afford a new one right now. But at least I can start making trips out to the storage warehouse now to get my things."

We made it through the meal and dessert, keeping the conversation on that level – punctuated dangerously every so often by Craig telling me how good I looked, how glad he was to see me, accompanied by his running a hand through my hair. The last gesture bothered me more than the unexpected kiss and hug when I arrived. I think I was afraid to let myself believe that he actually cared.

He still looked good, that's for sure. His hair was longer and he had progressed from the diamond stud in his right ear to a small gold hoop. If it was possible, he was even better-looking than he was the day I met him.

We left the restaurant and started walking down Ninth Avenue. I had planned to catch the bus home, until he asked me up to see his new place.

The apartment was tiny. It had a separate kitchen opposite the front door. A turn to the left down a short hall led to the bedroom and to the right was a tiny bathroom. Since there were no chairs, we sat on the bed. Before long, we were both out of our clothes.

"Do you think I can persuade you to stay the night?" he asked. He wrapped his arms around me and pulled me close to his chest. For someone who didn't work out, he had a nice body.

After a few moments, he said, "Michael, I don't want you to get the wrong idea. I can't believe you're here with me now. I don't know what happened to us last summer. Yes, I do, I was too busy, and pretty thoughtless. And I think I hurt your feelings."

"A lot," I said.

"A lot. I'm really sorry about that. But I'm just as busy now. Things are still just as complicated. I care a great deal about you. I enjoy being with you, and we connect. You make me feel good, and I don't want to lose touch again."

"But?" I prompted.

"I just don't know how much time I have to spare. I'm under a lot of stress at work, and that's not going to change."

"Listen, Craig. I'm leaving this up to you. I like you. I want a relationship, but I'm not going to sit around and wait for you to decide if *you* want one. You want a date? Call me up. You want more than just a date? That would be fine too. But do it this time."

I didn't get much sleep that night, partly because we made up for a lot of lost time, and partly because Craig's secondhand bed was a disaster and should have been thrown out. How he slept on it, I'll never know.

The next morning wasn't nearly as awkward as I imagined it would be. I think we were both tempted to stay in bed, but decided not to overdo things. I pulled on my clothes and Craig put on an old flannel robe that made me want to marry him on the spot.

He promised to call me, and I wished he hadn't. I'd had a nice time. I was tired but happy, and I didn't want to think about next steps or potential broken promises.

I got in a cab and was home a few minutes later. Anthony got up while I was rushing around trying to get ready for work. He staggered to the kitchen in his black-and-green silk kimono and began grinding beans for coffee. I came out of my room and he turned to me.

"So?" he asked.

"I slept with him."

"I *know* that. What did he have to say for himself?"

"He likes me, we connect, he missed me."

"Was the sex good?"

"As Miss Dorothy Parker once said, 'There was nothing more fun than a man.'"

"I can't deal with you this early in the morning. Are you gonna see him again?"

"You'll be very proud of me. I told him that I wanted to see him again, but it's going to be up to him this time. He'd better come to his senses and realize what a deal he's got here, or I'm putting myself out on the market again."

"It's about time!" he said, toasting with his coffee cup.

We spent the next few weeks finalizing the two spokeswoman spots for Lakeland. Tom informed us that they wanted the spots on the air by the first of the year, which meant we had less than a month to finish the scripts, cast, shoot and edit – an impossible task, especially considering all of this would be taking place at the height of the Christmas season.

Jo was able to get Patty as producer. She had been terrific on the Homestead Acres commercial, and Henry and I both wanted to work with her again. We just wished it could have been a better project than this nightmare.

Patty reviewed the scripts and said, "They must be crazy. This will be a twenty-hour day if we shoot the two of them at once. Set up a meeting with them. Let me see what I can do."

She wasn't able to do anything. Tom insisted that we shoot both spots in one day, and told us to finish the scripts and find a director. He also wanted to see print campaigns and radio scripts for both commercials as well.

I had heard from Craig just twice in all that time. He called me at work the morning after our dinner to tell me that he'd had a good time, and that he was glad we got together. I told him that I had had a nice time, too. I said I'd like to see him again. He told me how busy he was. He said that if he didn't have to work that weekend, he'd like to see me. I told him that would be fine and that he should call and let me know. He didn't call for another three weeks, during which I called twice (ignoring Anthony's advice not to) and left messages on his machine.

During the second call he apologized for not getting back to me. This time he never said a word about getting together. He was just calling to see how I was. I wish I could have answered, "married," but unfortunately, that wasn't the case.

I had actually had one date, with a friend of Anthony's who had been in Shades of Meaning one night when I stopped off to visit. Bobby had told Anthony that he thought I was interesting after I had left, and Anthony, taking his cue, badgered me into having dinner with him.

For a week, he kept telling me that Bobby was cute, that Bobby had a good job, that Bobby was a swimmer, that Bobby was a nice guy, that Bobby liked movies, that Bobby liked me.

"Anthony, Bobby doesn't even *know* me," I protested.

"So, give him a *chance*," Anthony said, drawing out the sentence like Ruth Gordon.

I gave him a chance. It was a perfectly nice evening. Bobby was pleasant. Bobby was cute. Bobby had a good job. Bobby was definitely a swimmer. He thought advertising must be fascinating. I assured him it was anything but. He asked me if I'd like to go out dancing some time. I told him that I didn't like to dance, since I once caught a glimpse of myself dancing in a mirror and decided that I looked like Carmen Miranda on too much coke.

He walked me home, gave me a polite little kiss and waited for me to ask him up. I thanked him for a nice evening and went up alone. Anthony was home. He was stripping a chair he'd found on the street, which he kept insisting was a Stickley. I only saw a ratty old painted chair with most of its upholstery gone.

He was using some incredibly pungent chemical to melt through generations of paint, varnish and grime, and had all the windows in the apartment open. The chair was in the middle of a sea of drop cloths and old newspapers covering the kitchen floor, and Anthony, in a T-shirt, shorts, a painter's cap and rubber gloves, was uncovering some previously obscured detail on the legs with a square of fine steel wool.

"What are you doing home so early?" he demanded as I walked in the door.

"Are you out of your mind? It's freezing outside. All the heat's going right out the window."

"Would you rather suffocate? It stinks in here."

"How much longer are you going to be working on that?"

"Another hour. Answer my question."

"I'm home because we ran out of things to talk about."

"Well, how was dinner?" he asked, pulling off his rubber gloves.

"It was okay."

"Just okay?"

"It was fine, Anthony, but I don't think anything's going to happen."

"Why not? Bobby's a nice guy."

"He's a very nice guy. He's a *peach*. But I don't feel anything for him."

"But he likes you. See him a couple of times. Maybe something will happen."

"Anthony, nothing's going to happen. There's no spark."

"Spark, *shmark*! That's the trouble with you. You're waiting for someone big and good-looking like Craig to come and sweep you off your feet like you're in some movie. Well, forget it, darling. Guys who look like that only break your heart. I should think you'd have learned that lesson by now."

"It has nothing to do with looks, Anthony," I said, tiptoeing around the mess in the kitchen to boil some water for tea. "I can't explain it. I don't know what I'm looking for, but your friend Bobby isn't it. I'll know it when I see it."

"Love grows sometimes, Michael."

"Listen to you all of a sudden. *You're* the jaded one and *I'm* the hopeless romantic, remember?"

"Well," he said, turning back to the chair, "I think you should at least have a second date with Bobby."

"That isn't fair, Anthony. If I'm not interested, what's the point? I'm not going to end up hurting Bobby's feelings by acting interested when I'm not. The meanest thing you can do to some man is to settle for him. And the longer it goes on, the harder it is to get out of."

"But he's such a nice guy, Michael."

"Anthony, I appreciate your wanting to help me out, but I'm just not interested, okay?"

"Do what you want," he said, looking up at me. "I think you're making a mistake."

"Fine, Anthony," I said, getting annoyed. "When I'm seventy-nine and living with three cats and haven't had a date in forty years I'll ask you for his number. Right now, I'm just not interested."

22
Soothing Relief

We started casting for Skin Therapy the second week in December. I knew the spots were bad, but when I heard fifty different actresses read lines like "It can actually make your nails less likely to chip, split and break," or "Sometimes my dry, flaky, itchy skin *really* needs help" – lines I had actually written – I wanted to run away and hide.

To save time and money, we had decided to do the casting in-house. We had a small production facility on the fifty-ninth floor. It was handy for casting sessions and having videocassettes duped and certain simple editing chores, but the slackers on staff there were, for the most part, incredibly inept and indifferent. As a result, everyone in the agency used them as a last resort, avoiding giving them anything more taxing to do than making VHS copies of rented movies, claiming it was research for a client.

Patty stopped at my door on her way to the session to ask for the scripts. I had just run off the copies, but hadn't stapled them yet. Patty said she'd do it and took the pile and my stapler over to Karen's desk and got her to help. I asked Patty if she had thought to have someone in the studio get us a table and a chair for the session. She hadn't, so I said I would call while she and Karen finished putting the scripts together. I got Lenny, who would be our cameraman for the session.

"Hi. It's Michael Gregoretti. We have the 9:30 casting session for Lakeland Labs."

"Yeah?"

"We need a table and a chair for the Hand Treatment session."

"We're not prop men down here. If you want a table and chair you have to get it yourself," he said, hanging up.

"I don't believe this," I said, slamming down the phone.

"What's wrong?" Karen called from her desk, where she and Patty were finishing up the scripts.

"I have to find a table and a chair for the auditions. Where am I supposed to go, the break room?"

"Take the table and a chair from Newark!" Karen said.

"That'll work," Patty agreed.

We got Henry, and went over to Newark. Howard was out and his secretary wasn't at her desk. We couldn't just walk off with the furniture. "We'd better ask Fran before we do this," I said. I knocked on her door and poked my head in. She was eating a scrambled egg and cheese sandwich and drinking a Coke. She moved the Coke behind her phone when I knocked, as if I were the Sparks Cola Police or something. (Being seen drinking the competition was *verboten* at Malcolm, and our vending machines dispensed only Sparks, Diet Sparks, Caffeine-Free Sparks, Lemon Sparks, Diet Lemon Sparks...)

"Fran, we have a problem, do you have a minute?"

"I'm eating breakfast," she said, coldly.

Probably for the third time today, I thought. "Well, it's a small problem, but it can't wait."

"What?"

"We have a casting session downstairs in about two

minutes, and they can't get us a table and chair."

"So what do you want from me, Michael?"

"I want to know if we can borrow the coffee table and a chair from Newark. We'd have it back by noon."

"I don't know. Howard might not like that."

"Howard is at the Sparks bottler's convention in Dallas. He'll never know."

"Well, write me a memo that you're taking it first."

"Thanks, Fran," I said.

Henry and Patty were waiting for me in Newark. "She says we can have the furniture, but I have to write her a memo first." Henry laughed and then pantomimed getting stuck in the eyes with two fingers by Moe Howard.

I went to my office, pulled a sheet of interoffice memo paper out of the drawer, rolled it into the typewriter and wrote:

> *This is to request the loan of one (1) round gray slate coffee table and one (1) stylishly moderne gray club chair from the area outside office #6152 (a.k.a. Newark), for use in a casting session for Lakeland Labs on the fifty-ninth floor. I promise to return the above in good working order sometime around noon today.*

I yanked the paper out of the machine, signed it, and took it back to Fran's office. She scanned it, and said, "There's no need to be sarcastic, Michael."

"That's not sarcasm, Fran. It's irony. Thanks for the furniture."

By the time we got downstairs, there were twenty women with shoulder bags and portfolios crowded around the reception area waiting to begin. They had to part like the Red Sea so Henry and I could get through with the table. The chair was on casters, and Patty sailed along behind us with it.

Jo was waiting for us in the studio, looking worried. "Where have you been? It looks like a Miss Subways reunion out there!"

I told her what had just happened with Lenny and Fran. "Is it my imagination or does everyone around here act like he's working for a different company?" I asked. "Why do I feel like everyone around here has his own private agenda?"

"Because, sweetie pie, everyone around here *does*."

We dragged the furniture into position while Lenny stood blankly by with his arms folded across his broad chest, looking like some Neanderthal contemplating his first blank cave wall.

"That table is awfully low," he said. "You gonna use a table that low in the spot?"

"No," I answered. "She'll be on a stool, probably, at a much higher table. But this is all we could find. We're not prop men either."

We were ready about ten minutes later, and started bringing the actresses in one at a time. I stood next to the camera and watched the auditions in the studio. Between takes, I'd check with Henry, Jo and Patty in the back room, where a monitor had been set up, to see what they thought of the performance. Jo always had some wonderful comment like, "What's wrong with her teeth?" or "That one says 'sue-this' instead of 'soothes.' Give her the hook!"

We saw several competent actresses, but no one really seemed right. Then Patty brought in Kate Mallory, a former Wilhelmina model and an absolute knockout. She had green eyes and flawless skin, and long dark hair parted slightly off-center that fell in light waves past her shoulders. I prayed that she could act.

After we had taped two readings, I asked her to wait before moving on, and went to the back room.

"She's just *fabulous!*" Jo said, clasping her hands

together.

"Isn't she?" I said. "I just wanted to see if you agreed."

Henry and Patty liked her, too. "There's just one problem," Jo said. "The client will never buy her. She's too beautiful, and they think beautiful women are bubbleheads."

We knew she was right. I looked at Patty and had a brainstorm. "Patty, can I borrow your glasses for a minute? I want to put them on Kate and have her do a take."

The glasses added something to her third reading — maybe just a hint of authority. It was pure Hollywood: putting glasses on a beautiful woman so the audience knows she's intelligent. But it worked. As far as we were concerned, we had found one woman who could put over these two horrible commercials.

We reviewed the casting tape after lunch and picked a second and third choice, then ran the tape for Ellen, Beth and Donald at a meeting in the conference room.

"They'll never go for her," Ellen said. "She's too pretty, even with the glasses."

"But having a former model talking about skin care would be wonderful," Jo said.

"I'm not arguing with you, I'm just telling you what's going to happen. They're not going to like your second or third choice, either. They're going to go for that scrawny blonde in the red sweater, because she looks like every other actress they've ever used."

Ellen was right. Tom mumbled something about hating to see a pretty girl in glasses, then said, "I like the blonde in the red sweater" in a voice that told us he wasn't open to further discussion.

Irene phoned me at work the next day. "I was just calling to see if you were still alive."

"I'm sorry. It's been crazed here. To make things worse, Henry and I just got a new assignment for Tinolate Athlete's Foot Spray. We're supposed to do two jocks in a locker room talking about the product."

"That's original."

"At least the auditions will be fun. All my life, I've wanted to say to an actor, 'Will you take off your shirt, please?'"

"Come have lunch with me?" she asked.

"I can't possibly have lunch with you today, Janie Clarkson!"

"Michael, stop doing Bette Davis! We're in the real world, not a movie. Look out the window. Those are real people down there."

"I know, I know. And Edith Head didn't dress them either."

"Too bad," she said, laughing. "So how about lunch?"

"I can't. In addition to everything else, I have a ton of print stuff I'm trying to get out of here, and Christmas is a week away and I haven't got any idea what anyone wants or any money to buy it with. Oh, I'm so in debt now, what's another hundred or two on my credit card!"

"My poor lamb."

"There's too much going on all at once. Remember that guy who used to spin plates on *The Ed Sullivan Show* to the 'Khachaturian Sabre Dance'? That's me. I feel like I've got all these plates twirling around on sticks in my office, and any minute there are going to be shards of china all over the joint."

"Have dinner with me, then. I haven't seen you in for-ever. Or Henry for that matter. You two are working way too hard."

"Irene, I'm so cranky."

"We can have Chi-nese," she sang.

"I really should attempt to shoehorn myself into

Macy's."

"Moo shu chick-en," she sang, an octave higher.

"What time?"

If Anthony's solution to all of life's troubles was a man, then Irene's was food. We met under the marquee of the Waverly Theater, got a bottle of wine and went to our favorite place, Ming Hudson Dynasty. I complained about work all through the appetizers, and then promised to stop.

Irene told me about working with Mara on her latest book, which I kept calling *Love's Savage Vicissitudes* to annoy her. It was actually called *Perfidious Love*, but I liked my title better.

As an economy move we had decided to split an order of moo shu chicken, since Ming Hudson Dynasty's portions were always more than enough for two. Irene dubbed them "Ming the Merciless" after trying to finish a portion alone the night we discovered this happy fact. We were on our first pancakes when she said, "I hate to ask, but you haven't mentioned anything about Craig."

"I got a Christmas card from him this week. He signed it 'Always, Craig.'"

"That's the problem," she said. "Always Craig. He should try being someone else."

"The time I wasted on that man!"

"I think it's a good sign that you're angry about this."

"Well, I am. Not just about Craig, but about everything. Why am I stuck? How come I have this dumb job and no money and no lover? I'm twenty-nine. I lived better when I was in college."

"You probably got more mail, too."

I told Irene I had been harboring a new theory – that we could blame everything on the baby boom and my parents for having me in 1957. There were just too many of us coming of age now and all the good ones were taken – jobs, apartments, boyfriends, size 14½ shirts. Someone else always got there first and creative types like us got the leftovers. I was getting a little tired of being creative and having nothing to show for it.

"I'm starting to think I should sell out and be like everyone else," I said. "I'd cut my hair and shave and go to work for Dow Chemical and dream up peacetime uses for napalm. Just give me the money."

"You wouldn't be happy, Michael."

"I'm so happy now? The difference is, those people don't know they're unhappy, so they think they're happy. If you think you're happy, then you're happy."

"Personally, I'd settle for more looks and a little less brains," Irene said.

"What's wrong with your looks?"

"Nothing, as far as I'm concerned. I'm happy in my pear-shaped Rubenesque body. But I'm not turning any heads. God, to be a gorgeous underachiever! Look at your brother. That's America. With looks I wouldn't have spent my whole adolescence reading books so I could be smart. Maybe we're just a couple of late bloomers."

"People our age are supposed to be on their way already."

"Says who?" she asked, dividing up the last of the food. "I think it's just this city. You're either married to your job here or you're on welfare. There doesn't seem to be any middle ground anymore. The ones with all the money also have no lives, because all they do is work."

"Maybe it's time to think about moving to another city."

"I think it's just as bad everywhere else, Michael."

"I don't know. I have these mornings when I could leave New York in a second, usually at the moment I attempt to change trains from the Number Two to the Grand Central Shuttle, and the whole world is trying to squeeze into the same car, like all of those old science fiction movies where an asteroid is going to smash into the earth, and they're sending out three rocket ships like interplanetary arks, and two have left already, and everyone is climbing all over everyone else to get on that last rocket. I mean, *clawing* like animals to get on a damn subway train. And when you finally get on one, you're shoved up against a hundred other people you *do* not want to know better and you see your reflection in the window and you look absolutely like hell, and some sad deranged panhandler is screaming about China and working the car for change. You have to ask yourself, why do you put up with this?"

"And what answer do you give yourself when you ask yourself this?" Irene said like a burlesque psychiatrist, trying to tease me out of the bad mood I was talking myself into.

"Because it's New York. Because every so often you get a little reward for being here. Like seeing Katharine Hepburn hailing a cab on your lunch hour and then, not two minutes later, some hunk in a suit gives you the glad eye on Third Avenue. Where else is that going to happen?"

Irene shrugged. I had a few more bites of food and fantasized about the day when all this would be behind me. I'd have enough money to live well and the rest wouldn't seem as bad. I wasn't thinking about having megamillions and a place on Central Park West, just a decent apartment on a quiet side street in the Village where everything's clean and there's still some porcelain left on the sinks and no cracked plaster ceilings. An orange tabby cat and maybe a husband. *Home.*

But then, maybe the present was all some sort of initiation rite – a fraternity hazing of epic proportions – and if I gave up now, I'd never get the knock on the door that says I passed the test and here's my basket of goodies and a key to the city.

"I don't think you're tough enough for New York, Michael. Sometimes I don't think I am, either."

"I think it's perfect that I work in the Chrysler Building. Neither of us belongs in this city. We both belong in some black-and-white, Max Steiner, *Ars Gratia Artis* New York that probably never even existed except in movies where they met under the clock in the old Penn Station or rode the upper deck of the Fifth Avenue bus."

"I think you're being a little hard on yourself. There are enough people in your life beating you up these days. You don't have to join in, too. It'll get better."

"When? I want the exact time and date."

"I wish I could tell you."

We finished dinner and left the restaurant. I took Irene's arm and walked her to the subway.

"It'll work out, Michael. It could be worse. Remember the year we met? You sat at that crummy little wood desk near the window and slapped mailing labels on book boxes and they wouldn't even let you listen to the radio while you worked. I think if you just find a new job, things will turn around for you."

I said, "I hope so," but I wasn't convinced.

"Michael, I don't mean to criticize. I know things seem bleak right now. But sometimes I think you just get stuck on how bad things are. You go over it and over it and you make yourself even more unhappy. Don't get me wrong, I'm here any time you need to talk, but sometimes I just wish I could hear you tell me something good about your life. Just say one positive thing."

"I'm positive that Ming Hudson Dynasty serves the finest moo shu in New York City."

"Well, that's a good first step," she said.

"Oh, don't pay any attention to me. It's the end of the year and I've seen one too many happy gay couples dragging home their first Christmas tree. I have what Jimmy Stewart had in *It's a Wonderful Life*, and I don't think Henry Travers is coming by anytime soon to convince me not to jump off the bridge. I should just go over to Fifteenth Street right now and check myself into Saint Zita's Home for Friendless Women."

"What are we going to do with you?"

"I don't know. But if you get a flash of inspiration, write a proposal. We'll consider any options."

PART TWO

23
Without Stomach Upset

I woke up the morning of Christmas Eve, decided I looked old and tired, and shaved off my beard. I kept the moustache, and when I finished, I told my reflection, "Now you look *young* and tired."

I took a late afternoon train to Long Island, and Joe was waiting in the car when we pulled into the station. Normally, I would have walked, since our house wasn't even ten minutes away, but I had a lot to carry, and it was cold, and Joe said he wanted to pick me up. I kissed him hello, loaded my things into the back seat, and took off my coat.

"Merry Christmas, Pop," I said, pulling the door shut.

"Merry Christmas, Michael. Hey! You shaved. You'll make your mother very happy."

"I'll tell her it was a Christmas present."

He started the car and backed out of the space. "We have to stop and get wine."

There was a liquor store on the way home, and to save time, I said I'd run in and buy a bottle while he circled the block, since the nearest parking space appeared to be in Connecticut. I wrapped my scarf around my neck and ran into the store, snatched the house white from its usual spot near the register and paid the cashier. I stepped back into the street and waited for my father to turn the corner in his big blue Oldsmobile. It was cold and windy, but there wasn't a cloud to be seen. Another Christmas without snow, I thought to myself as Joe pulled up.

The wind whipped my scarf and blew through my hair as I opened the door and climbed back into the car. "You look like Rock Hudson with that moustache!" Joe said, hastily adding, "I mean a movie star."

At the first red light he said, "I didn't mean that the way it came out before. I did mean 'movie star.' I can't help it, Michael. I guess I still can't believe it about Rock Hudson. Not that he was gay, because who cares? I always liked him. But the way he ended up."

There was an awkward silence until the light changed.

"Your mother and I worry about you. I don't want to preach. Just take care of yourself."

"Pop, there weren't that many before Tim, and fewer since. I'm being careful. I took the test and so far, I'm negative. They tell you to keep taking it to make sure because the virus takes awhile to show up. If I have it already, there's nothing I can do. I wish you wouldn't worry."

"I think the damn government is behind it. It's something that got out by mistake and now they're covering it up. Just like Kennedy."

"I don't know. Whatever it is, they'll figure it out someday, probably after it finishes with all of us and starts killing straight Republican boys, and maybe then that fraud in the White House will have something to say on the subject."

"Just don't get sick on us, Mikey, okay?"

I couldn't remember the last time he called me that.

"I won't, Pop."

Another red light, another awkward silence. He changed the subject. "Wait till you see the cheesecake I made for tomorrow. Best ever."

My father excelled at small things like flying kites and planting beautiful gardens that flowered late into fall. Lately he had been turning out a cheesecake I was convinced he could retire on, if only he'd try marketing it.

He had worked hard all his life and was a moderate success, although the repair shop he owned still wasn't worth nearly as much as the land it sat on. He wasn't like the other fathers on the block who went to the train station with briefcases and ties, and was all the more special to me because of it. He didn't exchange the baby teeth under my pillow for quarters, he left dollar bills and handwritten notes signed by Dentalina, the Tooth Fairy, telling me what a brave boy I had been when the dentist pulled them out. He told me the whining tone I heard under the test pattern every morning on TV while I waited for cartoons to start was the cleaning women vacuuming the studio. He taught me to ride a two-wheeler and how to throw a ball – all the things fathers did with sons. He also taught me how to find Cassiopeia among the stars. But what meant the most to me was the fact that he called me at school the day after I came out to him, just to say hi, adding before hanging up, "All I want for you, Michael, is to be happy. I don't care who with." I was afraid telling my parents I was gay would be a mistake. He made sure I knew it wasn't. I left my dorm room that night, walked down to a quiet corner of the campus and found Cassiopeia in the night sky.

While Joe was driving me home, Marco and Carla were having a long talk in the living room and my mother was putting the finishing touches on her traditional if-it-swims-in-the-sea-you'll-find-it-in-Rose-Gregoretti's-kitchen-on-

Christmas-Eve dinner. Marco asked Carla to marry him, got a yes and slipped the ring on her finger. Rose just happened to have some champagne in the refrigerator, and shortly after Joe and I came home, we all drank a toast to the new couple.

Rose told us to get to the table and started bringing food out from the kitchen, saying, "You know how much this fish cost? You'd better enjoy it!" (A remark I could count on hearing every year.)

As we sat down to eat, Carla asked me, "How come you didn't apply for that job at NBC?"

"What job at NBC?"

"There was an opening for a writer in Program Promotion. I saw the posting and told your brother about it. Didn't you tell him?" she asked Marco.

"Christ, I forgot. It's just been so goddamn busy at work," he offered lamely.

"How long ago was this?" I asked Carla.

"About a month. They filled it. But I'll keep my eyes open for you."

"Thanks."

Rose wedged one final platter on the table, this one overflowing with breaded lobster tails, and sat down. "Merry Christmas, everybody," she said.

Sometime during the meal, Rose started telling Carla about Christmases past: the time she fell off the chair decorating the tree; the year the tree tipped over and she had to rush out at the last minute to replace the ornaments that had shattered; the year Marco got a lump of coal in his stocking. I almost said, "He deserves one this year, too."

"We should show Carla the movies," Rose said.

"Oh, please don't," Marco groaned.

But Carla said she'd love to see them, so once the meal was finished and all the food was put away, Rose started the dishwasher and we all sat down in the living room to watch

Christmases past flicker by. We hadn't watched Joe's home movies in years, and I had practically forgotten what was in them. It was a strange feeling sitting there watching these two people I barely recognized. It was before I was born. Joe's hair was jet black. Rose was thin. At that time, they were only a few years older than I was sitting in the same room watching them. All around them were younger versions of all the relatives who, until recently, had spent every holiday with us. Cousins who had married and moved away, aunts and uncles who had died – all of them were back in the Gregoretti house that Christmas.

On screen, Rose walks into the room with Marco in her arms – a small, dark, crying bundle. The film jumps, and my father pops into the frame with his wife and first son; someone else had taken over for him as cameraman. He puts his arm around Rose, kisses her cheek, then leans down and kisses the baby. They laugh and wave at the camera, as Marco screams, and the whole scene is covered with little swirling blips of light – perforations punched into the end of each reel by Kodak that my father never seemed to have the heart to cut out, as if he couldn't bear to part with even one frame of the footage he'd shot of us.

"You can see what a happy child he was," Rose said to Carla. "I don't think he wanted to be born. If they hadn't gone in after him with forceps, I'd probably still be pregnant."

"Ma!" Marco groaned.

"Well, it's true. He was very high strung. They put him on tranquilizers when he was three and I was pregnant with Michael, but it only made him worse. He never slept. One day he dragged all the pots and pans out from under the cabinets and then started throwing Cheerios all over the kitchen while I was making beds. I came out here and got so upset, I took one of *my* tranquilizers, then locked him in the basement and called up Mr. Gregoretti and very calmly told him that if he didn't come home right away, I was going to strangle Marco and then kill myself. No one understood Alice Crimmins better than I did."

My father finished the story. "I rushed home and found Rose in bed, crying, and Marco down in the basement doing cartwheels."

A new panorama flickers across the screen – another tree standing in a sea of boxes in a corner of our then gray and red living room. A sleepy-eyed Marco, two years old and wearing green Christmas feety pajamas, is led into the room by Rose, whose long black hair is braided and coiled behind her neck. Together they began opening box after box.

"I remember that suit," Marco said, as he watched my mother opening a package thirty-one years ago, and holding a little red jacket up to Marco's shoulders.

Another Christmas flashed by. Grandma Renata in her black silk dress sits with her sisters and Grandpa Marco hands out presents.

"My mother and father," Rose told Carla.

On screen, my mother's younger sister, my Aunt Peggy, opens a box and mouths "Thank you" at the camera, as she holds up a blouse theatrically.

The blips swirl over the scene once more, and we jump to Christmas morning one year later. Marco is opening boxes without Rose's help. He races through toys and games and still more outfits.

"I remember that jacket," Rose said, fondly, in the darkness. "I bought it for you at Saks. You looked so cute when we dressed you up in it, but you hated it. And shoes! You never liked to wear shoes for some reason."

Christmas 1957 arrived and so did I. There on the screen my mother holds yet another dark bundle – fat Baby Michael. At her feet, Marco tugs on the hem of Rose's black silk "Five-thirty P. M. Fashion" cocktail dress, also from Saks.

"Look at your glamour girl mother," Rose said wistfully.

Cut to a shot of Grandpa Marco in his favorite chair next to the blazing fireplace. Martha, our painfully fat black cat, lies on her back in the fire's warmth, her tail swishing back and forth as a warning to all that she wants to be left alone. Grandpa sits with one arm around baby Michael and holds him on his knee. He waves to the camera, and then tries to make me wave my infant arm too.

"Now, Mikey was a happy baby," Rose said, keeping up the commentary.

At Grandpa's side is firstborn grandson and namesake, Marco, slapping Grandpa's leg again and again in a bid for attention. Grandpa looks at Marco, then back at the camera. We can read his lips as he says, "Jesus Christ! What the hell does he want?" My guess is he wanted Grandpa Marco to toss me into the fireplace.

Another Christmas passed. And another. And then it was Christmas 1960. More little-boy suits for Marco, now seven and opening packages with the same zeal, but making sure to keep one eye cocked on brother Michael's progress. Rose helps me open a box which Marco pulls away to inspect. My mother takes the box back gently and waves to the camera. I am laughing and smiling.

There is a jump as we cut to later that morning. I am still in pajamas and am chasing Mr. Machine around the living room, jumping up and down excitedly and clapping my hands. Martha the cat runs under the couch in terror as Mr. Machine zeroes in on her.

"That damn toy," my mother muttered, "I must have searched all over Long Island for it and finally found one on Christmas Eve in a drug store on Jericho Turnpike just as they were closing. I think I paid about nine dollars for it, which was a lot of money for a toy back then."

"I saw one in an antique shop not too long ago," I told her. "It was in perfect shape. They wanted sixty dollars for it."

"I think yours was broken before New Year's."

The blips of light signaled the end of one roll and the beginning of another. Cut to later that Christmas evening. I am mincing across the living room floor with a blue silk scarf on my head, wearing Mommy's shoes and her slip over my clothes. A silence fell over all of us. I tried desperately to think of something to say that would mask my embarrassment. I should have remembered this drag bit was coming, but I didn't. I don't think Joe did either.

I couldn't remember how or why, but someone had dressed me up like that, and Daddy must have thought it was cute, and out came the movie camera. I was too young to have done this without help from someone, even if it was my idea.

The shot zooms back from a close-up of me, Long Island's youngest Mae West impersonator, to a wide-angle shot of the living room. We can see Marco jumping on one of the couches and my mother watching from the dining room as I continue vamping down some imaginary runway.

I sat there feeling my face flush, watching myself shuffling around the room rolling my eyes, one hand on my hip like Tropic-Ana. I don't know why I was so embarrassed – probably because Carla was sitting in the room.

Finally, I turned to Rose in the darkness. "And I had to *tell* you I was gay?" I said.

Marco muttered, "Christ!" and went into the kitchen and opened the refrigerator door.

"Rose," I teased, "how come you bought Marco those cute little outfits every Christmas, but you stuck me in that old rag you wouldn't even use to polish the floor? I knew you always loved him best!"

"Michael," Marco shouted from the kitchen, "can we

get through one fucking night without you throwing the fact that you're gay in our faces?"

"Marco," my mother said sharply, "I may not have some big job in television, but I know rude when I see it. You apologize to your brother."

"Sorry, Mike," he called from the kitchen.

For a moment we all sat there, the uncomfortable silence broken only by the whirring of the movie projector. Then Rose spoke.

"Carla, I sure hope you know what you're getting yourself into here," she counseled. "Now, who wants more coffee?"

On screen, my mother sits on the floor with me, making a stuffed animal hop toward my feet and up to my knees. Then she makes it hop up to my face as if to kiss me and I throw my head back and laugh. The little blips pass over the scene.

24
Extra-Strength Pain Relief

About a week before we were originally scheduled to shoot the Skin Therapy and Total Hand Treatment spots, the spirit of the season must have taken hold of Tom, and he granted us an extension, pushing the shoot date into mid-January 1987. It was probably easier than giving us Christmas presents. At least it took some of the pressure off. We could only have been happier if they had canceled the commercials entirely.

The day we shot also turned out to be the coldest of the year. We had cast Bonnie, the mousy blonde in the red sweater, as the spokeswoman, and hired the best stylist we could find to unmouse her. I arrived on the set as the stylist and his two assistants were attempting to transform Bonnie from mouse to Blythe Danner. We were shooting in some low-rent studio Tom made us use in midtown, a far cry from Ed Harmon's setup in Chelsea. I found Jo off to the side of the set, drinking coffee and nibbling on half a croissant.

"Hi there, sweetie pie!" she said. "You look like you could use a hot drink of something."

"Can you stand this weather? How *cold* my little hand

is! Where's the food?"

Jo pointed in the general direction of a board on some sawhorses and added, "This is positively the worst coffee I've ever had. I recommend tea or hot chocolate."

"Thanks for the tip."

We shot the Skin Therapy spot first, since it was the less complicated of the two. Bonnie just sat in a plush chair, talked about how dry her skin was, picked up the product, rubbed some onto her hands and smiled a lot. We were picking up the snowstorm demo from the previous commercial, and would cut the existing footage into Bonnie's performance. Simple, except for the fact that Tom kept making her do it again and again. He was never satisfied with any of her readings; by the time we finished, we were already two hours behind schedule. I started wondering if he was related to Gwen Hammond.

We had lunch sent in rather than take an hour off, and everyone stood around the set absently eating sandwiches while they changed Bonnie's hair and makeup, put her in a new outfit, and got the cameras ready for the second commercial.

We were all tense from the morning's shoot. Once we started rolling on the second commercial, everyone was walking around looking like the stock market had crashed. There's nothing sadder than someone trying to be funny with bad material, and Bonnie's performance was sad indeed.

Sometime around six that night, she said she thought she might be able to give her delivery a little more energy if she were standing instead of sitting. At that point, we were willing to try anything, but it meant stopping the shoot while we raised the tabletop so Bonnie could stand behind it. We then had to raise and refocus the camera, adjust the lighting and raise the boom mike.

The result wasn't worth the wait. Sitting down or

standing up, it wasn't Bonnie's fault – it was my copy. And when Bonnie tried to give it a more playful reading, Tom said she was getting too ditsy and made her reel it in. It was hopeless. She was doing her best, but her performances were uneven – good on one line, flat on the next. She was just too tired. Instead of coming across like a fresh and breezy girl next door, she looked and sounded like a bored housewife. Worse, when they redid her makeup, they had put something in her hair to give it more body, and instead, it was working against her. She started out with bouncy curls and by the end of the evening was looking more and more like a flapper. We had to keep stopping between takes to fluff it up again.

Tom finally spoke up and asked to see the playback on what we'd shot so far. We gathered around the monitor and watched take after take. I kept trying to think of ways to save it. Maybe we could do just one more. Maybe Tom would decide to can the commercial.

But he decided he liked what he saw, and wanted to move on to the demo. His eye was on his watch more than on the quality of what we were doing at that point. "Let's just do the product shot and the close-ups and get the hell out of here before we go into triple overtime," he commanded.

We set up the kit for the product shot, but would save that for last. We still had to shoot the demos – Bonnie's nail tap-tap-tapping on the marble tabletop near the kit, and then the alternate version where she would press her nail down until the tip flexed. After we finished the two sequences, we could send Bonnie home and film the product shot.

Bonnie went to sleep in the makeup chair while they set up the shots. They left her alone, and used Jo's hand as a stand-in.

We roused Bonnie and took her back to the set. She

made a couple of practice taps on the marble tabletop as we watched on the monitor. Then we started filming.

After about ten stabs at the marble, Tom asked to see playback. "She's not coming down hard enough," he said. "She's really gotta smack that tabletop. I want people to think she's got nails like iron."

The director asked Bonnie to try giving her taps a little more emphasis. We shot a few more, but Tom still wasn't happy, and asked Bonnie to "really jab a couple home" for him. He was so busy studying her nail on the monitor, he missed the little winces of pain on her face each time she did it.

When he was satisfied that Bonnie was stabbing the marble with enough force to split it, he let us move on to the flex shot. To be sure the nail would actually flex, we cheated and made a tiny cut in the nail on the side away from the camera with a cuticle nipper.

Bonnie made a few gentle passes at the marble, and we got a graceful bowing effect. Impressive, but still within the realm of good taste. Tom was not satisfied.

His first complaint was that he could see the knuckles of her other fingers when she came in with her index finger pointed down. He wanted to see only the index finger. They tried moving the camera in closer, but we lost the package entirely, and Tom hit the roof.

"Am I working with a bunch of amateurs, or what? I want to see the girl's finger and the kit and no goddamn knuckles. How hard is that?"

They moved the camera back again, and the director had a brief talk with Bonnie in hushed tones. She held her three fingers as close to her palm as she could and wrapped her thumb tightly around them, but it didn't work. Her fingernails were pressing into her flesh, and it was difficult to hold that tight for very long. After the third try, Tom instructed us to tape her fingers against her palm.

This took a good twenty minutes to accomplish. She came back to the set, obviously uncomfortable, with her hand taped up like she'd just come from surgery. She started poking at the marble with her nail again. Tom wanted it to look really dramatic. After about ten tries, her nail was practically folding back on itself. I couldn't look at the monitor anymore – it was painful to watch. I kept hearing little groans coming from the pockets of people watching on various monitors scattered around the set. I said to Tom, "I really think we have enough footage of this. She's in pain, and we're going to break that nail."

"So what!" he snapped at me. "She has another hand. If she breaks it, we'll switch."

Bonnie did another series of takes for us and then the nail finally snapped. Her index finger was getting swollen. They soaked her hand in a big bowl of warm water so they could take off the tape while Tom watched the video play-back. He singled out one repulsive take where her nail bent like an 'L,' and told us to use that one and send her home.

Patty went into the makeup room to find Bonnie sitting in the chair with some ice in a washcloth pressed against her hand. She was crying, and told Patty she'd never do anything for Lakeland again. We really couldn't blame her.

The next day, Jo, Henry, Patty and I huddled behind two editors at a Moviola to watch the footage. The Skin Therapy film wasn't too bad. At least Bonnie looked fresh and happy. The Total Hand Treatment System footage was another story. Bonnie's delivery was flat, and you could see her grow more haggard with each take. The nail-bending sequences were disgusting.

We picked the takes we liked best for each spot, and left Patty and the editors to assemble a rough cut. I was beat, and told Jo I was heading home. She said it was okay, and told me to take a little extra time in the morning if I needed it.

I came home to find another airbrushed beefcake card from Craig. This one featured a man with the biggest chest in America standing in a doorway wearing white boxer shorts. There was a rumpled bed visible in the background. "I miss you" was all he had written inside. "Why are you doing this to me?" I said to the card. I sat down and called Anthony at Shades of Meaning.

"Are you coming home for dinner tonight? I thought I'd cook if you were."

"No," he said. "You sound awful. What's the matter?"

"I'm really tired. This commercial is turning out to be yet another disaster."

"And?"

"And I just got another card from Craig."

"What does he want now?"

"He said he misses me. That's all."

"What are you gonna do?"

"I don't know. I'm probably asking for trouble, but I want to call him."

"So call him, then. Maybe he's had some time to think things over, and maybe he's ready to make a commitment now."

"Or maybe he's just horny."

"Only one way to find out. Listen, I gotta run. We'll talk tonight, I promise."

I hung up the phone and poured a glass of wine. As tired as I was, I had bought some chicken cutlets and fresh broccoli on the way home, and decided to cook dinner anyway. It would be therapeutic, I figured, and Anthony could reheat the leftovers when he came in or eat them tomorrow. I worked in the kitchen for a while, losing myself in the process of breading the cutlets and frying them. When I came back into the living room to set the table, I noticed that it had started snowing. I went to the window and looked out onto Hudson Street.

The snow was sticking. Two men were heading toward Christopher Street, heads bowed against the wind. One of them was waving his arms emphatically as he spoke. The other man stopped, grabbed him by the shoulders and gave him a quick hug and a kiss. The man who had been talking hugged him back, and they continued arm in arm into the wind and snow. I watched until they turned onto Christopher, and I wished I were one of them.

I ate dinner and washed the dishes and did everything I could think of to put off calling Craig. Finally, I went into my room and called. He sounded genuinely happy to hear from me. He said he had debated sending that second card after I hadn't called at Christmas, then figured it was worth one more try. He asked what I had been doing, so I filled him in on my latest advertising nightmare.

There was an awkward silence when I finished. He ended it by saying, "If you got my card, I think you know what's on my mind. I really do miss you. I'd like to talk it over with you. Not on a phone, but over dinner some night. What are you doing Saturday?"

I kept thinking about the two men on Hudson Street. He'd better mean what he's saying, I told myself. I said okay, and he asked me to meet him at Fedora. We hung up, and I went back out into the living room with a book, and read until I dozed off.

I was a wreck all through dinner. Conversation was confined to safe areas – work, Craig's new apartment, and the Gay Men's Chorus, which he had recently joined. I don't know why, but somewhere during the meal, I decided that it was hopeless – he was as busy as ever, and as distant. Why had he sent that card, or more to the point, why had I called him?

It was snowing when we left the restaurant. We started walking and got as far as the token booth at the Christopher Street subway station. He turned and said, "Come home with me?"

I was suddenly so sad. I knew what would happen if I did. We'd go back to his apartment and have great sex on that awful bed, and he'd hold me in his arms and tell me all the reasons why he couldn't commit. The evening had already been enough of a replay of our last date to give away the ending. "Maybe some other time," I said.

"Okay." He ran his fingers through my hair, and leaned down and kissed me. "I hope you mean that."

We just stood there looking at each other, not knowing what to say next, until the train came rumbling into the station. He fished in his pocket for a token, gave me another quick kiss and said, "Thanks for seeing me tonight. It means a lot."

He went through the turnstile and hopped onto the train. As the doors slid shut, he turned and locked eyes with me until the train pulled out of the station. It was straight out of *Since You Went Away*.

I thrust my hands into my coat pockets and went back out into the snow. As I passed Christopher's, I heard a light rapping on the window, and looked over to see Anthony, with his cigarette lighter in hand, cigarette between his lips, motioning me inside.

"What happened?" he asked as I pulled up a vacant stool. "I saw the two of you pass a couple of minutes ago, and now you're alone. Did you have a fight?"

"No. It was probably the worst date of my life. Maybe I'm just tired, but I feel like nothing's changed. All he did was talk about work and how little time he has. So what's going to be different this time around? I'm just not strong enough for him to do it again."

I think Irene sensed how depressed I was getting. She called on Sunday morning to check in with me, and when I told her what a disaster my date with Craig had been, she asked if I wanted to take a ride with her to the Jersey Shore.

"Don't you think it's a little early? I mean, it *snowed* last night."

"Take a ride with me. The fresh sea air of Asbury Park will do you good."

Irene always said the car was the one luxury she could afford. Without it, she might have been able to move to a larger apartment. But then, without any means of impulsive escape, she'd really feel like a prisoner of the city. Given the choice, she'd rather have the car.

There were few people on the boardwalk. Most of the shops were still closed. At one that wasn't, Irene bought us a box of fudge, a Jersey Shore specialty.

"What do you think?" she asked as I tried some.

It took me a while to chew my way through to an answer.

"They should write 'Goodyear' on the box."

"When I was a kid, I used to love this stuff. It wasn't summer unless we stopped here and got fudge."

"Well you have your fudge, but it definitely isn't summer."

Irene had on a red plaid Woolrich jacket from the Fifties with a wonderful red printed silk scarf and I was wearing my black down jacket, but neither of us felt protected from the icy blast coming in off the ocean. "Does the phrase 'cooler near the shore' mean anything to you?"

"Want to get back in the car?"

"In a minute," I said.

We walked toward the rail. It was a gray afternoon. I could see a ship headed out to sea. I stared at it a long time.

"Hello in there," Irene said.

"Sorry. I'm just a little distracted. Irene, I've made such a mess of my life. I don't know how it happened but I certainly have screwed up. I'm starting to feel like I'm on God's B-list, and I don't know what to do anymore."

"What do you *want* to do?"

"I *want* to live in a Frank Capra movie."

"Okay, what's your second choice?"

"That's the problem. I don't know. I keep thinking if I could only finish my play, I'd be fine."

"Michael, you just need to be a little more disciplined about it, that's all."

"I don't know. It's a bunch of people saying witty things and a lot of doors slamming. Who cares? Who wants to see a farce set in an ad agency?"

"Don't make it a farce, then."

"It's about advertising. It *has* to be a farce. I just feel like I'm wasting my time. Sometimes I think I'm only writing so I can say I'm writing. Maybe once I finish it I can put it away and figure out what it is I really want to say. I haven't got a clue right now. Most of the time..." I turned back toward the sea.

"'Splain, Lucy. Most of the time, what?"

"Most of the time, I think I'm one of those people who loves a good story, but can't tell one to save my life."

"That's not true, Michael. It's that place. They have you believing you can't write."

"I'm not so sure. Remember a few weeks ago I mentioned I had an assignment for Tinolate Athlete's Foot Spray? They always do two jocks in a locker room talking about the product. So just to be different, I wrote a spot about a Russian waitress with bad feet and called it 'Pavlova's Dogs.' I liked it, but no one at the client got it. They just said 'No women!' Next I wrote a stand-up comedian in a nightclub arguing with a heckler in the audience.

The comedian was telling these really dreadful jokes, like, 'My athlete's foot is so bad, my shoes stuck their tongues out at me!' and the guy in the audience keeps yelling stuff back that turns out to be about the product. Jo loved it. Then Ellen said, 'The client expects a commercial that takes place in a locker room,' so that's what I gave them. I end up executing everyone else's ideas."

"Maybe once you're in the business a few more years, they stop cramming ideas down your throat and let you do what you want."

"It still happens to Jo, and she's been doing this forever." I looked out at the ocean again. I could barely see the ship now. "I had a dream the other night. I dreamed I was in the apartment, and I was on my way from my bedroom to the kitchen, and I noticed a door in the hallway, next to the closet. And I thought, 'This is odd, I don't remember a door there.' So I opened it, and there was an entire room back there that I never knew about before. It was beautiful — like that living room from the Frank Lloyd Wright house they have at the Met. Now, I'm not real big on dream interpretation, but I think this one meant something."

"What?"

"That maybe I have something inside I haven't really tapped into yet."

"Like your writing?"

"Like my writing. It's just that I don't have a lot of confidence in the play. I don't think it's very good."

"Just write and don't be so hard on yourself."

"I still think it's a warm-up."

"Speaking of warming up..."

"Yeah. Let's go."

We turned and started walking back to the car. Irene put her arm around me. "Poor honey. What am I going to do with you? Tell Rose it was just a phase and now you like girls and let's move in together."

"You deserve better, Irene. Like Henry."

"Henry doesn't know it yet, but he's going to marry me."

"Really?" I stopped walking.

"Really." She pulled me closer and we started walking again. "And you did that. He isn't like the guys I usually meet – the ones I feel like I can wipe up the floor with after five minutes. He's genuine and he's sweet. I like him, I approve of him and I'm hot for him. It's good with Henry, but different with you. Henry doesn't make me laugh the way you do. Henry doesn't get all my asides like you do. You listen better than anyone else, and you remember things. It's very flattering. Too bad I'm not a gay man – we'd be perfect for each other. Maybe I was a gay man in a former life."

"Or maybe this is training for your next life," I said.

"I could die young and come back as a beautiful struggling actor and you could keep me. You'd be a rich playwright by then and all your friends would be jealous that you have such a hunky young thing on your arm who adores you."

"I think we both deserve it *now*, Blanche."

We had reached the car. Irene unlocked my door, and then went around to the driver's side. I unlocked her door from inside. It was almost as cold in the car as it had been on the boardwalk. She started the car, and the two of us stared hopefully at the heating vent. It was throwing puffs of cool air at us.

Irene turned on the radio. WNEW was playing Ella Fitzgerald singing "Love Is Here to Stay." We looked at each other and smiled, and I said, "'I detest cheap sentiment'" in my best Margo Channing voice and turned it off.

"Okay, have it your way," she said. "Maybe we should have waited for spring to do this."

"I wouldn't have made it. Thanks for getting me out of the apartment. It was good therapy. I could have done without the fudge, though."

"Where to now?" she asked.

"Any place where I can get us burgers as big as the Ritz. My treat. I brought plastic."

"Yay!" she cheered in a little-girl voice. The car seemed to be warming up. She put it in gear and started backing out of the space. When we were on the road again, I said, "Do you think it's ever going to get better, or is it always going to be like this?"

"I vote for getting better."

"I think my problem is, I saw too many movies as a kid and my expectations are way too high. I came to New York hoping to be Audrey Hepburn in *Breakfast at Tiffany's*. I was convinced I would throw raucous parties in my little walk-up apartment and be the toast of *tout* Manhattan. They ought to ban that movie and burn the negative. I think it ruined an entire generation of gay men."

"Some pop psychologist should come along and do a book about it called 'The Holly Golightly Syndrome.'"

"What do you think, Blanche?" I asked. "Are we ever going to grow up and be happy adults with all the toys?"

"I don't think I'd recognize you happy."

"I'm a trip, I promise."

"I'd like to see it."

"You will. I hope so, anyway."

25
Now, Even Better!

I spent most of the next week in a dark editing room,
working on the rough cuts of the two Lakeland commercials. The editors had assembled a fairly good cut of the
new handruff spot, combining the existing demo footage
from the original commercial and the footage of Bonnie we
had just shot. Bonnie smiled a lot, and came across like a
good friend giving a little beauty advice to all the flaky-
skinned women of America. It wasn't exactly an acting *tour
de force*, but it was an improvement on the commercial they
already had, which wasn't saying much.

The Hand Treatment commercial, however, was
beyond hope. Bonnie had bright spots here and there
throughout her readings, but no single take was perfect.
We tried cutting pieces of various readings together – using
a sentence from one take, cutting to the product in her
hand, then picking up a line we liked from a different take,
but the effect was choppy. How many times could we get
away with jumping to a product shot? Worse, her hair
never matched in any of the shots – flat in one take, then
fluffier in the next. We had to sacrifice a couple of good
line readings for the sake of continuity. We tried lifting the

brighter vocal tracks from the takes we liked and laying them down on the scenes we were stuck with, but the dubbing was obvious, no matter how much we played with it.

We wound up assembling a cut we could live with, and that was the best we could offer Lakeland. Bad script plus bad performance equals bad commercial. But it was exactly the commercial Tom had asked for – and deserved.

We went back to the agency with the rough cut. Ellen had to see it, and so did Beth and Donald. Then, if they approved the spots, we'd set up a screening with Tom and finish them according to his instructions.

Patty, Jo, Henry and I trudged down to Ellen's office with the videocassette.

"You've got that look on your face again, sweetie pie."

"What look?" I said.

"That look you get when you think something bad is going to happen."

"I just don't want to be in the same room with Ellen when she sees those commercials for the first time. She's going to hate them, and hate me for doing them."

"Look, she saw the work that got killed, and she knows how these commercials got made. She can't blame you for that."

"It isn't exactly going to make my name the first one that springs to her mind when the good stuff comes up, that's for sure. I'm not exactly number one with Fran as it is, and without Ellen on my side, she'll have me working on Purina Rabbit Chow before the year is out."

We arrived to find Ellen sitting on the sofa scowling, as if she knew what was coming. "What have you got now, Gregoretti?"

"Well," I joked halfheartedly, "It ain't *Citizen Kane*."

We rolled the new handruff spot first. Ellen's comment was, "At least she sounds convincing and looks pretty.

That's about the best we can expect, I guess. But I don't want another one of these handruff commercials getting out of the agency." Why was she looking at me? I didn't think up the campaign and I certainly didn't want to make this spot. I wanted to do Joan Crawford in a beach house!

After seeing the Hand Treatment spot, she turned to me and said, "That's a terrible spot, Michael."

"Why *Michael?*" I said. "I didn't make this commercial alone, you know. I see at least six other guilty faces in this room. And I also had a little help from fat Tom Dolgen, the Wizard of Raritan. This was not a Michael Gregoretti production, folks."

"Okay, I'm sorry," she said. "I'm not blaming you."

"Not much."

"All right!" she shouted. "I said I was sorry, didn't I? Now you have to do something with this spot. Go back and look at all the footage you've got. There has to be something else you can use."

"That's about the best there was," Jo said. "Ellen, truthfully, these kids worked so hard to save the spot. There just isn't anything else. Tom wouldn't let us shoot anything peppy, so all her readings are flat."

"I don't know what to tell you," Ellen said, shaking her head, "but you can't show them this."

We had the wake for the commercial in Jo's office after work that afternoon. She sent her secretary out to buy a couple of bottles of wine and some cheese and crackers, and Patty, Henry and I sat glumly around her conference table trying to think of something to do with it.

"Maybe we could add some music," Jo said.

"How about a rap?" I offered, and went into rap mode, or as close to it as I could get for a white boy from Long Island. "I got a little magic for your hands and for your nails/It's got a special protein for the strength that never fails/Brush it on, rub it in/It feels just fab/Get a better pair of hands/from your friends at Lakeland Labs!"

"How much have you had to drink, Michael?" Jo asked, laughing and pretending to take my glass away.

"If only she didn't look so different in every take," Henry said.

"You know what's wrong?" I said. "We have nothing else to cut away to. Now, what if we shot another sequence upstairs in the TV studio. We do it on tape for now, and cut it in and if they like it at Lakeland, we go back and film it."

"I'm not following this," Henry said.

"Here's how we use all her best takes. We shoot a close-up sequence of a woman's hands holding the kit, then one where she's squirting a little on her nails, then one where she's rubbing it in. Then maybe we shoot a couple of extreme close-ups of the stuff squirting out of the spout or the brush dripping with solution, and we scramble it all together, and at the end of each line we like, we cut to one of these close-ups. She says, 'Bet you don't know what this is!' and we stick in a shot of this stuff squirting out. Then we pick up her next line from somewhere else and cut away again. We do the whole spot like that, using only her best readings."

"She's still going to look different in each take."

"Make some of it voice-over. Blow up the footage a couple of fields on an ADO so we're tighter on her face and you don't see her hair so much. Then we just trim it so it times out to thirty, add some stock music or a couple of sound effects. We could really inject some energy into this. I think that's all it needs."

"I like it," Jo said. "But I don't want to shoot this in the TV studio. That gang up there hasn't got a clue what they're doing. Do we have any money left, Patty? Maybe we can shoot it somewhere else."

"Some but not enough."

"Who owes us a favor?" Henry asked.

"Let me make a couple of phone calls. I bet I could find someone to shoot this for free," Jo said.

Jo did, but she swore us to secrecy. She had friends — four women who owned a small boutique agency — who let us use their studio. Jo had worked with them years ago, and in fact, had just done some freelance work for them on the sly, and was still waiting to be paid. Her friends, whom Jo referred to as "The Four Beautiful Girls Four," offered to do the taping as a favor if she'd agree to wait a little longer for her money. Jo agreed, gladly.

So the following afternoon, Henry, Jo, Patty and I kidnapped Karen, and on the pretext of going to lunch together, went to tape the inserts. We had cased Malcolm's female employees for a pair of hands that were closest to Bonnie's, and had chosen Karen not only for her beautiful hands, but also because we knew she could keep a secret.

We shot everything we could think of: product squirting through the air, being brushed onto nails, being massaged into the back of a hand, gushing out of the bottle. The Four Beautiful Girls Four were incredibly helpful, even suggesting some shots we hadn't thought of.

Patty had found the perfect piece of music, a very jazzy string bass with finger-snapping and female voices chorusing "oooh" and "yeah" every so often. And when we cut the new commercial together and added the music, we were floored by how good it became. True, it was an uneasy blend of tape and film, and the new footage looked a little amateurish, but it was just a demo, after all. The point was to show how we could improve this awful spot for not a lot of money and then get the go-ahead to actually do it.

Ellen watched the new cut and when it was over, made us play it again. "I can't believe that's the same spot.

It's still a little rough, but if Tom doesn't buy it, he's a jerk."

"Tom *is* a jerk," Beth said. "I love this commercial, don't get me wrong, but he'll never buy it in a million years."

"Fine," Jo said. "We were told to fix the spot and we did. These kids did a fabulous job with it, but if we can't sell it, we can't sell it. Maybe it's time to get Howard involved in this."

"Howard's going down to Tennessee for a conference at Sparks," Ellen said.

"Is it true they've put us on warning?" Jo asked.

"Yep. But you didn't hear that from me. So when are you showing this to Tom?" she asked, changing the subject.

"We can't get back to him until the middle of next week," Donald said, cute as ever in a blue wool suit today with a pale yellow cashmere vest. Oh, come to your senses, Donald, I wanted to say. Pierce that ear and marry me and let's go off into the sunset folding crepes together!

"Since you still have some time," Ellen said, "let me see if I can squeeze a little more money out of production for additional editing. I think you should clean it up a little more before you present it."

The extra polishing paid off. When we finished, we had a commercial with style, a commercial we could all be proud of, a commercial Tom called "a pile of shit."

We were crushed.

Jo did everything she could to convince him that our second version was superior to what we had originally shot, but Tom hated it. To further humiliate us, he made it quite clear that he wouldn't pay the extra editing costs for the new version, telling us we could "eat them" instead. He accused us of trying to ram ideas down his throat that he had made clear up front he didn't want, and trotted out his old favorite: how we didn't listen, didn't take direction and didn't understand his consumers. And once again we were berated for not being a model agency. "Why can't you people be more like Ogilvy?" he scolded in Mother Superior tones.

I only made it through the meeting without crying by imagining Tom roasting to death in a fire so big they'd have to shoot it in CinemaScope.

The next day's interoffice mail brought a terse staff memo from Herbert Malcolm, our CEO and grandson of the company's founder. He asked that everyone come to the area outside his offices for an important announcement at three that afternoon. There was much speculation throughout the agency on what the news could possibly be, and the guesses ranged from new business (we had just pitched Hallmark Cards) to important promotions ("He's resigning and naming Gwen Hammond his successor," said Jenny) to Jo's worst-case scenario (which proved to be true): "We lost Sparks Cola."

In all the time I had worked there, I had seen Herbert Malcolm exactly twice. Once on an elevator, when I kept giving him dirty looks for smoking a cigar, not knowing who he was, and that afternoon, when he stood before us and told us solemnly that, after thirty-four years, Sparks Cola had pulled the account. They would make the announcement the next morning from their corporate headquarters in Memphis, he told us: The business was going a couple of blocks up Lexington Avenue to McCann-Erickson. Nina DiSesa and Liz Chapple had pulled together a brilliant pitch on very short notice and had won the account, and the client couldn't be happier with their new team.

Then he dropped his other loafer. Howard had resigned his position as creative director and was being replaced by Richard Eisenstein, who had decided to return to Malcolm.

Richard Eisenstein! I felt as if the floor had opened beneath me and I was hurtling toward the pavement. I'd be working for Go-Get-My-Coffee Man again!

Mr. Malcolm assured us that Howard's decision was entirely his own, and it was with deep regret that he was leaving, which we all knew meant he blamed Howard for losing Sparks, and had kicked him the hell out. When he further assured us that the loss would not mean a significant cutback of personnel, you could feel a shudder go through the crowd – especially from the Sparks creative group – because we all knew that meant heads were about to roll.

Back in her office, Jo told me that she knew Richard only by reputation. "He did all that very piss-elegant, tasteful stuff. That 'I Am Fashion' campaign for the wool people was his. So was that Chanel stuff with all the clouds and Lena Horne singing 'Racing with the Moon' on the soundtrack. I mean, he does *fabulous* work, but I understand he's just a gray-flannel pill."

"He is. What did they promise him to get him to come back?" I asked.

"Money, I'm sure."

I told Jo about my history with Richard back when I was his secretary. I was sure he would have found a way to have me fired if he hadn't found another job first.

"Rule number one in this business is never, ever burn a bridge," Jo said. "And it sounds like you nuked this one."

"He was just some cranky group head when I worked for him. Who knew he was going to come back here and run the joint?"

"Well," she sighed, "maybe it won't be too bad. Maybe he's mellowed a bit and will look kindly on you since you're a writer now. *If* we're all still employed when the smoke clears, that is."

Howard left and Richard quietly took over. I expected him to march back, trumpets heralding triumphantly, in a scene right out of the second act of *Aida*, but at first, no one even knew he was there. We began to feel his presence, however. His first move as creative director was to have his office redecorated. The walls were covered in black fabric. Howard's big mahogany conference table was replaced by one that was all sleek black lacquer and smoke glass. Swooping Italian lighting fixtures that looked like they came from Buck Rogers' summer house on Fire Island illuminated the room with pinpoint accuracy, and Howard's brass lamps were sent out to replace the relics in the reception area. Next, sculpted black leather furniture that must have cost more than I made in a year was brought in. When it was all completed, Jo said that the only thing missing was Howard's body laid out on the new glass table.

We spent the rest of February finishing the Lakeland spokeswoman spots. I came back from the editors one afternoon to find a message from Craig among the pink While You Were Out slips Karen had left on my desk. She had written "He's in Columbia Presbyterian Hospital" under his name and then the number.

"Craig? It's Michael."

"Oh, Michael," he said softly.

"Why are you in the hospital?"

"Thanks for calling."

"Craig, what's wrong?"

"They're giving me Demerol shots. They make me very sleepy."

"But, Craig, why are you in the hospital?"

He filled me in piece by piece and out of sequence. He had rented a van and gone to the warehouse for the last of his cartons and furniture. A friend from the chorus was supposed to help him, but canceled at the last minute, so he did it alone. He strained his back lifting a box of books into the van. Then, a few days later, he slipped on the ice on his way to work. He went into spasms about an hour later and passed out. They called his doctor, who told them to call an ambulance and get Craig to the hospital right away. He'd been there a couple of days already.

"Michael, can you come see me tonight?" he asked, like a little boy.

"Sure I can. I can come up right after work. Do you need anything?"

"Can you bring me ice cream?"

"What kind?"

"Häagen-Dazs Butter Pecan."

It was snowing when I left the office. I got a pint of ice cream from the Lexington Avenue Gourmet and took the train uptown.

There were two beds in the room, and the one closest to the door was empty. The curtain was drawn around the other bed, and I could see the flicker of the TV screen through it. There was a warning taped to the door about infectious waste disposal, and a notice to visitors detailing how to scrub their hands after seeing the patient.

I knocked on the door and called his name, but he didn't hear me. I walked into the room and looked around the curtain at his bed. He was asleep. There was a big flower arrangement on the night table, with a card signed: *Love, Ray*. His dinner was sitting on a stand beside the bed. He had hardly touched it.

I unzipped my jacket quietly and draped it over the back of the chair, and put the ice cream on the coolish windowsill, where I hoped it wouldn't turn into slush.

I sat down and waited for him to wake up. When the national news was over and *Wheel of Fortune* came on, I took a book out of my backpack and started reading.

Craig stirred and opened his eyes. He squinted in my direction. He wasn't wearing his contacts. He smiled and held his arms out. "Michael!"

I went to give him a kiss, and he hugged me as tightly as he could, practically dragging me into the bed.

"MG, I'm so glad you came."

He wouldn't let me go. Then I realized he was crying.

"It's okay, Craig. Come on. It's okay. I brought ice cream."

"I'm scared, Michael."

"It'll be okay."

"You don't understand." His speech was still thick and sleepy. "They don't know what this is. All they're doing is giving me painkillers and trying to get the swelling down. But they tested me. I'm positive, Michael."

"You took the HIV test?"

"They made me."

"But you always suspected you were positive."

"Now I know."

"It doesn't mean you have AIDS, though. You're not sick."

"They act like I am. They won't even give me a shot without putting on gloves first." He hugged me again. "I may have to have back surgery. They don't know what I did to it, and they keep telling me it's too swollen to tell. I've had about eight doctors in here in two days, and they all say something different. One guy thinks I have a brain tumor."

"Just calm down, Craig. It'll be okay. Did you eat?"

"I hate the food."

"Do you want some ice cream? I got butter pecan."

"How did you know?"

"You told me to bring it."

"I did?"

"When you called today." I handed him the container and took one of the spoons from his dinner tray.

"Put that out in the hall," he said, waving the spoon at his dinner. "Maybe if they trip over it, they'll remember to take it away next time."

I removed the tray, then came back and sat on the edge of the bed. He held the pint on his chest with one hand, and reached for mine with the other.

"Thanks for coming up. And for the ice cream. I don't deserve you. I don't know why you even came."

"Oh, well. 'Fish gotta swim...'"

He squeezed my hand. "Not exactly the Valentine's Day I had in mind for us, but I'm glad you're here. Do you think we can start over again?"

"Let's take it a step at a time, Craig. How about getting you out of the hospital first? Eat your ice cream before it gets soupy."

"Maybe it's a good thing you didn't marry me when you had the chance. I'm falling apart."

"You're okay."

"I'm sorry I've been such a shit to you."

"Look, why don't we discuss this when you're strong enough to fight back, okay?"

When visiting hours ended, he gave me his house keys and asked me to get his glasses from his apartment and some shorts, T-shirts and assorted bathroom items. I promised to come back the next day. He kissed me and thanked me again for coming.

I called Craig from the film editors' the next day.

"How are you?"

"Not too good, MG. I can't keep anything down. They said it's the drugs."

"I'm coming up after work tonight. Is there anything else I can bring you from your apartment?"

"See if you can find my Walkman. And some tapes.

Look on top of my desk. Also, could you bring me one of
my crystals? On the nightstand. Bring one of the amethysts.
And could you pick up some more ice cream?"

"Butter pecan."

"Please. MG? I hope you understood what I tried to
tell you last night. You're very special to me. I'm glad
you're back."

Craig's apartment was a mess. He had given away or
dumped the last of Andrew's furniture, but had more than
replaced it with his own things from storage. There were
cartons everywhere, interspersed with random piles of
books and record albums, all bisected by a narrow, winding
path that led to the front door, kitchen and bathroom. It
looked like he had called in the Collyer brothers to
decorate.

I found a gym bag in his closet, and started filling it
with shorts and T-shirts. I threw in a couple of pairs of
socks and his sneakers and the amethysts.

I went into the bathroom for his shaving stuff. He had
a framed picture of Casey Donovan nearly naked on the
wall plus one of Michael J. Fox, clothed. To the mirror he
had taped a small, neatly hand-lettered sign that read:

MY GOALS

1. *To find a job that makes me feel useful
   and productive and gives me self-respect,
   and a salary that will let me live comfortably.*

2. *To find a place of peace within.*

I opened the medicine chest and took his toothbrush
and comb and whatever else he had in there that I thought

he could use, and grabbed the Walkman and tapes on my
way out.

When I got to the hospital, the nurse was just leaving.
The other bed was still empty. He gave me a big kiss and
thanked me for coming, and asked me to help him change
into a pair of shorts and a T-shirt. He had a big black-and-
blue mark on his behind.

"How'd you get that?"

"Demerol shot last night. She really jabbed me. She
couldn't get out of here fast enough."

"Craig, don't take any shit from anyone. You're in
here with a bad back, not AIDS. And even if it was AIDS,
no one has the right to treat you this way."

"They're starting me on an I.V. tonight to get the
swelling down in my spine. I told the doctor he has to put it
in. I'm not letting those bitches near me again."

When I got in that night, Anthony was sitting on the couch
in the living room watching television. He turned off the set
and met me at the front door.

"I got takeout from Ming tonight, and there's plenty
left. You want me to heat some up for you?"

"Thanks, Anthony, but I'm beat. I just want to go to
sleep. Maybe I'll eat it tomorrow."

"Take off your shoes and go sit on the couch, and I'll
bring you a cup of chamomile tea." He put a cassette in the
tape deck and went into the kitchen. I listened to the music
for a minute or two. Beethoven. Opus Thirty-six, Second
Movement. One of the few things I remembered from
college. That and other useless information such as: you
can't step in the same river twice, Prince Esterházy loved
the flute, and they killed Hypatia with oyster shells.

Anthony came into the living room with two mugs on
a red lacquer tray, and four fortune cookies in a small bowl.

"Oh, God," I said. "If only I could find a man who'd make me a cup of tea!"

"If only I could find one who'd *let* me!" he answered. "Most of the ones I meet make me sleep on the kitchen floor and call them 'Sir.' My mother still says the two of us should be lovers. She'd give us a dishwasher for a wedding present."

I sipped my tea. Then I reached for a fortune cookie.

"They're always more interesting if you add 'in bed' to whatever your fortune says," Anthony advised.

I cracked it open and read the fortune out loud. "Someone is thinking of you. In bed."

"See? How is Craig doing, anyway?"

"The same. The nurses treat him like he has the plague. No one's sure what he has. They're starting him on an I.V. drip of something. They want to do some tests on him – I don't know, an MRI or some scan, I think he said. But they keep telling him everything is swollen and the test won't tell them much. He's so doped up, I don't understand half of what he's telling me."

"But how is he acting toward you?"

"That's the strangest part, Anthony. He's never been this open before. I mean, he keeps talking about 'us' – like all of a sudden we're a couple. I'm not so sure I want it anymore. Why is that? I wanted him so bad when we first met, and now that he's ready, it's as if it's too late for me."

"You're just afraid of being hurt again."

"Can you blame me? You know what he told me tonight? In the beginning, when we first met, he was also dating some florist named Ray. He didn't say so in as many words, but I think he was having a hard time making up his mind who he wanted. And then he stopped dating both of us."

"So what do you want?"

"That's the problem. He keeps apologizing and asking

for another chance. A voice inside me keeps saying, 'You jerk! Don't fall for this line again.' I keep telling the voice to shut up. All I know is that I missed him the whole time we were apart, and kept wishing I could see him again."

"I think you should give it a little time. See him through this, and then see how you feel once he's out of the hospital. You earned your wings on this one, kiddo, that's for sure."

"I hope so. You know, tonight I was sitting there while he was on the phone with some friend who had called him from New Mexico, and he started complaining about his job taking over his life and how they're getting him a computer and computer stand for his apartment so he can work at home when he gets out of the hospital. Anyway, he's talking to his friend, but he looks right at me as he says, 'I want someone in my life again.'"

"This doesn't sound like Craig."

"No, it doesn't. That's what has me a little scared. I still can't help thinking it's not him talking, it's the drugs. What am I getting myself into here?"

"Just get him home and don't worry about the rest of it. I think you need some sleep, Michael. Finish your tea and hit the sack."

I reached for another cookie and cracked it open. "Oh, God," I said, looking at the fortune.

"What's it say?"

"'Don't lose sight of what you want.'"

"In bed!" we added.

26
Actual Unretouched Photo

By the end of the week, Craig had seen a number of specialists, and had discussed the possibility of everything from compressed vertebrae to spinal cancer. The fact that his condition had been prompted by a fall was a good sign, but there were complications: Craig had hurt his back skiing years ago, and had already had surgery once. It was hard to tell where old damage left off and new damage began.

They gave him a series of cortisone shots, which helped significantly, and were hoping to start weaning him off the Demerol. After a few days, they decided that his back wasn't in great shape, but with a brace, and eventually some physical therapy, he might be able to avoid a second surgery. It would have to be watched, they told him.

I hadn't been able to come to the hospital for two days, since we had gone to Raritan for yet another meeting, and then had to go back to the editors to make one final adjustment that Tom had asked for. The spots were still awful. The only good thing I could find to say was that they were done and we could move on.

Craig was in good spirits when I finally got to the hospital – he'd been told that he could go home soon. They

wanted him to get at least another week's bed rest before
he went back to work, and to start by going in for half-days.
He was still having trouble keeping food down, so they put
him back on Compazine and told him the problem would
go away eventually.

He celebrated his imminent release from the hospital
by calling Macy's and buying an electric piano that he'd
seen in an ad in the paper. Even on sale, it cost almost two
thousand dollars, but he had always wanted one, so he
called them and charged it.

When I asked him where he planned to put it, remind-
ing him about all the boxes already in the apartment, plus
the new computer and stand, he frowned. I guess I was
being a killjoy.

"All I keep thinking about is my new piano. I just want
it set up somewhere in the apartment for now where I can
play it. I was hoping maybe you'd give me a hand when I
got out."

"You're not moving anything, Craig. Get one of your
chorus buddies to help me and we'll move furniture and get
the piano set up. But you'd better plan on staying in bed for
a while."

"Maybe if I had some company," he said, taking my
hand.

"It's a little soon for that, don't you think?"

"We could be creative. I was hoping you could stay
with me when I get out. I'd feel better if I wasn't alone at
first. Just a night or two."

"Sure."

Jo knew that I had a friend in the hospital, and that I had
been rushing off every night after the editing sessions to
visit him, so when I asked for an afternoon off to take Craig
home, she said it wouldn't be a problem.

In the three weeks Craig had been there, he had accumulated more plants, magazines and books than we were able to carry home, but he insisted on taking it all. I got Craig down to the street and then made two more trips with all of his stuff. I loaded Craig and his cargo into the first cab that would stop. I can only imagine what we looked like – Craig, uncertain on his feet, with a bunch of Mylar helium "Get Well" balloons tethered to his wrist by multicolor ribbons, and me with this look of grim determination on my face, holding a faded azalea and waving at anything yellow that passed by, with three shopping bags and a gym bag scattered about at our feet.

It was a warm day for March, the first hint of spring we'd had after a particularly dismal, messy winter. I was grateful that we weren't trying to do this in the rain.

Craig needed to lie down as soon as we got back to his apartment. I hadn't been there since the piano had been delivered. Craig had called the super and told him to let them leave it wherever it would fit, and the delivery men, noting the condition of the rest of the apartment, decided that the small alcove between the front door and the kitchen was the best place for a piano. We had to squeeze past it in order to get through the front door or to walk from the bed to the bathroom, but until Craig could get his friend from the chorus to give me a hand with it, it had to stay where it was.

Once Craig was settled, he handed me a stack of prescriptions and some money, and asked me if I'd have them filled for him.

He was asleep when I got back, and didn't hear me come into the apartment. I put all of his prescriptions on the night table, although there wasn't much room thanks to his crystal collection. When he woke up, I asked him if I could leave for a little while to get some things at home, and he said that would be fine, that he just wanted to sleep.

I packed a change of clothes for work, and then left a note for Anthony telling him where I'd be. When I got back to Craig's apartment, he was up, sitting in bed watching TV.

"Hi there," he said, barely glancing away from the set.

"You're up."

He had changed into a pair of shorts and a T-shirt.

"Yeah. I just needed a nap, I guess. Do you think I could ask you a favor?"

"Sure."

"If I gave you some more money, could you run down to the grocery store and get some milk and some ginger ale, and a couple of other things? I made a list. There's nothing in the house."

I took the list and the money and left the apartment. I went down the stairs, which were just opposite his door, rather than wait for the ancient elevator, which always took forever anyway.

When I got back, he was on the phone, so I went into the kitchen and, maneuvering around the piano, put everything away. Then I sat down on the bed with a container of yogurt for dinner, pretending I cared about the story on *Entertainment Tonight*. Raquel Welch was plugging her latest TV movie, making yet another futile bid to be taken seriously as an actress.

Craig ended the call and said to me, "That was Danny, my boss. He wanted to know if the computer was up yet. He's going to send someone from the office on Sunday to get it going. By the way, can you use an attaché case? I got one free with the computer stand, and I have one just like it already. If you want it, it's yours."

"Sure," I said. I didn't really want it, but I thought I'd hurt his feelings if I refused. I could always use it for client meetings. His attention shifted back to the TV screen and a clip from Raquel's new movie. I finished the yogurt and got up to rinse out the container.

"Do you want anything? Ginger ale or water?"

"No, thanks," he said, eyes still glued to the screen.

Now what was this all about? Was he mad at me? I tried to imagine what I could have done.

The silence continued until bedtime. I went into the bathroom to wash up and brush my teeth, and came out to find all the lights out. The TV was still going, and Craig was under the covers, propped up on pillows. Now he was watching *L.A. Law*.

"Why don't you get into bed," he said.

I climbed in next to him, and after ten minutes of being ignored, rolled over and tried to sleep. *L.A. Law* ended and I heard the local news announcer do the lead-in for the night's show. Reagan was facing more criticism over the Iran-Contra affair. I heard Craig mutter, "Asshole!" at the president and snap off the TV with the remote. He swallowed a handful of pills and turned off the lamp. If he had moved any farther away from me, he would have fallen out of the bed. I wasn't expecting hot sweaty sex, but it would have been nice to sleep in his arms – or to have him even acknowledge the fact that I was there. I would have been happy if he had just said "Good night."

One of his pills must have been a sedative, because he seemed to drift off immediately. I kept moving around trying to find a comfortable spot in the bed. I couldn't believe he had just spent two thousand dollars on a piano – money he didn't have in the first place – instead of getting himself a decent bed. With his back in such bad shape, you'd think it would have been a priority. If it had been me, I would never have spent two thousand dollars on a piano unless it was made by Serta and I could also sleep on it.

I fell asleep sometime after midnight – only to be awakened by a phone call at two in the morning from some heavy breather who kept saying Craig's name between moans. Craig didn't even wake up. Whatever those pills he took were, I wanted some.

I lay there and watched the digital clock face click from two to three to four, before falling asleep again – to be awakened by the alarm what felt like seconds later.

I got out of bed and stubbed my toe on the piano as I made my way into the kitchen. I sliced one of the bran muffins I had picked up the night before and put it in the toaster. I knew I should have planned on leaving from my own apartment. I guess I'd had this vision of the two of us having a cozy breakfast together.

I ate in the kitchen, using the piano as a counter, and wondered what kind of person had no table and chairs in his apartment. How could he eat? Did he always sit on the bed? It must have been fun with soup.

I moved to the bathroom to shower and shave. When I was done drying my hair, I came out to get into my clothes. Craig was up and the TV was on.

"Could I have a glass of water, MG? I have to take my pills." He barely looked at me. What happened to the guy who kept making me climb into his hospital bed and wouldn't let go of me? I handed him the glass. He said, "You certainly got out of bed in a hurry this morning."

I lied and blamed work, adding that I was feeling guilty about missing the half-day yesterday, and wanted to get in early in case there was a problem. I must not have sounded too convincing, because he asked me what was bothering me.

"Nothing. I just didn't sleep very well."

"Can you come back again tonight?"

"After the gym. I'll be here around nine. Is that okay? Do you want me to come earlier?"

"I don't want to inconvenience you," he said, a little sarcastically, I thought. "Get here when you get here."

"Well, I mean, you don't have to wait for me to eat, if you don't want to."

"No, I'll wait. Tell you what. Get a pizza on your way up. Just call when you're coming. Take the keys." He started opening vials and spilling pills into the palm of his hand.

I finished dressing and got my things together.

"Well, I'm ready to leave," I said, giving him his cue to say something romantic and reassuring that would make me think I was imagining all this.

"'Bye."

It wasn't what I was waiting to hear.

I called Irene as soon as I got into work and told her what had happened.

"That jerk!" she said.

"I don't know what this is all about. He acted like I was the night nurse or something. No hug, no kiss, no thanks. Maybe I misunderstood him in the hospital."

"Or he changed his mind. It wouldn't be the first time."

"I wish you hadn't said that."

"Why not?"

"Because I'm thinking the same thing."

"Oh, Lambiekins. Why do you always find the shits?"

"I don't know, Blanche. Maybe he's just tired or something. Maybe I'm overreacting and being childish."

"I wouldn't say expecting a good-night kiss from your boyfriend on his first night home from the hospital was being childish. Especially not when you spent the last three weeks dragging your ass uptown with ice cream and magazines and doing his laundry and getting him to and from the toilet so he wouldn't fall down."

She had a point. "What are you going to do about it?"

"I told him I was coming back tonight with a pizza. But I'm not going to stay, that's for sure. Not unless he greets me at the door in his underwear, smirking."

Craig did not greet me at the door, nor was he smirking when I let myself in with dinner. He took one look at me and said, "Pizza! Yum!" and got up for some plates.

"Where should I put the box?"

"Put it on the bed."

I could see that the oil from the pizza was already penetrating the bottom of the box, so I found a newspaper and put it on the bed first, then put the box down on top of it and hoped for the best.

He turned down the TV volume, which I thought was significant progress, and sat down on the bed opposite me. He handed me a plate and a couple of paper towels, and opened the box. "You have no idea how good this smells after the food I've been eating for the past three weeks," he said, plowing in. As he finished his first slice, he said, "I want to ask you something."

"Okay." Here it comes, I thought.

"When I was in the hospital, did you meet my boss, Danny? I talked to him today and he asked how you were, and I didn't remember that you had met."

"You don't remember? He came up last Sunday with a Key Lime pie. I had a piece, Danny had a piece, and you ate the rest. You said it tasted better than the ones your stepmom used to make."

"I don't remember meeting his lover either, but he said they came up together once."

I wondered if he remembered all the conversations we had had about giving us a second chance. I was beginning to doubt it.

He got up and pulled the attaché case out of the closet.

"You forgot this when you left this morning." He put it next to my backpack, adding, "Make sure you take it tomorrow."

We ran out of things to say to each other before we ran out of pizza. I had had enough, and when he said he was finished, I took the remaining slices into the kitchen, wrapped them in foil and put them in the refrigerator. Then I folded up the greasy box and put it into the garbage.

Craig had propped himself up in bed again and was staring at the TV. I came out of the kitchen and stood at the foot of the bed and said, "I'm thinking about shaving off my moustache and all my hair and getting a bunch of biker tattoos."

"Mmmm. Okay," he answered absently.

I sat on the bed and started putting on my sneakers. During a commercial break, he said to me, "You're awfully quiet tonight. What's going on inside that head?"

"I don't know, Craig," I said. "I just don't know what we have here. It doesn't seem to matter to you whether I'm here or not."

"It matters a great deal."

"It doesn't seem that way to me. The TV hasn't been off one minute. You hardly talk to me, except to ask for a glass of water."

He sat up and hit the bed with a fist. "I won't have all this guilt laid on me!"

"I'm not trying to make you feel guilty. Craig, we're sleeping in the same bed, and you don't even touch me? How am I supposed to interpret that? All I wanted was a little hug last night. You could have driven a truck between the two of us."

"I happen to have a lot on my mind right now. I tried to lie still last night so you could get some sleep. If you wanted me to hug you, you should have said so. I knew you were bent out of shape about something this morning, but I let it go. Next I'm going to hear about all the money you spent on me while I was in the hospital, right? I never asked you for anything, Michael. I don't even know what you're doing here."

Nor did I at that point. I felt like he had hit me instead of the bed. Obviously, I had been wrong about him again. Whatever he wanted, it wasn't to be my lover.

"Listen," I said. "I'm tired and I think I'd better sleep in my own bed tonight." I got up and grabbed my backpack and coat and headed for the front door, leaving his house keys on top of the piano as I squeezed by. I knew I'd never be back. I was at the door, struggling with the third lock, when I heard him say from behind me, "Here."

"I can do it myself," I said, thinking he meant he was going to help with the lock, but when I turned, he had the attaché case in his hands.

"Don't forget this."

As I pulled the door open, he thrust the case at me from his side of the piano. "I don't want it tonight," I said. "I just want to go home. I'll get it next time."

If I waited for the elevator, he'd follow me out into the hall and I'd be cornered. The last thing I wanted was a big scene, so I opted for the stairs. I had made it halfway down to the landing, when he leaned over the railing above me and shouted, "Take it, or it's going in the trash!"

I turned on the landing and continued down. The attaché case hit the stairs behind me.

"It can stay there!" he shouted.

I just kept moving. Before I knew it, I was on Ninth Avenue. I stopped at a pay phone and called Anthony. "Please be home," I whispered. He picked it up on the fourth ring.

"Hi, it's Michael."

"What's wrong, kiddo?"

"I just walked out on Craig," I said, my voice breaking. "Let me tell you about it when I get home. I just wanted to make sure you were there."

I tried to remember how much change I had from the pizza. I knew I had at least five or six singles, so I hailed the first cab I saw heading downtown and went home.

"How could I have been so stupid, Anthony? Nothing's changed."

"But he told you he wanted you back."

"It was all a lot of hooey. I should have known better than to believe it. I think what upsets me most is that he turned it around so I'm the bad guy here. What is this? I get punished for caring about him? I liked him a hell of a lot better when he was on drugs. At least he was in touch with his emotions."

"He'll probably call and apologize tomorrow."

"He's not going to apologize, Anthony, because he doesn't think he did anything wrong. And if he did and I went back to him after this little display, then I'd deserve what I got. God! If I'm not the prize horse's ass of the decade, then I don't know who is."

"Well remember that, then, and don't be hurt."

"I'm just so angry at myself for falling for his line of crap again. I should have figured it all out when I saw that piece of paper taped up to the mirror in his bathroom listing his goals. There was no Number Three about some-one to share his life with."

"You're better off without him. Craig was just as bad for you as Vic was for me. Big, pretty and mean. Face it, darling, we both married hillbillies. Now what have you learned, Dorothy?"

"You've got the wrong Dorothy. Not Dorothy Gale, Dorothy *Parker*. The next time I'll know better than to put all my eggs in one bastard!"

I got the obligatory card from Craig two days later.

Dearest Michael,

I cannot begin to imagine how hurt you must be. I thought we were becoming friends again, but I guess you wanted something more than friendship from me — something I don't think I can give you.

I often wondered why you were being so attentive in the hospital, but it didn't dawn on me until after you left last night.

Obviously, I am not who you want me to be, and for that, I'm truly sorry.

I hope someday I can repay the debt I owe you, and that you'll be able to accept the gift.

Always,
Craig

"Yes! Always Craig!" I said aloud as I ripped it up.

27

Original And Cheese Flavor

Richard Eisenberg had spent his first few weeks at Malcolm keeping a surprisingly low profile. In a memo to the department, he asked us to bring in our portfolios so he could get to know our work. I'm sure I wasn't the only writer in Creative who had to call his headhunter to get his book back so Richard could inspect it.

I hadn't been having any luck with it anyway. I thought I had showcased my best work and some of my most creative spec pieces, but the headhunters I had shown it to were not terribly impressed. I had finally found one headhunter who grudgingly agreed to show my book around, but I still wasn't getting interviews. "The market's slow," she told me when I called to ask for it back. She politely suggested that I hang onto it, saying she had my résumé on file and that she'd call me.

Fran waddled around from office to office, collecting books and bringing them to Richard for his inspection. They were returned without comment.

One afternoon in early April, Fran called and said that Richard wanted to see Henry and me in his office. *Now.* I went to find Henry, and the two of us walked to Richard's office as if it were the last mile.

"This is like getting called to the principal's office," Henry said.

"It's worse. Do you think he's going to fire us?" I asked, hoping I was wrong.

"Maybe this is your last chance and he won't if you bring him some coffee," Henry offered.

"Yeah, but where will I find a chalice?"

After making us cool our heels in Newark for a couple of minutes, Richard summoned us into his office. He turned to us from a video monitor on a cart, looking grim.

"Production just sent me a copy of the two spots you did for Lakeland Labs." I thought he was going to spit at us. "I have to say that these are the worst spots I have seen in my entire career. You've certainly come a long way from your secretarial days, Michael."

"Richard," I said, trying to stick to the topic and ignore the insult, "we didn't want to do these spots. The client made us."

"Doing what the client wants is no excuse for bad work. This handruff spot is awful, and the nail and hand thing is worse. It's offensive."

Henry said quietly, "Richard, did you know that Michael and I cut a different version of that spot? The client would barely look at it, and it was a hundred times better. I'd like to show it to you. Maybe if you saw it, you could convince them to go with it."

He held up a hand to stop him. "Forget it. I'm killing this whole strategy. As much as I'd like to, I can't stop the handruff commercial. It's an existing campaign. But this other crap will never see the light of day as long as I'm here."

I thought he was warming up to fire us. "Richard," I tried, "it's not like this work didn't pass by Howard first."

"Well, maybe that's why Howard isn't here anymore."

He smiled, suddenly deciding to play Mr. Nice Guy. "Listen, the last thing I want to do is start pointing fingers and slapping wrists and getting off to a bad start with my people. I've seen your books, and I think you both have some talent. You just aren't getting very good direction. That's all going to change. Let's just say that these commercials are in the past now. And it will never happen again."

I could feel the sweat running down my sides. It was an ordeal, standing there watching him smile that barracuda smile, knowing he had probably made up his mind to fire us the first chance he got, citing work we never wanted to do as an accurate picture of our abilities.

"What are you two working on right now?"

"We have a couple of scripts for Tinolate Athlete's Foot spray in the running," I said.

"'Our success is measured in feet?'" he said, throwing the campaign line back at me with a sneer. God, he was more smug than ever!

"It's a pool-out," I explained, quickly adding, "but I didn't write that line." The enormously talented Ralph Graham had, as a matter of fact. I wanted to steer Richard toward Ralph's office and tell him to go pick up one of Ralph's baseball bats and beat *him* up with it instead of going after me.

"Okay, just so I know what's going on. We're going to do a little reorganizing around here, and I need to know who's on what. That's it, gentlemen. Thanks for coming by."

Like two first-time offenders, we were turned back on the street after promising not to transgress again. We went down to Jo's office and told her what Richard had said.

"Oh, my dears! How *awful*. Well, I can tell you this much, I think I know what he's up to on Total Hand Treatment. He'll find a campaign he hates, kill it, then do

something else and save the day. That was a fairly old trick
when I started in this business two hundred years ago. It's
just your bad luck that he decided to pick on your spot. A
couple of weeks from now, it would have been too late."

"But now he's got us labeled as a couple of hacks," I
said.

"Now, sweetie pie, everyone knows those commercials weren't your idea. Let Richard go fight with Tom.
Your spot is exactly what he asked for, and I'd like to see
Richard wrestle it out of Tom's chubby little hands. It
should be a very interesting clash of the Titans."

"Cripes! Every time I think things can't get worse
around here, someone comes along to show me just how
wrong I can be. Why didn't I just get his coffee the first
time around so he wouldn't hate me now? I'd introduce
him to Casper the Ghostly Friend if I knew who he was. I'd
even buy him a couple of gift certificates."

"It'll be fine, Michael, I promise you. I'll speak to
Richard myself. I'll get him to look at the alternate spot the
two of you did, and he'll change his mind."

Jo did her best with Richard. She was granted an audience,
brought our recut version of the Total Hand Treatment
commercial and did a five-minute promo for Henry and
me. It didn't work. He wanted to do a completely new
commercial himself.

I saw it on TV months later – an incredibly pretentious
thing with close-up shots of hands and bunches of Birds of
Paradise and harp music and a breathy female announcer
and lots of cuts to title cards with one word of copy
describing the product. Conceptually, it wasn't that far
away from "Tulip" – the commercial we showed in our first
presentation. But how Richard got Tom to agree to produce this arty confection, I'll never know.

The handruff disaster hit the airwaves May first. Lakeland must have got a bargain from the three networks, because they ran the damn spot day and night. I couldn't escape it. And when people at the agency mentioned to me that they had seen the commercial, it was always with a note of sarcasm. I started telling people I'd show them the dent on the side of my head where the client pressed the gun while I wrote it.

My favorite comment came from Rose one afternoon when she called me at work just to check in — and complain a little about Marco.

"Hi, Rose. What's up?"

"Don't ask. I just had another big fight with your brother on the phone."

"What now?"

"What else? The wedding. I wish they'd elope already!"

"What happened?" I asked, not really wanting to hear the answer, and knowing Marco would probably call later with his version of the same story.

"He started in again about changing the menu for the reception."

"Eighty-sixed the loaves and fishes, did he?"

"Don't be fresh, Mikey. He and Carla got it into their heads that they can change whatever they want. I told them they shouldn't, but why should they listen to me? I'm only paying for half of it. He's so damn bossy lately. I'm not gray under the Clairol for nothing."

"Rose, why don't you just stop arguing with him and letting him get to you?"

"I don't know. If I live through this thing it'll be a miracle. He came home this weekend — it was a disaster. He borrowed my car and went and worked out at the high school. I wasted the whole damn day waiting for him to come back and got nothing done. So after dinner, your father drove me to the drugstore to pick up a couple of things. Meanwhile, your brother came home and decided to do his laundry. He went downstairs and ran the machine just for those little red shorts of his and a shirt and two socks, and turned on every damn light in the house on the way, and left them all burning when he went back upstairs to his room. We got back, the house was lit up like Luna Park. Does he think I have stock in Long Island Lighting? I very nicely asked him to remember to turn off the lights he wasn't using, and he got furious and told me to stop picking on him. Now, was I wrong? What am I, a cigar-store Indian? I have feelings, too."

"Rose, don't get me started on this again. He's my brother and I wish we were closer, but he doesn't care about any of us. He treats you like dirt, and you can't even see it. You have this image of him as David Nelson, model boy. Well, he's not, and it's about time you realized that."

She sighed. "On top of everything else, I went to Bloomingdale's in Garden City yesterday to see if I could find something to wear to this damn wedding and everything I tried on made me look like Two-Ton Tony Galento. Oh, well. There isn't a hell of a lot I can do about any of it anyway. Some days I can accept it all and I'm fine, and some days I just feel sorry for Rosie. What can I tell you? So what's with you, anyway?"

"Not much. At least nothing good."

"You sound depressed. Is this still about Craig?"

"No, it's about work."

"I don't know. When I was your age, I had bigger problems than you do. I didn't have time to be depressed."

"I'm sorry, Rose. I want a refund on life. It doesn't live up to advertiser's claims."

"Life isn't fair, Mikey."

"Yeah, I know. Sinatra had a hit with 'New York, New York' even though he crucified the lyrics and it was Liza's first. If life were fair, *Liza* would have had the hit with it. Instead she's in and out of rehab. Life's not fair, I get it. But a joke's a joke, already."

"You need to get out of that place, that's all. Incidentally, I saw your commercial again last night. What's so terrible about it, anyway?"

"I don't know," I said.

"Well, I have news for that high-powered man, whoever he is, your new boss."

"Richard."

"Richard. If Richard thinks people sit around paying attention to that stuff on TV, he's crazy. If I want to buy Wisk, I want to buy Wisk, and no amount of singing and dancing is going to make me buy Tide."

"Richard thinks we're creating art here, that we do something sacred. As if no one knows he did those Palermo Pizza Pronto commercials at his last agency."

"Now *there's* a stupid commercial. I wouldn't order one of those if I was starving to death and they delivered it on a silver tray you could keep. At least your commercial is quiet and doesn't hurt my ears. She sits there like a nice lady and at least she's pretty. The flakes falling off her skin is a little stupid, if you ask me, but all right. She's a cute blonde. She's polite and she doesn't scream like that nut who goes crazy selling TV sets. And that's my opinion, and not just because I'm your mother."

When I repeated the conversation for Irene, she laughed and said, "You know, you are your mother's son! No one else could have had you."

28
50% More!

I hadn't had an assignment since I'd finished the Skin Therapy spots, and I was getting a little nervous about it. I went to see Fran, and told her that my schedule was light and that I'd be happy to help out wherever I could. She was engrossed in a lunchtime lasagna feast and doing a crossword puzzle, and barely acknowledged my presence.

I told Ellen the same thing, and she spoke vaguely about something fun coming up, which I began to sense was going to be her opportunity to fire me. She said she was waiting to see what happened after Richard announced his reorganization plan.

I got tired of sitting in my office with nothing to do, so I started working on *Dial Nine to Get Out* again. At least I looked busy. People saw me come in, sit down at the typewriter and start pounding away, and assumed I was doing something Malcolm-related. I was still ambivalent about the play, but as long as I had so much free time, I was determined to take advantage and finish it. I was rewriting a monologue for the third time that afternoon when my friend Frank called.

"'Do you always watch for the longest day in the year

and then miss it?'" he asked, like Mia Farrow in *The Great Gatsby*.

"Is that today?"

"No, but I like to say it. Want to go out for dinner? Billy's out of town and I don't feel like cooking."

We sat at an outdoor table at the Riviera Cafe, watching the passing parade of men. The conversation drifted around, as it always did when I had too much wine, to being coupled.

"Is it my imagination," I asked, "or are there more older men out with younger guys lately? It seems like everywhere I turn, I'm confronted with May/December Romance."

"I think you're imagining it," Frank said, picking up his cheeseburger and biting into it.

"I'm not. It keeps happening. I'll be out on the street wondering if I'm ever going to meet someone and I look up and there they are: Older Man with Generic Younger Boy in tow. I keep thinking it's a preview of my future walking toward me. And since it's a little late for me to be playing Younger Boy, I don't have to work too hard to figure out which part I *do* get. It's like all these couples are a sign or something."

"You think everything is a sign. If they play 'Moonlight Serenade' on the radio while you're trying to solve some problem, you take it as a sign."

"I don't do that."

"Yes, you do. Sometimes it just means they're playing 'Moonlight Serenade' on the radio, Michael. I don't think heaven sends us messages via the Glenn Miller Orchestra."

"Okay. The constant appearance of all these couples isn't a sign. But what if that *is* what's going to happen. What if I'm not destined to meet anyone until I'm, say, fifty? Or worse, sixty! Do you realize that means my next lover hasn't even been born yet? What am I supposed to do until he comes along?"

Frank started to laugh. Unfortunately, he was also in the middle of a swallow, and the laughing quickly turned to choking.

"Are you okay? Do you want me to Heimlich you?"

"I'm fine," he said. "Oh. I'm sorry. Your delivery was great, if ill-timed."

"I can't help it. I feel like time is running out for me. I've reached my peak and it's never going to be any better than it is right now. My hair is starting to turn gray, and I can see lines starting in my face. And I've had all these false starts that led nowhere. First Tim, then Craig. I'm thirty years old, and – "

"Michael! You are *twenty-nine*. Don't say 'thirty' yet. You are not *thirty*."

"I'll be thirty at the end of the month. I may as well get used to saying 'thirty.' I'm in my thirtieth year. Besides, twenty-nine sounds so phony. Like someone who's already in his thirties trying to buy back some time."

"I'm sure lots of people who are twenty-nine say they're twenty-nine. I said I was twenty-nine until the day I turned thirty. Don't be in such a big hurry."

"I can't *wait* to turn thirty," I said, with a little too much conviction. "I mean, it actually gives me some hope. When I look back at my twenties, you know what comes to mind? Being poor and lonely."

"So what's going to change in your thirties – being rich and lonely?"

"My thirties represent something new. I have big expectations. I was always a late bloomer. Everything happened to me long after it happened to everyone else. Getting a driver's license. Shaving. Sex. I ran out of hope for my twenties before I was halfway through them. But I can still meet someone in my thirties. I can find a better job in my thirties. I'd settle for finishing my play in my thirties.

But it's over for my twenties, so goodbye. Give it up. I'd like to believe it's all going to come together now."

Frank and I let a few moments pass while we turned our attention to our plates. "Maybe it's time to start dating younger men," he said.

This was not a new thought. I was out walking one day, and saw an extremely handsome young man walking toward me. I smiled. He smiled. I looked back. He looked back. I kept walking. I am an idiot. It was just that I couldn't get over how young he was. He couldn't have been more than twenty-two *and I was almost thirty*. I realized that I was now as old as some of my first dates were. And at the time, I thought thirty was so *old*. Can just eight years make such a difference? Suddenly, everyone looked so much younger to me. Even the cops on the street looked like babies. Not to mention the firemen.

"I don't know. I always liked them older," I said.

"Well, imagine dating a younger man."

"That's hard. Twenty is too young for me. Much too young. We won't have anything in common. I doubt if he'll know who Joni Mitchell is, much less Irene Dunne."

"*You* knew who Irene Dunne was at twenty."

"Honey, I knew who Irene Dunne was at *six*. But I am not the world," I said, adding, "'you think I'm a fool?'" in my best Irene Dunne voice. "Besides, a twenty-year-old probably looks at someone my age and sees a great big neon sign flashing overhead that says: DISEASED. Maybe twenty-seven. But considering my ill-fated career, he'll probably be making more money and be better established than I am, and I'll end up resenting him for it. We'll come to a bad end, I'm sure."

"You know, you don't answer questions, Michael, you devise scenarios."

"Well, we're talking hypothetical here, aren't we? I can't help it if I've seen too many movies. I always like to tack on an ending right out of *Summertime*."

"You still haven't answered the question."

"To answer your question, then, Frank Donovan, I don't see myself with a younger man. Someone my age or about five years older, yes. But not younger. If I dated someone younger, it would make me feel like I was supposed to be the more adult of the two. I don't want someone looking up at me all the time like he's about to say, 'Jeepers, Wally!' Anyway, I think I'm a lousy role model for Gay Youth of Today. I don't know too many thirty — twenty-nine-year-old men in advertising who still have the word 'junior' in their job title."

"Michael, you had an unconventional career path, that's all. You'll catch up."

"Maybe. Sometimes I wonder."

The waiter cleared the table and brought us two more glasses of wine.

"Would you want to be twenty again?" Frank asked.

"Twenty *now*? Christ, no! To be coming out in the middle of this nightmare would make what I went through look like a Technicolor musical. Being gay was just a leap of faith then, not the Red Badge of Courage. What I would like is to go back to when I was twenty, only this time knowing that things would work out. Not specifics. Not knowing I should put every cent I had in gold or something like that, but knowing that I would turn out okay. That I'd come to New York and make friends and discover that I liked myself and enjoyed being gay. None of that seemed possible when I was coming out. But to be twenty now? I can't imagine it. At least I remember life before AIDS, even if I did show up at the end of the party, and I was more of an observer than a participant. Maybe there's one thing I would change, and don't laugh at me."

"I won't laugh."

"I wish I had been to the baths just once. I never went.

I was just too insecure. I figured no one would touch me because I didn't have muscles. And now it's too late. It's all gone."

"Well, I never went either. And then I met Billy."

"God, you're so lucky. I can't imagine what it's like to have been with someone for nine years."

"I feel blessed, Michael. I mean, it's true what they say, the great thing about a lover is that you're never alone in bed, and the bad thing is that you're never alone in bed. But I have to admit, I've always wondered about the baths, too."

"Who knows? Sometimes you learn a lot more from what you miss than what you experience."

"Is that today's profundity?"

"You know what I mean. When I was twenty and finally sure that I was gay, I spent a lot of time sitting home thinking I should be out doing things and meeting men and being liberated. And all those nights I thought I was missing out on something, maybe all I missed out on was a virus. Is that a horrible thing to say?"

"It is, but I understand."

"It was all such a crapshoot – who gets sick and who doesn't – so 'wrong place, wrong time.' I have moments when I feel guilty that I'm healthy. I still don't understand it, and I can't, *I can't* sort it out. Why is David Summers dead? Or Rob or Bill or Bob from Jersey or David, that sweet, adorable painter from L.A. I met at Julius'? And how many others? And the rest of the world doesn't even seem to notice. All I can come up with is that life is shorter than we ever imagined. Who knows what's going to happen to any of us? The one thing I intend to do with my thirties is not waste them, like I did with my twenties. There's no time for all this bullshit that's been preoccupying me for the past ten years. My career, my career, me, me, *me*. It's excess baggage. I don't want to wake up one morning and realize my whole life's behind me. I have to focus on more important things and the rest of it, yo heave ho and over the rail."

"Such as?"

"Well, I don't know. I mean, where was I when all this started happening? What did I do? A couple of protests at *The New York Post* don't count. Marching in the Pride Parade or a candlelight vigil isn't activism. I want to find something to do that matters. All this focus on my career is just – it's as if I'm trying to distract myself from AIDS. Or hide from it. I want to volunteer for something."

"Go to GMHC. They need volunteers."

"*Craig* is at GMHC. Maybe the PWA Coalition."

"Or GLAAD. You're a writer. Go work for them."

"That's a good idea. I hadn't really thought about them. All of this is good. I need to find something that isn't selling hand cream on TV, that's for sure."

"And then what?"

"Finish writing the damn play and find a man!"

"Now you're talking!" Frank said, lifting his glass. "Here's to your thirties, Michael."

While I was still grateful for the time to write, the novelty of having nothing to work on every day started making me a little paranoid. I was convinced that they were going to fire me, and my joke about being on a Malcolm fellowship while I finished my play had begun to wear thin.

Richard still hadn't announced the promised reorganization, and the only news he had for us came after he'd roped in a new client: the tobacco giant Raleigh Brands and their new cigarette, Cachet, to launch.

Jo advised us not to panic, saying she'd been through dry spells before, and that as upsetting as it was to sit there day after day with nothing to work on, it was better than being unemployed.

But a few days later, she called me and told me to come down to her office. When I got there, she said, "Come on in, and close the door."

I did, and took one of the chairs in front of her desk.

"I found out something I think you should know so it doesn't hit you like a ton of bricks."

"They're going to fire me."

"No. I didn't want to say anything until now, because I was hoping I could fix it, but I can't. They're putting you in Gwen Hammond's group when they announce the reorganization."

"They can't."

"That's what I said. Believe me, sweetheart, I've been in Fran's office and Ellen's trying to make them understand, but they don't want to hear it. Now this part is strictly *entre nous*. I told them the two of you *detest* each other, and that it was plain bad chemistry. The round Miss Rotunda just waved me away and said, 'It's out of my hands! There's nothing I can do about it.' I think you're going to have to go talk to Richard yourself."

"Where are they putting you?"

"You'll find this amusing. They want to start two groups working on Cachet cigarettes, so I've got one group and your friend Gwen has the other. I have to share an account with that witch. We've already had one meeting, and she has the impression that I'm reporting to *her*. I'm ready to slap her into next week."

"Who's getting the Lakeland business, then?"

"It's staying with Ellen. Tinolate is going to Gwen and she'll have Ralph Graham supervise it and report to her. It was his account to start with. And he's keeping Muscovy. That's why they're moving you back into Gwen's group. You'll be reporting to Ralph. And Gwen. You've written for both accounts. It makes sense on paper."

"So did New Coke. But the thought of going back to Gwen. And Muscovy. And Ralph agreed to this?"

"Ralph does as he's told, but I'm sure he isn't happy about it."

"Is there any chance I can stay with you?"

"I would love that, Michael, but they won't listen to me. Ellen doesn't want to get involved. I think it was her idea, if you want to know the truth. I think Richard asked her what account she wouldn't mind giving up, and she picked Tinolate and they gave it to Gwen. Can you blame her?"

"Where's Henry going? He's been my partner for over a year."

"Ellen's keeping him in her group. I'm not sure who they're partnering him with now, though."

"Do you have anything else besides the cigarette?"

"No. There's talk going around about pitching Chanel, since Richard used to work on it, but that won't happen for a long, long time. And if we do get it, do you think Richard's going to let me work on it after the Total Hand Treatment disaster? It got back to me that he thinks I'm 'old hat.' I'm lucky he's willing to *give* me cigarettes."

"I just can't believe this is happening, Jo. I always swore I would never work on a cigarette account, and here I am, ready to go beg Richard to put me on one. Liquor was bad enough. I don't think I can do it."

"Michael, did I ever tell you about Marty Blumberg? Terrific writer, hysterically funny man. Then one day, they put him on the Lufthansa account. This was back around 1970. Now, Marty was the son of Holocaust survivors who came here after the war. He tried to do his best on the account, but it just wasn't working. First, he started slipping and kept calling the airline 'Luftwaffe' in meetings with the client, and you can just imagine how that went over. He begged and begged to be taken off the account, and they wouldn't do it. He was doing great work, the client loved him and everyone was happy except Marty. Finally one day, I guess he just snapped. He went into a presentation and gave the client an ad he'd done with a night shot of Big Ben and a headline that said: 'Who better than a German pilot to find London at night?' Then he walked out and we lost the account. You remind me of Marty in a lot of ways. You either work on what they give you or you don't. "

"I hate the whole idea of working on a cigarette."

"Sweetie pie, I don't like it either, but I like being out of work even less. I went to Richard and asked for something to do, and he put me on this. If he put me on a campaign promoting forced child labor in China, I'd have to hold my nose and do it! I put in twenty-eight years with this wretched company so that I could have a decent retirement, and unfortunately a lot of times it meant parking my moral objections to things out on Lexington Avenue on my way into the office. You can find another job at your age a lot easier than I can at mine. I made this deal and I'm stuck with it. You have to decide what you need to do."

I stopped in Lisa's office on my way back from talking to Jo. She had been idle for a month, too, and had spent her time working on her portfolio. When she confided in me about looking for another job, I asked her which headhunters she was using, and she started running down her list. I had seen the same ones, and agreed with her that they weren't very interested in junior people.

"I have found one woman I really, really like," Lisa told me. "Do you want her name?"

"If you wouldn't mind, I'd appreciate it. I mean, she might be sending our books out for the same jobs."

Lisa said she wouldn't mind at all, and gave me the phone number.

29
If Pain Persists, See Your Doctor

Marybeth Flynn was a big, earth-mother type, somewhere in her late fifties. She used a corner of her Upper East Side living room as an office, and her shelves were filled with advertising reference books and directories.

I went up to see her one evening after work. She invited me in, shooed two Maine Coon cats off a chair and handed me a glass of ice water. We started talking about my background and where I wanted to go.

"It's not hopeless, but I just want to tell you up front it won't be easy," she said, glancing at my résumé. "You've been writing for how long?"

"Three years. I've been at Malcolm about six."

"That's a long time to be at any one shop."

"Well, I did other things there before I got a chance to write."

"Let's have a look." She picked up my portfolio and started leafing through it, making little sighs as she read each ad. "You have to take some of this stuff out. These are all one-shots. You have no campaigns in here."

She got farther back in the book to the section where I had put all my radio scripts and TV storyboards. She flipped through it quickly, saying, "This stuff has to go too. If it wasn't produced, no one is interested."

"That's all I have. My spec stuff is my best work. The commercials I *do* have, I wouldn't show under torture. The only halfway decent thing I've got is this test commercial for Homestead Acres Dairy Spread, and even that's been compromised."

"I can tell you right now, these spec scripts are worthless. If it hasn't been produced and it isn't on a cassette they can watch, they won't bother to read it."

"But, Marybeth, that's ridiculous. Everyone in this business knows that good work rarely gets bought. You'd think they'd be more interested in what was rejected!"

"That's the way it is, kid."

"Well, what am I supposed to do? Go out and get a quarter of a million dollars and produce a spot myself?"

"If they look at your spec work at all, it has to be brilliant. Frankly, there's nothing brilliant in this portfolio. You can write, but..."

"You mean to tell me that all of this work from three years of being employed as a copywriter is useless?"

"Basically. That's the trouble with all this packaged goods stuff. It's just sell, sell, sell. No big concept behind it. None of this work is special enough to make an agency want to see you. All of the hot shops steal people from other hot shops. They see something they like on TV or in print somewhere, and they find out who did it and call him up and make him an offer."

"Fine. Maybe I can get a job sweeping their lobbies. It's a union job, it's got to pay more than I'm making now."

"Don't get defensive, Michael. I'm just telling you that this work doesn't prove how talented you are. I get glimmers of it here and there, but no one has ever taken the time to show you what to do. Big agencies just throw you in the pool and let you flail around. Let's have a look at your commercial," she said, putting the videocassette into the machine. I couldn't look at the spot or Marybeth's face while she watched it. I watched the two cats playing on the rug instead.

When it was over, she said, "Yeah," as if it was confirmation of my lack of talent. "This looks like everything else that comes out of Malcolm. It's a little goofy and that's cute, but it's your basic Malcolm commercial."

She was depressing me, and it must have shown on my face. "It's not hopeless. I think you should take a couple of classes at the School of Visual Arts. Learn to conceptualize. And maybe a couple of marketing classes too. There aren't too many good ones – most of the people who should teach don't. But there are a couple, and I'll give you their names. Malcolm has tuition reimbursement, right?"

"Yes."

"Then you should take some classes. And you need to clean up your book. Throw out most of these ads for Muscovy – they really are junior work. And get rid of this other stuff. I want to see some really brilliant work in here. Find an art director you like and can work with, and do some ads after hours. You have an entire agency at your disposal – use it. You can set type and make your spec look as good as produced work. It won't take more than a year."

"A *year*? You just said they're not interested in spec work. I have to find something right away."

"Not with that book. It just isn't special enough. And I'm not saying this to be mean. I'm telling you because I'd like to see you get out of Malcolm as much as you would."

I left Marybeth's apartment and started walking toward the subway. Her words kept coming back to me. All the work, all the fighting and all the late nights had been for nothing. I wasn't special enough. At least somebody finally told me. Now I knew why wherever I left my portfolio, it was generally returned to me without comment. It never got me interviews.

I kept walking until I was home. There was no sign of Anthony. I took two of his Xanax, set the clock radio and got into bed. I didn't eat or brush my teeth or do anything other than take off my clothes. I kept thinking about what Marybeth said as I lay there waiting for the pills to kick in.

I was just starting to float off when the phone rang. I considered letting the machine answer it, but picked it up instead. It was Irene. It was one of the rare nights when she wasn't with Henry, and the first chance she'd had to call me in almost a week. She was actually calling to apologize for disappearing, but I stopped her, told her I had just taken two Xanax, and repeated most of what Marybeth had said. I almost made it through the story without crying.

"What are you going to do?"

"I'd like to go eat the rest of the Xanax, if you want to know the truth."

"Stop it, Michael. You know you can write."

"But no one else knows it. I can't get another job, and I can't stay where I am."

"I think it's time to do a little reassessing here. It's time to try something else."

"Maybe." I was getting drowsy.

"Michael, you've been flinging yourself against a brick wall for how long now? It would be a different story if you liked what you were doing, or were really turned on by the industry, but you hate it. To be working this hard for nothing at your age, and then to be told on top of it that you have no talent? What's the matter with these people?"

"You're right, you're right."

"Go temp until you figure it out. The money couldn't possibly be worse. It's probably better."

"It's just the idea of being a secretary again. That was the worst job of my life."

"Because you worked for pigs. And you thought if you

played the best little secretary in the world, they'd promote you because you were so eager, and you were miserable until they did. What do you have to prove this time around? Just go in, type all day, collect the money and come home and write your play. Michael? Are you there?"

"I have to get off now, Irene. I can't keep my eyes open."

"Are you okay?"

"I'm fine. Thanks for calling. I appreciate it."

"My poor lamb. Get some sleep. I'll talk to you in the morning."

"Okay. 'Night." I was barely able to hang up the phone.

Suddenly, it was morning and the radio was blaring a Palermo Pizza Pronto commercial. Some idiot in a phony-baloney-whats-a-you-name-a Italian accent was singing to the tune of *"La Donna è Mobile:"*

> *I wan-na pizza pie!*
> *Anchovy piled up high.*
> *And lotsa sau-seege,*
> *And pep-pa-rrron-eeee...*

I bolted up in bed and said out loud, *"Sauseege!* This is fucked! I may not be brilliant, Marybeth Flynn, but I can be just as mediocre as whoever wrote this crap, which I suspect was Richard Eisenstein!"

I was able to get an appointment with Richard that afternoon. He sat with his arms resting on the glass table. In front of him was a yellow legal pad and one sharpened pencil. There was nothing else visible in the office — not a scrap of paper, or a computer, or even the phone. The VHS cart was gone as well. I knew there was an inner office somewhere and I supposed that was where he worked. This, I imagined, was where he *created*.

"What can I do for you, Michael?" he asked, flashing his flawless smile.

Richard was a handsome man in a glossy way. His clothes were immaculate and expensive. He had his hair cut so often it never seemed to grow. His hands and nails were perfect. But there was something unreal about him, and somewhat sinister, and I imagined that beneath his hand-made suit and imported shirt lurked a leather harness. Hitchcock would have cast him as a suave movie mogul about to have his wife murdered or a corrupt mayor with an attic full of dark secrets.

"I understand I'm being moved back into Gwen's group, and I was wondering if we could talk about that."

"Sure we can. Nothing is final."

"I'd like to keep working with Jo Fuller if I can."

"Well, she's on Cachet now, Michael. It's not really a writer's account. If anything, I need to get some art directors on it."

"What about leaving me on the Lakeland business with Ellen?"

I was feeling very disloyal. While I loved Jo and wanted to continue to work with her, I couldn't face the idea of working on a cigarette account. I wasn't too sure Ellen even liked me. But she had the best accounts in the agency, and I had to get better work into my portfolio if I was ever going to get out of Malcolm. I could always ask to get back into Jo's group when she picked up another account and needed a writer.

"Michael, I have to tell you something you're not going to like hearing. When I started working with Tom on the new spot for Total Hand Treatment, he said he didn't want you on the account anymore. I can't risk upsetting them by putting you back on it. Gabrielle keeps threatening to take the business to Ogilvy."

"She's been saying that since we got the account. It's probably the first English sentence she learned. Do you take her seriously?"

"I take all my clients seriously," he said. "Tom doesn't think you listen. He doesn't like you and I can't risk losing this account. You seem to get on the wrong side of almost everyone you work with. When you were my secretary I thought you were arrogant and uncooperative. Fran Rotunda tells me that you and Gwen were constantly fighting. You may have been promoted, but you haven't changed."

"Everyone fights with Gwen. She just never got any of my ideas. And I can't believe she'd take me back after all we've been through. Or Ralph Graham, for that matter."

"This business is about favors and horse trading, Michael. Sometimes you have to take something you don't want in order to get something you do. And I need team players here. I have very definite plans about how I'm going to run this department. There's a lot of waste here and I want things lean and mean. You're too much of a rebel and, frankly, I don't know what I'm going to do with you. You can't work with Gwen. You don't want to work with Ralph. I can't put you back on Lakeland." He turned his palms upward and shrugged.

"How about just leaving me in Ellen's group for the time being. Maybe she can use me on one of her other accounts."

He sighed. "You can talk to her, Michael, but she agreed that putting you in Gwen's group made the most sense for now. I'm not all that impressed with your work so far, but see what Ellen thinks, and if she wants you back, we'll see what we can do."

It was too good to be true.

Ellen was in a terrific mood when I got to her office. *Adweek* had done a small feature on her latest campaign for Buick and had called it the best work they'd seen coming out of Malcolm this year. Personally, I didn't think that was such a rave, considering our latest batch of mediocre commercials, but Ellen was overjoyed.

"That's the third accolade for that campaign this week!" she said, pinning the article to the wall with the others. She had a bottle of champagne on ice and some plastic cups set up on her desk. "I love getting good reviews on work that comes out of my group, which, incidentally, you're out of."

I didn't know what to say. "Well," I stammered, "I may not be going into Gwen's group after all."

"Why not?" she snapped.

"I told Richard how much I liked you and admired the work you were doing, and that I felt I could learn a lot from you if I could stay in your group." I touched my nose involuntarily to see if it was growing. I couldn't believe I was standing there flattering Ellen to save my job.

"I have nothing for you, Michael. You can go talk to Gwen and if she wants to let you come back here, fine, but it's up to her."

"Ellen. Gwen hates me."

"She doesn't hate you. Michael. You hate her. She's willing to give you another chance, and frankly I don't know why."

Oh, my God, I thought to myself. Why don't you just clock me with a Clio and put me out of my misery?

I went back to my office and brooded for an hour. I had painted myself into a lonely corner at Malcolm. I had fought for good work that got killed and had practically been killed by the bad work that got produced, and with the exception of the spray butter commercial, I had nothing to show for any of it. I had no other job prospects on the horizon. What choice did I have? I picked up the phone and called Gwen and asked if she had a minute to talk, and she said to come to her office.

When I knocked on her door, she asked me in, and if she didn't seem happy to see me, at least she was cordial and told me to sit down.

"So, Richard said that you and Ralph would be supervising me now."

"Actually, I am supervising Ralph and he is supervising you. But for the moment, we're still trying to figure out what accounts to put you on. You've stepped on a lot of toes this year, mine especially. I suppose we could put you back on Tinolate, but I would have to get Ralph's thoughts on that first."

"What if they put me back in Ellen's group?"

"Ellen doesn't need more writers. I think I did her a favor by agreeing to take you off her hands."

"Okay, so if I'm staying in your group, is there any chance I could go back on Forster Foods? I think I'm really tapped out on Muscovy and Tinolate. At least Forster would be new products to work on. And Maxine and I hit it off."

"Oh, Maxine," she said with a dismissive wave of the hand. "And anyway, we already have a writer on Forster. Michelle is on it now."

"One writer for all those products?"

"Lean and mean, Michael. That's the way it's going to be around here from now on according to Richard. Lean and mean." She made a point of looking at her watch. "I'm not making any promises. I think it's safe to say I'm about as happy at having you back in my group as you are about being here. Anyway, I have to go into a meeting with Richard in a few minutes, so why don't we continue this some other time?"

I had told her I would never work with her again, and here I was. I had told her I would cut off my favorite part of my anatomy before I would work with her again, and here I was. I thought about apologizing and promising to behave from now on, but I just couldn't bring myself to do anything more than stand up and thank her for seeing me. It hadn't gone that well and groveling wasn't going to help.

I don't know why, but my eye fell on Gwen's blazer as I turned to leave. She had tossed it on the conference table instead of hanging it on the hook behind her door. Poking out from under it was a cake box from the Lexington Avenue Gourmet, and through a little patch of the cellophane window I could see part of a row of powdered donuts. And as sure as I was standing there, I knew that Gwen was Casper the cocaine dealer. I had no proof, but I was as certain that she was Casper as if I had just witnessed her making a cash sale in the stairwell. I just knew. It was amazing how many suspicions and unconscious observations could collide in my head in that half-second and suddenly all fit together and make perfect sense. And at the same moment, I also realized that Gwen saw what I was looking at, and knew that I had figured it out.

In that one afternoon, I had spoken to Richard and Ellen and Gwen, and all that I had learned was that no one had any idea what they were going to do with me, and no one particularly cared if I stayed at Malcolm or not. But as I left her office, one thing was clear: I knew now that Gwen would certainly make a case for firing me and Richard and Ellen wouldn't argue with her.

Jo continued working on Cachet. "Cachet. For people who have it!" went Gwen's campaign line. The client bought it, and Jo was forced to execute it, and that's when we started calling the brand "Cliché."

Gwen had surprised me and given me a Whatta Wheat coupon ad to write. Maybe it was just to throw me off the scent, or maybe it was just a piece of business that no one else wanted, but that's what she gave me and that's what I was working on the day I was fired.

We all knew it was coming. Karen started handing out envelopes one payday morning and ran out of checks before she ran out of people to distribute them to.

"Michael," she said, "there's no check for you or Jenny." Karen had been at Malcolm almost as long as I had, and we both knew what this meant.

Jenny stopped at my door, looking terrified. "Fran just called me to say she has my paycheck."

"She has mine too, I think. She just hasn't called yet."

"Oh, Michael. I *can't* get fired."

"It gets easier each time it happens to you, believe me. This makes twice for me."

Lisa rounded the corner and planted herself in my guest chair, holding her paycheck. "Shit!" she exhaled. "If they were going to fire me, the least they could have done was wait until fall. Who the hell wants to be out of work in the summer? No one ever does any hiring until September. I should have taken a share in that house in the Hamptons."

They fired ten people that day. All of the juniors except for the ones Fran had placed were cut, plus some senior people. And, if the grapevine was to be believed, this was only the first wave of executions.

I was given my regular salary plus vacation pay and a generous two-weeks severance. I figured I could pay June's rent and have enough left over to feed myself until July if I lived like Gandhi.

I don't know why, but my first reaction was to call Marco. As briefly as I could, I laid out the scenario.

"What did you expect, Michael? The writing's been on the wall for you since you started at that place. I don't know why you stayed so long."

"Frankly, neither do I. But I was wondering if maybe you knew someone at ABC I could talk to."

It slipped out, but why had I bothered? The line was silent for a long time, and I braced for him to tell me to go to hell.

"There's nothing I can do for you at ABC, Michael."

"Well, thanks, Marco," I said, interrupting him. At that point I just wanted to get off the phone.

"You want to let me finish my sentence, Michael?" he said. "A friend of Carla's just got a job in Creative Services over at HBO. I'll ask her tonight, I promise. Maybe she can talk to him about getting you some freelance work."

Now it was my turn for silence. Had he really just said that? "Thanks, Marco. You have no idea how much that would mean to me."

"Don't worry about it. I have to go now. Let me know if you need money."

We said goodbye. I hung up the phone, folded my check and stuck it in my pocket, grabbed my backpack and headed toward the elevator. There would be plenty of time later to tell everyone I was leaving. In fact, I knew they'd all find out before lunch. I was taking the rest of the day off. What more could they do to me?

I walked past the receptionist's desk. The person sitting there was either new or a temp, and was so engrossed in a personal phone conversation, she didn't even look up at me. I pressed the call button and waited for the whooshing noise of the elevator's approach. The company motto, "We Think Global," mocked me from the wall as it always had. I knew I had a Sharpie somewhere in my backpack. I reached in and found it, checked to make sure the receptionist was still distracted, and with an adrenaline-induced speed and boldness that shocked me, deftly added a scrawled "L Y" to the "Global" in the slogan and returned the pen to my backpack an instant before the elevator doors opened. I stepped aboard, smirking like Cary Grant, and managed not to laugh until after the doors slid shut.

Once I hit Lexington Avenue, I started walking, and when I found myself at Rockefeller Center, I went up to Irene's office.

"Lambie!" She got up from her desk and started walking to her office door.

"I just got fired."

"Oh, honey, I know. Henry called me." She hugged me, then pulled me inside and closed the door. "What did they say to you?"

"Oh, the usual thing – the agency isn't having a good year and they need to cut back on staff. They blamed it on losing Sparks Cola. I knew it was coming after I spoke to Gwen, but when she gave me that assignment, I was hoping maybe they had changed their minds. I was surprised Fran even attempted to soften the blow. Everyone knows this is just Richard cleaning house. 'Lean and mean…'"

"Maybe it's a good thing, Michael. You hated it there so much."

"But I wanted to get out on my own terms. I wanted to quit for a better job, not get shoved out onto the street. I don't even have a thousand dollars in the bank."

"What are you going to do?"

"I don't know. I can't think about it now. I'm going to go out to my parents' house for a couple of days and sleep. Then I'm giving myself a week off. I'm going to pretend I'm on vacation until after my birthday, and then I'll start looking for something else."

The next morning, I went into work with a shopping bag and collected all of my personal things. I rolled up my posters and took down my collection of Matt Norklun ads.

Jo came to my office and said she wished there was something she could do, adding, "I feel just awful about this, but I think it's going to work out for you. I called The Four Beautiful Girls Four and they might have some free-lance work for you in June. They want you to call them."

I thanked Jo for the lead. She wanted to take me out to lunch, but I told her I had to catch a train to Long Island. She understood, but made me promise to go out with her one day during the following week to celebrate my birthday.

30
New And Improved!

I walked home from the train station. It was a chilly afternoon for May, with a cloudless, brilliant blue sky. I passed
my grammar school – an old brick building from the
Thirties with white columns. I used to pretend it was the
Selznick Studio as I reluctantly trudged up to the front door
and another day of torment at the hands of Miss Strom and
her unpredictable temper. ("Miss Strom, the Atom Bomb,"
we used to sing when she was out of earshot.) The bell was
ringing to signal the end of the day and the kids came
charging out, eager to begin two days of freedom.

I felt so old as I watched them in their jeans and baseball jackets, with their books in backpacks. Rose used to
send me off to school in a white shirt and tie, with a little
leather schoolbag and my hair neatly combed into place. I
looked like a tiny accountant. But, I realized sadly, how
long ago that was – before space travel, the Beatles, and
programs "Brought to You in Living Color." I still remembered very clearly the August afternoon Joe took me by the
hand and showed me how to walk to school from our
house. It was only four blocks away, but it seemed like
miles to me.

Rose wasn't home, so I let myself in through the back door and took my bag up to my room. I had packed hastily, throwing an extra pair of jeans and some sweatshirts into the bag and little else. The one thing I made sure I took was the script for *Dial Nine to Get Out*. It was in much better shape, thanks to my weeks without an assignment. I had an ending for it now, I thought to myself, tossing the bulky package on my bed: Hero Gets Fired. I still didn't think it was very good, but at least I was close to finishing it. I had planned to reread it over the weekend and do some editing. I thought it would be a good time to concentrate, and try to figure out how much more work it needed.

Rose was late getting home. She had decided to make a special dinner for me, I suppose because she felt all she could do was offer comfort, and had stopped to do some shopping. We had chicken Marsala, broccoli and roast potatoes, and drank half a bottle of wine that Joe had brought home. He said I hadn't given him enough time to bake anything, so he also bought a box of Entenmann's vanilla and chocolate cupcakes — my favorite when I was a boy.

I lit the fireplace before we ate. We seldom used it anymore, since Joe said it drew all the heat up the chimney, made the house colder instead of warmer and was bad for the planet, but practical or not, on this particular night it was comforting.

I helped Rose clear the table after dinner and started loading the dishwasher until she shooed me away, so I moved to the living room, poured another glass of wine, and spread out in front of the fire on a sofa cushion on the floor with the play.

Joe sat down in the club chair behind me.

"How are you fixed for funds?"

"I'm okay. I can pay this month's rent and probably next month's. I have enough money for food," I lied. "And

I'm sure I'll find something soon. I might be getting some freelance work, too. Jo has a couple of friends who may use me, and Marco said he'd ask Carla to get in touch with a friend of hers who just went over to HBO."

"He did? I'm glad to hear that."

"So I'll have something coming in. And I'm eligible for unemployment checks. I'm fine."

"Michael, you know your mother and I will help you out any way we can. I just hope you'll ask us."

"I know, Pop. Thanks."

"Just don't feel bad. It wasn't your fault." His dark eyes sparkled in the firelight. He looked at me and slowly grinned. "'Hey, Michael: What kind of electric lights do we have?'" he prompted. It was our standard routine when I was three, and it never failed to get applause and squeals of delight from my mother's cousins over how smart I was when I parroted back the answer he had taught me.

"'We have an incandescent light in the kitchen and a fluorescent light in the bathroom,'" I recited.

"How'd I get such a bright kid!" he said, ruffling my hair and completing the act. Then he gave my chin a squeeze and said, "You'll be fine, Michael."

He got up and went back into the kitchen to help Rose, and I returned to the manuscript. I was still at work on it long after they had gone to bed, and I had put the last log on the fire and filled the glass with what was left in the bottle.

My cheeks were warm – probably more from the wine than the fire. I sat on the cushion with my legs stretched out in front of me. I started reading the manuscript again from the beginning, and one by one, fed the pages to the flames until it was gone. It wasn't funny anymore. It probably never was.

I slept most of the weekend away, and stayed with my parents until the middle of the week. I had started to get antsy and decided to head back to the city. I hadn't planned on staying so long. There were things I needed to do. I wanted to go to the gym, and I still had to go sign up for unemployment. And I had a date for drinks with Irene on the night of my birthday.

Just before I was ready to leave, Rose called me into her bedroom. Joe had gone outside to start the car.

"You're still coming back the Sunday after your birthday for dinner, right?"

"Sure."

"Well, I was going to wait until then to give you this, but I decided to give it to you now instead." She handed me an envelope. Inside was a birthday card that read "I'm Glad You're My Son" on the cover. There was a check inside — her standard birthday present, or so I thought, until I read the amount. She was giving me five thousand dollars.

"Rose, what is this?"

"That's your rent for a year. Your father and I decided. You get yourself a part-time job for food money, and stay home and write."

"I can't take this!"

"Why not? After all the money I gave Marco for his wedding, I figured you should get some too."

"You don't have it to give away."

"It's done, so take it and shut up."

"But why?"

"Because I don't want you to take another job in advertising. You want to be a writer, so be a writer. Try it for a year."

"I don't understand, Rose."

"Mikey, when I was pregnant with you, it was probably the worst year of my life. I was thirty-seven. Your father and I weren't getting along, mostly because he didn't want to have another baby after Marco, and I sort of forced the issue. It was one disaster after another with you. First I was exposed to German measles, and who knew if you were going to be born in one piece. Then your brother started in with his 'Rock me' routine, and every night I had to sit on his bed and pat his back and rock him. I was exhausted. He never slept, so I never got any sleep either. One night I was sitting on the edge of the bed rocking him and I don't know what I did, but I slid off and fell on the floor and couldn't get up. When you were finally born, and you were healthy, I can't tell you how happy I was."

"I still don't understand."

"Let me finish. I'm sixty-seven years old, Mikey. I look in the mirror when I put on makeup, and I don't know who that is looking back. If I don't wear my glasses, it's not so bad, but then I can't see what I'm doing. I get a Social Security check in the mail every month, and it's got my name on it, and I think to myself, this *can't* be true. I can't be this old. What happened to the girl in the white bathing suit at Rockaway Point? What happened to the girl who used to lead the conga line at all the office Christmas parties? The one thing I did right was to have kids, even if I was the oldest mother in the maternity ward at Mercy Hospital.

"You're special, Mikey. From the moment you started talking, I always knew you were going to do something with your life. This past year, it's been torture to watch you. You've been unhappy before, but never like this. Whatever it was, I kept hoping it would pass, but it didn't. I know it was that job, and to tell you the truth, I'm glad they fired you.

"My life's over, and it was a big nothing. I raised two kids, and that's all I did. Maybe that's all I was supposed to do. But I know you can do something better with your life than write goddamn commercials, and I want you to try it. So take the money. Just don't tell your brother I gave it to you."

I hugged her and said "I love you." It was all I could manage without crying.

"Hurry up or you'll miss your train. He drives bad enough as it is. Don't make him rush. I'll see you on Sunday."

Irene said I deserved nothing less than to celebrate my birthday at the Plaza.

"Honey, you have only one thirtieth birthday, and you should launch the new you in style." I was instructed to put on my gray suit and meet her in the Oak Room at six.

There was a small combo playing Gershwin music for the cocktail hour. Irene sat at a back table, waving discreetly. She was wearing a gorgeous vintage black silk and velvet dress that I had never seen before and suspected had been purchased for this occasion.

"Happy Birthday, Lamb," she said, sliding a small, beautifully wrapped package and card toward me. I kissed her cheek and sat down.

"You look great," I said.

"*You* look great. Being unemployed agrees with you. Open your present."

The package was heavy and square. I tore off the wrapping paper. It was a travel-size Total Hand Treatment Kit embedded in a Lucite cube.

"Every writer needs a paperweight with a story behind it," she said. "Truman Capote had one that Colette gave him. I got the idea when they fired you last week. You should keep it on your desk for inspiration while you finish writing *Dial Nine to Get Out*. It's your medal of honor for lasting as long as you did in that dump."

"Irene. I burned it."

"What?"

"The play. I burned it last week when I went home. I don't know. I was so depressed about losing my job, and I took it home to work on it. I started rereading it and decided it was awful. So I burned it."

"Michael, why?"

"It just didn't seem funny anymore. There's nothing funny about advertising except the people who claim to love working in it."

"Oh, Michael, I thought it had potential."

"I didn't."

The waiter came to our table for our order. The occasion required champagne, Irene decided. Our waiter agreed and left discreetly.

"Are you sure you can afford this?" I asked.

"It's your birthday."

"I'll split it with you."

"You're poor and out of work, remember?"

"I wouldn't be too sure about the poor part. I'm going to be living rent-free for the next year."

"Please don't tell me you're moving back to Long Island."

"Not quite. Rose gave me a check for my birthday to pay my share of the rent for a year. Five thousand dollars. We had a long talk, and she wants me to stay home and write. I just have to find something part-time to pay for food."

"That's wonderful!"

"She gave me something else, and she doesn't even know it. For a long time, I've had another play in mind — something based on Rose. I kept putting it off because I was working on the other one. I think I'm ready to start this one now. She even gave me the title: *The Girl Who Led the Conga Line.*"

"Who are you going to get to play it, Anna Magnani by way of Jane Wyatt?"

"Let's not worry about casting. I haven't even started writing yet."

I looked around the room. We could have been on an ocean liner, or in Paris waiting for Scott and Zelda. I hoped that Irene was right, that if we launched my thirties in style, it would set the tone for the next ten years.

"What are we doing in this joint, anyway?" I asked her. "When we went out for my twenty-third birthday, you took me to Jimmy Day's for burgers. Now look at us. Two little kids from the 'burbs slumming at the Plaza. How did this happen?"

"Everyone grows up."

"You know what's a little sad? If I ever meet *Him*..."

"*When* I meet Him," she interrupted.

"Okay. *When* I meet Him, he'll never know me the way you do. He'll know me at thirty, but he'll never know that gawky twenty-two-year-old kid who used to work in publishing. I was such an innocent. I miss that kid an awful lot sometimes."

"You haven't changed so much, Michael. You may be older and you may be living a little better, but you're not as jaded as you'd like to think you are. You still have 'Somebody please love me' written all over you. And you know what? I think you're going to find it."

"Thanks. I like to believe that somewhere in this city there's a boyish, sensitive jock who appreciates good books, old movies, and Fats Waller and His Rhythm, who'll want to settle down and play house with me."

Our waiter returned with two champagne flutes on a tray. He set them down on the table with a flourish and slipped away.

"Well," Irene said, "you're the birthday boy, so you have to make the toast. Something poetic."

As I sat there, holding up the glass, searching for the words, the little combo launched into "Love Is Here to

Stay." I knew better than to try to top Ira Gershwin.

"To us. 'Not for a year, but ever and a day,'" I said, touching Irene's glass with mine.

"I don't believe it! You planned that, Michael, you had to! Things like that only happen in Frank Capra movies, and even then, you never believe it."

"Believe it. And drink," I said. "I was looking for an omen, and there it is. From here on, my life's going to be a Frank Capra movie. I'll make it happen. You see if I don't."

Irene reached across the table, took my hand and said, "'I'm glad I know you, George Bailey.'"

The camera pulls back. Michael and Irene are lost in a sea of couples at tables in a glittering room. Gershwin music swells up and over. Fade out. The End.

Acknowledgments

Many thanks to all of the people who read drafts and offered opinions and helpful suggestions over the long gestation of this book, especially Teresa Cavanaugh, David Groff, Carole DeSanti, Elisa Lichtenbaum, Michael Silver and Mary South.

Special thanks to Trent Duffy, who edited early drafts, and Diane Oatis, who edited the last three versions and made many great suggestions. Diane and Trent offered considerable help, support, hand-holding, and most of all, friendship, and Diane is responsible for making the paperback edition a reality.

Thanks also to Troy Schreck and Eric Whelan at Alfred Music Publishing, Jeffery Corrick and Sarah Laskin at Penguin Group (USA) and especially Lori Styler and Barbara Hogenson at The Barbara Hogenson Agency who helped steer me through rights and permissions.

And huge thanks to Maureen Panzera at Sanpan Design who gave me a fabulous cover, several days of her time and lots of advice. I appreciate all of it so much.

Finally, I'd like to thank all of the professionals I worked with during my eight-year career in advertising in New York — too many to name here. Unlike Michael Gregoretti and his stint at Malcolm & Partners, I was fortunate to work with the best and the brightest in the city, many of whom took me under their wings, taught me the business and helped me sharpen my skills. I hope they enjoyed working with me as much as I enjoyed and appreciated them. I am lucky to have been in the company of such talented and supportive people.

The works of novelist and playwright Thornton Wilder (1897-1975) explore the connection between the commonplace and the cosmic dimensions of human experience. This versatile artist was a successful adaptor and translator, librettist, actor, lecturer, teacher and screenwriter. He won the Pulitzer Prize for his novel *The Bridge of San Luis Rey*, and two additional Pulitzers for his plays *Our Town* and *The Skin of Our Teeth* in 1943.

For more about Thornton Wilder and his work, please consult **www.thorntonwilder.com**

About the Author

John Terracuso spent most of the 1980s working in New York City as an advertising copywriter. He then moved to HBO Home Video as creative services manager, followed by a stint in the New York PBS press office.

John has worked on several independent films, and wrote, produced, and directed both the video short *It's Someone's Wonderful Life*, and the faux documentary, *Non Dimenticar*.

John also wrote the pilot and several early episodes of *In the Life*, the pioneering LGBT news and variety program seen nationwide on PBS stations.

John grew up on Long Island and graduated Fairfield University in 1979. He lives in San Diego with his husband, Wendell Wyatt.

A Fool Among Fools is his first novel.

Made in the
USA
Lexington, KY